Yakima ran a dirty sleeve of his army-issue shirt across his mouth and pushed up onto his hands and knees. Out of the corner of his right eye, he saw the brave he'd thought he'd killed move. Not only move but raise one of Yakima's own pistols. He heard the brave click the hammer back and grunt.

Yakima looked over at the brave, who lay back down on the ground, his head a bloody, dripping mess. He was close to death and his hand was quivering, but somehow he was still managing to aim the barrel at a slant toward Yakima's own forehead.

"Oh, hell," the young scout whispered half a second before another pistol barked in the distance.

The bullet tore through the brave's already-bloody head, spewing the Indian's brains across rock and cactus. The brave triggered Yakima's pistol wildly before dropping the weapon, sighing, and dying.

Yakima turned to see his partner walking toward him, grinning.

"Ah, shit," Yakima groused. He didn't know what was worse—getting shot at by an Apache with his own pistol or being saved by Seth Barksdale, who'd surely never let him forget it.

The Southerner stood beside him, looking down at the dead Apache, whose brains were still dribbling out the side of his skull. He glanced at Yakima and grinned. "Kinda looks like you, don't he?" He slapped Yakima's chest with the back of his hand. "I reckon we know who'll be buyin' the drinks tonight."

continued . . .

Also Available By Frank Leslie

AMBUSH
AT APACHE
PASS

AN APACHE WARS NOVEL

Frank Leslie

A SIGNET BOOK

SIGNET
Published by the Penguin Group
Penguin Group (USA) LLC, 375 Hudson Street,
New York, New York 10014

USA | Canada | UK | Ireland | Australia New Zealand | India | South Africa | China
penguin.com
A Penguin Random House Company

First published by Signet, an imprint of New American Library,
a division of Penguin Group (USA) LLC

First Printing, September 2014

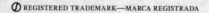

ISBN 978-0-451-46964-9

Printed in the United States of America
10 9 8 7 6 5 4 3 2 1

PUBLISHER'S NOTE
This is a work of fiction. Names, characters, places, and incidents either are the
product of the author's imagination or are used fictitiously, and any resemblance
to actual persons, living or dead, business establishments, events, or locales is
entirely coincidental.

For Matthew Mayo

Let me tell you, the Territory was wild in those days. Old Arizona! Wilder than a Coyotero with a too-tight breechclout. Ha! Wild—yessir, it had the bark on! This was just after the Little Misunderstanding Between the States. Old Fort Hildebrandt, or Fort Hell, as we who were stationed there all called it—was built in '57, but during the war, after the soldiers had pulled out to fight the graybacks, the Chiricahuas led by Geronimo himself sacked it. Damn near burned that sweet ole darlin' to the ground.

After the war, three troops of the Third Cavalry and one of the Fourth Infantry were sent back to rebuild the post there near Apache Pass, west of the New Mexico line, at the junction of Rattlesnake and Apache creeks. Creeks, my ass! Only if you call beds of sand, yucca, and Gila monsters creeks! Don't ever remember a spoonful of water in either. (I was raised back East, you understand.) Well, it was there between the Dos Cabezas Mountains and the Chiricahua Range, just north of Apache Pass, that we rebuilt that humble little 'dobe town, complete with a church and a couple hog pens (whorehouses)! Troops C, D, and H garrisoned her to protect the settlers, miners, prospectors, stagecoach passengers, freighting companies, and the U.S. Mail from them cutthroat Apaches—Chiricahuas, Coyoteros, and Mimbreños, mostly.

Camp Hell.

An oasis she became in a country drier than a lime burner's hat! Soldiers, wives and children of soldiers, teamsters, cold-steel artists, stock herders, horse breakers, whiskey drummers, prospectors, cardsharps, confidence men, and, by Jehovah, even whores and raggedy-heeled outlaws of every crooked stripe!—they all rubbed shoulders with the cavalry *yellowlegs and forted up for a time under them brush ramadas, amongst them tan 'dobe hovels the scorpions and salamanders squiggled around on.*

Wild as Apaches, all of 'em. Even some of the women and children. To go along with an Apache-wild land.

But them contract scouts for the U.S. Cavalry—they was even wilder. Old Gila River Joe, or "the sergeant," as he was known by the men under him, was chief of scouts only because no one else wanted the job, and he was too much soldier to say no when Colonel Alexander offered! Amongst the scouts were the Aravaipa trackers: Chiquito, Pedro, and One-Eyed Miguel. There was the former grayback and plantation owner, Seth Barksdale, and the half-breed, Yakima Henry. Ah, how well I remember young Henry. This was before he went on to become a legend of sorts. Or, maybe it was back at ole Fort Hell that Yakima Henry's legend really began.

Truth be told—an' I'm here to tell it, by God!—a whole lot of legends started at Fort Hell!

—from *Memories of Old Fort Hildebrandt* by Sergeant William "Blinky Bill" Everwine, quartermaster, Fort Hildebrandt, Arizona Territory, 1868–1876

Chapter 1

An agonized scream cut through the desert's eerie stillness.

First Lieutenant Henry L. Darling, B Troop, reined his cavalry remount to an abrupt halt and stared off across the rolling, creosote-bristling desert toward Apache Pass. Dread walked chilly fingers up young Darling's spine. He instinctively slid his hand toward the Army Colt .44 residing in the flap holster on his right hip.

Realizing the pistol wouldn't do him much good out here against Chiricahuas, he moved his hand to the butt of his seven-shot Spencer repeater. He pulled the carbine from its soft leather scabbard and rested its short barrel across the pommel of his saddle.

He'd made the movement without taking his eyes off the dun-colored desert rolling up gradually toward the pass, which was a low point along the lumpy purple horizon nearly straight ahead to the east, the green-brown lumps to either side being the ridges of the Dos Cabezas Mountains on the left and the Chiricahua Mountains on the right. His eyes scanned the chaparral slowly; he pricked his ears with such a concentrated effort that his eardrums ached. He

awaited another scream so he could pinpoint the scream-
er's location.

Wooden rattling rose behind him. So, too, came the
squawks of the light artillery wagon and the thudding of
the four-mule hitch drawing the wagon to the crest of a low
hill about sixty yards behind Darling. The lieutenant grimaced at the intrusion, and he glanced in frustration over
his left shoulder.

The canvas-covered wagon crested the hill, with four
sweaty, dusty mules drawing it down toward Darling, Four
soldiers in sky blue, yellow-striped slacks and navy blue,
leather-billed forage caps were riding lead. Their traditional yellow neckerchiefs were buffeted by the hot, dry
breeze.

When Darling saw the additional troopers trotting their
mounts to the crest of the hill behind the wagon, he turned
his head to again stare off toward the pass. Behind him, the
wagon's shrill squawking grew louder. The wheel hubs needed grease. Darling was beginning to wonder if the scream
he'd heard—or thought he'd heard—had really only been the
freighter's dry wheels. Not a man's scream at all.

It was easy to imagine screams in this country, the vast
silences of which had been torn by so many shrill pleas for
mercy. It was easy to imagine agony and carnage when you
so often expected it. Lived in dread of it. Even dreamed
about it, waking in cold sweats with the crazed yips and
yowls of attacking Apaches or the shrill screams of tortured, butchered men and women still echoing inside your
head. You'd find yourself clawing around in the darkness
for a pistol, and only after you'd drawn the weapon would
you realize you'd only been dreaming.

Or at least *this* time you'd been dreaming.

There it came again. Or . . . maybe not. Darling couldn't
be sure, because now the wagon was drawing up close on
the old mail road behind him and to his left, and there was
the rataplan of the horses and mules and the jangle of bit
chains and the squawks of the wheel hubs.

No, he couldn't be sure. He wanted to believe that what

he'd heard hadn't been a scream, because he had only two more weeks of duty out here in this den of iniquity, stationed at Fort Lowell, outside Tucson. Then he, Miriam, and their little baby, Kay, born just last winter, could return to Council Bluffs, Iowa, where the young lieutenant would begin reading the law under the supervision of his father-in-law, an esteemed attorney.

He'd exchange his carbine and army-issue .44, the cold night sweats, and the screams echoing around inside his head for law books and rose gardening and carrying his lovely, blond-haired, blue-eyed little Kay on his shoulders through lush green grass and sprawling cottonwoods along Lilac Creek, its placid surface dimpled by trout feeding on nymphs and mayflies.

"Lieutenant!"

Darling turned toward Sergeant Leonard Coffee, who was riding his bay gelding to the left of Corporal Bernard Sullivan at the head of the detail. Coffee thrust an arm and gloved hand toward the southeast, his bearded, sunburned face set in a wary grimace. Darling swiveled his head to see what the sergeant was pointing at, and the intestines in his lower belly writhed.

Charcoal puffs of smoke rose from the top of a distant, haystack-shaped bluff. More rose from another bluff farther south and east, smaller but unmistakable.

The young lieutenant's throat went dry. Dread pooled in his belly.

"Oh, shit," he heard himself say under his breath, barely audible now, because the wagon and the troopers were passing loudly along the trail behind him.

The sergeant yelled, "Any sign of Guzman?"

Again, the lieutenant scanned the terrain, hoping to see the burly scout galloping toward him across the desert. A voice in his ear, hushed with menace, whispered that he wouldn't. That if he was going to see Fort Lowell's chief scout and interpreter, Joaquin Guzman, again, he would have seen him by now. Guzman would have seen the Apache sign long ago and reported his findings to Darling when the contingent had still been three or four miles farther east.

"Lieutenant, did you hear me?" the sergeant shouted again.

Darling snapped a hard look over his shoulder. "Yes, I heard you, Sergeant! No, I haven't seen Guzman. Keep the column moving and alert the men—if that smoke hasn't already alerted them—to sit up smart in their saddles and keep a sharp watch out for Chiricahuas!"

"I don't like it that we haven't seen Guzman. That ain't a good sign!"

"No, it's not a good sign, Sergeant. Kindly follow my orders. Keep that wagon rolling. No stops until we've reached Fort Hildebrandt, understand?"

"All this for a goddamned piano."

Darling whipped his head back toward Sergeant Coffee, who was galloping at a slant toward the trail now as he tried to catch up to the passing double column.

"What was that, Sergeant?" Darling barked at the noncommissioned officer. But the sergeant continued galloping away, as though he hadn't heard the lieutenant's remonstrative rhetorical question.

The bearded noncom began barking orders to the soldiers, all of whom were looking warily off toward the smoke puffs rising in the south.

Darling hardened his jaw at the sergeant's insubordinate comment. But then he loosened it.

He really couldn't blame the sergeant for voicing Darling's own peevishness at being out here risking life and limb and a few other prized pieces of his anatomy to ensure that Colonel Ephraim Alexander's piano made it safely on the last leg of its journey from the Army Supply Depot in San Francisco to Fort Hildebrandt, more commonly and appropriately referred to as Fort Hell. Alexander was the commanding officer at Hildebrandt; he lived there with his daughter, Priscilla. Darling had led his nine-man, one-wagon procession out from Tucson to deliver the newly arrived piano, which the colonel had ordered for "Miss Priss," as everyone called her.

Miss Priss so loved to play the piano to entertain the officers and the officers' wives at Hildebrandt on weekends. Apparently, the old piano had either given out or been a casualty of Geronimo's attack when Hildebrandt had been abandoned during the War Between the States.

"Yes, Sergeant," Darling said to himself as he turned his horse toward the wagon and the soldiers riding fore and aft of it, "a piano, indeed!"

He didn't mind being out here to escort a Butterfield stagecoach or the mail or the army payroll or to see that a load of ore made it from the local gold and silver mines to Tucson or Lac Cruces. Such assignments were, after all, the reason Hildebrandt had been built here in the first place—in addition to holding one of the few sources of water out here, of course—and why he had been sent here after the War Between the States to help garrison Fort Lowell outside the slumbering Mexican village of Tucson.

He could live with dying for a legitimate government assignment. But he'd be damned if he died only two weeks before his mustering out of the service, for a gall-blasted piano!

Darling galloped up toward the wagon. Through the rear pucker he could see the large wooden crate jouncing around in the wagon box ensconced in a worn cream canvas, and he bit out another frustrated curse. The Apaches had probably seen the campfires last night, along Bone Creek, and had suspected the freight detachment was hauling arms or something else just as valuable out to Fort Hell, though at the moment, in their war against the whites, whom they saw as hoggish invaders swarming into their traditional homeland, few things were more valuable than guns and ammunition.

Darling wished that there were some way he could let them know that he was only carrying a piano. No shiny new Winchesters, Spencers, or Henry repeating rifles and ammunition for same, or mountain howitzers and crates of explosive shells. No food for the canteen or commissary storehouse, and no gold coins they might trade unscrupulous merchants for weapons.

Only a piano to appease the colonel's spoiled teenage daughter, Miss Priss!

"Any sign of Guzman, Lieutenant?" asked the wagon driver, Corporal McDuff, in a quavering voice as Darling rode past him. The man's voice was probably quavering from the wagon's violent bouncing along the trail, but Darling suspected the brittleness also stemmed from the smoke that he kept glancing at with worried eyes from beneath the brim of his salt-stained forage cap.

"Not yet, Corporal. Just keep the wagon moving. Under no circumstances are you to stop unless Sergeant Coffee or I order it, understand?"

"Yes, sir!"

Darling galloped ahead to trot his mount along beside the sergeant, who rode with his eyes narrowed beneath the brim of his yellow Hardee hat. He had his .56-56 Spencer resting across his thighs, and his gloved right hand wrapped around the neck of the stock. Neither he nor the lieutenant said anything as they continued moving at a spanking clip along the winding trail, around rock outcroppings and stands of barrel cactus and ocotillo.

A splash of red shone along the trail ahead, and the lieutenant tightened his hand around the neck of his own repeater. But the red was not the flannel of an Apache headband. It was only a roadrunner, vanishing as fast as it had appeared, weaving through the chaparral on the north side of the trail.

Darling looked to his right and behind.

The smoke was gone. Nothing moved out there except a watery mirage hovering above the creosote.

The two-track trace rose into bluffs on either side of the trail, and the lieutenant found himself and his command threading through what was known to the whites as Bayonet Canyon. A narrow wash ran along the base of the hundred-and-fifty-foot bluff on the right. It was sheathed in oaks, sycamores, and mesquites, old leaves littering the ground around it. The leaves of the trees rattled in the breeze as Darling's eyes scoured the rocky slopes rising along the trail.

Plenty of places for an Apache to hunker down and affect an ambush.

Darling's guts tightened again with apprehension as the canyon bent to the left, and he could see only about fifty yards ahead. The bluff on the left dropped gradually, and now more grass grew to either side of the trail amongst small boulders and mesquite snags.

Sergeant Coffee jerked back on his bay's reins and said, "Lieutenant, look there."

But Darling had already seen what looked like a man sitting under a tree about sixty yards ahead and on the trail's right side. He appeared to be on a chair, but of course there were no chairs out here. He must have been sitting on a stump partly shaded by the large desert willow towering over him.

He wore buckskins and was dark-complexioned, with a long, dark beard dropping halfway down his chest, and appeared to be holding his hat on his lap.

"Is that Guzman?" asked Coffee.

Darling waved his carbine in the air above his head. The man sitting beneath the willow did not move. He sat there as though he were carved in stone.

"I believe so," Darling said, holding his reins taut in his left hand, the Spencer in his right. He and Sergeant Coffee were both stopped in the trail, their mounts jittery. The double column had come to a halt behind them. Except for the blowing of horses and the rattling of bits, a tense silence descended over the shallow canyon.

"Sergeant, you and the column wait here." Darling dismounted and tossed Coffee his reins. "I'm going to check it out."

Coffee looked around, wagged his head slowly, gritting his teeth with dread. "Be careful, Lieutenant. Be awful damn careful."

Darling advanced ahead on foot. He had every intention of being careful, though he knew from experience that being careful in Apache country was, by itself, seldom enough to save you.

Chapter 2

"Guzman?"

Lieutenant Darling had stopped on the trail and was staring up the slight grade that the man was sitting on. The scout did not respond to the lieutenant's query. He merely sat, his ragged blue felt hat sitting upturned in his lap, staring. At least, Darling thought he was staring. The man's eyes looked as if they were open, though he couldn't be sure because the wedge of shade cast by the tree obscured his broad, bearded face with its single, bushy eyebrow.

The lieutenant squeezed his carbine in his hands. Sweat squished around inside his gloves. He glanced back at the two columns that remained mounted and quiet behind him, all round, dark eyes on the lieutenant.

Darling looked around carefully. He gazed up the trail and then he moved off the trail and climbed the steep grade until he was standing in front of Guzman. He'd been able to hear the flies buzzing as he climbed the slope, and now he saw them forming a gauzy, dark cloud over the stocky, middle-aged man's hat. Several clung to the deep, wide gash in the man's chest. The cut ran from just beneath his breastbone to just above the waistband of his buckskin trousers. His double cartridge belts were gone. The bloody gash gaped like a half-open mouth.

The air around the man was so pungent with the smell of rancid flesh and blood that Darling wrinkled his nose against it. He had to swallow to keep from gagging. He glanced around cautiously and then took one more step toward the dead scout, leaning forward to peer into the man's campaign hat.

The hat was nearly filled to the brim with bloody organs. The topmost organ was a fist-shaped heart.

The lieutenant wheeled and vomited. He glanced back toward the column. One of the horses whinnied shrilly and bucked. The ground rose in clumps along the trail and halfway up the sides of the bluffs on either side of the soldiers. Only it wasn't really the ground rising, Lieutenant Darling saw now, the bile churning in his belly. The clumps were Apaches wearing cloaks and headdresses made of woven brush.

Darling's mouth opened and he tried to scream, but he could not coax up any sounds from his throat.

As the Apaches began yowling like coyotes, Darling started down the steep slope toward the trail, while the soldiers and horses screamed, and thundering rifles lifted a vicious cacophony. He'd taken only two steps when he tripped over a rock and went rolling, losing his carbine. He rose onto his hands and knees, breathing hard, panic screaming in his ears beneath the roar of the Apaches' rifles. He saw his carbine, and just as he reached for it, something that felt fist-sized and hot slammed into his left shoulder.

It knocked him flat against the slope, at an angle to the trail below.

He lay stunned, staring at the sky. The rataplan of rifles and the bizarre yowling of the attacking Apaches . . . the agonized cries of soldiers and horses . . . sounded far away. In the periphery of Darling's vision, something moved. He lifted his head slightly. His bloody left shoulder, heavy and numb, was pinned to the ground.

Darling blinked as though to clear his eyes. Two riders were moving toward him along the trail, from the opposite direction in which the battle was being fought. If you could call it a battle. It was really a slaughter, the lieutenant knew in a vague, oddly disinterested way. He focused now on the two riders moving toward him at a slow, leisurely pace.

He squinted through the haze of pain flaring up behind his retinas. He couldn't be seeing what his eyes were telling his brain—a man and a woman riding side by side. But what was astonishing to the pain-racked lieutenant wasn't that they were a man and a woman, but the fact that the woman was a blonde dressed in the deerskins of an Apache, and the man was dressed in Confederate gray, though the War Between the States had been over for five years.

They reined up on the trail about thirty feet away from the lieutenant. The Confederate had a lean, raptorial face beneath the broad brim of his gray slouch hat. His thin red-blond beard was coated with butterscotch dust. Hawkish copper eyes slid to the lieutenant, and a wry smile tugged at the corners of his thin mouth. He had a nasty, jagged white scar across his long, sunburned nose. A captain's bars trimmed the sleeves of his soiled gray blouse over which he wore leather suspenders. He held a long-barreled Henry rifle with a brass receiver on his right shoulder.

"You want the honors, or shall I?" he asked the girl out of the side of his mouth, in a distinctly slow, Southern drawl.

The rifle reports and the yowling of the Apaches were dwindling now. The groans of the dying soldiers had turned to plaintive wails and groans and gasping sobs. Darling could smell the peppery odor of the powder smoke on the wind.

"Don't trouble yourself, Captain." The girl slung her right leg over the poll of her fine tobiano stallion, which boasted a long, flowing mane.

She strode off the side of the trail. Lieutenant Darling was mesmerized by the long-legged, bronzed beauty with blond hair so bleached by the sun that it was nearly the same white of her spotted stallion's. The horselike mane hung nearly to her hips, loosely bound by braided rawhide and held back from her face by a thick swatch of red flannel. Darling could see the rawhide-bound queue sliding out from each side of her back as she strode toward him. Her full, ripe breasts jostled behind the small, thin deerskin vest she wore only across her upper torso, exposing her flat belly.

The smooth, pale orbs curved out from behind the vest, beneath her slender arms.

A beaded medicine pouch hung from a thong around her neck.

As she approached, Darling smelled camp smoke, roots, sweat, grease, horses, and deerskins. She smelled like an Apache. The odor returned the lieutenant to some semblance of his senses, and, realizing he was about to die, he groaned and panted, reaching for the Army .44 holstered on his right hip.

He'd only gotten the flap unsnapped before the girl's shadow passed over him. She stared down at him with light blue eyes, like the lightest of blue lilacs, and owning such a feral coldness in a severely chiseled, sun-bronzed, savagely beautiful face that they nearly took his breath away.

So mesmerized was he by her startling eyes that he briefly forgot his attempt to draw the .44. And then, remembering the need to defend himself, he started to pull the piece from its holster.

The blond Apache beauty stepped down on the gun with her moccasin-clad left foot, and Darling cried out as her foot pinched his hand down against the handle of the revolver. The last thing the lieutenant saw was the long, wide-bladed, horn-handled knife glistening in the afternoon sun just before she swiped it across his throat.

Captain Lamar Chestnut chuckled as he said in his slow, Southern twang, "Darlin' Riona, I believe I'm going to rename you whatever name it would be in Chiricahua that means She Who Kills Without Blinkin' One Damn Eye!"

The young woman straightened while the lieutenant's body jerked and quivered. She cleaned the blade of her knife on the dying man's pants, slid the knife into the sheath hanging off her comely right hip, and strode back over to her stallion.

She glanced up at Lamar, who was smiling down at her from the back of his grulla gelding. Her expression was oblique as she lithely regained the tobiano's back, moving with the suppleness of a pouncing panther. Her long legs, sculpted by riding and climbing, dangled down over the horse's barrel.

She threw the queue of her long white-blond hair behind her shoulder and turned to Lamar again. She was neither smiling nor frowning but gazed at him as though she were staring right through him, as though she were still wondering what to make of him.

Lamar Chestnut was a decorated war hero. He'd killed scores of blue bellies on Eastern battlefields, and then, after the debacle of Appomattox, during his quest to secure arms and gold with which to build his own outlaw empire in northern Mexico, he'd killed as many more men south of the border.

He'd fought Apaches, but he'd never run into an Apache as striking and unnerving as this blond Chiricahua, Riona. Of course, she had not been born Apache, but she'd been with the People of the Winter Wolf band of Chiricahua Apaches long enough to have acquired their customs and language, and most interestingly, the subtle threat with which they all stared at you even when they weren't fighting you.

As if they were wondering if there wasn't a good enough reason to just kill you and be done with you so they no longer had to suffer the tediousness of your white man's ways.

That's how Riona was staring at him now. The look was so flat and cold that the former Confederate found his right hand itching to slide toward the butt of one of his brass-bellied Navy revolvers.

His heart hiccupped when she leaned toward him, wrapped her long, sinewy left arm around his neck, pulled his head toward her brusquely, parted her lips, and closed her mouth over his. Her breasts mashed against his chest. She kept her lips pressed to his for about five seconds. Then she slid her tongue against his and pulled her head away.

"Come on, Sergeant," she said, her eyes flashing coquettishly as she took her rope reins in both hands and ground her heels into her tobiano's flanks. "Let's see what these blue bellies have bestowed upon us!"

Lamar stared after her. His heart was still beating irregularly, apprehensively, but now his loins were heavy. An odd, beguiling contrast. But then, Miss Riona, as she did not mind him calling her, was a knot of beguiling contrasts—part coquettish white girl, part heartless savage. He watched her gallop along the trail toward the wagon and the dead soldiers strewn around it, the thick queue of her blond hair sliding back and forth across her supple, sun-bronzed back.

He grunted his desire and hoped he could talk her into sharing his blankets later tonight, a privilege she had not yet allowed him, though she'd teased him often enough.

The warriors were milling around the rear of the wagon. As Captain Chestnut put his steed into a trot, he saw that one warrior was running up the bluff to his left. Another man screamed. Chestnut saw that the brave was chasing one of the surviving soldiers—a bearded man with a sergeant's chevrons on his sleeves. The sergeant had fallen in his attempt to flee certain death. Chestnut watched with a mix of revulsion and admiration as the brave slowed to a fast walk and threw his head back, loosing a wolfish howl toward the broad sky.

Then he pulled the sergeant's head back by his hair, slashed his throat, kicked him over onto his back, and, with a shrill grunt, he buried the blade of his bowie knife into the still-writhing man's chest. He jerked the blade this way and that and then he switched the knife to his left hand. He thrust his right hand into the sergeant's chest, pulling out the heart, lifting it high above his head, and sticking out his tongue to catch the blood being pumped by the still-beating organ.

Lamar chuckled darkly and wagged his head. He was

damn glad he was fighting *with* them, because he sure as hell wouldn't want to be fighting *against* them. Miss Riona's People of the Winter Wolf were special, indeed.

Lamar stopped his grulla about fifty feet from the wagon. Several of the Chiricahua braves jerked back from it as though they thought it might explode. A couple ran into the brush and cowered behind boulders.

Lamar was about to lower his Henry from his shoulder and pump a round into the action when he heard what had frightened the Apaches. From inside the covered wagon rose the melodic notes of a piano.

The instrument was being played with a keen and practiced hand, though it sounded a tad wooden and muffled as the notes floated out from behind the dusty, threadbare canvas. Still, the sound was soft, whimsical, astonishingly melodic.

Lamar, who had been educated in the Deep South on his family's cotton plantation before the war, booted his steed forward slowly and smiled with incredulity as he said, "Brahms?"

Chapter 3

Yakima Henry was nineteen, and as green as spring willows lining a flooded wash, his sap running high. He was pondering ways to bleed some of it off—should he ask that comely young half Coyotero who worked for the sutler at Fort Hell to the dance Saturday night?—when he heard the hiccup of a distant gun report.

It was followed by a girl's shrill scream. A man bellowed, and then there was the hollow pop of a pistol.

"What in blazes you suppose that's all about?" asked Seth Barksdale, Yakima's fellow contract scout from Fort Hildebrandt, or "Fort Hell" as the remote outpost was called by those who had been unfortunate enough to be stationed there in the shadow of the Chiricahua Mountains, between Mesilla and Tucson.

Barksdale was kneeling by a spring, which was dribbling out of rocks in a hollow beneath the ridge that Yakima had climbed. The former Confederate scout held the hide-wrapped canteen he'd been filling at the spring in both hands, and spring water dripped down the thick tuft of his light brown spade beard as he turned his head this way and that, looking around.

Yakima had been sitting on a boulder to rest and entertain his youthful fantasies as well as to scout for a particularly vicious pack of renegade Chiricahuas that had attacked a mail detail from Lordsburg two days ago after they'd wiped out an entire nine-man freighting detail out of Tucson. The young half-breed rose as a pistol popped in the east and a low clattering sounded, and he shuttled his gaze in that direction.

A red-blown blur gradually clarified, as did the shapes of horses and riders converging on it. The young, black-haired, green-eyed scout dropped down into the hollow, and said, "Looks like we found them broncos. Or the Tuesday stage from Lordsburg did."

"Ah, hell!" Barksdale said, quickly capping his canteen. "This is Wednesday! There ain't no stage on Wednesday!"

"There's a Wednesday stage today or my eyes ain't workin' right," Yakima said, marching over to where his buckskin gelding stood ground-reined, a sack of cracked corn hanging down its snout by its ears. "They was workin' well this mornin' when I spied Miss Lucinda washin' her drawers out in a big tub on Suds Row, and those are pistols poppin', all right. And now I can hear those Chiricahuas howlin' and that old jehu, Melvin Beltrami, shoutin' curses back—so, yep, I reckon there's a Wednesday stage, all right."

Yakima removed the feed sack from his horse's snout, shoved it into a saddlebag pouch, and was adeptly threading the latigo through his saddle's D-ring while he stared through a notch in the hollow toward the eastern desert.

Barksdale tightened his own mount's saddle strap, saying just to vent some of his own young man's excitement, "Damn, you got diarrhea of the jaw! I thought Injuns was supposed to be quiet folks."

"I'm only half," Yakima reminded his Southern partner, toeing a stirrup and swinging up into his saddle. "My ma was full-blood Cheyenne. My old man was German. You couldn't get two words out of Pa all day, but Ma'd talk your ear off over mornin' coffee!"

Yakima touched spurs to the buckskin's flanks, and the fleet-footed gelding was instantly rocking through the notch in the hollow and out onto the open desert.

"Come on, you patch-bearded grayback, before they run that 'stoga into the ground!"

But Barksdale was already twenty feet behind him, hunkered low in his saddle, his long brown hair flying out behind him in the wind. His tobacco brown planter's hat was tipped low on his forehead. "Yep, that's old Beltrami," he shouted as the stage driver's bellows cut across the desert once more. They were followed by the hammering thunder of what could only have been a ten-gauge shotgun. "And that's Jubal Dent's Greener!"

"He's givin' 'em hell, all right!" Yakima yelled as he watched a Chiricahua turn a backward somersault over the rump of his galloping mustang, the horse giving a shrill whinny and veering away from the red-and-yellow Concord coach it had been bearing down on.

The shotgun's thunder reached Yakima's ears half a second later, as the Apache hit the ground in a puff of tan dust and rolled, arms and legs and long black hair flying.

As Yakima whipped his horse with his rein ends, closing on the stage as well as the half dozen or so whooping and hollering Chiricahuas, he saw another brave fly from his horse, pivoting and turning in midair before hitting the ground on his head and rolling wildly.

The thunder of the shotgun's blast had reached Yakima's ears while the brave was in midair, falling.

As Yakima urged even more speed from his desert-born-and-bred buckskin, he drew closer to the stage and the braves pursuing it. He saw the braves now racing to within twenty or thirty yards of the flying coach, several of the Chiricahuas obscured by the roiling cloud of adobe-colored dust churned up by the stage's iron-shod wheels.

There were seven, maybe eight braves still mounted and

skillfully flinging arrows at the Concord and the jehu sitting
in the driver's box, whooping and yelling at his team, and
the shotgun messenger, who lay prone on the stage's roof,
amongst the luggage and a strongbox strapped to the stage's
brass bars. Just now the shotgunner, Jubal Dent, was breaking open his Greener and plucking out the spent shells.
Someone inside the bouncing, lurching coach was triggering
a pistol through the door at the attacking Indians.

Yakima could hear the faint cracks of a small-caliber
pistol.

The young scout reached forward with his right hand
and slipped his .56-46 Spencer carbine from its saddle
boot. As one of the braves ahead of him flung an arrow
toward the stage, the shotgunner, Dent, lurched backward
and grabbed his left shoulder with his right hand, dropping
his shotgun in the process. The Greener bounced off the
stage's roof and fell over the side to disappear amongst the
creosote and Spanish bayonet that was about all that grew
in this stretch of the *malpaís* south of Fort Hell.

The brave who'd pierced Dent with an arrow whooped
louder, thrilled by his success, and reached into the deer-
hide quiver jostling down his brown back for another
arrow. But before the brave could knock the arrow to his
bowstring, Yakima raised his Spencer to his shoulder,
rocked the heavy hammer back to full cock, and fired.

Smoke and flames lanced from the carbine's barrel. The
report echoed out over the basin, drowned quickly by the
howling of the Indians, the clattering of the stage, and
the thunder of galloping hooves. Yakima watched through
his dispersing powder smoke as the brave jerked forward
on his blanket saddle, straightened, and then crouched low
over his horse's poll and fell forward against the mustang's
crest.

The brave slid down the mount's right side and disappeared for a second before he reappeared a moment later,
dancing off into a snag of rocks and cactus obscured by the
stage's billowing dust.

Barksdale triggered one of his two Confederate pistols

over the head of his rangy roan, and started whooping and hollering so loudly that he nearly drowned out the Indians. Yakima followed suit, yelling like a moon-crazed coyote, as he took his horse's reins in his teeth before racking a fresh cartridge into his seven-shot carbine's chamber.

He aimed quickly, expertly, and fired, and whooped again as he watched another Apache go flying from a lunging horse's back. He didn't see the brave land, for just then he was distracted by a loud banging, cracking noise and saw the stage lurch sharply on its rear offside. As that point of the coach sagged, the wheel from that same side of the axle rolled off behind the coach while the coach itself slowed, kicking up even more dust because of the missing wheel, and skidded to a halt.

The Chiricahuas between Yakima and the coach all turned to look behind them, and then they stopped and wheeled their horses. Their whooping and hollering stopped for maybe three seconds, but then, realizing they'd been flanked, about half of the war party galloped off to the north. No Apache Yakima had ever encountered enjoyed surprises; they would not fight unless they were relatively certain the odds were in their favor. They were not cowards by any definition. But they were practical. They believed that when either surprised or outnumbered—or both—they should flee to safety and live to fight another day.

Two of the braves, however, apparently did not live by this creed. Instead of joining the others that were galloping around the now-stopped stage and heading north toward the Maverick Mountains, these two turned their horses and took off straight toward Yakima. The young scout dispatched one attacker with his carbine and then slid the rifle into its boot.

Just as he'd begun to raise one of his two 1860 Dragoon Colts that had been converted to metallic cartridges, the other brave was literally on top of him. Yakima's buckskin slipped straight out from beneath the young half-breed's butt as he and the brave, limbs entangled, flew out behind the horse and hit the ground like two wildcats chained to the same wagon. That was the comparison Yakima made in his own mind possibly because the brave's stench was like that of wildcat dens the young scout had once investigated.

Yakima's back slammed to the ground. The howling renegade landed on a shoulder just beyond him to his left and went rolling before gaining his feet, a knife flashing in his hand. The knife had been honed from strap iron. Yakima had seen his share of such knives—though all of them until now he'd found on dead Apache bodies. Now he saw one up close—to within six inches of his face, in fact—as the brave stormed toward him, holding the knife down low until he was on Yakima again and was driving the knife up toward his throat.

The brave's black eyes were round and bright, his thin lips stretching a victorious leer.

The Chiricahua was all catgutlike sinew, with springs for feet, but his head was bleeding from where he'd landed on a rock. He was a little dazed. Otherwise, Yakima likely wouldn't have been able to step away and bound on top of him, driving him to the ground. The brave squirmed, trying to thrust again with his knife, but Yakima grabbed the nearest rock and used it to smash the brave's left temple.

He had to drive the rock down on the brave's head five or six times before he felt the short, muscular body relax beneath him. When it did, Yakima slumped to his side, exhausted from the rushing of his own blood, and a little dazed himself with his unceremonious meeting with the sandy-bottomed *malpaís*.

He'd only killed two other Apaches, one Mimbreño, and one Lipan, since he landed the scouting job at Fort Hell a little over a year ago—one year after the camp had opened back up again for military service. Those had been the first Indians he'd ever killed, and each killing had horrified and sickened him. Though he'd killed white men before in self-defense, and he himself was half white, killing Indians felt more like killing his own people.

Why that was, he had no idea.

He saw now that the killing wasn't getting any easier.

His guts recoiled, and he rolled over onto his left hip and shoulder and spat in disgust onto a yucca plant out from beneath which a salamander scampered. In the distance, he could hear the stagecoach driver, old Melvin Beltrami, cutting loose with a string of epithets so foul they would have caused smoke to curl from a nun's ears.

Yakima ran a dirty sleeve of his army-issue shirt across his mouth and pushed up onto his hands and knees. Out of the corner of his right eye, he saw the brave he'd thought he'd killed move. Not only move but raise one of Yakima's own pistols. He heard the brave click the hammer back and grunt.

Yakima looked over at the brave, who lay back down on the ground, his head a bloody, dripping mess. He was close to death and his hand was quivering, but somehow he was still managing to aim the barrel at a slant toward Yakima's own forehead.

"Oh, hell," the young scout whispered half a second before another pistol barked in the distance.

The bullet tore through the brave's already-bloody head, spewing the Indian's brains across rock and cactus. The brave triggered Yakima's pistol wildly before dropping the weapon, sighing, and dying.

Yakima turned to see his partner walking toward him, grinning.

"Ah, shit," Yakima groused. He didn't know what was worse—getting shot at by an Apache with his own pistol or being saved by Seth Barksdale, who'd surely never let him forget it.

The Southerner stood beside him, looking down at the dead Apache, whose brains were still dribbling out the side of his skull. He glanced at Yakima and grinned. "Kinda looks like you, don't he?" He slapped Yakima's chest with the back of his hand. "I reckon we know who'll be buyin' the drinks tonight."

Chapter 4

Yakima told his friend and partner, Seth Barksdale, to do something physically impossible to himself. Barksdale returned the sentiment using sign language, stepped into his saddle, and galloped over to where the stagecoach sat at an odd angle along the far side of the stage trail, while Yakima retrieved his stolen pistol.

The walnut-gripped Dragoon Colt was speckled with the dead Chiricahua's brains and blood. Yakima cleaned it on the brave's deerskin leggings and calico shirt, and looked at the brave's eyes. They were open and staring at nothing. The young scout gave a shudder and felt foolish for feeling so revolted. Seth, who'd fought in the War Between the States as an officer under General Nathan Bedford Forest, seemed immune to death. By all indications, the young Southerner was immune to fear, as well.

Yakima had not fought in the recent war but had spent his childhood traipsing around the remotest regions of the West with his taciturn German prospector father and his Cheyenne mother. He'd lived so wildly and remotely before and after his parents had died, that he'd only heard the

Eastern battles mentioned a few times over the years, and he'd been so busy prospecting and breaking horses for ranchers or riding on cattle drives and roundups to help sustain himself that he'd given that faraway trouble little thought.

Having hunted and killed only animals for food until he was sixteen—and the two men who'd wanted to steal his horse and make him a "good Indian"—killing human beings was new to young Yakima Henry. He secretly admired Seth for his cold-bloodedness. Sometimes Yakima thought he would have been better off if he'd remained a horsebreaker, which had been his first job at Fort Hell, until the chief of scouts, Sergeant Joe Tunney, had volunteered him to fill a scouting vacancy.

Somehow, after Yakima had gone out hunting with some civilian game hunters, word had gotten around about his excellent tracking and shooting skills, and the sergeant, also known as Gila River Joe, had long-looped him, as Barksdale had called it.

"You're one of us now, breed," the young Southerner had said, jerking the brim of Yakima's hat down over his eyes when young Henry threw his gear down in the scouts' adobe brick bunkhouse near the stables at Fort Hell. "Like it or not, you'd best get used to it. And you'd best get used to ole Gila River Joe's ways of doin' things. He don't say much, but when he does, you'd best jump or he'll make you dance. He might be old, but don't let that fool you." Seth had winked conspiratorially. "The sergeant'll make you dance!"

The stage driver was still cursing a blue streak. Yakima ran down his horse, which he'd trained not to stray far under any circumstance, and rode over to find Seth and the stage driver, easing the shotgun rider, who had a Chiricahua arrow sticking out of his left shoulder, down from the driver's boot. The shotgunner, Jubal Dent, was groaning and cursing, his fleshy face sweating and creased with pain, while Barksdale and Beltrami, a Cajun from down south of New Orleans, eased him down over the stage's left front wheel. Beltrami harangued Seth with "I thought you boys was supposed to be patrolin' this damn stage road so we could make it through from Lordsburg without getting punched so full of arrows we look more like porcupines than men!"

"There was a stage through yesterday," Seth said, grunting beneath the shotgun messenger's considerable weight. "We wasn't expectin' one through today."

"Well, we had so gall-dang many passengers we had to send another one from Lordsburg, and Albert Bauer sent a courier last night from the Rattlesnake Creek Station to give you dog faces at Hildebrandt the word!"

"'Paches!" Dent was spitting out through gritted teeth. "Hate every damn one of 'em. Mice on horseback and flingin' arrows—that's what they is!" He cursed as Barksdale, the driver, and Yakima set him down on the ground and eased him back against the front wheel's wooden spokes.

Hearing voices from inside the coach, Yakima realized that no one had yet checked on the passengers. As he walked over to the door, which had three arrows sticking out of it, someone kicked it open from inside, and Yakima glimpsed a man's dusty brown, store-bought boot beneath a brown broadcloth pants leg.

"Oh, for Christ's sake," the man was saying. "I've heard about these goings-on, but I thought the army was out here to protect us from those savages!"

"Here, let me help," Yakima said, reaching inside,

The man jerked his arm back and glared at Yakima from behind dust-smeared spectacles that flashed in the brassy, late-autumn Sonoran sun. He was sharp featured, with a thin red beard, maybe thirty-five, his nose peeling from sunburn. He'd lost his hat in the fracas, and he was holding a carefully folded silk handkerchief to his forehead.

"Unhand me," he barked at the young scout, his eyes raking Yakima up and down, his gaze finally settling on the young man's broad-faced, chiseled Indian features. "Glory be to God—but they're all over the place!"

Just then a young woman's face appeared over the man's left shoulder. With thick dark brown hair and lustrous gray

eyes beneath a decorative straw hat trimmed with silk
flowers and paper berries, she was a heart-stopper. Yakima
felt himself take one involuntary step back as she said, "Let
me help you, Mr. Tatum."

The girl—she was probably not quite Yakima's age,
though her bold gaze was frank and mature and she carried
herself with surprising confidence in light of the terrifying
ride she'd just taken thanks to the Chiricahuas—rose from
her seat and slipped between Tatum's knees and the man
sitting across from him, to the open door.

Yakima was standing back, customarily bashful when
around people in general, and women of better breeding
than his own in particular—which included just about
everybody—but when the girl extended her hand to him, he
started clumsily forward to take it. He was too slow, though,
for Seth Barksdale appeared out of nowhere, stepping between Yakima and the brown-haired, frosty-eyed beauty to
gently take her pale, delicate hand in his gloved one.

"Don't mind him, miss," Seth said, glancing ironically
at Yakima. "He was born in a cave. I, on the other hand,
was raised amongst gentlemen and ladies, so allow me the
rare good fortune of assisting your destaging."

All of this while accentuating his petal-soft Tennessee
drawl, which Yakima often heard him use while sparking
the percentage girls of the Sonora Sun Saloon operated by
the Mexican sutler, Armando Palacio Valdez, and Valdez's
softheaded son, Jorge, at Fort Hell.

The girl glanced around him at Yakima. Her mouth corners lifted in a faint smile, and then she hitched up the
long, pleated skirts of her dusty traveling dress, said, "Why,
thank you, kind sir," and stepped down out of the stage.

There were two other passengers, both men who Yakima
assumed, judging by the cut of their suits and their crisp
hats and superior demeanors, were ranching or possibly
mining speculators. Arizona was attracting more and more
business entrepreneurs now that the war was over. Neither
of the other two appeared to be injured, though both looked
more than a little indignant.

While they smoked and talked amongst themselves in low, confidential tones, looking around at the dead Indians—they'd probably never seen Apaches before—the girl cleaned Tatum's head wound with the man's own handkerchief and water from a canteen. He was leaning back and groaning against the stage's left rear wheel.

Seth hovered over her with that sleepy-eyed look he always got when a particular female had attracted him. "Are you all right, Miss, uh . . . Miss . . ."

"I'm all right," the girl said coolly, glancing over at the wounded shotgun messenger, who sat passed out now against the wheel, still holding his right hand around the arrow embedded in his left shoulder. "How's that poor man over there?"

"Oh, he'll be all right," said the driver, Beltrami, who was sixty or possibly older. Heavy-shouldered, stooped, and with a gut like a sagging flour sack, he had a long gray-brown beard and long, greasy gray-brown hair hanging from a low-crowned, straw Sonora hat.

His face was scarred from knives, fists, and the blazing frontier sun so that it looked like patched and tanned cowhide. A bite from a diamondback several years ago had left him with a twitch on nearly his entire left side, from that eye and cheek to his foot. "He's been pierced so many times by Chiricowy and Coyote arrows, he don't feel right without one stickin' out of him. We'll have him back to the camp straightaway, and Doc Sawchuck'll make him good as new, though first I'd better go back and see if I can't find our wheel."

He gave one of his characteristic twitches, kicking his left boot at a horse apple, and limped off in the direction from which the stage had come.

The girl stared after the man curiously and then glanced at Yakima. "Coyotes sling arrows out here?"

Barksdale was leaning against the coach, one low-heeled cavalry boot cocked with a flourish. He wore a brown-and-white pinto vest over a cream wool shirt, a string tie dancing down his chest. He had a red ostrich feather sticking out of the braided gator-skin band of his tobacco brown planter's hat, which he wore instead of a regulation kepi. "Coyoteros," Seth corrected. "Some call 'em coyotes because it's just easier to get their tongues around. But they're Apaches, just the same."

The girl's eyes were still on Yakima, which the young half-breed scout found a little disconcerting. He might have been half white, but the fact of his having any Indian blood at all made him a full-blood in most non-Indian eyes. Which made white girls, especially white girls of better breeding than the usual frontier fare, strictly off-limits.

It even made them dangerous.

"How are you?" the girl asked Yakima.

The scout's ears warmed. He wasn't sure how to answer the question. Had this pretty girl in all that finery and with such captivatingly bold eyes and straight, fine nose really addressed him?

"I saw what happened back there," she persisted, adding more water to Tatum's handkerchief but keeping her eyes on Yakima. "You're a marvelous horseman. I saw the Indian bull into you. Quite a tumble you took. But you held your own, didn't you? Apache scout, I take it? I heard that Apaches are quite magnificent mounted." She quirked another, slightly broader smile than before, her bold gray-blue eyes sparking in the warm sunshine. "Let's see—Papa said there were Aravaipa scouts at Fort Hell. Are you one of those?"

"No, ma'am," Yakima said, clearing a thick frog from his throat and finding himself not totally capable of meeting the girl's gaze. "I'm half Cheyenne."

"Ah," she said, narrowing her eyes admiringly. "You've the most amazing emerald gaze. . . ."

Seth grunted his disapproval of the turn in the conversation that had left him in the metaphorical dust. "Don't he got just the purtiest darn eyes?" he said, turning away. "I reckon I'd best go help Beltrami run down his wheel."

Yakima ground his jaws at his partner's ribbing. He

wanted to give Seth a hard right cross, and he would
have . . . if the girl hadn't been staring at him as though she
were peering right through him. "Emerald eyes . . . and
shy," she said, dabbing absently at Tatum's forehead. "I like
that."

"Allow me to remonstrate you, Miss Tunney," her patient said, scowling at Yakima. "Half-breed or full, it don't
matter. He don't deserve your . . ."

Tatum let his sentence trail off as thudding hooves
sounded in the distance. Yakima wheeled, instantly drawing both his Colts from the holsters he wore on both
fringed-buckskin-clad thighs and clicking the hammers
back.

He stared nearly straight south from the stage.

Several riders were barreling down on him, spread out
in a ragged line from left to right, their fleet ponies weaving through the desert scrub and leaping small patches of
prickly pear and Spanish bayonet. Dust billowed behind
them.

Yakima holstered his pistols when he recognized the
lead rider straddling a rangy cream mare. The willowy
frame and lean, craggy, leathery face that appeared nearly
black beneath the blue, broad-brimmed Hardee hat belonged to the chief of scouts himself, "Gila River" Joe
Tunney. Just then, recognizing Tunney and the three Aravaipa scouts galloping to either side of him, Yakima realized that the pretty pilgrim girl had been called Tunney by
Tatum.

He turned to the girl, frowning curiously. Surely she
was not related to the old desert rat, Gila River Joe, whom
Yakima saw as belonging as much to the Sonoran sands
and sun-blasted rocks and cactus as the Gila monsters
themselves. Hell, the old warrior had even been nicknamed
after a mostly dry desert watercourse. That's how long Gila
River Joe had called Arizona home.

He was so much a part of this land that he hadn't even
been sent east to fight in the War Between the States, but

instead had been one of the few soldiers who'd remained to garrison a remote outpost up near the little desert cross-roads settlement of Apache Junction, in the shadow of Superstition Mountain.

Nah. This pretty, gray-eyed, brown-haired girl clad in taffeta and crinoline couldn't be any relative of old Joe's.

Chapter 5

Yakima stood back, incredulous, as Gila River Joe Tunney, or simply "the sergeant," as Yakima and most everyone else addressed him, reined his mare to an abrupt halt not twenty yards from the stage.

The horse whinnied and skidded another six yards, and turned as it stopped. The sergeant, lean as whang leather and short—he came only to Yakima's shoulder, and he probably didn't weigh much more than a couple of bags of parched corn though he was the last man Yakima would ever want to fight—slipped smoothly out of his saddle and strode over to where the girl was just now rising, lowering the wadded, blood-spotted handkerchief.

"Samantha?" the sergeant said, tentative, his eyes worried in his craggy, hawk-nosed, Indian-dark face.

"Sergeant? F-father?" the girl said, in the same tentative fashion as the sergeant, as though she wasn't quite sure how to address him, or if she wasn't exactly sure about how she felt, seeing him.

Yakima stood back in stunned silence. He'd never given much thought to the sergeant's past or to his personal life.

A man like the sergeant didn't seem to have a personal life, let alone a family.

The sergeant was married to the cavalry, and outside of the service in general and the scouts in particular, he had no life. Or so Yakima had sort of semiconsciously opined. He'd never known the sergeant to drink much or even cavort with the percentage girls over at Valdez's saloon, much less father a child.

But the man had apparently had a woman, after all. And here stood the man's beautiful, gray-eyed product of that union, who didn't look half as bold as she'd looked before but now appeared as cautious as a doe with coyotes on her trail.

"I heard the caterwaulin'," the sergeant said. "Me an' the scouts were on top of that ridge yonder." He jerked his head to indicate the crest of a rocky butte humping up in the south. The sergeant and the Aravaipas had split from Yakima and Barksdale earlier that morning to look for the Chiricahuas. Well, they'd found at least a portion of the ragtag band. Or rather, the stage and the sergeant's daughter had.

The sergeant continued. "I was expectin' you on yesterday's stage. When you didn't show, I figured you'd be on Saturday's."

"We sent a courier from the Rattlesnake Station," said the driver, Beltrami, a little defensively as he and Barksdale rolled the wheel toward the coach. "A second stage came in from Lordsburg. Your daughter, Miss Samantha, was on that one, Joe."

Beltrami smiled at the sergeant. The driver continued wheeling the wheel over to the opposite side of the stage alone, for Seth, hearing the words *Joe* and *daughter* in the same sentence, stopped and turned to curiously regard the girl.

Barksdale glanced at Yakima, who shrugged, and then the sergeant said, "You all right, Samantha?"

She nodded, moving forward slowly, like a doe investigating a possible trap. She looked straight at him for a time—they were roughly the same size—and then she threw her arms around the sergeant's lean waist to hug him. The sergeant didn't seem to know what to do with himself. Only after Samantha had been embracing him for several seconds did the chief of scouts finally raise his arms and slowly, as though each weighed a good twenty pounds, wrap them around the girl.

Yakima had never seen the sergeant so uncomfortable, and he'd started to turn away in embarrassment but stopped when father and daughter separated.

The sergeant said, "Well, I'm glad you made it safe . . . uh . . . Samantha. Truly, I am. You're a rare sight for these sore old eyes. Look how you've grown. Good Lord. Well . . . you're not far from the fort now. Soon as Melvin gets that wheel back on the axle, we'll get you on over to Hell. I mean, uh, Hildebrandt. The colonel's got a room waitin', and Two Feathers will prepare you a hot bath."

"Two Feathers?" Samantha asked.

Before the sergeant could reply, the shotgunner, Dent, who was still sitting back against the coach's left front wheel, said, "Lookee there, the sergeant's got him a daughter. Who'd have known? A fine-lookin' little filly, too. Must take after her ma, eh, Joe?"

The sergeant looked relieved to be distracted from his uncomfortably intimate and unexpected reintroduction to his daughter, even though it had come by way of rude remarks from a notorious lout in this neck of the desert, Jubal Dent. The sergeant walked over to Dent, and Yakima felt his stomach muscles tighten. The sergeant was fair and generally kind, though always brusque. Small as he was in stature, he took nothing from anyone. Most everybody knew that and steered clear of climbing his hump, as the expression went.

But not Jubal Dent.

The sergeant stared down at the shotgun messenger. Yakima knew it was going to be bad when the sergeant smiled. He hardly ever smiled. His eyes, which were nearly the same gray as his daughter's, flashed when he was either pleased or angry, but he rarely smiled. When he did smile,

Yakima, Barksdale, and even the Aravaipa scouts ran for cover.

"Good Lord, Jubal—what did those savages do to you?" the sergeant asked in mock concern.

Dent stared up at him, closing one eye against the sun. His lips inside his thick, sweaty, dirty beard were stretched apprehensively. "I'll . . . I'll be all right, Sergeant," the shotgunner said. "Doc Sawchuck'll . . ."

He let his voice trail off as the sergeant said, "We need to get this out of you before it festers."

"I'm all right, Sergeant!"

"Pshaw," the sergeant said, crouching and closing one of his gloved hands around the point of the arrow protruding from the driver's back. He closed his other gloved hand around the arrow's fletched end.

Dent kicked and squirmed and shouted, "I'll be all right, Sergeant. Sawchuck'll fix me up good as n—!"

The sentence cut abruptly into a yelp as the sergeant snapped the arrow in two. Tossing away the arrow's fletched end, he pulled the pointed end out of the man's back. He tossed that end away, as well. Dent sat straight up against the wheel. His lower jaw hung nearly to his chest, and he was panting raggedly through his wide-open mouth.

His eyes stared off, glassy with shock.

"Joe!" Beltrami called from the other side of the stage. "Come over here, Joe. You're gonna wanna see this!"

The sergeant glanced at Yakima and Barksdale.

"Oh, Lord—don't tell me we're about to be attacked again!" exclaimed Tatum, still sitting against the stage's left rear wheel, holding his neckerchief against his forehead.

Gila River Joe strode over to his daughter, squeezed her forearm. "You stay here, Samantha. Don't wander far from the stage."

She said nothing as both Yakima and Barksdale gave her one more, incredulous look and then wheeled to follow their boss around the backside of the coach and into the brush beyond it. The three Aravaipi scouts dismounted. Chiquito, Pedro, and One-Eyed Miguel had been sitting

their mustangs with customary silence and patience,
though Yakima had been half-aware of One-Eyed Miguel
translating the white folks' conversation out one side of his
mouth for his two partners, neither of whom was fluent in
English. Aside from the cusswords, that is.

Both Chiquito and Pedro took unabashed delight in
swearing in the white man's tongue.

Yakima followed the sergeant with Barksdale close on
his heels. All three had their pistols out, cocked and ready.
The two stage passengers followed the three cavalrymen
cautiously.

Gila River Joe stopped beside Melvin Beltrami, who
stood looking down at something on the other side of a
clay-colored boulder beside which a barrel cactus grew
crooked. What they were looking at was a dead Apache.
No. At first, Yakima thought the dead man was an Apache,
because he'd only taken in the knee-high deerskin leggings
turned down at the tops, the pointed-toed javelina-skin
moccasins, and the red flannel bandanna wrapped around
the top of the man's head.

Not a man. A boy. A white boy.

The young man, maybe fourteen or fifteen years old, lay
twisted on his back, legs crossed, dark blue eyes staring
upward. The eyes were glazed in death. Blood trickled
from the corner of the boy's red lips. The blue eyes and the
blond hair were what was most noticeably white about the
kid. His skin was dark. Almost as dark as Yakima's. It had
been tanned by several years of desert wind, desert sun.

Like an Apache, he'd likely lived mostly outdoors even
in the winter.

Like *an Apache, hell,* Yakima thought. *This kid—this*
white *kid—must have been living as an Apache.* He must
have been with the Chiricahuas who'd attacked the stage,
and that was why he was lying here dead with two bullet
holes in his sun-bronzed chest. Either Yakima or Seth had
shot him. Blood trickled from both holes that shone between the flaps of his beaded deerskin vest, which, besides
the beaded breechclout, leggings, red sash, and bandanna,

was all he'd been wearing. A quiver and spilled arrows lay nearby; an ash bow strung with javelina gut and wrapped tightly with rawhide lay a little farther away.

Beltrami fingered his long gray beard as he shuttled his perplexed gaze to Gila River Joe. The driver's face twitched and his left arm jerked, and then he said, "I'll be damned if that ain't a white boy, Joe. A white boy ridin' with 'paches."

The sergeant again looked perplexed, downright stunned. Twice in one day. Yakima never thought he'd see the like.

Gila River Joe hitched his sky blue trousers with the yellow stripes running down the outside, up his skinny thighs. He slid his big Walker Colt back a little on his right hip, adjusted the bowie knife he wore in a beaded sheath on his left hip, both hanging from a wide black belt, and dropped to one knee beside the white Apache.

He leaned far over the dead boy, closely studying the dead child's face. Then so softly that Yakima wasn't sure that he'd heard the sergeant clearly, Gila River Joe said, "Angus?"

Before anyone could ask the sergeant what he'd said, so they could all be sure, the sergeant picked the boy up in his arms. The white Apache was probably nearly as tall and heavy as Joe himself, but the sergeant had no trouble hefting the child off the ground from his kneeling position.

He turned with the boy in his arms, brushed past Yakima and the rest of the onlookers, and stopped before the three Aravaipas, who, knowing their places in a mostly white gathering, had kept several yards back. The sergeant stopped directly in front of One-Eyed Miguel, or *El Tuerto*, as he was known in Spanish, and said nothing. He gave the Aravaipa a significant look.

One-Eyed Miguel, who wore hawk feathers in the many braids that fell past his shoulders, and whose face was long and crooked, his eyes set close against his long, slender nose, stared down at the boy in Gila River Joe's arms. His right eye, which was half-closed, was the blind one. It sat in a badly sunken and knotted socket in which you could occasionally glimpse the eggshell white eye that resided there. Yakima did not know how he'd lost the eye, but he assumed in battle with other Apaches. Apaches hated Apaches of other bands even more than they hated whites.

The sergeant said something in the Aravaipa dialect of the Athabaskan tongue, which was the guttural language of the Apache, to One-Eyed Miguel. The Aravaipa opened his mouth in surprise as he stared down at the dead white boy dressed as a Chiricahua, and responded to the sergeant's question. Yakima had picked up enough of the Apache language for rudimentary communication with his Aravaipa brethren, but both Gila River Joe and One-Eyed Miguel had spoken too low for him to have heard what they'd said.

The two men stared at each other across the dead boy's body hanging slack in the sergeant's arms.

"What's going on?" Yakima wanted to ask. "Who's the dead boy?" But he kept the questions to himself as the sergeant and the Aravaipa stared at each other in silent, grave communion. Obviously, they'd recognized him.

The sergeant had muttered what Yakima had picked up as "Angus."

Who was Angus?

Samantha broke the spell when she called from the other side of the stage, "Sergeant?" She hadn't said it loudly, but loudly enough and with enough tension that Yakima knew that she, too, had found something of significance.

The two young white scouts were the first to reach the other side of the stage. They stood staring off toward the south where many cream-colored, rocky buttes rose, foreshortening into the distance. From the tallest of these buttes, which was standing a little back from several others, puffs of gray smoke rose. The signals were answered by more smoke puffing from atop another butte still farther back and a little east.

The smoke had the brunt of Yakima's attention until his keen eyes caught movement on a low mesa fronting the nearest butte from which smoke signals rose. Several horseback riders were milling there. They were too far away to count, or to reveal many details, but Yakima could see the spots on a few of the horses. He also saw one of the riders thrust a war lance high in the air and hold it there for about five seconds before he thrust it upward three more times.

The quick, angry moves were sending a dark message to the bunch gathered around the stalled stage.

Then the rider with the lance wheeled his horse and disappeared. The others atop the mesa also turned their own horses and followed the leader down the far side of the mesa and out of sight. Gradually, the smoke signals dwindled until only a few gray strands drifted like cotton on the hot, dry breeze.

The Aravaipa scouts grunted their excitement, turning to the sergeant, who stood near the stage, holding the white boy in his arms and staring off toward where the smoke and horseback riders had been. Gila River Joe turned to One-Eyed Miguel, and said, "No. They want us to send a contingent after them. You know as well as I do what would happen if we did. We'll deal with them later."

One-Eyed Miguel spoke passionately in his guttural tongue.

"No," the sergeant repeated, rasping out the single word and shaking his head. He glanced at the other two Aravaipa scouts, Chiquita and Pedro, both of whom had already mounted their mustangs and sat tensely, shuttling eager looks between One-Eyed Miguel, the sergeant, and the mesa where they'd all seen the Apaches.

"Get 'em settled down," Joe told One-Eyed Miguel warningly.

Apaches, even Apaches who worked for the cavalry, liked nothing better than a challenge. They loved a fight. They loved war. Yakima often wondered how any Apache could ever settle down. They were proud and fiercely territorial. How could Arizona Territory itself ever get settled down enough that Indians and whites could live together in peace? To the young Cheyenne half-breed, such an aspiration seemed like foolish fantasy of politicians who didn't live here and didn't understand the Apache.

Oh, well, he often thought, when thinking about the

larger predicament became too much for him. At least he
had a job. Most nights, he even had a roof over his head and
enough pocket jingle that he could afford one of Valdez's
percentage girls one night a week. Girls and roofs over his
head had been rare until he'd come to Fort Hildebrandt.

To Fort Hell . . .

Samantha stood staring at the dead boy in the sergeant's
arms. She looked pale, shaken, confused. All of this—the
deadly fracas, the Apaches, and now the dead white boy
clad in Apache garb hanging slack in her father's arms—
seemed to be almost too much for her to take in. The girl
turned away suddenly. Gagging and hitching her skirts
above her ankles, she ran around the far side of the stage.

The sergeant turned to Yakima and Seth. "You two
keep an eye on her. Don't let her stray."

"You got it, Sergeant," Seth said, and he and Yakima followed the girl at a discreet distance as she ran into the desert,
retching.

"The rest of you—Beltrami, One-Eye, Chiquito, Pedro—
get that wheel on the stage so we can get back to Hildebrandt. Pronto!"

Just before the sergeant left his field of vision, Yakima
saw Gila River Joe staring down in shock and dismay at the
dead boy in his arms.

Angus . . . ?

Chapter 6

Samantha Tunney thought that she must be Gila River Joe's daughter, after all, for as the stage pulled back onto the trail after the long delay, she glanced out the window to her left. Her gaze landed on one of the dead Apaches whose lower face and upper chest were all blood and gristle. The warrior's jaw hung askew by only a few strands of ragged tendon.

The brave had obviously taken the full brunt of a shotgun blast.

Samantha turned her head away abruptly and clamped a hand against her chest. She did not want to vomit again. Certainly not in the stage amongst these men. But, realizing that she did not feel as weak as she had felt before, and that she'd turned away only fearing her own reaction, she slid her gaze out the window once more.

The dead brave was sliding back away from the stage as Mr. Beltrami pulled the coach back onto the trail, popping his whip over the backs of the four-horse hitch. Samantha stared at the blood and viscera, noting how the body lay at an odd angle, half on its side, for it had landed on a rock about the size of a wheel hub. She stared at the dead man whose bandanna had slid up to half cover the top of his head, turning her own head to follow the body until it grew small behind her. When it was out of sight, she fished a small sketchbook and pencil out of her leather satchel, opened the book's pasteboard cover, and flipped past the figures she'd sketched on her way west from Utica, New York—figures of farmers, Mississippi steamers, cowboys, long-horned cows, tar paper shacks standing alone on the prairie, log saloons with facades, a gaudily dressed young girl of the streets she glimpsed at Fort Smith, crude-looking men carrying guns and knives on their hips, railroad cars—until she found a fresh leaf.

From memory, Samantha sketched the dead Chiricahua, her pencil making quick slashes and curves across the top of the page. Before she knew it, her heart was fluttering with the excitement of inspiration, and she was done with the Chiricahua. At least, she had enough that she could fill in the details from memory later.

She had moved on to the second half of the page to sketch the shotgun rider sitting beside her slumped against the coach's far wall, groaning, half-conscious. Before they'd loaded Dent onto the stage, she'd helped her father stuff makeshift bandages into the man's two wounds, and Beltrami had given Dent a couple of big drinks from a hide-wrapped whiskey bottle he'd produced from a footlocker beneath the driver's seat. That had rendered the man semi-conscious, though he continued to groan as the stage jostled and rocked him where he sat beside Tatum, who Samantha realized had turned his attention on her, looking down at her with an expression of reproof on his mustached, bespectacled face.

Tatum didn't approve of her drawing a suffering man, apparently. But Dent would be suffering whether Samantha sketched him or not. Tatum could mind his own business. Besides, from what she'd overheard him saying to the other two passengers, he was a pimp returning to his saloon in Ehrenburg on the California line. Pimps had little room to judge others, Samantha thought, though she was more consumed now with her drawings than with what Tatum or anyone else thought of her.

She was fascinated by her surroundings. No longer as revolted as before, though of course the fear and revulsion were still there. How could she be human and not feel repulsed by all she'd seen this day?

But she no longer felt a driving desire to return to Utica, which was what she'd yearned to do when the Chiricahuas thundered out of the chaparral, screaming like banshees and flinging arrows, one of which had missed Samantha by a whisker to graze Tatum's forehead before embedding itself in a corner of the inner carriage. Samantha had vowed during the attack that if she survived, she would forget about visiting her father out here on this backside of hell. She would return to Utica and do just as she'd promised her mother: marry a moneyed man in business, who had nothing whatsoever to do with the military, and raise a family.

Her father had visited her only twice in the twenty years Samantha had been alive. If he wanted to do so again, she'd thought, he could visit her in Utica at his own bidding.

But now, she realized, she wanted to visit him here, in this strange, forbidding land more than ever—that strange, dark, cold-souled little military man with eyes like flint. The sergeant was a stranger to her. As strange as anything she'd so far encountered west of the Mississippi River.

"Samantha, you're twenty years old now, a young woman," her mother had said. *"If you really want to visit the sergeant out there on that savage frontier, there's little I can do to stop you. Especially when it is quite evident you have a will as indomitable as his!"*

She finished sketching the wounded shotgun rider and flipped the sketchbook's cover closed. So many thoughts were flinging themselves at her that now after the shock of the attack and of encountering her father again out here in what her mother had called the savage frontier, she found herself too distracted to continue drawing. Distracted, fascinated, even fearful. But she no longer felt any desire to return home—that is, not until after she'd had her fill of this place.

Maybe she was like her father. He had to be brave to remain out here for so long. Thirty years or more since he himself had left his home in Kentucky, spent a brief time in a military school, and then ventured west to fight the Indians. He had to have an adventurous spirit. Samantha had always considered herself adventurous, though, bound by the restraints of wealthy Eastern society, she hadn't been able to fully explore that adventurousness.

Now she considered the handsome, black-haired, green-eyed young man she'd seen galloping to her rescue, shooting Chiricahuas until one had driven him from his horse. The green-eyed young man—he had to be around her age—fascinated her even more than the Indians she'd seen on her trip so far. Yakima, she thought she'd heard the oily-eyed Southerner in the ostentatious hat call him. A half-breed. A man even more exotic than the Indians, because while he was half Indian, he was also half white.

Could there be a more lonely, precarious place for a man than this savage frontier? She'd heard that half-breeds were even more reviled than full-blooded Indians.

Samantha had to admit that her views were probably tainted with the quixotic influence of all the dime novels she'd read against her mother's forbidding, as well as the romantic yarns by Mr. Fennimore Cooper that she'd consumed before traveling here. Still she couldn't help smiling at the prospect of becoming more familiar with her strange frontiersman father on his own wild terrain, and the handsome young half-breed named Yakima.

Samantha stuck her head out the window, holding her small straw boater on her head. She blinked against the dust as she looked behind the stage. The half Indian clad in a blue chambray shirt, suspenders, buckskin pants, and broad-brimmed black hat rode about forty yards behind the coach, on his clean-lined buckskin gelding. The Southerner, who was just a little too much like the well-bred, overly confident young men Samantha's mother was always trying to match her up with, rode beside Yakima. Samantha smiled and pulled her head back into the stage.

The coach began to climb, slowing slightly.

"Fort Hell dead ahead, folks!" Beltrami shouted from his perch in the driver's box. "Or . . . uh . . . Fort Hildebrandt, if you'll beg my pardon!"

The jehu laughed at that. Again, Samantha smiled. She'd heard the fort's moniker way back in Utica, as the rebuilding and garrisoning of Fort Hildebrandt had been the subject of several articles in the Washington *Globe* and in several magazines that the girl had subscribed to while away at finishing school in New York City—many without her mother's or stepfather's knowledge, of course. But, then, they'd never known about the small bohemian circle of young artists and writers she'd run around with, either.

Nor, of course, of the private drawing sessions she'd attended with sittings of nude models, including several nude *male* models. Ever since those sessions, Samantha had found herself imagining what certain attractive men she met would look like with their clothes off.

She snickered quietly at the thought, wondering what Yakima Henry would look like in his birthday suit, and then, feeling both sheepish and finding herself squirming a little, turned her attention to the buildings that had started appearing outside the coach's windows.

They were climbing between high, rounded buttes tufted with cactus and stippled with rocks. Near the bottom of one of the buttes, on the right side of the coach, was a brick chapel with a belfry. Out in front of the chapel a man in a long brown robe, obviously the priest, was playing tug-of-war with a beefy yellow mutt, the priest laughing and the dog growling and shaking his head as he pulled on the rope. The priest and the dog turned to the coach, and the priest shaded his eyes with his hand to scrutinize the carriage, and the dog barked and gave chase, nipping at the turning wheels.

"Where's your shotgun messenger, Melvin?" asked the priest.

"Inside the coach with a Chiricowy arrow in his shoulder!" shouted the driver as the team continued pulling the stagecoach up the slope between the buttes.

A ways beyond was a larger building marked COMMISSARY. Like the chapel and the other buildings scattered amongst the buttes, the commissary was constructed of mud bricks with straw and gravel embedded in the bricks. The commissary had a buggy pulled up to it, and two women and several children were milling amongst the barrels and crates of goods arranged on the wooden loading dock, which stood high atop stone pylons. The dock was shaded by a broad brush ramada.

Samantha turned her head this way and that, taking it all in—or, at least what she could see of the post's fringes from inside the lurching coach, dust billowing in the windows and causing her to blink and cough. Out the coach's left side a long, low building came into view, identified by a crude wooden sign as BUTTERFIELD STAGE STATION NO. 10, another smaller sign announcing Z. W. HAWKINS, STATIONMASTER. A man who Samantha assumed was Mr. Hawkins himself, wearing suspenders over a white, sweat-stained shirt and a bowler hat, with a fat cigar protruding from one corner of his mouth, was staring incredulously at the coach.

"Jubal's been hit!" the driver shouted by way of explanation. "Headin' for the hospital!"

The stationmaster removed the stogie from his mouth and began striding along the trail behind the stage, waving at the dust. He was walking past another building just west of the stage station that a large, bold sign stretching across its second story identified as SONORA SUN SALOON. This structure, built of sun-bleached vertical boards, had little color itself, but brightly colored curtains hung over most of the first- and second-story windows, and the three girls milling and smoking on the building's front gallery were dressed, however skimpily, in all colors of the rainbow.

"What happened?" one of the girls, clad in a pink corset and thin blue wrap, called to the stationmaster striding past the saloon's porch.

The stationmaster ignored her as he kicked at the priest's dog, which deftly dodged and wheeled away from him, the stationmaster shouting something that Samantha could not hear above the clomping of the team's hooves and the squawking and rattling of the coach's wheels.

As the coach swung sharply to the right, Samantha grabbed a rawhide strap hanging from the ceiling to brace herself.

The coach passed under a wooden portal announcing simply FORT HILDEBRANDT. Two uniformed guards armed with rifles stepped aside as the coach continued on along a trail, more and more mud-brick buildings revealing themselves to Samantha's wide-eyed gaze. To the right was a building with a narrow gallery marked POST COMMANDER. A short, thickset young officer with a black mustache and goatee stood near the log porch rail, staring concernedly at the coach, which stopped before him.

A great cloud of dust overtook the coach, even more than before, and Samantha found herself having to squeeze her eyes closed against it, coughing. When she opened her eyes again, the driver and Yakima and the Southern scout were helping the shotgun messenger out of the coach's far side.

Samantha's father was standing on the porch of the post commander's office, talking to the short young officer as well as to another man—the post commander?—who was now standing on the porch, as well.

The gray-haired man was stroking a cream kitten that was crouched on his right shoulder. He was not clad in the traditional blue uniform tunic, but in a soft light tan buckskin jacket and with a red kerchief knotted around his red-weathered, deeply lined neck. He was tall and broad-chested, his shoulders thrust back with authority while one knee, clad in brown corduroy, appeared bent at an odd angle. In his free hand was a black wooden cane topped with a stallion carved from obsidian. He wore a crisp cream stockmen's hat banded with a skin of some kind.

Samantha's father and the stocky young officer, who

wore a monocle on his right eye, both seemed to be deferring to the older gent. Though the older gent was not wearing a uniform, nor showing his rank in any way, Samantha had a feeling that this man with the broad, leonine head, the thick gray muttonchop whiskers, and the brick red, weathered cheeks was indeed the post commander, Colonel Ephraim Alexander. The stocky young man, who had lieutenant's bars on his shoulders, was likely the colonel's aide, whose name, if Samantha remembered correctly from her father's letters, was Lieutenant Gunther Geist.

While the two scouts helped the wounded shotgun messenger around the back of the coach and over to an infirmary sitting opposite the post commander's office, the other three male passengers climbed out of the stage on the post commander's side. The stocky, young lieutenant leaned into the door, smiling. He was no longer wearing his monocle, the black silk ribbon of which dangled from the breast pocket of his gold-buttoned tunic. With a faint German accent, he said, "Miss Tunney, welcome to Fort Hildebrandt. I am the colonel's adjutant. May I assist?"

The young lieutenant, who had a square head and a broad, pale face that did not take well to the sun, and dark brown eyes, slid a small, soft hand through the open door and into the coach.

"Yes, of course," Samantha said, aware of the young lieutenant's eyes roaming all over her body as she accepted his hand. He was not at all handsome, but his teeth were large and white, though one gold one peeked out from behind his right eyetooth. "Thank you, uh . . . Lieutenant Geist, is it?" Samantha said as she stepped onto the small, portable step situated before the coach's open door for her benefit, and planted her other side-button shoe on the ground.

She must have been dizzy from the jouncing ride, which did not surprise her, as it had happened before on the long trip she'd taken by train, steamboat, and stage, the stages naturally being the roughest form of all three methods of travel. The ground seemed to slide out from under her, and she gave a startled "Whoa!" as she pitched to her right . . .

and into the open arms of Lieutenant Geist, who laughed as he helped her regain her balance.

"A little unbalanced, I see," the lieutenant said, keeping his thick left arm wrapped a little too tightly around her slender waist. "A stage road as well as a Chiricahua ambuscade does that to a person. Fortunately, I've caught you and promise not to release you until you've regained your equilibrium."

"She'll be fine, Lieutenant." This from Samantha's father, Gila River Joe, who'd come down off the porch and was standing nearby with the man who Samantha assumed was the post commander. The sergeant was scowling at the young lieutenant from beneath the brim of his tan campaign hat, his sun-leathered nose slanting down over his upper lip like a menacing knife. "You keep holdin' her like that, she won't be able to take a breath."

Samantha gave a nervous laugh and brushed stray strands of her hair from her eyes as the lieutenant removed his arm. "Yes, I'm fine now, Lieutenant. Thanks for your help." The dust was still lifting around them, and Samantha wrinkled her nose at it and waved her hand again.

Crisply and in what the girl decided was her father's customary authoritative tone relieved by no warmth whatever, the sergeant said, "Samantha, this is Colonel Alexander. The colonel is the commander of Fort Hildebrandt. Colonel Alexander, this is my daughter from Utica, New York—Samantha Tunney."

The colonel smiled and held out his hand. "A pleasure to meet you, Miss Tunney. I've been waiting for you ever since your stepfather, the lieutenant governor, informed me . . ." The colonel hesitated, cutting his eyes somewhat sheepishly to Samantha's father, whose own craggy, dark face remained implacable beneath the shading brim of his hat. "Uh . . . well, that Mr. Biddles informed me of your wish to visit us here at Fort Hildebrandt. To visit your father, I mean, though it's my own great pleasure to have you, as well."

Samantha smiled brightly and shook the colonel's hand.

She could tell that Colonel Alexander felt chagrined to have mentioned that instead of her own natural father it had been Samantha's stepfather, the lieutenant governor of New York State, who'd first informed the colonel of the girl's intention to visit the Arizona Territory. Lieutenant Governor George T. Biddles had made all of the arrangements on behalf of Samantha and Samantha's mother, Katherine.

Samantha's stepfather was nearly as doting on Samantha as the girl's mother. Samantha knew that her stepfather and Colonel Alexander had exchanged at least a dozen letters on the subject, though she hadn't received one word from her own father, the sergeant.

Uncle George, as Samantha had dubbed her mother's husband when he married Katherine when Samantha was only seven years old, had wanted to send a bodyguard along on Samantha's journey to the Wild West, but the headstrong girl had steadfastly refused, insisting she was savvy enough to travel alone. While Samantha had taken full advantage of her privileged upbringing, she had always resisted its constraints, and that had been part of the reason why she'd wanted to make this journey.

"Thank you ever so much, Colonel," Samantha said. "I can't tell you how happy I am to be here. All of this is terribly new to me. Quite novel." She looked at her stoic father. "And it's been a terribly long time since I've had the pleasure of my long-lost father's company."

There was an awkward silence. The colonel glanced at Gila River Joe and then turned his gaze back to Samantha. "I do apologize for the attack. You would have had an escort if we'd been expecting you, but apparently the courier from the Diamondback Creek Station didn't make it through."

"Oh, that wasn't your fault. Besides, it turned out we were in quite good hands," Samantha said, turning to the two scouts, Yakima and Mr. Barksdale, who had returned from the commissary to mill around behind the sergeant and the colonel, probably awaiting orders. Samantha had noticed that the Aravaipa scouts were all waiting some distance away, in the shade of the infirmary's brush arbor.

They were squatting there; one was drawing in the dirt with a stick.

"Yes, well, good," the colonel said. "I'm glad you're all right, and I hope you find the accommodations here at Fort Hildebrandt comfortable. I'm sure they won't be anything like what you're accustomed to."

"I wasn't expecting that they would be!" Samantha laughed.

"My housekeeper, Two Feathers, has been awaiting your arrival. I'll send for a hack and have Corporal Diamond take you and your luggage over to my quarters straightaway." Uncle George had arranged for Samantha to stay in the colonel's house, as it wouldn't have been fitting for her, the stepdaughter of a lieutenant governor, to stay anywhere less accommodating. Most guests of any status at all at Fort Hildebrandt stayed with the officers' families and were served by the officers' servants.

"If you don't mind, Colonel, I'd like to take a leisurely walk," Samantha said. "I think I've done quite enough riding for a while, and I'd love to take a look around. This is all quite exotic to this city girl's eyes." She tried not to look at the blanket-wrapped body draped over the back of her father's cream mare, which was tied to a hitch rack near the front of the stage team.

She knew that the blankets shrouded the dead white boy dressed as an Indian. And she had a feeling that her father was waiting to discuss the boy with the colonel. The colonel called for a wagon to pick up her luggage, which formed a small mountain on the boardwalk in front of his office, and then he shook the girl's hand once more.

"Your father will want to accompany you, no doubt," the colonel said.

"I would like to, Colonel," said Gila River Joe. "But I'm afraid I'll have to catch up with Samantha later. I have a matter to discuss with you. A pressing one."

"That's quite all right, Sergeant," Samantha said, pushing through the strange apprehension she'd found herself feeling around her father, who was so different from everyone else in her life, and planted a kiss on Gila River Joe's cheek. "I don't want my visit to impede on the sergeant's duties."

"I'd be happy to escort Miss Tunney over to your quarters, sir," piped up Lieutenant Geist, clicking his bootheels together sharply and smiling broadly at Samantha. "If Miss Tunney herself feels so inclined, of course."

Samantha couldn't very well say no. And she supposed that she did need someone to show her the way. So, while she'd have preferred the company of Yakima Henry, who was leaning back against the hitch rack, trying as hard as he could to keep his eyes off her, Samantha accepted Lieutenant Geist's proffered arm.

She said good-bye to her father and the colonel. The colonel smiled. Her father did not. The strange, dark little man could have been carved out of granite. But Samantha did not take offense or lose heart in the reason for her visit.

She was going to crack through that hard outer crust and probe her father's depths. In doing so, she was convinced that she would gain an understanding not only of who Gila River Joe was, but also of herself, as well.

While passing Yakima, Samantha turned and offered the handsome half-breed an ever so faintly devilish smile, which he met straight-on before jerking his eyes away and fidgeting with his horse's reins.

Chapter 7

The sergeant was relieved when the girl had gone, though he hadn't liked the way Lieutenant Geist had been staring at her, as though she were a big plate of food he was about to shove his thick snout in. Geist was a big eater. A big womanizer, too, though as far as the sergeant had heard, most of his womanizing was one-sided. His sundry advances toward every female who moved through the fort's cottonwood gates were roundly thwarted.

During his free time, Geist was known to prey on the washwomen of Soap Suds Row behind the quartermaster storehouse, where the fort's clothes and bedding were boiled, dried, and steamed by a dozen women—some of them noncommissioned officers' wives, some of them women who did double duty in the cribs behind the Sonora Sun Saloon and the post trader's store after dark.

The colonel, however, was fond of the stocky lieutenant, a supposedly well-bred immigrant from Germany. The sergeant supposed the colonel had his reasons, not the least of which was probably that Geist was efficient in his duties, most of which pertained to the overwhelming task of

ensuring that the fort was continuously provisioned by the
army's western storehouses, which lay over a thousand miles
away in San Francisco.

Anyway, Geist was no business of the sergeant's. That
the colonel valued him was good enough for Gila River
Joe. As far as the sergeant was concerned, Colonel Alexander himself was an exemplary officer, the very best that
any soldier could be. That any *man* could be. Oh, the colonel had gotten a little softer in his later years, allowed
himself a tad too much food and drink. But while he might
overindulge himself and his daughter a bit, he'd given his
life to the military. He'd even sacrificed most of his family
to the taming of the Western frontier. He'd lost much and
he deserved to pamper both himself and his only surviving
child now in the late autumn of his career and his life.

The sergeant felt an almost religious devotion to this
proud, straight-backed, aging soldier, who could do no
wrong in his eyes. Though the sergeant never could have
expressed such sentiment, he loved and respected Colonel
Ephraim Alexander, only ten years his senior, like a wise
old uncle. They'd been together on the frontier a long time,
and in light of the old man's history and personal and professional tragedy, the sergeant felt not only devoted but pro-
tective of him.

That was why the matter he wanted to bring up with the
post commander was a particularly hard one to broach.

"She's a beautiful girl, Sergeant," the colonel said, watching Samantha walk away with Geist while the stagecoach was turned around and driven back in the direction
of the relay station. The two uninjured passengers headed
with their luggage for the Dragoon Mountain Hotel, a pri-
vately owned flophouse that flanked the post trader's store
and that also housed a small saloon.

Alexander smiled at the sergeant. "You must be very
proud." Then, as he searched the smaller man's face, which
must have betrayed the sergeant's consternation, Alexander's smile faded, and he said, "Joe, what is it?"

The sergeant turned to his two young scouts, Henry and

Barksdale, and then cut his eyes toward the blanket-wrapped body lying over the cuppers of the cream gelding standing at the hitch rack. The scouts walked over to the horse and untied and removed the body from behind the cantle of the sergeant's saddle.

"Joe, you know we don't bring dead Apaches back to the fort," the colonel said, looking and sounding befuddled. "We let their own people care for them."

"This one's different, Colonel," the sergeant said as the two scouts carried the body up onto the porch fronting the colonel's office. To the scouts, the sergeant said, "Take him on inside, boys."

The colonel looked even more incredulous. "Joe, what on earth is the meaning of this?" He chuckled without mirth and pointed toward the scouts with his cane. "You're not bringing that Chiricahua into my office!"

The scouts stopped just outside the open office door, looking questioningly back at their two superior officers. When the sergeant nodded, they glanced at each other, shrugged, and continued carrying the body into the colonel's office.

The sergeant said, "You'll understand in a minute, Colonel."

He climbed the porch steps, ordering the scouts inside the office to lay the body on the map table in the office's outer area, where Geist and Corporal Diamond worked at separate desks. The sergeant stepped inside, blinking against the heavy shadows. The scouts were laying the boy's body on a table along the office's left wall, under a framed map of Arizona Territory. Several wooden filing cabinets and bookshelves lay to the right.

The single, sashed window in the front wall, left of the table, spread a trapezoid of yellow sunlight upon the blanket-wrapped body, the head of which lay two feet from the window. Some of the boy's blond hair shone through folds in the blankets. His moccasin-clad feet poked out the other end of the package, the pointed toes curled. The right moccasin's seams were parting, offering a glimpse of the young man's pale little toe.

The sergeant canted his head at his men, and the two scouts retreated to the dense shadows near Corporal Diamond's unoccupied desk. The corporal was fetching a buckboard with which to transport the sergeant's daughter's luggage to the colonel's large house on Officers' Row. The colonel clomped heavily up onto the porch, slightly dragging his left leg from having taken a rebel minié ball in the knee back in '64.

"Good Lord, Sergeant," the older man said, "I can't imagine why you—"

He cut himself off as he gazed at Gila River Joe, who was untying the rawhide straps around the boy's body. The sergeant had already unwrapped the boy's head, and it must have been the blond hair that had silenced the post commander.

Colonel Alexander limped over to the table and stood to the right of the sergeant. "A blond Chiricahua?"

"No such thing," the sergeant said.

Alexander scowled at the sergeant. Then he looked at the boy lying before him atop the blanket.

"Good Lord," he said. "This is no Apache." He ran his arthritic right hand down the boy's slender arm. Even with the deep bronze tan, it was apparent that the young man was naturally fair-skinned.

"Look," the sergeant said, turning the boy's right arm, which had a rawhide thong tied around it just above the elbow, until he and the colonel were looking down at the almost fish-belly white of the boy's inner arm.

"Take a look at his eyes," the sergeant urged quietly.

"His eyes?"

The sergeant nodded. "Take a look."

The boy's blond head was turned slightly toward the colonel. His eyes were half-open, but you couldn't really see their color, as they were partly hidden by the pale lids.

Flies buzzed in the air around the boy's chest that was matted with congealed blood. More blood had dried as it had run down the left corner of the boy's mouth, the ends of his white teeth revealed by the lips stretched in a slight grimace. He was missing one tooth.

The colonel hesitated, bent down as though to see under the half-closed lids, and then said, "Well, here . . . ," and used his left thumb to pry up the young man's left eyelid. A blue eye stared glassily up at him, the bright sunlight reflecting off the cornea.

The colonel stared down at the eye for a long time. He removed his thumb from the eye, and the lid dropped about a third of the way down over the eyeball. The colonel was breathing hard. The sergeant could hear him wheezing softly, his broad shoulders rising and falling heavily. The sergeant said nothing, his boots cemented to the floor.

The colonel stepped back but he kept his hands half-raised, opening and closing them. He looked at the sergeant, who looked back at him, Gila River Joe's eyes saying nothing. The sergeant's heart was heavy. Sweat dribbled down his back under his shirt, and down his leathery, clean-shaven cheeks. He knew that the colonel was beginning to come to the realization of this blond Chiricahua's identity.

The sergeant turned to the two scouts waiting in the shadows, both with their heads canted to one side, frowning curiously at the sergeant and the colonel. The sergeant said quietly, "You boys go tend your horses. Get yourselves something to eat. Tell the others." He glanced out the window at the Aravaipas squatting on their haunches in the shade of the infirmary's ramada. "I'll track you down shortly."

The scouts shuffled out of the post commander's office.

The colonel looked at the sergeant. He rolled the boy onto his side, so that he faced away from him and the sergeant. With his red, arthritic hands, the colonel parted the long, coarse bleached blond hair that had been cut unevenly, probably cropped with a bowie knife. It hung around the boy's neck, and the colonel parted it several times before he stopped and stared.

A salmon-colored, vaguely liver-shaped birthmark shone between his slightly quivering fingers.

"My God," the colonel whispered. He paused for a long time, took a deep, raspy breath. "His mother called that an angel's kiss."

The colonel removed his hands from the back of the boy's head. The crudely cropped hair fell back into place along the boy's neck, hiding the birthmark. The sergeant had been holding the young man up on his left shoulder, but now he released him and the boy rolled onto his back. His partly open, cerulean eyes stared at the ceiling.

"Angus," the colonel said, a sob choking out of him. He stumbled back and before the sergeant could catch him, he'd dropped to one knee in front of the table. "Oh, Christ— *Angus!*"

Chapter 8

Lieutenant Geist wasn't the tour guide Samantha would have chosen. The guide she'd have preferred was the young, bashful half Cheyenne, Yakima Henry. However, the stocky, monocle-wearing lieutenant—did he think the eye-piece made him appear sophisticated?—was definitely informative as he led the young New Yorker through the heart of Fort Hildebrandt.

As they strolled along together, he identified many of the buildings surrounding the long, dusty parade ground that was furrowed with the prints of many horses and on which not a single tuft of grass grew. He pointed out a butcher shop, the quartermaster's storehouses, the blacksmith and farrier shop, a tailor shop, several sets of cavalry barracks, an oil house, two kitchens, a mess hall, several granaries. Perched on a hill to the east were the charred brick remains of the old hospital, which had been burned along with the rest of the fort when the cavalry abandoned it back in '62. Samantha inquired about a mound of brown soil lying up a slight grade toward the north and flanked by rocky bluffs.

"Oh, that," said Geist, eager to answer the girl's every question, "is the source of all the fresh water here at Fort Hildebrandt. Do you see that dark line running up into the hills to the north and west?"

Shading her eyes from the hammering sun, Samantha said she did.

"That's the ditch that carries the water from Cedar Spring to the reservoir. A pipe carries the water from the reservoir to that holding tank over there," Geist added, pointing toward a large wooden tank propped on stone pilings not far from the reservoir. A young, black-haired, dark-skinned girl in a checked dress was filling a bucket from a spigot near the bottom of the tank. "That's Norma Yellow Bird. She's the housemaid of Lieutenant and Mrs. Vincent."

"Apache?"

"Full-blood Mimbreño, also known as Gila or Warm Springs Apache. Almost all of the officers' wives have at least one Apache girl working in their house. All except for Lieutenant Myers's wife, Millicent. Mrs. Myers knew a woman who did the laundry out here before the war. The laundress was badly stabbed—pardon me, but *butchered* might be a more precise description—by one of the Apache girls she had working for her. A young Coyotero. Mrs. Myers saw it happen and she refuses to let any Apache into her home. She employs, at her own expense, a young white woman from Wilcox."

"I see."

"Was that too much for you?" Geist asked, turning to regard Samantha with concern. He clamped his right hand over hers resting on his left forearm, his monocle winking in the sunlight. "I shouldn't have said anything about the murder, after your unlucky experience along the trail. Please, accept my apology, Miss Tunney."

"I'm no shrinking violet, Lieutenant," Samantha assured the man crisply. "What I saw earlier was quite horrifying, but I've read enough about the horrors and depredations out here that it didn't take me entirely by surprise. Your description of the murder of a single woman sounds quite tame by comparison. I assure you—I won't lose any sleep over your story tonight."

"Will you lose any over the Chiricahuas?"

Samantha frowned as the lieutenant led her up the north side of the parade ground on which three groups of men were skirmishing with their horses, hooves thudding, the soldiers' voices rising in the hot, dry air around the flag buffeting in the wind.

"I don't think so," she said. "Maybe I'm still in shock, but I feel as if I'm over it now. I've never seen anyone killed before, and it was indeed startling, but, yes—I don't think it will bother me unduly. More than anything, I guess I'm . . ." She paused as she searched for the right word. "I guess I'm more fascinated by this new experience I'm having. This world out here is so different from my own back in New York State."

Geist chuckled and digressed for a moment, pointing out a row of small but neat, two-story, wood-framed houses set back behind a white picket fence and with scraggly, transplanted trees bristling from the otherwise desolate yards. He said that those were the homes of the married officers' families.

Samantha looked around, taking it all in—the little, neat houses with porches on which wicker chairs were arranged, the parade ground and skirmishing soldiers, thumping horses, tack squawking, dust rising, the guidon flapping in the wind. There were the smells of cooking emanating from a kitchen as well as the stench of horse manure and dust and the peppery tang of the few desert plants. Occasional voices or the soft tinkling of a piano rose from one of the houses that Samantha and Geist passed as they walked. From one came slightly louder, jovial voices and then a woman's delighted laughter.

Suddenly, she realized that Geist was smiling at her from behind his dusty monocle. As she turned her face to his, he said, "Sergeant Tunney's daughter." He shook his head. "Who'd have thought he even had a daughter?"

"Didn't talk too much about me, I gather," Samantha said with a wry chuckle.

"Well, the sergeant, I'm sure you know, isn't the most talkative of soldiers. Of all the sergeants at Fort Hildebrandt, I probably see your father the most, since he's such good friends with the colonel, and all . . . but he's also the one sergeant . . . the one noncommissioned officer at the fort I know the least about."

"That's interesting."

"Interesting?"

"Yes, it's interesting to hear that about him," Samantha said as she and the lieutenant stopped walking at the same time and turned to each other. "You see, Lieutenant, I—"

"Please, call me Gunther. I don't feel worthy of having one as beautiful as you addressing me so formally. Besides, most everyone at Fort Hildebrandt has followed the colonel's lead in loosening regulations just a tad."

"Well, then—Gunther it is," Samantha said, offering a pleasant smile but feeling as uncomfortable as she usually did under male fawning, especially when she wasn't nearly as interested in said fawner. She was grateful to Geist for the tour, but she felt no attraction to the man whatsoever. He seemed too full of himself, too in love with the sound of his own voice, his own measured cadences, and something told her that a cold shrewdness, a selfish arrogance lay not far beneath his unctuous surface.

She knew such quick judgments were unfair, but she couldn't help herself.

"You were going to say before I so rudely interrupted?" Geist asked as they stood facing each other, the soldiers skirmishing behind him. Somewhere, someone was blowing a bugle none too artfully, and a dog was barking.

"I was going to say that as little you know about my father, I probably don't know him half so well. I've seen him only twice before. My mother says he was with us for a few years after I was born, but they divorced when I was three. I hardly remember those first three years. Since then, I've seen the sergeant twice. Both back East. Both times for half a day each. And he probably never said more than twenty or thirty words to me during each of those half days."

Geist placed his hand on her shoulder. "I'm very sorry."

"Don't be. I've had a good life. I was raised well with nearly all the comforts a girl could imagine. I was sent to the best finishing school in the country and got an education that I hope has given me depth and the beginnings of an understanding of the world I live in. I love my mother and my stepfather dearly. But now it's time to get to know my blood father." She hiked a shoulder. "That's why I'm here."

Samantha studied Geist's face as he regarded her dubiously from behind his monocle. She thought she knew what he was thinking. "Wish me luck." Then she chuckled, and Geist held out his left elbow and she hooked her right arm around it. They turned and resumed walking.

"If you don't mind, I'll be frank, Miss Tunney."

"Only if you'll call me Samantha, Gunther. Fair is fair, after all."

"Ah, thank you. Samantha it is. What a lovely name. Frankly, I find it a wee bit difficult to fathom you as the sergeant's daughter. You're so personable and charming, and you obviously enjoy conversation. You must have inherited those qualities from your mother, I would assume?"

"So would I," Samantha said. "But if you look closely at photographs of me and the sergeant, you'll see a familial resemblance. We have some of the same facial features, the same natural coloring. Our builds are similar."

"Ha!" Geist said, flirtatiously. "I think we'll have to agree to disagree on that point."

Samantha laughed and kicked playfully at a stone, aware that the man was ogling her breasts whenever she wasn't looking directly at him. "I mean, in a family sort of way, though I'll admit we do seem to come from two different worlds. Have you noticed that even I call him sergeant?"

"I did notice that, but I didn't want to make you feel self-conscious about it."

"I'm hoping that by the time I leave Fort Hildebrandt,

I'll be able to address him as Father and make it come out sounding halfway natural."

"Well, here we are," Geist said, stopping in front of the largest house that Samantha had seen so far on Officers' Row. They'd climbed a slight hill, and here, nestled in some mesquites at the end of Officers' Row, and with a large, scraggly cottonwood partly shading it, stood a sprawling structure built of wood and brick, with a stately gambrel roof. The house was certainly nothing like what Samantha had grown up in, or what she was accustomed to seeing back where she hailed from, but it was an impressive dwelling given the otherwise barrenness and crudeness of what she'd so far observed on the Western frontier.

A broad porch with a painted wooden floor, white pillars, and a sturdy white rail appeared to abut the south and east sides. A long, leather-padded cradle swing hung beneath the porch roof, and its chains squawked faintly as the breeze jostled them. A potted palm tree stood between the swing and the large stained-glass window, which bore the same pattern as the transom window over the heavy oak doors.

Beyond the house to the south were a few more adobe outbuildings, and a large brick barn with an adjoining corral in which four or five clean-lined Thoroughbreds stood idly. In addition, there were also a two-hole brick privy and several more sheds as well as a stylish, red-wheeled chaise with its leather top folded down.

"Oh, my goodness . . . how unexpected," Samantha said.

"The colonel has been criticized for the opulence of his private quarters by several of his underlings as well as by several newspaper reporters who'd visited the fort just after it was rebuilt after the war. To them I say bunk. The colonel is a civilized man accustomed to the finer things in life. He's devoted most of his life to his country. He fought bravely in the War Between the States, suffering a shattered knee for his trouble. And he returned here after the war—here, to a place of great, remembered sorrow. I say he deserves to retire to such luxury after the long days he puts in. After all, who knows how long he'll be out here? The Apaches certainly show no signs of going anywhere, or of settling down, and we need old warriors like Colonel Alexander."

Geist nodded to indicate the buckboard wagon pulled up in front of the house. "Ah, Corporal Diamond is here with your luggage."

Samantha had seen the wagon being driven at a spanking pace along the far side of the parade ground and roll off ahead of her and the lieutenant. Now she watched a young, uniformed man in a forage cap—who she assumed was Corporal Diamond—step out of the house and stride out to the buckboard to retrieve the rest of her luggage, which lay in the wagon's box. The corporal paused to salute the lieutenant and then, nodding cordially to Samantha, continued his chore.

"Shall we, Samantha?" Geist said, extending his hand toward the house's open front door. "I'll introduce you to Two Feathers."

Samantha was staring at the corporal, but her mind was elsewhere. Now she absently turned to Geist again and said, "Please, unless I'm being overly nosy, explain to me what you mean about *great, remembered sorrow*, Gunther."

"Beg your pardon?"

"You said that after the war, the colonel returned here to this place of *great, remembered sorrow*. What did you mean?"

"The lady's luggage has been placed in her room, Lieutenant Geist."

Samantha turned to see Corporal Diamond, who didn't appear to be much over thirteen or fourteen years old, though of course he had to be, standing at the bottom of the porch steps, saluting the lieutenant, his oversized blue uniform blouse hanging loosely off his shoulders.

The lieutenant returned the corporal's salute. "Thank you, Corporal. That will be all. I'll see you back at headquarters."

"Thank you, sir!" The corporal strode over to the wagon, climbed aboard, and headed off down the hill along the parade ground.

Something told Samantha that Lieutenant Geist had welcomed the interruption. He looked a bit flushed and fidgety when just before he'd been the picture of self-assured, fawning servitude.

"Ah, there's Two Feathers," he said, sounding relieved. With a dip of his chin, he indicated a full-bodied, middle-aged Indian woman in a cream dress printed with purple flowers, waiting in the house's open doorway, her brown-eyed, coffee-colored face expressionless. "I'll introduce you in a minute, but first—"

"I'm sorry if my question was out of line, Gunther," Samantha said, her iron will compelling her to press the matter, though she knew she was crowding the border of discreetness. She'd always been overly inquisitive. She knew that if her mother were here, she'd be horrified.

"Well . . . uh . . . no, not at all." The lieutenant's swarthy, fleshy cheeks above his thick black mustache and goatee were flushing crimson. "It is a delicate matter, and one that should be continued at another time. How about if you allow me the privilege of accompanying you to the weekly dance at the mess hall Saturday night? Punch will be served, and several of the men here at Hildebrandt are quite adept with a squeeze-box, guitar, and harmonica. Corporal Paddy Graydon plays a right mean fiddle!"

"Oh . . . a dance." It was Samantha's turn to fidget. She didn't feel any desire to join the overly ingratiating young officer to an entertainment of any kind, but guilt needled her. He had, after all, shown her around the fort, and he'd been awfully nice. The poor man, a bit of a loblolly and not overly handsome, probably didn't have many lady friends. He seemed so desperate for a companion that Samantha found herself saying, "Yes, of course, I'd love to accompany you to the dance on Saturday night, Gunther."

Immediately, however, she regretted the response.

What if she'd wrangled an invitation from young Yakima Henry, the young, green-eyed half Cheyenne who so thoroughly intrigued her?

"Wonderful!"

For a second, Samantha thought Geist was going to levitate off the heels of his polished, high-topped black boots. Instead, he turned and gestured again to the Indian woman waiting in the open door of Colonel Alexander's residence. "Shall we?"

Chapter 9

Yakima Henry and Seth Barksdale were carefully grooming their horses under the brush arbor that ran down the middle of the quartermaster's corral, which sat outside the main fort and was ringed by a six-foot adobe wall. Yakima and his buckskin were in one stall, Seth and his sorrel in the next stall beyond a partition composed of woven ocotillo branches.

There were three stable calls each day at Hildebrandt, for the soldiers to tend the horses without whom there would be no cavalry. At the moment, however, the soldiers were involved in other occupations, and the two young contract scouts were the only men in the corral. The horses lazed in the sun around the brush arbor and switched their tails in the shade.

The Aravaipa scouts had returned to their *ranchería* in the ravine at the fort's west end, where they tended their mustangs and lived with their families in their traditional ways.

"So," Seth said as he trimmed his sorrel's right front

hoof, "you gonna give the sergeant's daughter what she's obviously pinin' for?"

Yakima snorted as he slowly curried his buckskin, watching the dust rise from the short, bristling hairs. "What do you think she's pinin' for?"

"You know what she's pinin' for same as me. Why she's pinin' for yours, though, and not mine, is way beyond me."

"Maybe she's just got a good sense that I'm better . . . uh . . . *equipped*."

Seth tossed a horse apple over the partition; it clipped the brim of Yakima's hat. "If you don't stop starin' at me in the bathhouse, I'm gonna shoot you, you lascivious bastard."

Yakima frowned. Lascivious? The vocabulary of the gentrified Southerner, whose family had been rich before the war had broken them, never ceased to befuddle the half-breed, who'd never traveled west of the Missouri, much less the Mississippi, and could only read at the level of a second grader, though he hoped to improve himself in that regard.

They worked in silence for a time, and then Seth said, "You didn't answer my question."

"She's all yours."

Yakima knew that Miss Tunney would be trouble for him, a half-breed. He had to be careful in choosing which girls he turned his attentions to. Young men with Indian blood—*any* Indian blood—were not to fraternize with non-Indian girls. Especially those of better breeding, which pretty much meant any white girl. Yakima had known his share of young Indians, either part- or full-blood, who had ended up stretching hemp in the shade of a stout cottonwood for their indiscretions.

It wasn't only the family of the white girls who might object. Many whites saw the union of an Indian and a white girl as scandalous at the very least, and often good reason to fetch a long riata. It wasn't only the men who suffered in such a situation, either. White girls or women caught fraternizing with boys or men sporting skin a shade darker than fashionable suffered, as well. The punishment might range anywhere from ostracism to public whipping and tar and feathering.

The young half-breed had to admit that Tunney's daughter was right fetching. But for him, she was fetching trouble. The flirtatious way she'd acted toward him had puzzled him, for few white girls had ever given him the time of day.

"Nah, I don't think so," Barksdale said. "She's the sergeant's daughter as well as a Yankee, and even if the sergeant allowed her to cavort with a rebel, albeit one as galvanized as I obviously am"—the ex-Confederate first lieutenant paused to grin at the irony through the ocotillo branches—"I know a few other girls without such thin pink Yankee blood who look just as good in taffeta and crinoline."

"You'd better get your eyes off Captain Hendricks's oldest," Yakima warned his friend, "or you're gonna be screamin' mighty loud when the captain fills your Tennessee ass with Yankee buckshot."

Barksdale laughed through his teeth.

"What I don't understand, though," he said, ignoring his partner's warning and clipping his sorrel's left rear hoof, which he'd clamped between his bent knees, "is how such a delectable little morsel ever sprouted from old Gila River Joe's seed."

They were back to the topic of Samantha Tunney again. Yakima sighed. He didn't want to talk about the beautiful brunette who'd regarded him so brashly. Doing so made his belly tighten with young male yearnings, and he'd already had enough of those before the sergeant's unlikely daughter had arrived.

"If you find out, you let me know. Here's a question I got for you and that's been chewin' at me ever since the skirmish." Yakima was working on his buckskin's tail, gritting his teeth as he brushed through the coarse hair to remove several nasty burr clumps woven with cholla thorns. "What's

with the white boy we killed today? The one dressed like a
Chiricahua?"

Seth frowned over the stall partition. "Shit, I was gonna
ask you the same damn thing. You don't know?"

"No idea."

"The sergeant called the kid Angus," Seth said, scowling beneath the brim of his planter's hat. "Must be a captive settler's boy who—"

A sudden shout cut him off. Yakima had heard it, too—it
had sounded like a loud grunt or groan. As both Yakima
and Seth rose from their crouches, looking around, a woman's raised voice spewed a string of Mexican epithets so
quickly that Yakima, who'd picked up a fair working knowledge of the local variety of border Spanish mixed liberally
with Apache, could understand only a word here and there.
The woman was as mad as an old wet hen, though. There
was no denying that.

Yakima turned toward Walt Munroe's post trader's store
that sat on a wide, barren hill southeast of the corrals, on the
other side of a shallow arroyo. The store was a large mud-
brick adobe with viga poles sprouting from just beneath its
flat roof. A corral and brush arbor flanked it. Yakima
couldn't see the place's front door from his vantage, because
several wagons, horses, and mules blocked his view. Dust
lifted in the yard like wisps of tan fog.

There appeared to be a commotion between the wagons
at the front of the store. Yakima could see heads moving
around through the dust, some hatted. Some were moving
in jerks, with violent twists and turns.

A man laughed from that direction. Other men were
speaking not quite loudly enough for Yakima to hear what
they were saying, though he could tell it was Spanish. The
woman's angry voice could be heard beneath the voices of
the men.

Yakima put down his currycomb and walked slowly out
of the stall and into the corral, staring over the adobe wall
toward the post trader's store. Seth did the same, matching

his partner stride for stride, holding a hand up above the brim of his hat to shade his eyes against the sun. He held a hand over one of the two Griswold & Gunnison conversion .44s he wore up high on his lean hips.

"Does that one wagon there—the one closest to the store—look familiar?"

Yakima squinted shading his own eyes with his hand. "Not to me."

"I believe that's old Ramon Ortega's rig," Seth said. The girl screamed and cursed as the figures continued moving around quickly between the wagons and the store. Seth picked up his pace, heading for the corral gate. "Come on."

Barksdale continued increasing his speed until, after he'd crouched between mesquite poles constituting the corral gate, he was striding quickly down the slope toward the dry wash and the trader's store beyond. Yakima increased his own pace, regarding the wagons and the jostling figures cautiously, automatically closing one hand around the walnut grips of his right Dragoon.

Walking side by side, he and Seth crossed the wash and climbed the other side, the wagons, horses, and mules growing larger before them. The post trader's store was L-shaped; the front door was located about halfway down the longer side and flanked a boardwalk that ran down the entire inside of the L and had a brush ramada covering it, offering shade most times of the day.

The sunlight blazed down upon the mud brown adobe bricks of the store's front wall. Several men dressed in rough trail garb stood on the boardwalk, observing the goings-on in the yard fronting the store. One—a portly, bearded gent in a red-and-black calico shirt and suspenders—sat on a hide-bottom chair swing, rocking slowly back and forth on the balls of his stovepipe boots.

Yakima recognized him as one of the freighters whom Walt Munroe did business with in Tucson. The other three men Yakima didn't know, but they were watching the festivities and smiling with amusement.

As Seth and Yakima approached the store, heading for

a ten-yard break between the nearest loaded freight wagons, Yakima could see four men milling around a girl in a ruffled cream blouse with Spanish-styled embroidering, and a long dark red skirt. The blouse hung off one of her brown shoulders, though she was doing her best to hold it up, crossing both her arms on her chest. The four men around her were Mexicans wearing palm-leaf Sonora hats and deerskin *charro* slacks, the belled cuffs of which flared out around their spurred boots.

"I will give you two pesos if you show us more—eh, senorita?" one of them was saying, waving a slender knife in the girl's face.

Yakima and Seth had slowed their pace and were crouching behind the wagons, keeping the wagons between them and the men accosting the girl. As they drew nearer, Yakima saw that a man lay in the back of the wagon to his right. At least, his upper body lay in the wagon. His legs clad in patched deerskins and his moccasin-clad feet hung down over the wagon's open tailgate. He appeared to be sound asleep.

It was on the other side of this wagon and another, larger wagon that the men were harassing the girl, who continued to curse her assailants viciously at the tops of her lungs. The men laughed and jeered, and the three others encouraged the man with the knife to cut the rest of the girl's blouse off.

"If you do not take off your clothes and show us your lovely body, senorita," said the man with the knife in Spanish, "*I* will do what is necessary, and I cannot guarantee you I will not cut your heavenly body, as well!"

The girl lurched forward and shouted in a blaze of Spanish something like "Do it, you thorn-peckered javelina whose mother is the whore of mules, and I'll cut your balls off and shove them down your throat with the point of a butcher knife until you shit them out your asshole!"

Yakima could see only the girl's profile from his vantage, but he had recognized her voice. He could tell from the way Seth glanced at him, smirking slightly, that his partner had recognized it, too. Her father was the deerskin-clad Mexican asleep in the back of the small supply wagon near Yakima. When Seth gestured toward the supply wagon with a mere flick of his eyes, Yakima knew exactly what Barksdale wanted him to do.

The young half-breed usually took Barksdale's lead without hesitation, for Seth was seven years older, he'd been a scout at the fort nearly two years longer than Yakima had, and he'd been a decorated officer for the Confederacy.

You couldn't tell any of those things by looking at Seth, however. In his pinto vest and befeathered planter's hat with the chin thong hanging to his chest, you'd think he was a dude from Memphis or New Orleans, maybe a banker's son acting out his boyish fantasy of drifting west to seek adventure. With his soft, round face, his devil-may-care attitude, light blue eyes, and scraggly light brown mustache and goatee that never seemed to fill out like it should, the Southerner appeared younger than his years.

But Yakima, who had grown up on the wild frontier, himself as wild as a coyote, bouncing around from place to place, surviving by means of his outdoor skills and his wits, knew Seth to be as capable a frontiersman and as fierce a fighter as Yakima had ever known. And the young half-breed, alienated by white society, growing up more alone than not, with a knife in one hand, a pistol in the other, had crossed with a whole passel of fierce frontier fighters.

He moved stealthily over to the wagon, peered over the top. None of the Mexicans were facing the wagon directly. As easily as a cat, he leaped up and over the side of the wagon and hunkered down amidst bags of flour, sugar, coffee, and feed heaped inside.

He glanced at the man asleep on a horse blanket at the end of the wagon.

The man's low-crowned straw sombrero hid his face, wobbling slightly as he breathed, snoring loudly under the hat. He wore a faded red calico tunic that was sweat-pasted to his soft, lumpy chest. An empty bottle leaned against his left hip, a black spider climbing around the lip.

Yakima snorted wryly as he sat down on a flour sack and

doffed his own, flat-crowned coal black hat, keeping his head low as he peered over the large, tarp-covered freight wagon, which was just beyond the smaller wagon he was hunkered in. About halfway between the larger wagon and the store, the girl stood surrounded by the four Mexicans.

Yakima could see them well enough now that he recognized them from previous encounters in the desert. They were scalp hunters, a savage breed of border tough who hunted the scalps of Apaches that the *rurales* from their own country paid dearly for. The Apaches were as much a problem for Mexico as they were in the American southwestern territories.

Of course, the *rurales* wanted only scalps taken from Apaches in their own country, but who would know where any given scalp came from? Apaches recognized no international boundary. If the hunters couldn't find enough scalps in Mexico, they crossed the border and hunted them in what had only recently become Arizona Territory.

Officially, the scalp hunters were breaking no laws. They were just killing Apaches. Still, they were every bit as savage as the Apaches they hunted. Possibly even more savage. Yakima knew they often killed innocent women and children as well as Mexicans, knowing that a black scalp was a black scalp, indistinguishable from any other. The man with the knife now accosting the girl was their leader—a particularly savage amongst savages who went by the handle of *La Escorpion*.

Chapter 10

Grinning maniacally, two braids of his own black hair falling down his red-and-black calico shirt in back, the Scorpion was still urging the girl to disrobe, waving the knife in her face. But the girl was having none of it. She lunged at him, shoving him away from her, but the man only laughed and threatened her again with the knife as he tried to pull at her blouse and skirt with his free hand.

Suddenly, he threw himself at her, wrapping his arms around her and kissing her. She wriggled, grunting in his arms.

"Cerdo!" she cried, pulling her head back from his.

He laughed again and gave her blouse another hard tug, ripping it off her shoulders so that it hung now by a couple of jagged strands from her waist.

"Bastardo pig suckling of mules!" the girl screamed, releasing the blouse and kicking at him furiously, her long black hair flying, her brown breasts jostling.

Yakima was wondering where in hell Seth was. He was starting to slide both his Colts from their holsters, grinding his molars angrily, when Seth strolled out from behind a

stout wagon on the far side of the yard, to Yakima's left.
Seth must have plucked a hunk of braided chewing tobacco
from one of the wagons, because now, as casually as though
he were just strolling to the privy, he sliced off a chunk of
the wedding cake, and said, "Senor Scorpion, may I have a
moment of your time?"

He'd said it loudly enough that the Scorpion had heard
above his own laughter as well as the laughter of his com-
patriots, and he spun around on a heel, slapping a hand to
the butt of a Remington riding his right hip. Yakima tightened his hands around his Dragoons but kept both guns in
their holsters.

Seth already had one of his Griswold & Gunnison .44s
out so fast that Yakima hadn't even seen the move. Seth
was aiming the iron popper at his belly. He grinned his
casual Seth grin, using only half of his mouth, with his
other hand holding the cut piece of wedding cake on the
blade of his knife up close to his chin.

"Now, Senor Scorpion, if you're tryin' to finagle a date
with that purty li'l miss there, you're goin' about it all
wrong. If I woulda known you had a hankerin' to ask her to
the ball, you shoulda come talk to me. I know how to spark
a fetchin' belle. Sparked a few even outta their bloomers,
don't ya know?" He winked at the girl. "I can tell you right
here that cuttin' her blouse off with a pigsticker in front of
your friends"—he shook his head, grinning and deftly
sliding the chunk of chaw through his lips with the knife
blade—"ain't gonna work fer shit. *El usted comprende?*"

He lowered the knife, chewing the hunk of tobacco
slowly, openmouthed, grinning.

"This here?" the Scorpion said, raising his own knife to
show Barksdale. "This is the *chiquita*'s own stiletto. I took
it away from her just before she would have cut my *cajones*
off. She is half animal, this one. Like father like daughter,
I guess, huh? I don't know about you, Senor Barksdale, so
good to see you again, by the way"—he gave a cordial dip
of his pointed chin around which his long black mare's tail
mustaches drooped toward his chest—"but I think that

trying to cut a man's *cajones* off when he's just trying to have a conversation is terribly rude."

"It is at that. It is at that. Tell you what, ole hoss, you turn Senorita Ortega over to me, and I'll give her a good old-fashioned tongue-lashin'. Teach her the error of her ways. Your oysters will never be in danger again. I assure you of that, Senor Scorpion." He flashed his crooked, dashing smile again as the breeze curled the longish light brown hair feathering down over his ears. "At least, not from the senorita, anyways."

"Pigs!" the girl said, throwing her long hair back wildly, holding what was left of her blouse across her chest with one hand. Her back was facing Yakima, so he couldn't tell if she was accomplishing the task or not. "They are all pigs! Seth, shoot them!"

She attempted to remove herself from the line of fire, but one of the other men who'd been standing behind her grabbed her arm and jerked her violently toward him. Even from over the man's left shoulder, Yakima could tell he had a hard, enraged look on his face.

Shouting, "Here, why don't you take her head?" he snapped up a big machete from a long sheath hanging off his right hip. As he raised it, the girl screamed and cowered. Yakima plucked his Arkansas toothpick from the hard rawhide sheath he wore behind his neck and right shoulder, and flicked it from behind his right ear.

The man with the machete, nearly the size of a bear and with thick, frizzy black hair covering his shoulders, gave a shrill yelp. The machete dropped to the ground. The hide-wrapped wooden handle of Yakima's toothpick protruded from the man's forearm near his elbow. He lowered the arm and, folding it over his belly, turned his enraged face toward Yakima, who had leaped from the small supply wagon to the top of the tarpaulin-covered larger wagon about twenty yards from the Mexican whose arm he'd perforated.

The young half-breed grinned down at the man and his cohorts, his fists now filled with both of his Dragoons, cocked and ready to fire.

The girl had pulled away from the big man and was backing away to one side. The big man's dark eyes blazed with exasperation and fury as he wrapped his right hand around the toothpick's handle and pulled the five inches of Damascus steel from his forearm, screaming. He held the bloody knife threateningly in his right fist. Yakima narrowed his eyes, aiming his right-hand Colt at the center of the big man's forehead.

"Just go ahead and drop it," Yakima said. "I'll fetch it later, after you boys have moved on."

All the Mexicans were standing around looking incredulous, their eyes on the lean, young half-breed standing atop the covered freight wagon. They all had their hands on their guns, which they had plenty of—holstered on hips, over bellies, or hanging down their chests—but none seemed willing to pull iron from leather.

The girl was looking up at Yakima now, too. As he glanced at her, what struck him first was that she wore a black leather patch over her left eye. The strap slanting over her head had been concealed by the thick hair that hung to the small of her back.

Like a full-blood Indian's, her hair was so black that it had a blue sheen. Her face owned the high, wide cheekbones and narrow jaw of an Apache. Yakima didn't have time to inspect her too carefully, but he was astonished by her rugged, feral beauty, which was only accentuated by the eye patch.

Her lone molasses black eye blazed at him like some trapped animal's. There was no gratefulness in it but only the wild wariness of an animal released from a trap, as suspicious of its rescuer as it was of its captor.

"Now, what in the hell'd you have to go and do that for?" Seth feigned astonishment at his partner's actions. "Look what you did to that poor man's arm. Sir, let me apologize! My half-breed partner ain't fit for civilized company! You know what I'd do if I were you boys at this moment?"

Seth paused as though awaiting for a response.

The Mexicans had switched their glares to him now. All

except the big man with the bloody left forearm, that is. He kept his gaze on Yakima. If his eyes had been mountain howitzers, they'd be spitting explosive shells at the still-grinning young half-breed standing with his boots spread shoulder-width apart atop the freight wagon.

Seth said, "I'd skedaddle. I'd make like longhorns ahead of a cyclone. Sure enough, I'd climb aboard my hosses and ride for the border so fast a mountain lion runnin' downhill couldn't catch me!"

Seth had replaced the knife in his left hand with his second Griswold & Gunnison, the cocked pistols in his hands belying the mock-affable smile beneath his mustache.

The Mexicans slid their testy gazes between him and Yakima. The girl stood back against a wagon wheel. Her eyes glittered victoriously as she curled her nose at her attackers.

The Scorpion turned back to Seth and opened his hands in supplication. "Senors," he intoned, "I think there has been a misunderstanding. We were only having a friendly little visit with Senorita Ortega. After all, it has been a while since we have seen her and her most . . . uh . . . *gallant* father, Senor Ortega."

He glanced toward the legs hanging over the end of the small supply wagon Yakima had leaped out of. "Senor Ortega was otherwise occupied, as you can see, so we were just catching up a little with the senorita. But that is all right, Senor Barksdale." The Scorpion put some dark steel in his voice as he glanced at the girl. "We will catch up with the senorita later. And I have no doubt that my friend Pepe will likely catch up later with Senor Henry." He smiled. "Somewhere down the line. . . ."

Yakima hadn't known the names of the other men in the gang, only the leader's. But he had a pretty good idea he knew another name now. Pepe glared up at him again, hardening his heavy anvil jaw as he clamped his right hand over his bloody left forearm and grunted. He had a skull-and-crossbones tattoo on the nub of his left cheek, beneath the broad brim of his Sonora hat, and it stood out against the enraged crimson of the rest of his face.

"*Sí*," Pepe wheezed, saliva bubbling through his clenched teeth, "we will meet again, green-eyed Siwash. When we do, you will be howling for your *madre* to save you from the slow skinning I will give you, after I have cut the tendons in your arms and hung you from a tree."

"This is all right cheerful as hell," Seth said. "Why don't you boys skedaddle, like I done suggested, before that crazy half-breed does somethin' else to embarrass us both and just make you fellas all the angrier? This fandango's *over.*"

The men looked at one another and then strode stiffly off to a string of saddle horses and packhorses tied to one of the several hitch racks fronting the store. They mounted up and, continuing to glare at Yakima and Seth, rode their horses between the wagons and out of the yard, galloping down a shallow gully that twisted through the buttes to the west.

When they were gone, Seth holstered his Confederate pistols and sighed. Yakima holstered his own revolvers and leaped down off the freight wagon and into the yard. The girl glanced at him and said to Seth, "Who's the Siwash?"

"Yakima Henry, meet Luz Ortega. Luz, meet Yakima Henry."

"Apache?" the girl asked Seth.

"No, ma'am," Yakima answered on his own behalf. He offered nothing more.

She gave him a cool appraisal and then, turning to give her back to Yakima and Seth, flung her tattered blouse into the dirt. She walked over to the wagon in which her father, Ramon Ortega, still slept, snoring loudly. Yakima watched her blue-black hair, coarse as a horse's mane, slide back and forth across her slender brown back.

Yakima glanced at Seth. Seth merely grinned at the stunning girl and shook his head.

At the back of the wagon, she stopped and kicked one of the man's dangling legs, yelling in Spanish, "Thanks for the help, Papa! If not for your intervention, I might have been raped in the dirt and left with my throat cut!"

The old man jerked with a start, groaning, and then

flopped back down on the wagon's floor. He kicked both his legs, and then, as the girl continued walking around the far side of the wagon, he resumed snoring.

Yakima looked down at the unconscious man and then asked Seth, "That's *Ramon Ortega*?"

Barksdale grimaced, sighed. "Don't match up to his reputation, does he?"

"He sure don't."

Ortega was legendary around this part of Arizona Territory. Or at least, he had been, back when Arizona was still considered New Mexico, and he was guiding and interpreting for General Carleton's storied column of California Volunteers, who'd first established Fort Hildebrandt and opened up a mail road between Mesilla and Tucson before that fateful shot was fired at Fort Sumter. Ortega had been forced to retire because of drinking and for some years had been raising his half-Mimbreño Apache daughter and trapping wild horses at their rancho in the foothills of the Dragoon Mountains. His wife had been a daughter of Mangas Coloradas.

Yakima had never met the legendary scout, though he'd seen him from a distance, the way you usually only saw Apaches, and he had heard his name bandied about with a rare combination of quiet laughter and awe. Yakima returned his attention to the girl, a granddaughter of the fabled Mangas Coloradas, with renewed interest.

Luz Ortega did not bother to cover herself with anything more than her hair as she walked up to the seat of the wagon. When she turned toward the wagon, Yakima could see her round, uptilted, brown-nippled breasts jostling around behind the thick strands of the hair hanging down her chest.

"Those pigs will be after me now," she said as though half to herself, curling her upper lip and flaring her nostrils. "They know where we live. They have visited the rancho before. When they show up again, I will be waiting with a Winchester, and they will sing me to sleep with their girlish wails."

Seth walked up to the back of the wagon and stared

down at the unconscious man. "How long's this old reprobate been out like this?"

"He passed out in time that he didn't have to help with
loading. He bought a bottle from Senor Munroe and drank
it on top of what he drank on our way here from the rancho." Munroe was standing on the ramada, gazing sheepishly into the yard. Now that the show was over, several of
the freighters were heading for their rigs and preparing
their horses or mules for travel. One was greasing his wheel
hubs and casting the one-eyed girl lascivious smirks.

Luz reached beneath the wagon seat and rummaged
around before pulling out what she was looking for. She
shook out a man's blue linsey shirt in front of her and then
shrugged into it. She let it hang from her shoulders, not
buttoning it, while she reached under the seat again and
pulled out a stubby pocket pistol. Walking back around the
wagon, she wedged the pistol behind the waistband of her
skirt and then began buttoning her blouse from the bottom.

"Want me to escort you back to your rancho?" Seth
asked her.

Leaving the shirt unbuttoned halfway down her chest,
she shook her hair out of her lone eye and away from her
eye patch and gave him a cool smile. "No, but you can buy
me a drink. After all that, I could use one."

Seth stepped aside and gestured toward the post trader's
store. "Right this way, senorita."

Chapter 11

Yakima followed Seth and Luz Ortega toward the post trader's store from several feet behind, giving them plenty of room. He was feeling like the proverbial third wheel, for he knew that Seth had an interest in the girl. Young woman, rather. Yakima thought she must be close to Seth's age, in her mid-twenties.

Seth hadn't talked much about her, but Yakima knew he'd ridden out to the Dragoons several times to visit her and her father. Because Seth hadn't talked much about the visit, Yakima had suspected that it was the young granddaughter of Mangas Coloradas he'd been visiting mostly, as opposed to her legendary father. Seth talked a lot with Yakima about women in a frivolous, joking way, but he'd never said much about Luz Ortega.

For that reason, Yakima sort of vaguely suspected he might have feelings for her. And now he could understand why. Even without the eye patch, the young woman would not have been beautiful in the traditional way, but there was a savage mystery and dark, erotically feral appeal about her.

She was like a wildcat who'd just walked out of the Sonora Desert, looking to rend and feed.

And she was the granddaughter of the fabled Mangas Coloradas, killed in '63 by soldiers at Fort McLane, for chrissakes. . . .

Yakima would have left the two alone, but he was curious about the young woman. Also, he was hungry, and Munroe, the post trader, usually served a cheap, hearty lunch.

Munroe stood on the gallery near the door that was propped open with a rock, grinning sheepishly and rubbing his hands on his threadbare, checked trousers.

"Thanks for the help out there, you cowardly bastard," Luz said to him as she brushed past the portly, square-faced gent with the light red handlebar mustache and dark blue eyes. He wore a dirty green apron over a soiled white shirt and suspenders. His longish hair was parted in the middle and swept back behind his ears.

"I was just about to send Martin to the guardhouse over at the fort when these two showed up," Munroe said, glancing at Seth and Yakima walking about ten feet behind.

Luz strode coolly past the trader.

As Seth stepped onto the boardwalk, Munroe looked at him and then at Yakima, and threw his beefy arms up in supplication. "Honest, boys!"

Yakima didn't say anything, either, as he walked past the man. He wondered how long Munroe would have enjoyed the entertainment before he or one of the others had stepped in and done something. Even so-called civilized men this far out in the desert were only marginally so, and Yakima had to admit that even he enjoyed a glance or two at the girl's breasts.

But then, that's why he liked it out here. The wildness of it. He'd spent a few months at a boarding school for orphans in Denver just after his mother died, and those few months before he'd run away had only made him appreciate the wild all the more. The nuns at the orphanage had been even less civilized than Munroe and the freighters. In fact, in many ways, they made the Apaches look tame in comparison.

"You got any menudo?" Yakima asked the trader who'd followed him, Seth, and Luz into his dim, low-ceilinged store.

"Sure, sure, I got menudo," the trader said, truckling now in light of his recent transgression. "I got menudo, bread, cheese . . ."

"I'll have a bowl of menudo," Yakima said. "Bread and cheese."

"Make it two," Seth said. "Luz, you want some menudo?"

"No, I want a shot of tequila," she said, dragging a chair out from a table in the portion of the dark, cluttered, maze-like store used as a crude dining room, near a billiard room and saloon for officers.

"Make that two," Seth said.

"Make it three," Yakima heard himself say for Luz's benefit. He wasn't about to order a bottle of his preferred sarsaparilla in front of the girl, though he probably would have done so if she hadn't been present. He'd not yet acquired a taste for liquor or tobacco despite his best efforts. Not smoking or drinking in a fort teeming with smokers and drinkers made him feel like a hind-tit calf.

He'd have to work on it.

When they'd sat down at a table near a cold woodstove, Seth sitting to Yakima's left, Luz sitting across the table from him, no one said anything. Yakima sat back in his chair, lacing his hands across his flat belly. Seth sat back in his own chair, turned toward Luz. He crossed his legs and smiled the way he usually did, ironically, as though he had a secret opinion and wanted you to guess what it was.

He shuttled his gaze from Luz to Yakima and back again.

Luz stared off into the store's dark shadows, where Munroe could be heard stomping around and talking to his helper and stepson, Martin, who hadn't been right in the head since he'd been kicked by a Spanish mule when he was ten.

Luz didn't seem at all uncomfortable with the silence. After a time, she turned to Yakima, looked at Seth, and said, "He's good with a knife, this Siwash."

"That's about all he can do. Can't ride for shit. Or shoot. Tunney hired him for a tracker and he can't find his way to the privy after sunset."

Yakima didn't say anything. He looked blandly off through one of the windows, though he could see Luz's eyes sparkle briefly at the funning.

"They'll be looking for you now," Luz told Yakima from across the table, her lone eye grave. "They'll be waiting to get you alone. Maybe not soon, but just when you've forgotten about them. Both of you, but you most of all. You shamed Pepe."

"I'll be looking forward to it," Yakima said. "That's a fight I'd like to finish."

Seth and Luz shared an oblique look, as though they were the only two grown-ups at the table. It rankled Yakima a little.

Martin, a towheaded young man in his twenties, appeared with a bottle and three glasses. He set the bottle and glasses on the table, rubbed his hands on his pants, hesitating as though wondering if he'd forgotten something, then shuffled away, stumbling, as though he were moving too quickly for his oversized feet.

Seth filled the shot glasses.

Luz took one, threw her it back, and said to Seth, "You haven't visited us for a time."

"You been pinin' for me, Miss Luz?" Seth asked, refilling her shot glass.

"I pine for no man," Luz said, glaring at him over the rim of her glass. She took a small sip, threw her hair back, and changed the subject. "I heard you ran into Chiricahuas today."

"Word gets around fast."

"They attacked the stage," Yakima said, turning his shot glass around on the table, not really wanting to drink it but knowing he would, with Luz here. "One of 'em was a white boy decked out like a Chiricahua warrior."

Luz frowned. "A *white* boy?"

"A young blond kid, maybe fourteen, sixteen at the most."

Martin brought a tray with two steaming bowls of menudo and a plate of thickly sliced, crumbly brown bread and cheese. He set the bowls down in front of Luz and Yakima, and he set the bread down between them. He rubbed a hand on his pants again, muttered something Yakima couldn't make out, and then stumbled away.

Luz slid her bowl and her spoon over to Seth, who said, "You don't seem all that surprised."

"By the white boy?" Luz sipped her tequila, set the glass back down on the table. "I've seen one around. There's been a group of Apaches moving around the mountains near the rancho. They haven't come into the yard, and so far they've left our horses and mules alone, so Ramon said not to worry about them. I've seen a white boy riding with them. There is a white girl, as well. Older than the boy. She has hair the color of straw, very long—as long as mine—and she rides a tobiano. A very distinctive horse with a mane as long as the girl's hair, and as well tended. I saw her and the others once from a short distance, when they were taking water from one of our springs. I hid in the rocks above the spring and watched."

Seth held a spoonful of menudo in front of his chin. "A white boy and a white girl."

"Captives?" Yakima said. Plenty of whites had been taken by the Apaches over the years. Some had been rescued, some had been killed, but the fate of many was a mystery and likely always would be. "Not all that uncommon."

To Luz, Seth said, "I don't know if the sergeant was addlepated or what, but he called him Angus and took him to Alexander. They were palverin' over the dead boy in the colonel's office when we left to tend our horses."

"Angus," Luz said, nodding slowly.

Shoveling the menudo into his mouth, Yakima looked from Seth to Luz and then back to Seth again. He stopped eating, frowning. "Will one of you tell me what's goin' on with this kid, Angus? I take it the sergeant and the colonel thought they knew the boy, but *how* did they know him?"

"I never caught the colonel's son's name," Seth said still to Luz. "The one who was taken."

Yakima scowled. "Taken?"

"Angus," Luz said. "I know the story. Ramon told me. Everyone around here knows it."

"I don't know it," Yakima said.

"Everyone who was here before the war knows it," Luz said to him. "It was a great tragedy." She refilled hers and Seth's shot glasses, made a pass over Yakima's glass, but, seeing that his drink hadn't been touched, set the bottle down. She glanced at Yakima, who lowered his eyes and shoved bread and cheese into his mouth.

Luz said, "It's not talked about much anymore, with the colonel back at Hildebrandt."

"A great tragedy," Seth said, nodding. "That's how the story always begins."

He set his spoon in his bowl and looked around to see if anyone was within earshot. Keeping his voice discreetly low, he turned to Yakima, and said, "Before the war, the colonel had most of his family out here—wife, son, two daughters. His wife, son, and one of his daughters were headed off to Wilcox to shop one Saturday morning. They had a small escort, maybe four men. There had been a lull in hostile activity around the fort, so the colonel let them go. There wasn't much to the fort back then—maybe ten buildings was all. Mail came through maybe once a month. His family was probably goin' stir-crazy along with everybody else.

"Anyway, the contingent was attacked. The soldiers were killed. Their bodies were found around the burned Dougherty wagon that the colonel's wife and young'uns had ridden in. The bodies of the colonel's family never were found. It was assumed they'd been taken."

Yakima sat up straight in his chair as he pondered the tragedy. The attack itself wasn't all that surprising, for such horrors happened all the time out here. What was surprising was that this was the first time Yakima had heard the story. It cast Colonel Alexander in a new light for him—a man who'd returned after the war to the scene of what must have been the worst tragedy of his life.

Why would a man do that? Surely, given his rank and war record, he must have had a choice.

Keeping his voice low, Seth continued. "Many, many scouting parties were sent out looking for the colonel's family. The colonel himself headed up several of them. But then the first shot was fired at Sumter, and orders came from Washington—the fort was to mostly be abandoned. All that remained were about twenty volunteers from the Fifth Californian Infantry. The Apache war was shoved to a warming rack, as most troopers were needed to fight the Confederacy. The colonel was ordered back, as well. He sent out one more scouting party, and they came back waggin' their heads."

"No sign?"

"About all the sign that had ever been found were a few strands of cloth from the hem of the colonel's daughter's dress. The heel of his wife's shoe was found up Cavalry Gulch a month later. Parts of a few horse tracks near the burned Dougherty had been found right after the attack, but that was all. It was like they and their attackers were swallowed up by eternity, never to be seen or heard from again."

"Until now," Yakima said.

"Maybe," Luz said. "Who knows? If the boy is the colonel's son, the colonel had better bury him and forget him." She threw the last of her tequila back, slammed the empty glass down on the table. "He'd better forget the girl, too."

"Why's that?" Seth asked.

"Because she has been a captive so long that she is probably more Apache now than white."

Luz slid her chair back, rose, and started for the door. She glanced over her shoulder at Seth. "Stop out at the ranch sometime. I'll kill a pig."

Luz Ortega moved through the door and was gone.

Chapter 12

Lamar Chestnut struck a match to life on the stone floor of the cave and sat back against his saddle, lighting his half-smoked cheroot and staring through the billowing smoke at the blond Apache playing the baby grand piano.

Chestnut chuckled too quietly for Riona to hear above the light, delicate notes fluttering like golden-throated little birds from her fingers that so adeptly manipulated the piano's ivory keys. *What a sight,* he thought. If he didn't know better, he'd have thought he was drunk or high on opium or Mexican marijuana, and was imagining the blond, bronze-skinned Apache beauty playing parlor piano in a cave in the middle of nowhere in the south-central Arizona Territory.

A piano in a cave in the heart of Apacheria.

Chestnut's men and Riona's had had a hell of a time back-and-bellying it out of the wagon and into the cavern. Chestnut himself had helped until there were too many men for the size of the cave. Then he had happily stopped assisting and rummaged up a stiff shot of tequila to quell the ache in his lower back.

Wrestling a piano into a cave.

Chestnut chuckled again and shook his head, as he stared in open admiration at the dazzling blond Apache. There was no denying the girl. Not only because she was so damn pretty and commanded so much authority by her demeanor alone, but because she likely would have shot any man who hadn't complied with her wish to have the piano in the cave. All the Apaches as well as Chestnut's own former Confederates were so mesmerized by the girl, they wouldn't have even thought of defending themselves against her.

A fire cracked and sputtered in the stone ring just outside the cave. On a flat rock beside the flames, a coffeepot gurgled and steamed, the sounds all but drowned by the notes echoing eerily around the small stone cleft in the sandstone mountain wall. The cavern, likely hollowed out by wind, was just large enough to house the piano, its lovely player, the fire, Chestnut himself, and their gear.

The acoustics were not that good in here, but the girl didn't seem to mind. On her sculpted, war-painted face was a look of utter distraction, absorption.

She stared down at the keys as her hands fluttered so effortlessly back and forth, as though she were staring far into the misty reaches of her more civilized, Victorian-Eastern past.

She closed out the song she was playing with a subtle flourish, and left her hands on the keys while the last notes resounded off the stone walls and the crackling of the fire moved in to take their place. The quiet was deeper now than before, and mysterious. Despite the men sitting around their own two fires in the darkness beyond the cave—nursing their aching backs, no doubt—it seemed quite intimate in here.

"Mozart?" Chestnut asked, exhaling cigarette smoke.

"Bach, you fool."

"Ah, Bach." Chestnut heaved himself to his feet, grabbed his tequila bottle, and moved a little uncertainly over to the piano. He sat down beside her on the bench and took a swig from the bottle. "Play another one. I like how you play. I like watchin' you . . . play."

He leaned toward her, fingered the *hoddentin* pouch dangling over her deep cleavage, and very gently kissed the lobe of her left ear. She leaned away from him, smiling as she began to play again.

"Is my brother back yet?"

"Haven't heard. I been listenin' to you playin'. Can he play like you?"

"He didn't have time to learn. He's eight years younger than I am, and was only six when we were captured."

"That's all right—I don't think anyone could play like you, my sweet." Chestnut continued to nuzzle her fine tan neck while she played. The notes of the sonata chimed lightly around the cavern. The tequila was exaggerating his Southern accent, dragging each vowel out nearly in harmony with the music. "You got your special way of doin' pretty much everything . . . don't ya, Miss Riona?"

"You're very sweet."

"Ain't ah?"

She chuckled as she continued to lean away from him.

He set the bottle on the piano and caressed her bare thigh with his hands.

"Don't," she said, sweetly.

"I got an idea."

"Oh?"

"Let's make this a special night, Miss Riona. I mean, with the music an' all, it's already special. Why, your deft touch across the keys is remindin' me of the debutante balls back home . . . once the hour got late and little groups of us dashin' young gentlemen and the belles in their hoop skirts broke up and went to stand together in quiet conversation under the mossy oaks out in the yard . . . under the only slightly less strict scrutiny of the girls' chaperones, of course."

He chuckled.

"You know that thing you're doing with your hand?" she said, a little breathless.

"What's that?"

"You'd best stop."

He moved his head around in front of hers and kissed her. "Why's that?"

He opened his eyes to see her smiling at him, but the smile did not reach anywhere close to her eyes, which were hard as polished blue stones. She did not say anything. She didn't have to. Chestnut removed his hand, sat up straight, and grimacing in frustration, lifted the bottle.

"Miss Riona, I do not understand why I repel you so. Do you not find me the least bit attractive? The girls back home once did. Why, back before the war, I promised to marry one of 'em."

She continued to stare at him in that hard, flat, cold way. Just as he shook his head and began to rise and turn away from her, she placed a hand on his forearm. "It's nothing personal, Captain." There was a slight tone of relenting in her voice. "It's just that . . . well . . . I'm reluctant to mix business with pleasure."

Chestnut turned back to her, hope kindling within him once more. "Why, Miss Riona, I see no reason to forestall what will certainly come to pass between us. Surely, it will. Why delay any longer? You an' me—why, we're partners for the long haul. I can feel that very deep in these old Southern bones."

He wasn't entirely convinced of what he'd just espoused. But so far, joining up with the strange blonde and her bronco bunch of wandering outlaw Apaches to pillage and plunder isolated ranches, mines, and stagecoaches had proven lucrative, indeed. Chestnut needed all the capital he could get his hands on in his quest to build up his outlaw empire.

"Why, Captain," the girl said, a reluctant smile tugging at her lips, "you do flatter me so."

Chestnut placed his hand on the back of her neck and was surprised and pleased when she did not draw away as he slid his face once more to her. He'd just closed his mouth over hers when the sound of guttural Apache voices and the approach of unshod horses rose outside the cave.

"What in tarnation did you fellas get into?" Chestnut heard one of his own men say in the quiet night.

More Apache voices rose, and horses snorted.

Chestnut groaned in frustration as Riona pulled her mouth away from his, having given him only an enticing taste of what he'd been longing for. She turned toward the cave's entrance.

"My brother's back." She rose from the bench and strode quickly around the piano. "Sounds like they had trouble."

"Oh, my dear, sweet darlin' Riona!" the captain complained, grabbing the bottle, poking the cigar back into his mouth, as he followed her out of the cave and into the little canyon they'd all bivouacked in.

As he moved away from the fire at the edge of the cave, the shadows in the canyon composed themselves into man-shaped silhouettes, the watery light of the two others fires flickering off guns and knives.

The seven or eight Apaches who'd gone out after the stagecoach had returned. Only, it seemed that several had returned lying belly down across their blanket saddles. Four braves were leading the dead men's horses on foot, and their dark eyes flashed anxiously as Riona pushed through the standing, gray-clad Confederates and other Apache warriors to confront the stocky brave who'd led the group after the stage.

This young warrior, Zuna-Ki-Yen, stepped forward. His eyes were wide beneath the green flannel bandanna holding his hair back behind his round, flat face that bore a long, eyelash-shaped scar across his left cheek.

The brave spoke quickly and anxiously, using hand gestures, and then lowered his eyes in shame when he had finished. The other Apaches said nothing but stood in customary stoicism around their blond leader and this sublieutenant.

One of Chestnut's men, Hap Brindle, looked curiously at one of the other Confederates, Lawrence Cline, standing beside him, and said, "What'd he say, Law? What hap—?"

Before he could finish, Riona gave a keening screech,

lifting her face toward the stars over the canyon, and then dropped to her knees in the dirt.

Chestnut stumbled forward but stopped himself. *Oh, shit,* he thought. *The girl's brother . . .*

Silence hovered over the canyon, the darkness of which was only partly relieved by the flickering umber flames of the campfires. Chestnut stood just outside the cave, staring into the canyon, and none of the figures before him moved or said a word. He could see Riona's blond head. She was collapsed on the ground. She was silent, as well, unmoving, until she slowly lifted her head and her shoulders. She sniffed, wiped away tears with the back of each hand in turn.

Kneeling there, looking up at the stocky brave standing before her, his chin lowered in shame, she said, "And you did not bring him back?" She repeated the question in Apache—a harsh, grunting, furiously accusatory question.

The brave muttered something that Chestnut could barely hear, though he wouldn't have been able to understand the Apache, even if he'd heard it clearly.

Chestnut was too drunk on tequila to react when Riona's right hand flicked down to her right thigh, where she carried a bowie knife in a beaded buckskin sheath. She rose quickly, fluidly, like a puma rising from a crouch to pounce on its prey, and then Chestnut saw her right arm move violently.

The stocky Apache stumbled backward, mewling, and closed his hands over his belly.

Chestnut sucked a startled breath.

All of the men around him—Confederate outlaws and Apaches alike—took one step back. Hap Brindle said, "Good *Lawd*!"

Zuna-Ki-Yen dropped to his knees, whimpering.

Riona took one step forward and swept the bowie across his throat.

Thick blood gushed from the brave's neck, appearing like tar in the darkness. His arms sagged to his sides as he pitched forward onto his face and lay still.

Riona swung around, returning the bloody knife to her thigh sheath. "We always bring back our dead. . . ."

She strode over to Chestnut, stared up at him coldly, her blue eyes now dark as coals. "Best tuck your men into their bedrolls, Captain. We'll be up at first light."

Haltingly, his drunk mind slow to process all that had happened in the last three minutes, Chestnut said, "To . . . do what?"

"We're going to make use of that Gatling gun you stole from the cavalry patrol in New Mexico."

"Uh . . . to . . . do . . . what exactly, Riona?"

"To make a special delivery to Fort Hell." She smiled, and it was like the door of a very cold icehouse being opened. "I miss my father, you see. And I want to see him again. I want to show that gutless bastard what happens when you kill one of my own."

She brushed past Chestnut and entered the cave.

A moment later the precise, vibrant notes of what Chestnut recognized as a Mozart concerto fluttered out of the cave and into the quiet canyon.

Chapter 13

"What do you think, Joe?" asked Colonel Ephraim Alexander. "Do you think they're alive? Matilda and Riona? Just as Angus was?"

The colonel and Sergeant Tunney were sitting alone on the porch of the colonel's house, overlooking the parade ground down the hill to their right. Tattoo had just sounded, and now the night was rolling like dark smoke from the red ball of the sun teetering on the jagged western horizon.

A lone coyote was yammering somewhere in the north.

"I don't know, Colonel. Your guess is as good as mine. Obviously, young Angus was a strong boy. He survived. As I remember, Riona was a spirited little filly. They both took after you."

"What about Matilda?"

Gila River Joe leaned forward, resting his elbows on his knees. The hide-bottom wicker chair creaked against his shifting weight. He swirled his brandy snifter in his right hand, looking down at it, his Cuban cigar smoldering between the first two dark brown fingers of his other hand.

The sergeant had grown weary of the conversation. It

was a repeat of the one they'd had when they first sat down out here after a supper meant to introduce Samantha to some of the senior-most officers at Hildebrandt, and the officers' wives. It had included the colonel himself, of course, and his fourteen-year-old daughter, Priscilla, Two Feathers, the sergeant, Samantha, several other officers and their wives, as well as Lieutenant Geist, the colonel's adjutant. The supper had been in Samantha's honor, but it had turned out to be a sullen affair, since the news of the colonel's son's discovery and death hovered over the dining room like a storm over the desert.

Afterward, the only one of his visitors whom the colonel had invited to remain for a cigar and brandy was the sergeant. The two old warriors had been through hell and back together many times. Other soldiers came and went, but for these two wizened soldiers, their only true friends were each other.

Despite their separation in rank, it was a fact that the colonel made no bones about. He'd made the excuse to the others this evening that he and Joe had to discuss a scouting party, and go over maps, and there was no point for any non–field officers to remain for the meeting. It would simply be a pointless waste of their time. This would be a job for the scouts of Fort Hildebrandt.

This, ostensibly being the search for the colonel's still-missing wife and daughter.

But it had been no meeting, and Joe had known it wouldn't be. It was a private conversation. Actually, few words had even been spoken. Joe had mostly just sat here with the colonel, smoking and sipping his brandy, watching the soldiers return to the parade ground after the last stable call, listening when the colonel felt like speaking, and nodding or shaking his head as the situation warranted. The sergeant was here mostly to lend an ear to his old friend's sadness at having discovered at one and the same time not only that his long-lost son, Angus, had been alive all these years, but that he was now dead, killed the very same day he'd been found.

Could there be any greater irony than discovering only by finding your son's dead body that he had actually been alive?

"No, probably not Matilda," the colonel said, answering his own question about his wife. "Apaches take the young and healthy men, the women of childbearing age. The old . . . the frail . . . they don't waste their time with."

Gila River Joe said nothing. He'd let the colonel go on talking and asking and answering his own questions for as long as he needed to. Joe was here to listen, to be present with his old friend.

"But Riona," the colonel said, sitting back in his chair and blowing a long plume of smoke out into the gathering darkness. "There's a good chance she's alive. If so, I wonder if she's become, like Angus obviously became, one of them. . . ."

"Most likely," the sergeant wanted to say but didn't. The colonel knew. The only way Miss Riona could be alive was if she'd become Apache. He also knew that she'd probably given birth to several children by now, because that's why they would have taken her in the first place—to help increase their numbers and thus their odds against the white invaders. They'd taken Angus to be a warrior. Riona would be a wife and a mother.

There was a long silence.

"She's a real beauty, Joe."

The sergeant looked at the colonel, whose long, freckled face framed by thick gray-blond muttonchops was burnished with the last red light of the sunset. His Celtic-blue eyes glinted. He was smiling wistfully, showing the tips of his large, strong yellow teeth. "Samantha. A real beauty. I see a lot of both you and Katherine in her. She's a strong girl—quite witty and precocious, obviously intelligent. I overheard her talking with Marion Stryker during dinner; she yearns to be an artist. She's going to draw pictures while she's here. Hopes to sell them to *Harper's Bazaar* and the *Knickerbocker*."

"Takes more after her mother's side of the family in that regard," the sergeant joked. "One of her uncles went to

Paris to draw pictures. Being from money, he never really had to concern himself with practical matters."

"She was a few years younger than Riona, as I recall. Good Lord—eight years, Joe! I doubt I'd recognize her."

Taps sounded and both men sat quietly listening to the plaintive notes bugling up from the parade ground. The sun had tipped beyond the mountains, and darkness was fast rolling over the hills, though the roofs of Fort Hildebrandt were still brushed with salmon.

When the last bugle note had dwindled to silence, the sergeant drained his snifter, set the glass on the porch rail, and rose heavily from his chair. "Time for a pillow."

"Joe?"

The sergeant looked down at the colonel sitting in his chair, staring down pensively at the brandy snifter in his hand. Finally, he looked up. The last of the light shone on the surface of his deep-set eyes. "Find her for me, will you? If she's alive, find her and bring her back?"

The sergeant stared down at the bereaved old battler curiously.

"Stay for Angus's funeral tomorrow. There's no big hurry after eight years. Stay tomorrow, visit with your daughter, and then take your scouts out and bring Riona back."

"Of course I will, Colonel. If she's alive, I'll find her. She's likely nearby."

Colonel Alexander heaved himself slowly and creakily up from his chair and stood towering over the slighter but straighter noncom who was ten years younger but whose soul seemed just as ancient. He placed a hand on Gila River Joe's shoulder and said quietly in his deep, lumbering baritone, "I can't order you, Joe. This is a personal matter. Fighting Apaches is one thing. Locating and retrieving my daughter is another."

Gila River Joe felt his ears warm slightly. He was always a little uncomfortable when a conversation, even one with the colonel, drifted this deep into intimate, personal territory. He preferred to confer as two soldiers, not as one father to another. That was unfamiliar territory to the sergeant, a fact that had become all the more apparent earlier this evening, when at dinner he'd sat beside his daughter, a beautiful young woman of his own flesh and blood but who was just as alien to him as someone from the moon.

He cleared his throat and squared his shoulders. "I'll stay for the funeral. And then I'll take the scouts out and look for Riona. Good night." He clicked his heels and saluted as he always did. The colonel gave a wry chuff at the sergeant's insistence on formality even during a private, personal conversation, and obliged the noncom by halfheartedly returning the salute.

Gila River Joe gave a moment's consideration of going inside to bid Samantha good night but then relieved himself of the chore with the excuse that she might already be in bed after such a trying day. He'd see her tomorrow. He drifted down the porch steps and, donning the dress helmet and straightening the shell jacket he'd worn to the dinner, walked down the road and past the parade ground.

His quarters were the original post surgeon's cabin lying halfway between the rebuilt fort and the original, smaller fort that had been sacked while the army was away fighting the War Between the States. It was nothing more than an adobe box little larger than a Conestoga wagon with a sagging front stoop under a brush ramada. A privy sat behind it, near a dry wash sheathed in catclaw and paloverdes. The sergeant was always killing scorpions and spiders climbing up and down the walls.

Unmarried noncommissioned officers had a designated quarters near the enlisted men's barracks, but the sergeant, a loner by nature, preferred the more rustic quarters set off away from the parade ground.

He went inside and lit a Rochester lamp he'd salvaged from the original fort and which hung over his small wooden table from a rusty wire. The sooty lamp cast wan, reddish yellow light over the hovel. It was sparsely furnished with just a table, a couple of rickety hide-bottom chairs, an army cot, a beehive fireplace crouching in a corner, and several shelves holding mostly airtight tins and a couple of pots and pans.

Gila River Joe built a small fire in the fireplace and set a pot of water to boiling for tea.

While the water boiled, he sat on the deacon's bench on his porch and ate a snack of embalmed beef and a can of stewed tomatoes. His mind was frustratingly busy with conflicting thoughts and emotions, all having to do with the colonel's dead son and the presence of his own daughter here at the fort. Her visit was not unexpected, of course, as he and Samantha had exchanged letters on the subject, but the problem was he simply did not know what to make of the girl.

More specifically, he did not know what to make of him being her *father*, and what she expected of him. Obviously, she expected something or she wouldn't have made the long, arduous trek out from New York. Gila River Joe was afraid of few things in his life, but the truth of the matter was that he was afraid of his own daughter. If he had reflected on it closely, he probably would have said he'd rather have fought a horde of armed Chiricahua braves barehanded than to have to be alone in the same room with the girl.

He'd anticipated her arrival with mixed feelings of fascination and dread, the fascination stemming from the fact that she was his own flesh and blood, after all, and he'd often wondered with a father's curiosity what she looked and acted like now that she was a young adult. The last time he'd seen her she was a very awkward, though precocious, thirteen-year-old.

The dread was a result of his having little idea how to relate to the girl. Of how to be a father to her when he'd had so little experience at it.

When he heard the teapot hissing, he went inside and dumped some green tea into the pot, swirled it, and let it steep as he stared pensively out the single window over the table at the fast-fading, lime green light and the thickening shadows. He filled a stone mug with the brew, which he brought back out to the stoop. He took his place once more on the deacon's bench and was continuing to try to follow the millrace of his thoughts while drinking the tea, when gravel crunched in the darkness beyond the stoop.

Automatically, he reached for his big Walker Colt still holstered on his right hip but stayed the movement when he heard a young woman's voice say, "Sergeant?"

Chapter 14

Gila River Joe's heart thudded. He stared into the shadows beyond two scrubby mesquites, in the direction of the parade ground.

Soft, crunching footsteps sounded. "Sergeant Tunney?"

"Samantha?"

She laughed. "My gosh, what did you do to get yourself hidden away out here, so far from everyone else?" A bray rose to the west of the sergeant's shack, from the quartermaster's corral. "Out here with the mules?"

A slender, pale figure appeared in the shadows beyond the now-abandoned adobe that once housed the post's head laundress. Samantha ducked under a tree branch and continued forward. The sergeant gained his feet slowly, removing his right hand from his pistol, his tea steaming in his left.

"Good Lord, child—you shouldn't be out here. It's dangerous. Apaches are everywhere!"

Samantha stopped and folded her arms across her stomach, glancing around cautiously. "Do they come right into the fort?"

"From time to time. At least, it's not unheard of." Tunney set his tea down on the bench, dropped down his three porch steps, and strode out to his daughter's side. "If you're going to walk around after dark, you should have an escort."

"Oh, I didn't realize that. I thought I was safe inside the fort. Isn't there a wall around it?"

"No. Hildebrandt's not a defensive fort. Apaches are not known for attacking when they're outmanned. Very practical that way. But that doesn't keep one or two from sneaking in from time to time to steal horses or mules. A herder was killed a couple of weeks ago and several mules stolen."

"I didn't realize how dangerous it was, though I guess I should have after my greeting from the Chiricahuas earlier."

"I didn't mean to frighten you."

"Oh, you didn't."

"I just meant that it's wise to be careful. And that you shouldn't walk anywhere without an escort."

"It is rather wild out here, isn't it?"

"You're a long ways from Utica, Samantha."

There was a brief, awkward silence. Samantha studied the small cabin hunched before her. A nighthawk gave a shrill scream over the hills to the west. "So, this is where you live."

"These are my quarters," the sergeant said. "Mine and the scorpions."

She smiled at him. "May, I"—she shrugged—"see inside?"

"Of course," the sergeant said. "I'm sorry. I'm, uh"—he chuckled self-consciously—"I'm not used to having visitors." He took her by the arm and began leading her to the porch. "Watch your step. That second board there is half-rotten."

He released her arm and then followed her up the steps and into the cabin. She stopped just inside and looked around at the shack dimly lit by the lamp that, hanging slightly off-kilter, was issuing sooty smoke from its cracked mantel. As she looked around, Tunney became conscious of the contrast between his humble quarters and the fresh, young woman standing beside him. She'd obviously bathed before supper. She smelled fresh and sweet, and she wore a crisp albeit slightly wrinkled pink cambric blouse, her rich dark brown hair piled and pinned fetchingly atop her pretty head.

He was again nudged by a half-conscious elbow of amazement at the improbable fact that he'd fathered this girl. He even remembered the night it had happened at Fort Beaumont in southwestern Texas, right after the Mexican War. He and Katherine had just been married and had taken up housekeeping in a married officer's quarters not unlike this one, though cleaner. Joe Tunney had been a brash young second lieutenant back then, before his bar had been taken away because of circumstances not entirely of his own making. . . .

"I do apologize, Samantha," the sergeant said. "I didn't know you'd be visiting me here. Once in a while Sergeant Bertram's wife comes over and straightens up and shovels out the dust and dead spiders, but she hasn't been by—"

"No, it's wonderful!" Samantha moved around, turning her head slowly this way and that, perusing the cabin's shabby furnishings as though she were strolling past the fancy shops on Fifth Avenue in New York City. "I mean, it's wonderfully rustic. You don't know how often I've wondered where and how you live."

"Humbly, by your standards."

"Oh, hush, Sergeant."

She stopped near his cot and bent down, sliding a loose lock of hair behind her ear, to peruse a wooden shelf he'd fashioned from a tomato crate. She reached out and lifted the brass ambrotype case that housed two hand-tinted oval photographs—one picture was of Samantha herself at thirteen, braids wrapped atop her head, and the other featured him and Katherine. Tunney was young and straight, with a full, upswept mustache. In full dress uniform complete with a Solingen saber, he stood beside the velvet armchair on which the lovely Katherine sat, resplendent in her wedding dress.

The photograph had been taken in a photographer's tent

in Amarillo, where they'd been married, but the stage ornaments flanking the newlyweds made it appear as if they were posing in an elegant drawing room back East.

She showed him the frame over her shoulder, giving him a conspiratorial little quirk of her lips. Tunney felt his cheeks warm. Samantha returned the frame to the shelf, and the sergeant said, "Would you like some tea?"

"I would love some tea."

Tunney reached for a mug—his only other one—removed the teapot from the makeshift spit he'd erected over the bee-hive fireplace, and filled it with the tea. "It's been hanging there awhile. Probably a little bitter," he said, handing his daughter the cup.

"Please don't worry so much about things, Sergeant," Samantha chided him quietly, taking the mug in her hands and blowing on it.

Tunney shrugged and gestured toward a chair at the table.

When they'd sat down across from each other, Samantha blew on the steaming tea again and sipped. She sat sideways to the table, her back to the front wall, looking around with bright, wide eyes.

It was nearly dark outside now, and the only sounds were the occasional calls of night birds, the braying of a mule, the whinny of a horse, the mournful wails of a coyote in the hills and bluffs beyond the fort's perimeter, the sputtering of the coals in the stove, and the scratching of the breeze around the sergeant's shack.

Tunney was racking his brain for something to say, when, to his great relief, Samantha herself broke the silence, turning to him with "So, what should I call you?"

"What should you *call* me?"

"I can't seem to settle on any one thing. I discussed the matter with Mother before I left, and she laughed and said I should call you *Pa*, because you were more of a *Pa* type of a father than a *Father* type. But I'll go on calling you Sergeant, if you like."

"No, I—"

"Or Joe." Samantha leaned over the table, resting her chin on her fist, studying him in the wan, flickering light of the lantern. "Hmmm . . . Gila River Joe. You know, I think that's my favorite."

Joe chuckled.

"Please tell me how you acquired that handle, Joe or Sergeant. Or *Pa.* I've heard it was because you involuntarily spent an entire winter camping along the banks of the Gila River when your entire patrol, save for you yourself, of course, was wiped out by kill-crazy Apaches!"

"Kill-crazy Apaches!" Joe chuckled again and sipped his tea. "You been readin' them little yellow-covered books. Imagine—with your education!"

"Tell me."

"About what?"

"The Gila River!"

"Oh, that. Well, hell . . ." Joe winced and ran his hand across his mouth. "I do apologize. I know better than to curse in front of the ladies."

"Don't worry, I will not inform Mother of my father's scandalous tongue. Now, please, tell me how you came to be known as Gila River Joe."

The sergeant took another sip of his tea. "It was back before the War Between the States broke out. Maybe five years before. We'd just acquired all this territory out here—you know, after the Mexican War, the Gadsden Purchase, and all that. I and a column headed by a good lieutenant rode out from Camp McCaslin in New Mexico. We were out a month and were riding up along the Gila River northeast of Tucson, near where Camp Grant would be established in the months ahead, when we were attacked by White Mountain Apaches led by Zanna, one of the fiercest of all the White Mountain subchiefs. They hit us hard early one morning, wiping out nearly half our column in the first couple of hours. Scattered our horses and pack mules from hell to breakfast."

The lieutenant sighed as he stared down at his nearly empty mug. "They looted our dead and started comin' at us with our own cap-and-ball Colts and muskets. We all scrambled and hid amongst the rocks and cactus. We were scattered all over those slopes and canyons on either side of the river. Zanna's warriors kept coming at us night and day, for several nights and several days. They picked us off one by one, two by two"—he could still hear the screams of the tortured and the dying men in his head—"until I was the lone survivor. I forted up there as well as I could, in the hills and bluffs and rocks along the Gila."

"You survived by sheer stealth, filling canteens at the stream, and eating the meat of the dead cavalry horses," Samantha added.

Joe scowled at her. "You know the story?"

She nodded, smiling. "I heard it from an old soldier at Fort Union, on the way out here."

"What was his name?"

"Captain Ravely."

"Ah, Gerald Ravely. He'd been stationed at McCaslin at the time." The sergeant frowned. "Well, if you already knew the story, why—?"

"I wanted to hear you tell it."

"Straight from the horse's mouth, huh?"

Still resting her chin on the heel of her hand, Samantha gazed at him dreamily. "You survived alone out there nearly all winter. More soldiers were sent out to look for your patrol, but they all met with stiff resistance from the Apaches and had to turn back. The Apaches had you surrounded, without a horse or ammunition for your pistol. All you had was the bayonet blade from your musket. You spent nearly the entire winter living by your wits—eating horse meat and sneaking down to the river at night for water."

The sergeant shook his head and continued the story as he stared somberly out the opaque wax paper window to his right. "I hardly ever dared go down to the river. Zanna had it too well covered. I found a small tinaja hidden amongst the rocks that the White Mountains apparently didn't know about. I stayed pretty close to that spring all winter, scuttling around only at night for food."

He remembered stumbling over the bodies of the decimated patrol on those dark nights. The bloody, bloated bodies, the stench tempered only slightly by the chill air in the canyon that winter. He remembered the long, cold nights, the nearly impenetrable fear that seemed to have no end, the constant, desperate need for sustenance as well as total concealment, which meant that he had to cover every track he made.

"I'm sorry, Sergeant." Samantha stretched her arm across the table, placed her hand on top of his. "It's more than a story to you. I was callous in asking you to recite it."

"No," Joe said, liking the feel of his daughter's hand on his. "I enjoyed telling it to you. Funny—you're the first person I've told in years. The first person I've told that many details to."

He threw back the last of his tea and leaned back in his chair. "Well, when Zanna's bunch finally pulled out the next spring and headed for Mexico, I made my way southwest to Tucson, eventually crossed paths with a cavalry patrol from Fort Breckenridge. By hook or by crook, after that I started being called Gila River Joe—I think a newspaper fella from Phoenix hung the handle on me—and I guess it stuck."

"May I call you Joe, then?" Samantha asked. "I mean . . . *Pa* doesn't seem right somehow, since we really hardly know each other. And *Father* seems too formal. *Joe* seems to be the right balance." She smiled brightly, proudly. "*Joe*, short for *Gila River Joe*."

"All right," Joe said, feeling embarrassed by the intimacy of the conversation but also enjoying it. He felt less uneasy now about this frank, lovely girl—who was his own fresh and blood—having tracked him down. "*Joe* it is. Now that we got that straightened out, what shall I call you?"

"Please, call me Sam. All my friends at school did, though Mother abhors it. She says she didn't raise her daughter to be addressed as a boy."

Joe threw his head back and laughed with abandon. "Oh, dear Lord—that sounds like Katherine!"

They laughed together for a time, and then Sam said, "Joe, I don't want you to feel any pressure about my being here. I mean . . ." She looked down as though the words she were searching for might be on the floor near her feet. Then she looked up, sliding that defiant lock of hair back behind her ear again. "I mean I don't want you to think you have to suddenly be my father. My stepfather, Uncle George, has filled that role quite well for a good many years."

"Of course he has," Gila River Joe said, guilt poking his ribs like a rusty nail.

At the same time, he was well aware that George Biddles had fulfilled his role for him, and grateful for it. Biddles had been a much better father than Joe could have been not only because of his family's deep pockets, but also because the man obviously wasn't as selfish as Joe Tunney was. When Katherine had grown weary of frontier-post life before the War Between the States had broken out and had given Joe the choice of either following her and their young daughter back East or divorce, he had chosen divorce.

Complicating his and Katherine's marriage had been the humiliating matter of his demotion from first lieutenant to second sergeant, which Katherine had taken harder than Joe himself had. But he'd still obviously been more in love with the rugged Western frontier than his family, a fact that his conscience had wrestled with for a long time.

A fact that he was still wrestling with this evening.

Samantha reached across the table again and squeezed Joe's hand. "What I guess I'm saying is, I don't want you to feel any pressure. I didn't come here looking for a father. I came here looking for the man who *is* my father, whoever that man may be, regardless of whether I'm here or not." She swallowed, gazed at him levelly beneath the smoking Rochester. "But I would like your help with one thing."

"What's that?" Joe said, his voice thick as her flesh fairly burned against his.

"I would like your help in getting to know who that man is."

Sam stared at him, tilting her head slightly, with faint

beseeching. The red-tinted lamplight glowed softly as it followed the curvature of her large gray-blue eyes.

Gila River Joe felt his heartbeat quicken.

He cleared his throat, offered an uncertain smile, feeling a whole passel of strange emotions—the most potent of which was pride in having fathered such an arresting young woman—and said, "Why, all right, Sam. It might not come fast or easy for me, but if you hold my feet to the fire, I think I can swing her."

Chapter 15

"Careful, partner," warned Seth Barksdale the next day. "You're treadin' into dangerous territory."

"I did that when I started bunkin' with you, with all your dreamin' an' screamin' of a night, and lungin' for pistols and knives. It's a wonder you haven't cut my throat."

Yakima shifted the saddle on his left shoulder as he stared toward the cavalry stables and corrals southwest of the fort, where he and Seth were heading. It was nearly midday, hot, and the hoof thuds and yells of soldiers practicing the Charge rose raucously from the parade ground.

"Well, I'll be damned—look there," he mused, slowing his pace slightly.

"Them three savages are gettin' their pictures drawn."

The six-foot-high adobe wall of the southernmost corral, and its peeled pole gate, lay before the two contract scouts. The three Aravaipa scouts were outside the front gate. Chiquito and Pedro were mounted on their bayo coyote mustangs trimmed with colorful *bayeta* blankets and dyed breast straps and rope halters. One-Eyed Miguel was squatting on his haunches before his bayo lobo, which was sniffing the greased braids wrapped around the top of his rider's head. The tracker's half-Mexican wife always braided his hair with hawk feathers, as was the custom of the band to which he belonged.

One-Eyed Miguel looked very serious as he stared gravely into the distance, as though at enemies gathering on the distant horizon. He was squinting his lone eye. He didn't always wear his snakeskin patch over his badly scarred, blind eye, but he wore it today, which was a good thing since the sergeant's comely daughter was sketching his picture in the big, leather-covered sketchbook.

As Yakima and Seth continued walking toward the corral gate, Samantha closed the book with a satisfied smile and said, "Thank you so very much, gentlemen. I've sketched the outline and I can fill in the details. . . ." She let her voice trail off, apparently hearing the *ching*ing of approaching spurs, and turned toward Seth and Yakima. "Oh, there you are, Mr. Henry." She glanced briefly at Seth. "Good day, Mr. Barksdale," she said cordially before returning her smiling eyes to Yakima. "I was looking for you earlier."

"Of course she was," Seth grunted in Yakima's ear.

Yakima did not react. One-Eyed Miguel straightened, looked at Samantha, then at Yakima, and grinned broadly, showing all his chipped, tobacco-stained teeth. The lead Aravaipa scout turned and swung fluidly up onto the back of his bayo lobo and said in his guttural tongue, using his hands for emphasis, "She was looking for you earlier because she awakened wet and horny this morning in her room at the colonel's casita. She was looking for you, Green Eyed Siwash, so that you could give her the mounting she's been moaning for. If you are not man enough to please her"—the bawdy-tongued scout hoisted himself up slightly in his saddle—"perhaps I could perform the task in your honor. You must warn her, though, that after tumbling with One-Eyed Miguel she will never again get satisfaction from another man—white or red!"

Miguel threw his arm up with a high-pitched howl, ground heels into his mustang's flanks, and galloped off to the west. Howling with jubilation, the other two Aravaipas galloped after their leader, heading north on their second scout of the day.

Seth glanced at Yakima. "Poetic devil, ain't he?"

"What was all that about?" Samantha asked. She'd been staring after the galloping Apaches, but now she turned to Seth and Yakima, frowning.

Seth nudged Yakima with his elbow, sighed, and headed through the corral gate with his saddle on one shoulder, his Spencer carbine in his other hand, leaving Yakima to fend for himself alone against the comely daughter of Sergeant Tunney. The girl held him with a look.

"Uh . . . ," Yakima said, absently kicking a horse apple, "they was just commentin' on how we'd best be hittin' the trail. Three scouts today, before we go out on a long run tomorrow, after them Chiricowys . . ."

The girl's eyebrows arched upward. "Why is it I don't think that's really what he said?"

"Well . . . you're just the suspicious type, I reckon."

"Oh, I'm the suspicious type? Hmmm." Samantha Tunney hugged the sketchbook to the corset of her dark brown shirtwaist edged with white ruffles and lace. It matched her plumed felt riding hat and the flowing, pleated skirt that dropped to below her ankles. The subdued colors probably meant she'd be attending the funeral of the colonel's dead son later. "I was looking for you earlier, Mr. Henry. I guess you were out on your morning scout. At least, that's what I was told by Lieutenant Geist, who's been very helpful." Irony gave a dry pitch to her tone.

"Why were you lookin' for me, Miss Tunney?"

"Please, do call me Samantha."

Yakima stared at her. At least, he tried to. He wasn't accustomed to being in the company of beautiful young women, least of all a well-bred white woman who was the daughter of Gila River Joe Tunney, his commanding officer. This was the man who controlled his poke and whether Yakima woke up at Hildebrandt the next day or was hoofin' it off to God knew where looking for other employment. For some cow-brained reason, he liked it here at Fort Hell.

It had become home to him.

And he wanted to stay.

Her beauty made it hard for him to look straight at her for longer than a couple of seconds or so at a time.

She continued. "Joe tells me I need an escort if I'm going to wander very far from the fort proper, and I was wondering if you'd escort me sometime. Show me around. I'd really like to get to know the place better. I overhead a couple of soldiers this morning speaking about a couple of *hog ranches* in a canyon near here. Something in the gentlemen's tone led me to believe that these ranches are something other than pig farms."

She curled one side of her mouth. "I thought maybe you could introduce me to those ranches so I can become acquainted with all aspects of life here at Fort Hell, as I believe it's called."

Her eyes raked him up and down with a feminine brashness he'd rarely seen outside the hog ranches she'd mentioned. "Also, I'd like to draw you, Mr. Henry."

"Why would you want to make a picture of me, Miss Tunney?"

"I'm writing and illustrating an article about the frontier, and I have a vague notion to make my thesis something about the clash of cultures. You, being half Indian and half white, would be a wonderful . . . and might I add a *handsome* . . . representation of this clash. A man straddling a high fence between two worlds, not really at home in either one."

"Yeah, that sounds like it'd be a right entertainin' story, all right, but if you wouldn't mind, Miss—"

"Samantha!"

They both turned to see Lieutenant Geist walking toward them from the direction of the fort commander's office. He was in his full-dress uniform complete with epaulettes, polished helmet and boots, crimson sash, and saber snugged down in a brass-trimmed steel sheath. From head to toe, he was flashing in the sunlight. Even his monocle!

"I say there, Miss Tunney!"

"Oh, hello, Gunther."

Geist smiled as he came to a stop near Samantha and Yakima, and removed his monocle with a black-gloved hand. "I say, it's probably . . . well, it's probably best not to fraternize too closely with the lower-ranking folks here at Fort Hildebrandt." He glanced at Yakima distastefully. "Especially . . . uh . . . with those men who have no rank at all. These are contract scouts, you understand, and, well, Mr. Henry here is a half-breed *Indian*."

He rose up and down on the heels of his boots, beaming down at Samantha as though he'd just given her an invaluable bit of new information that would make her visit to Hildebrandt so much easier.

"Yes, I understand they are contract scouts, Lieutenant. And I also understand that Mr. Henry is a half-breed Indian, but I don't see how that—"

"Geist is right, Miss Tunney," Yakima said, sidling away from the two, heading toward the corral gate that Seth had left open for him. "You'd best stay away from me. I think I'm probably a whole lot more interesting to think about from a distance than to know close up, and I don't bathe half as much as Geist here. When I do it's usually in one o' them stock tanks yonder where the horses are drinkin' out of."

He nodded toward one of the wooden stock tanks inside the corral, which a young private on stable duty was pouring a bucket of water into.

"That's *Lieutenant* Geist, mister," the lieutenant said, spreading his mustached lips in a brightly phony smile.

"Go fuck yourself, Geist," Yakima said, turning full around and heading through the corral gate. "I don't answer to you."

Behind him, the corners of Samantha's mouth lifted up into a small smile.

"I'll . . . I'll . . . have you written up for that, you mangy rock worshipper!" Geist belted out, one hand on his sword handle, as though he was pondering drawing it. His fleshy face around his black mustache and goatee was as red as an Arizona sunset.

"You've done it before. You'll do it again," Yakima said lazily, slouching away toward where Seth was grinning as he saddled his bay in a brush-covered stable.

Yakima and Seth rode out of the fort just as the officers, the officers' wives, and sundry civilians close to the colonel were marching up the hill north of the fort to congregate in the cemetery for the colonel's son's funeral. The fort's chaplain, Father Dunleavy, and his dog were already standing beside the freshly dug grave, his robes ruffling in the breeze.

An hour or so later, Yakima and Seth were riding along a piñon-studded bench on the long, gradual slope of Apache Pass, scouting for Chiricahua sign. Their job was to locate the *ranchería* of the main group of Chiricahuas that had been plaguing patrols out of Fort Hildebrandt and causing trouble for passengers along the stage and mail road.

Sergeant Tunney wanted to gain some idea of the *ranchería*'s location before sending out a larger cavalry contingent to attack the Apaches. Attacking them was going to be tricky, however. Since the colonel's son had been riding with them, there was a chance the colonel's daughter, who was five years older than the boy had been, would be at the *ranchería* with the rest of the group's women.

So far today, the scouts had found no sign indicating where the *ranchería* lay. The traditional Apache encampment would likely be, as they usually were, a small collection of brush *jacales*, stone fire rings, and makeshift corrals for housing their horse herds hidden in a deep canyon or along a wash well concealed by brush and cacti.

Sometimes looking for Apache encampments was like looking for matchsticks. Yakima had lived out here for a time as a boy, when his strange, silent father had been prospecting this country east of Tucson, so he knew the terrain well, as did Seth, who'd been out here since a year after the war.

Still, it was a vast landscape, shoved, pinched, churned, buffed, and tortured into all forms of wind- and sun-blasted barrancas and cordilleras.

Only the Apaches themselves, to whom it was home, really knew it. Yakima and Seth were newcomers here, and Yakima was made painfully aware of that fact every time he rode out to scout it.

They were riding down off a rocky slope onto a broad flat between cactus-spiked hogbacks, when Seth leaned out from his saddle to scour the ground beneath him and said absently, "Which one of us you suppose shot the colonel's kid?"

The question had nagged at Yakima—mostly in a vague sort of way—ever since they found the dead white boy in the brush. He tried to sound more casual about it than he really felt.

"Does it matter? He was runnin' wild with them Chiricahuas, and his bullets or arrows would have perforated our hides as certain sure as those the full-bloods was slingin'."

"Yeah, I know." Seth stopped his horse, swung down from the saddle, and plucked a clump of scat from between two catclaw shrubs. "I was just wonderin's, all." He broke up the clump of the old, dried-up chunk of burro shit and let it fall to the ground. "You think the colonel holds it against us?"

"I don't know," Yakima said, staring off toward the northwest. "Why don't you ask him?"

"Could have been Dent who shot him, too. Or one of the stage passengers. Them two fancy Dans were shootin' pistols out the stage windows."

Yakima looked at his partner. "Why does it matter?" He tried to sound incredulous, because he didn't want the killing to bother him, though it did. They'd been fighting Indians, for chrissakes, and the colonel's son had obviously become a Chiricahua as deadly as the rest.

"I don't know," Seth said, straightening and slapping his hands together. "I guess I just feel guilty about shooting the old man's kid. I thought I was done killin' white boys. And the colonel's obviously pretty torn up about it. He seems like such a sad old man. Proud, but . . . sad. He was hopin' to maybe get his kids and his wife back alive one day, and—"

"All right, all right, for chrissakes!" Yakima was suddenly annoyed. Seth giving voice to the source of their guilt wasn't making the young half-breed feel any better about his. In fact, it only caused him to ruminate on it harder. "There's nothin' we can do about it now, and since the old man didn't lock us in the guardhouse, let's forget about it. The kid's probably been buried now, anyway. Look over there."

"Where?"

Yakima pointed.

Seth walked around to the other side of his horse and stared off toward the lower country to the north. A wagon and several blue-uniformed soldiers were sliding along the trail that rose out of the chaparral to traverse Apache Pass from the west. The entire group was little larger than two thumbnails placed side by side from this distance—just a slight splash of blues and duns and the cream of the covered wagon. Light tan dust billowed up around and behind the slow-moving procession.

"You suppose that's the colonel's piano?" Seth asked, his voice pitched with irony, though neither he nor Yakima begrudged the old man a piano for his daughter. Colonel Alexander was a fair, even-tempered commander. And while he was notoriously extravagant when it came to spoiling his thirteen-year-old daughter, few faulted him for it, given his circumstances and exemplary record. No one on this side of the sod had sacrificed more for his country.

"Could be," Yakima said. "It's been due any day now."

"Let's ride down and have a chat with them boys," Seth

said, stepping up into his saddle. "Maybe they've seen some Chiricahua sign."

"Might as well give it a shot," Yakima said, touching spurs to his buckskin's flanks. "We sure as hell aren't findin' any up here."

Chapter 16

The two scouts galloped down the side of the slope, swung right, and headed down the long, slow grade toward the stage and mail road.

They soon picked up an old Indian hunting trail that meandered north through the mesquites and creosote shrubs, and gained the road to see the covered artillery wagon, accompanied by a contingent of soldiers from Fort Lowell and the district supply depot at Tucson, rounding a curve and climbing a low hill along the trail to the west of Yakima's and Seth's position.

Over the bristling desert flora and through the rising dust, Yakima counted four soldiers riding ahead of the wagon with four more bringing up the rear. Yakima and Seth waited in the trail, slouching in their saddles.

As the wagon crested the hill and started down the other side, Yakima could see the heads of the soldiers swiveling to stare toward him and Seth. All were holding carbines with butts either pressed against their cartridge belts or across the pommels of their saddles. As they drew closer, not unexpectedly, the young half-breed saw that their bearded, sunburned, dust-caked faces were set with caution.

For some reason he couldn't explain, Yakima felt a twinge of unease. And when Seth gave him an incredulous frown, Yakima knew his partner was feeling a might wormy in his squirmy parts, as well. But Seth didn't say anything, so Yakima didn't say anything, either. He wanted to unsheath his Spencer, just in case, but he knew he couldn't. Since he and Seth were not wearing uniforms, they could easily be mistaken for the road agents, who were known to prey as heavily upon the trail as did the Apaches.

The wagon descended the hill and continued toward Yakima and Seth. It followed a long curve in the trail, avoiding a pile of eroded black rock deposited here by some ancient glacier or maybe heaved up from the earth's bowels a handful of eons ago. A Cooper's hawk perched atop the escarpment, taking a break from hunting rabbits and kangaroo rats to watch the human activities below with raptorial interest.

The wagon clattered loudly, while water sloshed in a barrel strapped to its side. Occasional breezes snapped the soiled canvas tarp draped over the wagon's boughs. Hooves clomped, and tack squawked.

One of the two lead riders wore a lieutenant's single bar on his filthy uniform that was more gray than blue, Yakima saw now from close-up. The man looked as though he'd literally climbed down off his horse and rolled in alkali.

The lieutenant was tall and lean. His long, copper-eyed, hollow-jawed face owned a hungry, buzzardlike look. His chin jutted severely, and a saber scar lay in a slanting white knot across the middle of his long nose. He wore a red sash and a cavalry saber, though the rest of his uniform was not regulation dress. The butt of a Henry rifle jutted from his saddle boot.

Staring skeptically toward Yakima and Seth, he slowly raised his left hand. The man beside the lieutenant was his age but stockier, and he wore a full, bushy black beard and three yellow chevrons with a single stripe over the top, making him a quartermaster sergeant.

The driver of the wagon was leaning forward, elbows resting on his knees, the reins of the four-mule hitch resting easily in his gloved hands. Glowering over the mules at the two men sitting in the trail facing him, the jehu worked up a wad of chaw with his tongue, spat it down over the dashboard, and snorted.

"From Lowell?" Seth asked, breaking the silence.

Yakima jerked slightly when the hawk took wing from the rocky pinnacle to his right, cawing. The bird flapped low over the wagon, banked sharply, and disappeared back along the western trail, its raucous cries dwindling gradually beneath the snorting of the mules and horses, the scratching of the breeze in the brush.

"That's right," said the lieutenant in a low, slow, gravelly voice that bore the hint of a slight Southern accent. "Piano for Hildebrandt. Don't understand hauling a piano way out here in this 'pache-infested canker on the devil's behind, but to each his own, I reckon."

Seth chuckled and shifted his weight in his saddle, leaning harder against the horn. "That piano's gonna put a mighty pretty smile on the colonel's daughter's face."

"That's Colonel Alexander, I take it. It's nice seein' a girl smile out here." The lieutenant canted his head slightly. "You two from Hildebrandt?"

"That's right," Yakima said. "Contract scouts."

"If you fellas don't mind," said the sergeant sitting beside the lieutenant, "we got us a timetable to keep."

The lieutenant glanced at him with mild reproof, and then he turned back to Seth and Yakima, spreading a slight, affable grin that somehow seemed out of place on his otherwise stony face. "The sergeant's all about timetables. Me, I'd just like to get rid of this piano and get started back to Lowell. We heard at the last stage station the Chiricahuas been kicking up the dirt somethin' fierce out here. They said that after yesterday they was lookin' for a new shotgun rider."

"Jubal Dent took an arrow," Yakima said.

"That's too bad. Not unexpected. Dangerous profession. But too bad, nonetheless. He gonna be okay—Jubal?"

"He'll be all right," Yakima said.

"No thanks to Gila River Joe," Seth added, grinning at Yakima, who returned the smile.

Seth turned again to the lieutenant. "You see any Chiricahuas on your way out from Tucson?"

"Seen some smoke back that way," the lieutenant said, glancing back over his left shoulder. "Just above Ten-Mile Ridge. Seen plenty of 'pache smoke talk in my time out here." He shook his head gravely. "Never fails to make me all mushy down around my shell belt."

"Ten-Mile Ridge, eh?" said Yakima. "Well, then, I reckon we'll let you boys be on your way."

Seth pinched his hat brim to the lieutenant. He and Yakima turned their horses off to opposite sides of the trail, and the lieutenant yelled, "Forward!"

When the procession had passed, the two Hildebrandt scouts booted their horses back onto the trail, staring after the wagon. The driver's yells and the cracking of his blacksnake over the backs of the mules were dying away as the troopers and the wagon disappeared around another bend in the powdery trail, the vast desert swallowing them.

"Anything about them seem strange to you?" asked Seth.

"Yeah, but I can't put my finger on it."

"Me, neither."

They were both too preoccupied with the Chiricahuas to give the wagon escort further thought. They turned to the southwest, the direction in which the lieutenant had said he'd seen smoke signals, and booted their mounts across the desert, heading toward a red escarpment jutting like a dinosaur spine out of the desert, a mile or so away. It was the highest point in several miles and they decided that it would be the best spot to reconnoiter Ten-Mile Ridge through their army-issue field glasses.

Half an hour later, they lay on their bellies near the top of the dinosaur spine. They'd left their horses directly below, for the ridge was too steep for the mounts, and they were both standing in the shade cast by the ridge, munching on wild grasses and mesquite berries. Seth stared through his field glasses, stretching his lips back from his teeth, running his gloved index right finger across the binoculars' focus wheel.

"Anything?" Yakima was sucking the nourishing pulp of a barrel cactus, the juice running down the corners of his mouth. Two eagles were slowly circling the ridge, riding thermals pushing up off the hot desert floor.

"Not a damn thi—" Seth cut himself abruptly off. Lowering the glasses, he turned toward Yakima, frowning. Sweat was carving shallow troughs through the dust on his cheeks.

"Hey, did you notice that lieutenant kinda talked like me?"

"He talked *like* you, yeah, but he didn't talk near as much as you do. You accused me of talkin' too much. Christalmighty, sometimes I do swear you'd talk the ears off a corncob!"

"He was a first lieutenant."

Yakima studied his partner. "So?"

"He was Southern. That was a Georgia accent. Since when did they start puttin' lieutenants' bars on the shoulders of Johnny Rebs?"

Yakima squinted. "You mean graybacks can't be officers?" He'd heard that some time ago, but he'd forgotten about it. He'd been so removed from the war, living and wandering in the West during those years, that it had been little more than a vague rumor to him. It still sort of was.

"Nope, ain't allowed. At least, in most cases. Can't get no further than a first sergeant. That's why I didn't join the Union blue out here but decided to be my own contractor."

"Well, maybe he threw in with the Union. Some o' them fellas from Dixie musta fought for the North."

Seth was fingering his chin whiskers. "That sword he was wearin' . . . wasn't no Union saber. I saw so many of 'em durin' the war that I didn't think nothin' of it, but it had a little copper plate up around the hand guard. If I'd been closer, I woulda seen that that copper plate had the initials CSA on it!"

"Confederate States of America?"

"Didn't Luz mention she'd seen gray-clad men riding with the Chiricahuas around her and her old man's ranch?"

Yakima froze with his mouth half-open, his heart thudding in his ears. "Yeah. Yeah, I think she did."

Seth turned to stare off in the direction of Hildebrandt. "Their uniforms was awful dusty. Like they rode through a windstorm, or . . ."

"Or rolled in dust to cover bloodstains."

The two scouts stared at each other in hushed silence for about five seconds. They were both seeing that wagon again in their minds' eyes, and they were wondering what the soiled wagon cover had concealed.

Simultaneously, they leaped to their feet. Letting the field glasses hang by the lanyard around his neck, Seth followed Yakima to the other side of the escarpment. They moved quickly down the steep side—too quickly, for both of them lost their footing in the loose gravel and dropped to their knees, almost falling and rolling straight down to the ground.

They followed a cleft between rocks to the formation's base, and their horses started whickering as the two scouts ran at them, quickly grabbing the ground-tied reins and swinging into the saddles.

"How far you think we're out from Hell?" Seth asked, crouching low and driving spurs into his gelding's flanks.

Yakima was bent low over his horse's billowing mane as the buckskin stretched its stride, fairly gliding over the desert. "This may be my first and only time I'd say we're too far from Hell, Seth!"

He whipped his rein ends against the horse's flanks, urging more speed.

Chapter 17

Samantha Tunney frowned beneath the wide, floppy brim of her sunhat.

She wished the drilling soldiers on the parade ground before her would hold still for a minute so she could draw a few clear lines. The images in her head were all a blur of scissoring horses' legs and jostling, mounted troopers, with dust sifting this way and that beneath the fort's regimental guidon and the American flag flapping high atop their wooden poles.

At the moment, the drill sergeant, mounted on a horse on the far side of the parade ground, was yelling at the soldiers riding in a loosely formed circle before him. The sergeant's Irish accent was so thick that Samantha couldn't understand much of what he was yelling, but they must have been drill commands. He seemed to be commanding the mounted troopers' movements with the sword he was wielding high above his head, similar to how a symphony conductor commanded the notes that flowed out of the harps, cellos, oboes, and violins of his musicians.

The post bugler sat on a cream horse beside the sergeant,

and as the mounted cavalry soldiers formed a line at the end of the parade ground to Samantha's far left, the sergeant bellowed, *"Charge!"*

The bugler began blasting away on his horn. The mounted troopers raised their brass-tipped sabers and began yelling and batting their heels against the flanks of their sweaty bays. The horses lunged off their back hooves and began racing toward the opposite side of the parade ground, to Samantha's far right.

Over there stood several large frames constructed of peeled poles. From the top beam of the frames dangled little white men without arms or legs, though of course they weren't men at all. They were sheets filled with straw and shaped into the trunks of living men, and they hung from the frame, billowing slightly in the slight breeze, billowing to the point of dancing when the breeze gusted, which it did now just as the soldiers reached them.

Following the charging, blue-clad troopers with her eyes, Samantha swiftly scratched lines onto the cream leaf in her sketchbook, and found herself chuckling. Some of the soldiers managed to drive their swords into the hanging white dummies, but several missed their targets altogether, evoking a fusillade of groans and shouted epithets from the rotund, red-faced Irish sergeant.

As Samantha looked up, one of the windblown dummies slammed against one of the mounted troopers. The young man screamed and flung his sword away from him as he flew back over his buck-kicking mount's left hip. The horse turned abruptly with the others, and as the young soldier lost his hat and loosed another, horrified scream, his head and shoulders hit the ground.

The horse kept running with the others toward the opposite end of the parade ground, from where they'd started, the young trooper screaming as his upper body bounced along the ground beside the horse.

"Oh, my . . . !" Samantha jumped to her feet in astonishment, casting her concerned gaze at the poor soldier who, having apparently gotten his boot caught in his stirrup, was being dragged right past her. The horse's hooves hammered the ground; she could feel the pulsating vibrations beneath her feet. The young man's fair-skinned face was red with terror, eyes wide and beseeching the sky as he grimaced against the pain of his shoulders and head bouncing off the hard-packed dirt beneath him.

About fifty feet to Samantha's left, the poor soldier's boot broke free of the stirrup, and the trooper rolled wildly, limbs and dust flying, before he finally came to a stop. Samantha clamped a hand over her mouth. As a couple of the other mounted troopers rode toward the man, who was grunting as he attempted to regain his footing, the sergeant laughed heartily from across the field and said to Samantha, "Don't worry yourself, my little teacup. It's just one dummy taken down by another!"

He threw his red-bearded head back and laughed raucously, as though at the most humorous joke he'd ever heard. He cut himself off abruptly, and his face crumpled with what appeared genuine fury as he said, "Private Schwartzenheimer! On your feet, boyo! Grab your rifle and start runnin' laps! You'll run laps until stable call!"

"Oh, my gosh!" Samantha gasped, watching the poor trooper get helped to his feet by two of his now-dismounted comrades. To herself, she said, "Talk about adding insult to injury!"

The young trooper, slight and pimple-faced, brushed himself off and retrieved his dusty kepi. With not so much as a glance toward Samantha, his cheeks flushed with embarrassment, the poor boy raised his rifle in both hands above his head and began jogging around the parade ground.

He appeared to be all right, and the other troopers resumed their drills, so Samantha sat back down in her chair and took up her sketchbook. She'd drawn only half an image of the trooper tumbling off his horse, as best she could remember it, when something caught her eye to the south of the fort.

A covered wagon was climbing the long hill from Apache Pass. The driver was yelling and cracking his whip over the backs of the weary-looking team. Samantha could see the man standing up in his driver's box, and she supposed he was yelling, though she couldn't hear him above the yelling of the drill sergeant and the thudding of the hooves before her.

The wagon was being led up the hill by several mounted troopers, the blue of their uniforms showing vaguely behind the liberal coating of dust they'd obviously acquired along the desert trail. More soldiers followed.

The wagon was likely loaded with freight headed for either the post trader's store or the quartermaster's warehouse, Samantha silently opined. She'd been at Hildebrandt for only a day, but, an eminently curious girl, and not shy about asking questions, she was already learning how the fort functioned.

As the wagon continued climbing the hill, it drew the interest of several soldiers who rode sentry around Hildebrandt's perimeter. Two of these sentinels rode out to meet the wagon and then turned their mounts around to accompany the procession on up the hill. About a hundred yards down the southern slope, the trail forked, one tine leading off toward the chapel, the hotel, the saloon, the post trader's store, and the corrals, while the other angled toward the parade ground. The wagon and its accompaniment of soldiers took the latter tine and followed the trail up along the far side of the parade ground, stopping momentarily at the small post headquarters building, near the infirmary.

While the leader of the freight detail conferred with the officer of the day—the colonel had taken the day off, as he'd just buried his son only two hours earlier—the drills in front of Samantha continued, and she continued with her sketching. But when she glanced up again, however, she was again distracted.

This time it was by two horseback riders galloping hell-for-leather, as they say, up the same hill that the freight detail had climbed a few minutes before. The riders were mere bobbing specks from this distance of what must have been nearly a mile away, but for some reason they held Samantha's attention.

Why would two riders gallop so quickly up that low hill from the pass unless compelled by great urgency?

Samantha glanced around.

None of the soldiers milling about the perimeters of Hildebrandt appeared to have noticed the fast-moving newcomers yet. All seemed preoccupied with the arrival of the freight wagon, which was understandable, since the fort was so isolated and visitors were few and far between. The only news from the outside world came from the sporadically delivered U.S. Mail, the infrequent visits of soldiers from other forts, or from civilians riding the Butterfield stage.

"All right—this way to the colonel's quarters, Lieutenant!" said the mounted sentry, gigging his sweaty bay ahead along the trail skirting the far side of the parade ground.

He kept his horse at a walk so that the wagon could keep up to him. The wagon pulled ahead to the far end of the parade ground, and the slow-moving procession turned around that end of the parade ground and came up the trail on Samantha's side, heading toward the colonel's large quarters beyond her, to the south.

As the wagon's rattling grew louder, Samantha turned toward the trail climbing the slope from Apache Pass.

The two galloping riders had dropped down out of sight as they climbed the last leg of the hill into Hildebrandt. Meanwhile, the soldiers and the wagon clattered past her, and she closed her sketchbook and rose from her chair to watch it pass, squinting against the dust kicked up by the wagon and the horses.

As the wagon passed, the bearded driver turned toward Samantha. His pale blue eyes studied her for longer than was appropriate, in the most craven way, looking her up and down. And then as the wagon continued on past her, the driver smiled lasciviously and winked.

Gila River Joe Tunney stood on the colonel's front ramada, holding a dainty china cup in one hand, a matching saucer in the other hand. He was staring down the gradual hill toward the wagon and the mounted soldiers heading toward him, on his side of the parade ground.

Most of the other soldiers who had gathered for a light meal on the lee side of the brief funeral for the colonel's son were still inside, visiting with the colonel. Some of the women were helping Two Feathers in the kitchen. All of the other soldiers here were officers, Tunney being the only non-com invited owing to his long-standing, rank-transcending friendship with Colonel Alexander.

Samantha had also been invited but had excused herself some time ago, a fact that amused the sergeant. Gila River Joe, too, had never had much patience with social gatherings. Yet Samantha, who barely knew the colonel or anyone else here, had made a graceful escape, while he felt compelled to remain at least until the others started leaving, even though he was probably more disinclined to social formalities and idle conversation.

The sergeant studied the dust-caked procession curiously as it continued past his daughter, who'd changed out of her funeral attire and had gone down to draw pictures of the parade drills, which she seemed fascinated by. The freight procession had traveled past the quartermaster's storehouse, so the wagon must be heading for the colonel's place. They were probably hauling in more furniture to make his house more of a home to young Priss and to make his infrequent but important visitors, such as the territorial governors of Arizona, Colorado, and New Mexico, more comfortable during their stay in his quarters.

As the wagon came to a stuttering halt, Corporal Winston Clark, who'd been heading up the afternoon sentry duty and who'd led the freight wagon over from the fort commander's office, dismounted and gave a salute to the sergeant, who returned it.

"Freighting contingent from Fort Lowell, sir. They're delivering the colonel's new piano!" said Clark, unable to stop his mouth corners from quirking a wry grin.

Tunney jerked his head toward the front door, and Clark mounted the porch steps. He went on inside, and soon

Tunney could hear the colonel calling for Priss, whom Tunney had seen slip out the back door with the daughter of Captain Stryker.

Tunney sipped his coffee and blinked against the dust rising from the horses, the mules, and the wagon. One of the mules brayed in its traces. A horse of one of the troopers riding drag behind the wagon whinnied. The weary mounts had likely smelled the hay from the corrals as they'd passed around the far end of the parade ground.

Tunney found himself studying the troopers, all of whom were so dusty that the blue of their uniforms was barely visible. They must have ridden through a dust storm.

The sergeant riding to the right of the detachment's commander, a first lieutenant, called for the soldiers to dismount and give their horses a breather. The lieutenant also dismounted. The tall, rangy gent with a sandy blond mustache and pointed sideburns glanced out the corner of his copper left eye at Tunney and then he gave his back to the sergeant as he busied himself with his McClelland saddle's rigging.

Tunney narrowed his eyes as he lowered his coffee cup. There appeared to be a faint red sheen over the man's left shoulder, partly hidden by the dust. As the colonel and young, sandy-haired Priss came out onto the veranda, hand in hand, and followed by several of the visiting officers and their wives, the colonel saying, "Your piano is here, just like I promised, Miss Priss! And we couldn't have asked for a better day for its arrival, could we? You can play 'The Old Rugged Cross' for our guests!"

"Oh, Papa, I can't wait to see it!"

One of the immaculately coifed and gowned officers' wives cooed and clapped.

Tunney was only vaguely listening to the commotion around him. His eyes had left what appeared a faint bloodstain on the lieutenant's uniform to the sword hanging off his right hip, behind the conversion Navy Colt holstered there, as well.

Now the lieutenant turned. He glanced once more at

Tunney, flat-eyed, and then he saluted the colonel and said, "Colonel Alexander?"

"Yes, Lieutenant," the colonel said, narrowing his eyes as he scrutinized the dusty stranger. "And you are . . . ?"

"I, sir, am the soldier who is about to deliver a present that you and your daughter will never forget!"

Pistols crackled in the distance.

Tunney's heartbeat quickened as voices yelled from across the parade ground. The sergeant turned to his right to see Samantha walking slowly, cautiously toward him, clutching her sketchbook to her chest. Her eyes beneath her straw sun hat, however, were staring to the southeast, the direction from which thudding hooves were growing louder.

Tunney saw them then—two familiar riders racing toward the colonel's quarters from across a corner of the parade ground. Yakima Henry and Seth Barksdale were shouting and triggering their pistols into the air.

"What on earth is that commotion?" asked the colonel.

Tunney said around a sudden hard knot in his throat, speaking out of the left corner of his mouth, "Colonel, take Priss inside *now*!"

He hadn't gotten that last word out before the world exploded.

Chapter 18

There was a high-pitched, oddly feminine wail.

The sergeant dropped his coffee cup and saucer, which shattered on the floor between his boots. At the same time, a deafening clatter rose. Immediately, even through his shock, Gila River Joe recognized the raucous, thumping reports of a large-caliber gun.

The thumps sounded like an exploding string of Chinese firecrackers, but they were as loud as thunder peals. Several large holes appeared in the canvas over the wagon, on the side facing the colonel's quarters. The holes quickly grew larger until Tunney could see the smoking maw of the brass-canistered Gatling gun mounted on a tripod inside the box. The .45-caliber bullets tore one hole after another in the canvas, starting near the front of the wagon and moving down the side toward the rear, arcing toward the sergeant.

Through the growing, ragged-edged holes, a female face appeared over the swiveling barrel of the eight-mawed machine gun, which she was cranking with her right hand. Long blond hair hung down over the girl's naked shoulders.

Her tanned face was smeared with ochre and green and blue war paint—it was swirled and striped with the stuff—and her mouth made a large, dark *O* as the girl-warrior screamed, crumpling her face and slitting her light-colored eyes with animal fury.

The sergeant glanced quickly to his left to see the bullets the girl was flinging punching into the veranda's ceiling support posts, into flowerpots, into the front wall of the house . . . into the blue-clad officers and their well-dressed wives, punching them back against the wall of the house off which they bounced and, twisting, spurting blood from their fancy clothes, fell.

The men shouted. The women screamed. Miss Priss screamed shrilly as her father picked her up and threw himself straight back into the house's open door and into Two Feathers, who had been standing behind him. As he did, the colonel grunted and went down hard. Though Tunney couldn't see him anymore, because he was inside, he could hear the loud thud of the big man hitting the foyer floor.

As the Gatling gun's maw swung toward the sergeant, the bullets punched into the folks to his left and hammered chunks of wood from the house's front wall, causing a water olla hanging from the porch ceiling to explode. As the bullet spray came within two feet of the sergeant, he turned and threw himself through the window behind him.

Joe felt a bullet clip the edge of his left boot as he hit the floor inside the colonel's foyer on his left shoulder. He rolled over, feeling the glass cutting into his arm, and lay on his back, dazed and bleeding, as he watched several more bullets arc through the broken window and punch into the newel post of the nearby stairs and ping off the suit of Spanish armor that the colonel had found years ago in the desert and had mounted on the foyer wall.

And then the Gatling gun's barking grew slightly less loud as the crazed blond Apache girl firing it swung it farther toward the west.

West . . .

That had been the direction from which Samantha had been approaching the house when all hell broke loose probably less than fifteen seconds before, though to the sergeant it had seemed like half a lifetime.

Samantha!

The sergeant shook off his confusion, heaved himself to his feet, grabbed his big Walker Colt, and began to sling lead out the broken window and into the covered wagon.

Yakima Henry had taken his reins in his teeth and now he was firing both his Dragoon revolvers into the "soldiers" riding wildly on their buck-kicking horses as they spoked away from the wagon from which the thunderous clattering of a Gatling gun rose.

One of his bullets punched into the shoulder of a dusty rider, and the man jerked back in his saddle, gritting his teeth and clapping his gun over the wound. As he thrust his pistol toward Yakima, still galloping toward the colonel's quarters enveloped in sooty powder smoke, the man's horse suddenly reared. The rider screamed and went tumbling into the dirt at the far northeastern corner of the parade ground.

Yakima's buckskin took two more strides.

Yakima looked at the wagon—its dirty cream tarpaulin was buffeting madly. The brass canister of the Gatling gun swung to aim straight out of the wagon's rear. Half a second after Yakima's swirling brain registered that a blond Apache was turning the belching machine gun's wooden-handled crank, he saw Samantha Tunney standing frozen in shock as the bullets hurled toward her, kicking up dust to her right.

Yakima dropped both his pistols whose hammers had clicked onto empty chambers, and kicked loose of the buckskin's saddle. He hurled himself in a broad arc off the right side of his horse, smashing his right shoulder into the brown-haired girl's own. She screamed as Yakima drove her to the ground and his buckskin loosed a shrill whinny as the bullets from the Gatling gun hurled over Yakima and the girl and into the still-galloping horse.

Yakima was only vaguely aware of the horse falling and rolling as more bullets were slicing the air around them and blowing up dirt and gravel. When they stopped rolling, Yakima found himself staring up into the girl's wide, shocked gray eyes, a lock of her hair caught between his lips.

He rolled her over, covering her body with his, as she squirmed beneath him, and stared toward the colonel's quarters. An insane cacophony was rising around him, nearly as loud as a freight train—full of the sounds of screaming men and women, and the bawling of fallen horses in every direction around the parade ground.

Some of the soldiers who'd been drilling earlier had been running toward the colonel's house just after the Gatling gun had opened up, when Yakima and Seth had galloped into the fort, shouting and triggering warning shots into the air. Now the wagon was swinging around, the mules bawling and buck-kicking in the leather harnesses and traces, the driver cursing and laughing and whipping the reins over the team's backs.

As he made the maneuver, there was a pause in the fire of the Gatling gun, but the so-called soldiers, identifiable by the heavy dust coating their blue uniforms, were riding madly around the parade ground, triggering revolvers, carbines, or in some cases, Henry sixteen-shot rifles at Hildebrandt soldiers scrambling for cover or returning fire too hastily for accurate shooting.

Yakima looked around for a pistol. As he did, he saw that the wagon was heading straight for him and the girl. The lead mules were growing larger and larger before him, and the wagon driver's bellowing laughter was growing louder beneath the clattering thunder of the wagon boards and the iron-shod wheels.

Yakima wrapped his arms around Samantha Tunney and rolled sharply to his left twice. One of the mules kicked his left ankle as the team and the wagon brushed past him with less than a whisker's breadth to spare. Yakima saw a rifle lying on the ground near a groaning soldier from the parade ground. He scrambled over to the Spencer repeater, jacked a cartridge into the breech, and holding the butt plate against his right hip, looked wildly around for a target.

Near the house, Sergeant Tunney was limping over to where one of the so-called soldiers was down on the ground, wounded. Tunney's hat was off, his hair was blowing in the breeze, and his wizened face was deep burgundy with rage as he kicked the downed man in the face, driving him over onto his back. Tunney planted a boot on the man's chest and aimed his cocked Colt at the man's face. But Yakima only heard the report of the sergeant's big horse pistol as he shuttled his glance toward the parade ground, where he saw Seth down on one knee beside his own dead mount.

Yakima's partner had his other leg extended. Crimson shone on the outside of his buckskin-clad thigh. Seth's hat was off, his sweaty, sandy brown hair hanging over one eye. He was gritting his teeth, probably cursing, as he quickly reloaded one of his revolvers from his shell belt. His dead horse was lying on his Henry repeater, only the stock of which was visible where it lay flat against the ground.

The wagon and the belching Gatling gun were turning a broad circle around the parade ground. The canvas cover hung in burning shreds around the ash boughs arcing over the box, fully revealing the bronzed, blond-haired, war-painted, half-naked young woman hunkered over the machine gun, which she must have reloaded with a fresh clip of .45-caliber cartridges.

She turned the crank, howling wildly, hair blowing like a mane, smoke and flames leaping from the canvas that fell in tatters from the wagon boughs.

Bam-Bam-Bam-Bam-Bam-Bam-Bam!

The bullets cut into the barracks and the commanding officer's headquarters. They chewed into scattering soldiers and hammered into the rain barrels, which in turn spewed water onto the boardwalks beneath the ramadas. Ollas popped, wooden shutters splintered, and more horses went down, screaming. One of the horseback marauders galloped toward Yakima, howling like a banshee and aiming a rifle with both of his hands while he held his reins in his teeth.

Yakima dropped to a knee just as the man fired at him, the wayward bullet plunking into an unmoving soldier lying behind Yakima. Yakima raised the rifle he'd taken off the dead soldier, aimed carefully while the marauder bore down on him, racking a fresh cartridge into his Spencer's breech, and the young scout drilled a neat round hole between the howling man's eyes.

Both eyes rolled back into his head as he jerked back in his saddle, hat tumbling forward down his chest.

The horse swung away from Yakima, whinnying shrilly, throwing the dead marauder into the dirt at Yakima's boots.

The half-breed grabbed the horse's reins, holding on as the horse half dragged him several yards before he got the mount stopped. He'd meant to go after the wagon, but now he saw that the wagon housing the still-hammering Gatling gun was rattling back toward him behind its four-hitch team of wild-eyed, horrified mules.

"Holy shit, amigo!"

Yakima turned to Seth, who was hurrying in Yakima's direction—hurrying as fast as he could while dragging the foot of his wounded left leg. He had both of his Confederate revolvers in his hands and he was whipping anxious looks toward the far end of the fort. Still clinging to the horse's reins, Yakima followed his partner's gaze, and the cold water of grave apprehension flowed down his spine.

Sergeant Tunney ran up near Yakima and dropped to a knee beside his daughter, who was now bent over the young soldier from whom Yakima had confiscated the pistol. The young soldier—Humphreys—was sobbing and begging Samantha not to let him die as he clung to her arms. Yakima only half registered that heartbreaking moment, because the scene that Seth had first pointed out was even more blood chilling.

A handful of howling Apache warriors were hazing what appeared most of Hildebrandt's remuda—a good seventy or eighty horses and mules—straight toward Yakima, Seth, Samantha, and the sergeant. Not only that, but the wagon housing the Gatling gun and the demented white girl was bearing down on them even faster, and judging by the thunder, the female gunner wasn't out of bullets!

Yakima released the horse's reins. The mount wasted no time in bolting off through a break between the colonel's quarters and those of Captain Stryker's. Both on one knee and spaced about ten feet apart, Sergeant Tunney and Seth fired their pistols at the oncoming raiders. The Sergeant's Colt barked only once before its hammer pinged, empty. Seth fired each of his two guns once before bullets fired by the charging marauders hammered into the ground to his right. He jerked toward his wounded leg and lost his balance.

"We gotta pull back, boys!" Gila River Joe shouted, tugging on his daughter's arm. "Samantha, run!"

"We can't leave him!" the girl screamed as she gazed horrifically down at the pimply-faced Private Humphreys, who lay wide-eyed and slack in death.

"Daughter, that soldier is dead!" The sergeant pulled her to her feet, glanced at Yakima and Seth. "Come on, fellas! That's an *order*!"

The wagon was bearing down along the north side of the parade ground, fifty yards and closing in fast. The herd of horses and mules was barreling in from the parade ground's southwest corner, sixty yards away and moving even faster.

"You heard the man!" Yakima moved to Seth, crouched, and shoved his shoulder in his partner's left armpit, heaving the Southerner to his feet. Seth yelped as Yakima half carried and half dragged him into the break between the buildings, where Tunney was shoving his daughter to the ground and standing in front of her to shield her.

Yakima swung around to face the parade ground just as the mules of the wagon hurled into view, moving from left to right across the mouth of the break.

The half-breed's heart was a charging grizzly inside his chest. It was that grizzly inside him that must have dictated what he did next, because he had no idea what other madness could have sent him hurtling out of the mouth of the break and into the side of the wagon, kick-stepping off the ground and hoisting himself into the driver's boot around the brake handle.

"Look at that demented half-breed!" he heard Seth shout in the crazed energy of the moment, the Southerner's voice all but drowned by the clattering of the wagon, the thundering of the Gatling gun, and the hammering of Yakima's own heart. "I'll bet my rifle against my dead horse we'll never see his loco ass again!"

Chapter 19

The driver, yelling and shaking the reins over the mule team's backs, snapped a hang-jawed, wide-eyed look at Yakima, who lurched forward into the boot around the brake handle. The driver dropped half of the reins onto the floor near his boots and reached for the Remington revolver riding in the cross-draw position on his left hip.

The wagon lurched, swayed, and bounced as it cut past the last of the fort's original adobe buildings and headed for open desert to the east, and Yakima threw himself at the stocky, bearded gent, grabbing his right hand just as it started to come up, filled with iron.

Yakima drove the man to the floor beneath the spring seat, and pressed his right forearm across the man's bearded neck, trying to cut off his wind. As he did, he looked down at the pistol. The barrel was snug against his ribs. The driver was trying to cock it, but Yakima had two fingers clamped over the hammer.

"You lousy dog eater," the man raked out through gritted teeth, spittle flecking his lips as he glared up at Yakima.

As they wrestled, the gun came up slowly, the driver

trying to hold on to it and cock it, Yakima trying to take it away from him. Yakima was vaguely aware of the galloping horses surrounding the wagon—some riderless cavalry remounts, some belonging to the marauders. A couple of those riders were closing in on the wagon, yelling and raising pistols. A couple of those pistols popped. One of the bullets slammed into the seat not far from Yakima's head.

Yakima clamped his forearm down harder against the driver's throat. The man convulsed and gagged, his eyes growing glassy as he kicked desperately. When his right hand started to go slack, Yakima wrapped his hand around the grips, poked his index finger through the trigger guard, turned the barrel until the end of it was snug up against the underside of the driver's stout, furry jaw, and squeezed the trigger.

The Remy lurched and hiccupped.

The bullet exited the crown of the man's skull in a spray of blood and white brain matter. Beneath Yakima, the driver fell instantly slacken.

Yakima glanced up. A rider had closed in on the right side of the wagon—the lean, copper-eyed gent with the arrowhead sideburns. He flared his nostrils as he barked out, "You son of a bitch!" and aimed his Colt at Yakima's head. Yakima pulled his head down against the driver's still-quivering chest.

The copper-eyed rider's bullet clanked off the iron part of the wooden seat. Yakima lifted his confiscated Remington and fired twice. The wagon was bouncing so violently that his first shot sailed wide, but his second caused the galloping rider to grimace and clamp his left hand against the right side of his neck. His horse faltered and turned away and fell back behind the driverless wagon.

Then Yakima remembered the blonde and the Gatling gun.

As he grabbed the seat and carefully gained his feet, careful not to be thrown to either side, he glanced into the wagon's box. The girl lay back against the tailgate, behind the Gatling gun that stood like a big brass mosquito, the canister flopping this way on the tripod that had been bolted to the wagon bed.

The girl had a cut lip and a scrape on her forehead. She'd probably made a play for Yakima but had been thrown back there by the wagon's violent lurching. She was smiling as she clamped one hand over the top of the tailgate and extended a pistol straight out in her right hand, aiming at Yakima.

She glanced at the Remington in his hand. "Throw it over the side!"

Yakima looked around. He was surrounded by uniformed marauders and Apaches—most likely, Chiricahuas—along with fleeing horses. Dust roiled, tinged with the scent of sage and the musk of creosote. He looked back toward the fort that had become a small, insignificant brown lump in the bowl in the hills behind him.

The last thing he wanted to do was give up the gun, but he did so, just the same.

"Stop the team!" the girl yelled, that smile still curling her upper lip.

A couple of the men galloping around the wagon, which was angling to the north now as the team instinctively picked a path of least resistance despite still galloping hell-for-leather, snapped off shots at Yakima. One hammered the side of the wagon not far from the blonde, who glared at the riders and angrily waved them off.

Cowed, they lowered their pistols.

Yakima looked at the gun she was aiming from ten feet away. He looked at the riders, which included a good dozen or so war-painted Apache braves, and suddenly realized that his move back at Hildebrandt had been a tad reckless, and most likely, suicidal. He picked up the reins that were drooping over the steel-banded dashboard and dancing along the floor, carefully turned to face the team and leaned back, applying steady, even pressure on the reins.

When the mules began to slow, Yakima jerked back harder, shouting, "Whoaahh! Whoaaahhhh, now!"

It took a while, for the team seemed intent on running

all the way to New Mexico, but when he finally got them stopped on the near side of a broad, gravelly wash, he heard hooves rattling around him. The marauders were closing, horses snorting, tack squawking and rattling. The hawk-faced gent he'd grazed rode up to the right side of the wagon, still holding his left hand against the side of his bloody neck, aiming his Colt at Yakima.

His copper eyes were hard, reflecting a cold, angry light beneath the brim of his dusty dark blue campaign hat. His upper lip was curled in silent fury.

The Chiricahuas had closed in on the wagon now, too. Yakima felt a tingling in his loins. The tingling of dread. He could smell the wild smell of the Indians—the bear grease and the pungent scent of *hoddentin*, their medicine powder. Their eyes were darkly savage as they regarded the half-breed standing in the wagon's driver's boot, wishing like hell a hole would open up beside the wagon and swallow him.

The hawk-nosed white man raised his pistol and clicked back the hammer, narrowing an eye as he aimed down the barrel at Yakima's forehead.

"Hold it," said the girl behind Yakima.

The wagon jerked.

Yakima turned. She stood behind him, smiling coldly.

She smelled like the Apaches, though she was definitely a white. A blond-haired, blue-eyed white girl in Chiricahua garb, burned and honed to one hell of a beautifully, frighteningly savage visage by the desert sun and wind. She reminded Yakima of a fine, wild mare. She raised her pistol, grimacing. Yakima thought she was going to shoot him. He felt himself start to recoil but caught himself. He wasn't about to gift this savage beauty with his fear.

That was why he didn't raise his hand to defend himself when she smashed the butt against his right temple.

His harsh landing upon the floor of the driver's boot, half on and half off the dead driver, was his last sensation for a while.

At least, his last semicoherent one.

He was aware of much pain and misery for what seemed, in the deep, cold soup of his unconsciousness, a very long time. There was a large, swollen flame red heart pounding in his head, and someone kept poking it with a razor-edged Apache war lance. He heard voices, but mostly he just heard the pounding of that wounded heart in his head.

And then he felt as though he were lying on a bed of cactus thorns.

His eyes must have opened, because he found himself staring up into the face of a dead man. He watched several faces float around him in the murky soup of unconsciousness— the long, dark, severely chiseled face of his mother, the craggy, bearded, green-eyed face of his father wearing the sweat-stained canvas he'd worn most of the years Yakima had known him.

He saw the face of the male teacher who'd tried to literally beat the ways of the civilized white man into him back at the orphanage school in Denver. He saw the face of a benevolent white rancher he'd worked for after he'd run away from the orphanage and had gone back to what he knew best—drifting and gentling horses.

This face was just another one of those. His mind wanting, for some strange reason, to scare him.

But no.

This face staring down at him was real. Sunlight bathed the left side of the dead man's face. The man was grinning at him. No, not grinning. He was grimacing around something protruding from between his lips. Yakima realized that that thing in his mouth was his own penis, and that the man's eyes had been cut out of his head. The dark, crusty stuff running in stripes down his cheeks was blood.

Dried blood.

The man's eye sockets were dark and empty.

Yakima looked around to see three more dead men hanging from trees around him. They'd all been stripped. They were pale, shaggy-headed corpses hanging by their arms, which had been pulled back behind their backs, their tied wrists jutting straight above their heads.

Their wrists were tied with long strips of rawhide to the limbs of fir trees. The muscles that had held their shoulders in their sockets had been cut. Two of the dead men's tied ankles were tied lower down on the same tree to which his arms were tied. The other one had probably been tied similarly, but it was hard to tell. Each of the three was missing part of one leg. A ragged, bloody fringe was all that remained of the mangled limb.

That wasn't the work of Apaches. Some wild animal had been feeding on the corpses, likely jumping up and pulling off chunks.

Pale, waxy skin shown through the dried blood that all but covered the dead men.

They were all giving Yakima horrific death stares, grinning around the severed members stuck between their teeth.

Yakima tried to move his arms and legs. No doing. He lowered his gaze, grunted, and groaned. He was tied spreadeagle on a patch of gravelly ground in a clearing amongst tall fir trees, surrounded by dead men who'd obviously been tortured before they'd died.

His wrists and ankles were tied with rawhide to wooden stakes that had been driven into the ground. He wasn't wearing a stitch—as naked as the day he'd been born. He blinked to make sure his eyelids had not been cut off, which was a favorite practice of the Chiricahuas in the torturing of their prey. It allowed the Sonora sun free access to the eyeballs, which it would then slowly turn to coal.

When he found that he could blink, he lowered his chin to look down past his broad chest and flat belly to his crotch. His manhood was still there. He swallowed, gave a ragged sigh. He hadn't been tortured in that way, either.

At least, not yet.

He had a bad feeling that he would be, though. The dead men hanging around him were the Apaches' promise of that. They'd let him lie here awhile and look at the tortured dead men in anticipation of his own slow, excruciatingly painful demise.

He grimaced as the wounded heart continued to throb in his head, sending railroad spikes of pure misery through his ears from the inside out.

He pulled at the spikes securing him spread-eagle to the ground. None of them budged. They were likely long, and they'd been hammered deep. Two feet, at least. The rawhide had been wrapped several times, tightly, around each wrist and ankle. It was stout stuff, too—toughened by a good long soaking in water and then dried quickly by a hot fire.

Terror caused Yakima's heart to beat faster. He winced as the heart in his head beat faster, sending even more severe pain into his ears. He took several deep, slow breaths until he calmed down. A terrified man was a useless man. He had to keep his courage up, keep his mind calm, so he could think through his options and find a way to survive.

Continuing to take deep, slow, regular breaths, relaxing, he looked around again, shunting his gaze beyond the dead men. He was in a deep valley. The firs told him he was high in some mountain range. Probably the Chiricahuas or the Dragoons. The tall pinnacles of wind-blasted volcanic rock looming behind and above the firs looked more like formations he'd seen in the larger, higher Chiricahua Range.

The air was autumn cool, though the sun was warm on his naked skin. Fallen aspen leaves scratched around him in a slight breeze tainted with the smell of wood smoke. That meant he wasn't entirely alone out here. His captives were here, somewhere. Occasionally, as he worked against the rawhide ties and tried to remain calm, he could hear voices on the wind. He thought back through the tangle of his brain-damaged memory until he had the image of the blond Chiricahua princess in his mind's eye. And the man with the thin red-blond sideburns shaved into the shapes of arrowheads, with the hawk nose and copper eyes.

And the Chiricahuas. How many of those? He'd seen close to a dozen, at least.

Chiricahuas running with white men. And a white woman—though Yakima had a pretty strong hunch she was more Chiricahua than white. He remembered the wild smell of her, the feral glint in her eyes. She reminded him a little of Luz Ortega. Somehow that blond hair and those blue eyes set against that bronzed skin made her seem even more savage than a full-blooded Chiricahua.

Why in hell were they all running together? And why had they attacked the fort?

The fort.

Yakima had been so preoccupied with his own dire situation that he'd forgotten about Hildebrandt. He'd seen so many soldiers dead, that Gatling gun having cut them down, that they'd likely be easy pickings if the same group attacked again.

Fort Hell. Damn appropriate name for it.

Or for what was left of it.

Chapter 20

"Get something around that leg, Barksdale," Sergeant Tunney said as he and the young scout hurried out from the break between the two officers' quarters, where they'd taken cover when the Gatling gun had charged through the fort.

Tunney had given the order absently, as a matter of course, his eyes on the parade ground over which a fog of smoke and dust hung thick. He could still smell the horses that had run past less than a minute ago, and the stench of powder smoke burned in his nostrils. The groans of the wounded and dying soldiers recalled memories of the battles that Tunney had been a part of many times in his soldiering past. Only, these male pleas for help were shot through with the cries and screams of women, as well.

The sergeant turned to Samantha walking slowly behind him. She was covered in dirt, and her hair hung disheveled about her rounded shoulders. Her dress was torn and bloodsplashed. Seeing the blood on the girl caught the sergeant up short, and he said, "Are you all right, Sam? You're not . . . you're not *wounded*, for chrissakes . . . ?"

Samantha stared in wide-eyed shock at the parade ground. She shook her head slowly, her lips parted, her chest rising and falling heavily.

"You stay here between the buildings," Tunney told her, squeezing her arm. "You stay here, out of sight. All right?"

He couldn't tell if she'd heard him or not. She stopped walking but continued to stare, her eyes glazed with shock. The sergeant squeezed his daughter's arm once more. "Stay here, Sam!"

He ran out from the break as Barksdale limped out beside him, dragging his left foot, looking around wildly, tracking in every direction with his old Confederate revolvers, looking for targets. Tunney looked around carefully but holstered his empty Colt. He wouldn't take time to reload the old cap-and-ball revolver just yet. Something told him all the attackers had left with the horses and the Gatling gun.

His mind was on the colonel. He swung up onto the porch steps of the Alexander quarters and paused on one foot, grabbing a roof support post to steady himself. Three officers lay in blood pools on the broad veranda. Four women were down, as well. Another lay in the arms of Captain Stryker, who was down on one knee, shaking the inert, pale woman and calling, "Louise! Good God—Louise!" he paused, staring down at the woman as though he couldn't believe his eyes. *"Louise!"*

Tunney cleared his throat. "She's dead, Captain."

Captain Stryker jerked an enraged look up at him. "What in the hell happened, Sergeant? Who . . . Who in the hell *were* they?"

"Your guess is as good as mine, sir." Tunney stepped around the man, over the blood, and through the open door. He was relieved to see the colonel being slowly helped to his feet by Lieutenant Geist, whose cracked monocle hung from the collar of his dress coat by a black silk ribbon. The lieutenant looked unharmed but shaken. The colonel's sky blue, gilt-trimmed shell jacket was torn and blood-spotted across the top of the man's left shoulder, and blood shone on his side about halfway between his shell belt and that shoulder.

"Priss!" the colonel yelled. "Priss, where are you, daughter?"

The last Tunney had seen, the colonel had pulled the girl in off the porch and had been falling over her to shield her from the bullets. At the moment, however, she was nowhere in sight. Neither was Two Feathers.

"I'll look for her, Colonel," the sergeant said, helping Geist maneuver the big man into a straight-backed chair by a bullet-shattered grandfather clock near the bottom of the varnished oak stairs. "How bad you hit?"

"Just scratched," the colonel said, trying to push himself to his feet, staring in wide-eyed horror through the open front door. "What in the name of hell's fury happened here, Joe?"

The sergeant and Lieutenant Geist pushed him back in the chair. To Geist, Joe said, "Keep him here. Don't let him move around. I'll look for Priscilla."

"Joe!" the colonel yelled behind him. "Did you see who was firing that *Gatling gun*?"

"Take it easy, Colonel," Geist urged. "You gotta hold still until we can get that bleeding stopped. Sergeant Tunney is looking for Miss Alexander."

The sergeant stormed through the first story of the house, yelling for Two Feathers, the colonel's housekeeper and cook, and then he saw movement out a back window. He rushed through the kitchen, which was at the rear of the house, and out the back door and onto the rear veranda.

"Two Feathers, no!" Tunney held both his hands up, palm out, in supplication.

The Coyotero housekeeper, who was in her mid-twenties and dressed in crisp dark blue gingham and a white apron, had just cocked the old .31-caliber pocket model revolver, the four-inch barrel of which she was holding against the head of one of the two girls she was crouching with in the porch's far corner. Both girls, roughly the same age and dressed in their Sunday finest, long hair brushed and neat,

were bawling into their upraised knees, hugging each
other.

Two Feathers looked at Tunney. Her brown eyes were
round and nearly black with fear.

"It's over," the sergeant said, slowing moving toward
the three. "For now, they're safe. You're all safe."

Two Feathers pulled the pistol away from Priss's head
and depressed the hammer. Guiltily, the housekeeper stared
up at Tunney. "The colonel, he told me that if we were ever
attacked, and it looked like the Apaches were going to overrun the fort—"

"I know," the sergeant said. The colonel had told her to
kill Priss rather than let her be taken captive. "I know. But
it's over now. Take the girls upstairs. Whatever you do,
don't let them go out onto the porch." He held the Coyotero
woman's gaze with his, silently conveying the gravity of
the situation.

Two Feathers rose, slipped her short-barreled revolver
into her apron, and pulled the sobbing girls to their feet.
When the Apache housekeeper had ushered them inside,
the sergeant stepped out to the edge of the porch and stared
across the cactus-spiked hills rolling away to the northeast.

The stone and adobe remains of the original fort lay in
that direction, on a hill a little higher than the one the current fort was spread across. Tunney slid his cautious gaze
across the crest of that hill, looking for more ambushers.
Apaches were known to attack a single location multiple
times, each attack usually coming when their prey was still
reeling from the previous one.

He saw no sign of the sentry riders. Where were they?
The attack from the white marauders had been a surprise
to everyone, but why hadn't the sentry riders warned of the
Apache attack?

Something moved against the skyline above the old fort.
Joe's right hand automatically slid toward the Colt on his
left hip. He drew the gun as he watched three horses emerge
from the far side of the hill and stand against the bright blue
sky, switching their tails and lowering their heads to graze.

The sergeant's eyes were keen. Even at a distance of a quarter mile, he thought he recognized the three horses tied tail to tail. They appeared to have packs on their backs. Or maybe something else had been slung over their blanket saddles. . . .

Gila River Joe removed the spent cylinder from the big Colt and replaced it with a fresh, fully loaded one from the leather cartridge pouch on his shell belt. The sergeant was so accustomed to the big cap-and-ball revolver that he continued to use the outdated weapon despite the ease of the newer ones that fired metal cartridges. He always kept four or five extra loaded cylinders in his cartridge pouch.

He turned the Colt's wheel as he stepped down off the porch and tramped into the backyard of the colonel's quarters. He moved past a row of transplanted shrubs and a flower bed partitioned off by a short white picket fence, and quickened his pace as he headed toward the old fort.

Cries and yells rose from the direction of the parade ground on the other side of Alexander's and Stryker's quarters. The breeze was out of the south, carrying the rotten-egg smell of powder smoke.

The sergeant dropped down into a crease between hills and quickly strode up the next hill, angling toward the horses. As he did, he saw a splash of blue and yellow sprawled across a patch of Mormon tea. He stopped and looked down at the dead sentry rider, three Chiricahua arrows bristling from his back. His horse was nowhere around.

The sergeant looked around carefully, holding his pistol half out in front of his right side, his thumb caressing the hammer. The Apaches could hole up tight as rattlesnakes and make themselves just as hard to see against the grays and browns and greens of the desert. Not spying any more attackers—at least, no near ones—the sergeant continued on up to the old fort. When he was sixty yards away from the horses grazing beside the hollowed-out shell of the old sutler's store, which had been burned by Geronimo after the army abandoned the fort in '62, he could see that they indeed were tied tail to tail by their braided hemp Aravaipa-style hackamore reins.

Joe got a sick feeling. His feet grew heavy, and he unconsciously slowed his pace. He recognized the desert-bred mustangs, all right. They weren't carrying packs, either. They were carrying men who'd been slung belly down over their backs. Three short, muscular, black-haired men.

The Aravaipa scouts.

Joe stopped when the horses shied away from him, and he had to follow them quite a ways as they sidled away from him, nickering fearfully, until he managed to grab the rope reins of the lead horse—a bayo lobo. When he had the three horses settled down, Joe scrutinized the man slung belly down over the bayo lobo's back.

He wore the calico shirt and deerskin armbands of One-Eyed Miguel. The man's hair was trimmed with hawk feathers and dyed red rawhide. His back was bloody. So was the back of the neck. He'd likely been shot with arrows, and the arrows had been pulled out. Blood also matted his long black, braided hair that was threaded with the silver of a middle-aged Apache.

"Christ," Joe heard himself mutter, turning to the two other dead Aravaipa, each slung over his own horse.

Chiquito was on the next horse's back, a bayo coyote. Then Pedro. Their arms hung slack toward the ground, fingertips brushing the weeds. Flies buzzed in the air over the dead men.

Suddenly, a hissing sounded. Joe looked around. The hissing grew gradually louder. It became a rising murmur that grew more and more melodic until he realized that it was an Apache death song, muttered low, softly, haltingly.

Joe looked down at the back of One-Eyed Miguel's head. Frowning, he squatted and looked at the side of the man's blood-smeared face. The man's lips were moving and the very soft strains of the dirge were emanating from his lips. One-Eyed Miguel was beseeching the People on the Other Side, those family members who were already dead, to assist him in crossing over. He was telling them he had no eyes, so he could not see his way in the darkness.

Joe slipped his bowie knife from his belt sheath, cut the ropes binding the scout's wrists to his ankles beneath his horse's belly, and then he eased One-Eyed Miguel down off his horse. He gentled him into the dry brush, on his back. He grimaced when he saw that the Apache's lone eye had been cut out of its socket, leaving a jellylike red mess. The scout's ears had been cut off, as well. His enemies, the Chiricahua, had wanted to make sure he could neither see nor hear his way through the darkness—and also so that he could neither see nor hear them when they, too, crossed over to the other side.

They wanted no retribution in this life or any other.

Chapter 21

One-Eyed Miguel fell silent. He reached up with both his bloody hands and curled his fingers to his palms. He was beckoning.

The sergeant got down on both knees beside him. "I'm here, my friend. How did this happen?"

The scout started to speak in such quiet rasps that the sergeant had to put his head down close to the dying man's mouth. In Apache, the scout told the sergeant that he and the others had been lured into a small canyon, one which woodcutters had named Spanish Cañon because it was there they'd found several Spanish artifacts including an old conquistador helmet. The smoke had been a ruse—a trap that the three scouts had discovered too late.

Four Chiricahuas had snuck up on them from behind and shot them all down with arrows. After they'd finished their artwork with their butcher knives, they'd tied the scouts over their horses and slapped their horses back to the fort to add to the soldiers' fear.

They did a good job of it, Joe thought, as One-Eyed Miguel fell silent. Any Apache who could sneak up on

One-Eyed Miguel, Chiquito, and Pedro, veteran scouts and trackers and formidable warriors in their own right, had to be some intrepid fighters, indeed. And they'd also put a lot of forethought into the raid on the fort, using the colonel's piano shipment as the primary trap. The blond young lady and the Gatling gun had done a good job of diverting the soldiers' attention from the fort's perimeters, including the corrals, which were left vulnerable for the Apaches.

One-Eyed Miguel lifted his hands again slightly, curling his fingers and opening and closing his mouth.

"Yes?" the sergeant said. "What is it, Miguel?"

The scout spoke softly, hoarsely in his native tongue.

The sergeant nodded, rose. He drew his pistol, stepped back, and cocked the hammer.

"*Ka-dish-day*, my friend," he said, and squeezed the trigger.

One-Eyed Miguel's head bounced with the force of the slug slamming through it. The scout gave a long, slow sigh and relaxed against the earth. Mother Earth, Father Sky. The sergeant cursed, holstered the smoking revolver, lifted the scout's bloody body up over his shoulder, and then slung him back onto his horse. Miguel was roughly the sergeant's size, maybe a little heavier, but the wiry older man had no trouble with the maneuver. Gila River Joe was fifty, but he was still as tough as a Sonora panther, and he moved like one, too.

He pointed the horse in the direction of the Aravaipa *ranchería* so that the scout's families could tend the bodies, and all three horses galloped off after the leader, heading west.

The sergeant scouted around to make sure that another attack wasn't imminent, and then he walked back down the hills to the fort. He was shocked by the devastation, the men and women—mostly officers' wives but a few maids and laundry women, as well—dead and wounded.

The post's two surgeons, their orderlies, and many uninjured soldiers and laundresses were tending the wounded, stopping the bleeding where they'd fallen and carting them off on stretchers to the post hospital. In the meantime, Joe corralled several dazed and enervated but otherwise healthy soldiers and ordered them to summon as many others as they could find, who were not on death's doorstep, to arm themselves with carbines and to keep watch from the high points around the fort. He wanted several on the roofs lining the parade ground, as well.

"At the first sign of any suspicious movement out there, boys—I don't care if it's just brush moving odd—you trigger three shots as fast as you can, all right?"

"You got it, Sergeant," said Corporal Erik Whately, whose cheek was grazed, but who otherwise looked fit, if nervous. He and five others ran toward the enlisted men's barracks, waving to others milling around, hang-jawed in shock from the suddenness and ferocity of the attack.

"Take some buglers with you!" the sergeant shouted. "At the first sign of trouble have them start spitting out 'Boots and Saddles' so loud that President Juarez will hear it from Mexico City!"

"Yes, sir, Sergeant!" one of them shouted over his shoulder.

Three soldiers were moving toward him, two supporting the wounded man between them. The wounded man had been hit in the lower leg, and he was groaning and cursing as the other two led him around one of the several dead horses littering the parade ground.

"That's it, Daniels," the sergeant said. "You're looking spiffy. I've cut myself worse shaving. You'll be good as new in no time!"

"Yes . . . yes, sir, Sergeant," Private Daniels said half-heartedly, sucking air through his clenched teeth, his chubby, freckled cheeks drawn up into two, bright red balls beneath his pinched eyes.

When the sergeant saw that no injured man was lying unattended, he began making his way back to the colonel's quarters. He wanted to check on the man's condition and learn what the colonel's orders were. Joe knew what he'd do—he'd make sure the fort was secure, first and foremost, and then he'd send enough armed men as he could spare from the fort to retrieve as many horses as they could find. With orders to be doubly aware of traps.

But he wasn't the commander. Colonel Alexander was, and for good reason. The colonel might have been a bit stove-up and compromised by personal tragedy, but he'd seen the elephant more than a few times, and he was the best battlefield tactician the sergeant had ever known— short only of General Crook himself. They'd fought many a hard battle out here against the Apaches, and the colonel had gained further experience in the War Between the States. The sergeant knew that Colonel Alexander would know exactly what to do in this most extraordinary of situations—with a good two-thirds of the officers at Hildebrandt either dead or wounded!

The Apaches didn't attack military posts! They waited for the soldiers to come to them!

The sergeant started toward the colonel's quarters, and stopped. Two people were helping another soldier— Sergeant Vernon Whitney of D Troop—across the parade ground to Joe's left. The two helping him were Sergeant Bernard "Scotty" Mulligan, who had been leading the C Troop drills on the parade ground earlier, and Joe's own daughter, Samantha. She had one of the wounded sergeant's arms draped over her shoulders and she was holding a bandage over a wound on the man's neck, while she and Scotty led Whitney in the direction of the hospital.

Samantha was nearly covered in blood. She looked horrified and downright stricken as she continued on past her father, not glancing his way but instead keeping her attention on the wounded man to whom she was muttering encouragement. Horrified but strong, the sergeant thought, turning his head to follow his daughter with his gaze. Sam was dwarfed by the big, barrel-chested man she was helping. His weight was nearly driving her to the ground.

She was scared but she was strong, too. And she felt compelled to help when most folks when confronted by such a disaster so far away from the comforts and familiarity of hearth and home would likely be cowering under a bed somewhere.

The corners of the sergeant's mouth lifted in an unabashedly proud smile, and his pale blue eyes glinted from deep in their dark, craggy sockets. He brushed a fist across his nose, swung his head around, and continued in the direction of the colonel's quarters. Lieutenant Gunther Geist was walking toward him, sweating and looking confounded, his dress uniform streaked with blood that didn't appear to be his own.

"Sergeant!" the pale, stout-legged young lieutenant said, almost breaking into a run. "Sergeant, there you are! The colonel's been wondering where you are. He wants to speak with you." The lieutenant turned to walk along with Gila River Joe.

"How's he doing, Lieutenant?" the sergeant asked, continuing in the direction of the colonel's quarters, stepping around dead horses and two fallen soldiers who'd been drilling on the parade ground when that infernal Gatling gun had started blasting away, gunning down soldiers and horses like fish in a barrel.

"I think he'll be all right. He wants to see you. Apparently, he prefers to confer with you than with me, though it appears that I am now the highest-ranking officer at Hildebrandt capable of performing his duties, with most of the others either dead or wounded in the infirmary."

"I wouldn't take it personally, Lieutenant."

"Personally?" Geist snorted his incredulity. "I don't take it personally. I take nothing personally, Sergeant. I take it professionally. This is a professional affront. It's most irregular. You're a first sergeant, and while you're highly capable and the most senior person here at Hildebrandt, I am a first *lieutenant* as well as the colonel's adjutant! *I* should be the one he's conferring with!"

The sergeant marched up the veranda steps of the colonel's house. The wounded had been carted off the porch, but four dead officers and two dead officers' wives remained in bloody piles on the porch and in the foyer, flies buzzing around and over them. Joe shook his head. He'd seen many dead men before, but he'd never seen dead women clad in silk and taffeta. The scene shook him to his core, though he didn't let on.

"What would you like me to do about it, Lieutenant?"

Geist grimaced at the dead, blankly staring women, and then followed the sergeant into the foyer. He suddenly pitched his voice low. "I'd like you to remind him of military hierarchy!"

The sergeant didn't have to ask where the colonel was. He could hear his and his daughter's voices rising from the direction of the parlor. The sergeant moved between two open French doors and headed down a short hall to the parlor whose windows looked off toward the forbiddingly shadowed Chiricahuas lumping up in the southeast. The room was filled with plants, two round tables covered with flowered cloths, a cello, several upholstered chairs, a sofa, and a few wooden cabinets housing cloth-bound books.

Priss knelt beside her father, where he lay on a fainting couch over which a red-and-gold cloth had been thrown, and which was outfitted with pillows covered in the same material. The colonel lay with one leg up on the couch, the other slack on the Chinese rug on the floor, his booted foot resting on its heel. That leg had a bandage wrapped tightly around it. A lump under his coat and over his left shoulder showed where another bandage had been stuffed.

The thirteen-year-old girl was holding the colonel's hand to her cheek and sobbing, "Please don't die, Papa. Please, don't die! I couldn't bear to live without you, Papa. You're all I have in this entire, miserable, godforsaken world!"

The sergeant had stopped in the doorway. He'd removed his dress helmet, which now, under the circumstances, he felt foolish for wearing. He was running his thick thumb along the slightly frayed aiguillettes festooning the sloping crown beneath the gold-chased insignia of the American eagle.

"Oh, dear, girl, your father is fine," said the colonel, though he was breathing hard and his face was swollen and red. "Please stop crying and go pour your dear old pop a glass of brandy, won't you?"

"Of course, Father."

The sergeant cleared his throat. He was aware that Geist had not entered the parlor with him but was lingering out in the hall. The colonel's fainting couch ran along the wall to the sergeant's left, and he was facing away from the sergeant. The colonel glanced over his shoulder and said, "Ah, there you are, Joe. Good God, how do things look out there? Thank you, Priss. Why don't you go on upstairs and join Two Feathers and Glynette?"

"I refuse to take a sedative, Father! Glynette may need one after what happened to her mother, but I want to be aware of what is happening with you at all times!"

"All right, all right," the colonel said with an air of defeat, letting his head loll on his shoulders as though its weight alone wearied him. "You do not have to take a sedative, my dear. But run along now. I've important business to see to. Stay in the house, though."

The thirteen-year-old swung around and brushed past the sergeant without so much as glancing at him and left the room, sniffling and rubbing tears from her cheeks with her small, pale hands. The colonel opened his mouth to speak but kept the words in his throat when his young daughter's voice echoed in the hallway outside the parlor, "Good Lord, Lieutenant, you frightened me! I thought for a minute you were one of those *savages*! What on earth are you doing lurking out here in the dark hall, anyway?" Priss raised her voice with open insolence. "Father, are you aware that Lieutenant Geist is out here in the hall?"

The colonel chuckled wryly, shook his head, and said, "Lieutenant, please do that head count for me now, won't you? I need an accurate count of every man who can ride a horse and wield a carbine!"

Geist's sheepish voice rose from the hall. "At once, Colonel! At once, sir, of course!"

"And don't forget to pick out two couriers and two fast horses—if the Apaches left us any!"

"Right, Colonel!"

Geist's boots thudded off down the hall. Priscilla's little dress slippers pattered into the distance, as well, and she could soon be heard creaking up the stairs over the parlor.

"That girl's a scandal, I tell you!" The colonel chuckled, sipped his brandy, coughed, and then gestured with his free right hand. "Sit, Joe. Sit, sit! Tell me—how bad is it out there?"

The sergeant pulled a chair out away from the table nearest the fainting couch. On the table was a glass-covered humidor filled with Havana cigars. "It's bad, Colonel. We were hit hard. I'd estimate the dead at around twenty. That's not counting the women. I must have seen twice that many wounded out there, a good many of them officers. Also . . ."

"Also, what? Spit it out, Joe! You know you can be frank with me."

"We lost our Aravaipa scouts, Colonel. They were led into a trap and butchered, sent back to the fort draped over their horses."

"God*damn*!"

"The Apaches killed our sentries with bow and arrow. That's how they were able to raid the corrals."

"White men and Indians running together." The colonel stared at the Chiricahua Mountains rising out the southeastern windows. "I thought I'd seen everything out here."

"We probably lost the half-breed, Yakima Henry, as well. The fool kid pulled an idiot stunt trying to jump aboard the wagon carrying that Gatling gun. He's likely lying dead at the bottom of some arroyo. We still have Barksdale, but he took a bullet to the thigh."

"Are the wounded being well tended, Joe?"

"We could do with more medicos, but the surgeons appear to be getting adequate help from the survivors. Many of the housekeepers and even some of the doxies from the Sonora Sun are out there, as well. Tragedies like this tend to bring out the sand in everyone. Everyone seems to be pulling together."

Joe thought of Samantha and indulged in another, fleeting prideful flush. "I've posted men on the hills around the fort as well as on as many rooftops as possible. We may not be able to hold off another attack without suffering more casualties, but we'll damn well know when they're coming and from which direction." He gave his head a fateful wag. "Tonight, however, is another question. I don't like that Gatling gun one damn bit."

"Where did they get it, Joe?"

"I haven't heard of any arms shipments being hit lately. They must have raided a supply link in New Mexico, maybe Texas, and hauled that belching cannon out here. I sure wish we had one!"

"I've had a couple on order from San Francisco for nigh on a year now, Joe. Go on and pour yourself a glass of brandy. You could use one."

"No, thanks," the sergeant said. "It's going to be a long night, and I'll need to be on my toes."

"Yes, you will. I'm putting you in charge until this ordeal is over and I'm back on my feet. You're ahead of Lieutenant Geist. Consider yourself a brevet captain."

"That's highly irregular, Colonel."

"Yes, well—so are you and so am I." The colonel laughed, choked, and sipped his brandy to clear his throat. "Geist is a wonderful clerk, but he's no field officer." He sipped his drink again and cocked an eye over the rim of his glass. "Joe?" The colonel stared at him gravely. "Why haven't you said anything?"

"About what?"

"The blond Apache girl who was firing that Gatling gun."

The sergeant didn't know how to answer. For a second, he considered pouring himself a brandy, after all.

"That girl is my daughter, Joe."

The colonel stared at him, waiting for him to say something, so the sergeant said, "Well, given the boy was your son . . . yes, that's probably right, Colonel."

"Joe?"

"Yes, Colonel?"

"Run her down for me, will you?"

"All right. She's one of them now, you know?"

"If it's possible at all, Joe"—the colonel threw back the last of his brandy and stared through the window behind the sergeant with haunted, drink-rheumy eyes—"bring my daughter back to me."

Chapter 22

Yakima Henry looked down at his private parts.

In the fading light, with the night closing down fast over the canyon, he looked up at the hanging dead men whose own private parts had been stuffed into their mouths. The young scout gritted his teeth and pulled against his ties once more, grunting and grinding his naked ass into the sand and gravel beneath him.

He groaned and laid his head back against the ground, cursing.

It was no use. He'd been fighting the rawhide ties binding him to the stakes for the past several hours. They wouldn't give. All that was giving was his skin beneath the hide. Both wrists and ankles were scraped and bleeding. The blood felt cool now as the heat left the canyon. The chill was like a cold breath wafting over him, burrowing up under his exposed scrotum to probe his bowels.

The sun plunged farther behind the western ridge. It was as if someone had turned a lamp down low, so that only a small, thin flame guttered above the kerosene-soaked wick.

Beyond the saberlike firs and pines jutting around him, the ground was a murky, ever-dimming salmon green.

Chicken flesh rose across his shoulders and thighs.

The temperature must have dropped a good five degrees in the past five seconds. It was continuing to drop. It would get cold up here in these mountains. Might get down to the fifties, even forties.

He wasn't sure if it actually got that cold. But it felt as though it got damn cold. At one point during that long, bitter night, his heart seemed to shrivel up to the size of a walnut and beat only one or twice per minute. He forgot about the cold, however, when a low growl sounded in the ink-black darkness around him. His heart beat faster.

He knew the sound a wildcat makes when it's stalking a meal. . . .

He lay listening.

The growl sounded again, a little farther away this time. Again, closer. The sounds were shifting as though the beast was shifting directions, inspecting the scene of its feeding ground from several different angles. Yakima could hear the soft thuds of its padded feet, the crunching of leaves and pine needles, the faint snap of a thin branch.

It was taking its time, being cautious, because it smelled something different here from what it had smelled the night before. It smelled not only dead flesh, but living flesh now, as well. That would probably make it extra cautious. It might think it was being led into a trap by a hunter.

The padding and the growling stopped.

Maybe, sensing something out of the ordinary, it would not come all the way into the circle of dead men where one naked, living man lay staked out on the ground, coldly sweating, heart now fluttering like a frenzied bird in his chest. Staked out here like a Thanksgiving dish served up hot on a table!

Yakima lay holding his breath, turning his head slowly this way and that, staring into the darkness, listening.

Another growl sounded. The thumping resumed. The cat was moving toward Yakima and the dead men. Slowly, surely. The thumps were gradually growing louder, as were the low, cautious groans and hungry growls.

Ah, shit.

His pecker tingled. His bowels writhed. And as the slow, crunching thumps continued to grow louder, Yakima gritted his teeth and pulled desperately at the rawhide ties binding him to the stakes. Nothing was giving. He wasn't going anywhere.

Then he smelled a faint, cloying sweetness.

He stopped struggling and looked around. The darkness shifted like a curtain straight out beyond his feet between two of the hanging dead men. What appeared like two copper pennies floating in midair moved slowly toward Yakima. The pennies flickered. The cat had blinked. Its eyes grew brighter. The starlight flashed on them dully.

Yakima froze. He stared down his chest and belly at the cat padding slowly toward him. It was a black panther, as black as the night. Yakima could hear the animal growling deep in its chest. He could hear it softly sniffing its prey, lowering its head.

The wild, sweet stench became a heavy musk in Yakima's nose.

Yakima's testicles drew up tight in his scrotum, which shrank to clench them like a fist. He stared at the beast.

From four feet beyond, the cat regarded him suspiciously, hungrily. Its eyes were like two lamps, each subtly pulsating. The cat gave a louder growl and moved forward. It came around the side of Yakima, its padded feet almost silent on the gravelly ground, and lowered its big head. That head must have been the size of a water bucket. The ears formed two stiff triangles nearly directly above the glowing eyes.

The head came down still farther. The animal shoved its nose toward Yakima's face. The young half-breed could smell the rotted stench of its breath, feel the soft rake of its whiskers against his cheeks as it sniffed his mouth and then his neck and chest. Its breath was oddly cool against his flesh. It smelled like moldering chicken left too long in the sun. The beast slid its head still farther down Yakima's body, and the young scout gritted his teeth until he could hear them cracking from the strain, as he felt the cool puffs of the wildcat's breath on his exposed member and scrotum.

"Ah, Jesus," he said silently. "Ah, Jesus, Jesus, Jesus . . . !"

He closed his eyes awaiting the chomp of the animal's no-doubt razor-sharp teeth.

But then he could feel the cool puffs of fetid air moving back up across his belly and his chest. When he opened his eyes, the cat's eyes were six inches above Yakima's face, staring into Yakima's eyes. He could see the scalelike faults and clefts of the wildcat's corneas, the varied shades of copper and orange encircling the coal black pupil that looked as large as the tip of one of Yakima's fingers.

The nose worked. A low mewling rose from the beast's throat.

Yakima thought the beast was going to open its jaws and rip into his face. The young half-breed clenched his entire body. The cat pulled its head back and away. Continuing to mewl almost inaudibly, it turned around and slinked off into the darkness from which it had come. Its soft foot thuds and crunches dwindled quickly.

And then there was only silence save for the brutal drumming of Yakima's heart.

"What the hell?"

He'd said it aloud. The sound of his own voice sounded inordinately loud in the funereal silence, and it startled him. Incredulity rippled through him as he stared off in the direction that the panther had vanished. He waited, expecting the cat to return. When the minutes passed and became nearly half an hour, his heart slowed slightly.

His fear remained, however. He was still tied helpless, and there were likely other cats in these mountains. Cats, wolves, bobcats, coyotes . . .

The night trudged slowly on. It was like a waking dream. First, there was a chill that caused his teeth to clatter and then heat fell like a hot iron on his chest. The day lingered, the warm iron sliding across his body.

Crows cawed. A hunting hawk gave its ratcheting hunting

cry. Throughout the day, between the times when he drifted from unconsciousness, he heard men's voices and occasional laughter and the thudding of hooves somewhere over his shoulders from about a quarter to a half a mile away. The voices and the horses came and went.

He must have passed out again, because when he opened his eyes there was only a wash of pale green light in the otherwise purple sky over the jutting western ridges. Immediately, he had the sense that someone or some *thing* was staring at him.

"Oh, Jesus," he tried to say, but his tongue was too swollen from thirst and from the dry mountain air he'd been exposed to in his frozen position for more hours than his sluggish brain could calculate.

For several minutes, he looked around, squinting, trying to probe the thickening darkness beyond the hanging dead men, whose foul stench had seemed to grow stronger over the past day or however long he'd been out here. He was staring off to his right, past the mangled leg of one of the corpses, when he heard a soft sound to his left. He swung his head that way, wincing at the stiffness in his neck.

The darkness was shifting. A figure was moving toward him—the tall, straight, voluptuous figure of a young woman. Bare, bronze skin glistened in the fading light. Long, coarse blond hair flickered. The light also shone on the white and ochre paint striping her cheeks and across the bridge of her long, fine nose.

She came up and stood over Yakima, staring down at him. She was barefoot and bare-legged clear to her upper thighs. Yakima could smell the short deerskin vest and short skirt that she wore. He could smell the gamey, Apache smell of her. There was another smell, too. Something sharp. Maybe mescal.

An elk-hide *hoddentin* pouch hung from a rawhide thong around her neck and snuggled against her breasts. She wore a large knife in a beaded sheath strapped to her thigh just above her knee. A bladder flask hung from one shoulder by a braided rawhide lanyard.

Yakima stared at the knife, the handle of which, jutting from the top of the sheath, was curved staghorn. He could see the shape of the savage blade in the sheath. Suddenly, he felt very much like when the panther had visited.

"You must not taste very good," the girl said. Her voice was hoarse, raspy. She blinked her cornflower blue eyes.

Yakima stared up at her. Even in his miserable state—thirsty, hungry, weakened by temperature extremes and fear—he could appreciate the girl's beauty. Her body was strong but curved in all the right female places—her breasts curved out from the sides of the vest drawn tight against them—but her eyes were every bit as cold and feral as a panther's.

Yakima grunted. He cleared his throat, tried to work up a little saliva to oil his tongue, and raked out, "Water . . ."

The young woman squatted on her haunches, knees in the air, and plucked a .45-caliber brass cartridge from the mouth of the canteen. She held the flask over Yakima's head, tipped it. The water poured out of the flask and onto his face—first in his eyes and then on his nose before a refreshing couple of tablespoonsful landed on his desperately extended tongue.

She smiled as she poured, narrowing her eyes and spreading her lips. Her prominent eyeteeth were vaguely feline.

Yakima sucked down as much water as he could. Coughing spasms racked him as he sucked some of the water into his lungs. He lifted his head, feeling as though he were drowning. For nearly a minute, he thought he was going to drown there in the dry desert on a few tablespoons of water. With every breath, he seemed to suck the dribbles deeper into his lungs.

When the spasms subsided, and he lowered his head again to the ground, the girl was smiling down at him delightedly, apparently amused by his discomfort.

"Who the hell are you?" Yakima asked, anger burning through his misery. He coughed up a little more water, swallowed it down the right throat this time.

"The name I was born with is Riona Alexander," she said

in a vaguely taunting, amused voice, still smiling. She corked the canteen, set it down beside her, and ran her right index finger down Yakima's chest, starting at his throat. "My Chiricahua name has changed some over the years. First it was *Sango*—'foreign one.' Then it became *Koni*—'crazy one.' And now and forever more, they call me *Nant'an*, which, roughly translated, means 'ruler.' In your tongue, I am a queen. Queen of my small band of misfit Apaches, anyway."

"Queen, huh? You ain't no queen. You're the colonel's daughter."

"I *was* the colonel's daughter. As my brother was the colonel's son. Who killed Kq'na'ilchiihe, or Firefly, in your tongue?" The girl arched an eyebrow. "You? I saw you out there."

"Maybe."

She stopped the slow slide of her finger just below his belly. She looked down there, smiled again. "You are either strong or very lucky."

"I used to think I was both."

"You were foolish to pull that stunt the other day. Leaping into the wagon. But sometimes the fiercest fighters are also the most foolish. They don't live very long, but their fire burns very bright for as long as it does burn."

Riona Alexander began sliding her finger slowly back up Yakima's torso. She was digging her fingernail into his skin just enough to hurt and kindle the expectation of more pain to come. "The wildcat was afraid of you. She must have respected your power."

"How did you know about the wildcat?"

"I know many things. I see things. I always have, since I was a very young girl. They said back home that it was the Celtic blood of my ancestors. Very much like the wild, prescient blood of the Apache witches, and the *diyini*, the medicine men. From seeing things, I know that you have a fighter's blood in you. Cheyenne blood. The blood of the Light Horsemen, some of the fiercest fighters ever known. The *ndōicho* knew it, too. She sensed the power in your blood, just as I am sensing it now."

The colonel's daughter ran her finger up Yakima's throat, over his chin, and used it to trace his cracked, wind-burned lips. "It is a very raw power. Untamed. That's what caused you to be foolish. What caused your death here tonight."

Yakima's heart thumped as he watched her pull her hand away from his face and use it to slide the big, nasty-looking knife from the sheath on her bronzed right thigh.

Chapter 23

Out of the frying pan and into the fire, Yakima thought.

He watched the colonel's long-lost daughter flip the bowie knife in the air over his belly. The blade flashed as it turned end over end twice, glinting in the last wan rays of the setting sun, and just before it would have landed point down and hilt deep in his private parts, she wrapped her hand around the handle and snapped the blade out of the air.

Yakima sighed.

"Not bad for a girl raised in Boston, eh? One educated at the Miriam Pendergrass School for Girls?"

"No, that was pretty good," Yakima pinched out, though he wouldn't know the school she'd mentioned from Adam's off ox. "You ever thought of maybe going on back to your old man? I hear he's pretty het up about you and your brother and mother bein' missin' all these years. If you want, I could take you back, just you and me."

She laughed huskily. "I will never go back to my father," she said, setting the knife down tauntingly close to where Yakima's left hand lay against the ground, tied to the stake. "Apaches never leave their loved ones behind." Her voice had attained a hard, angry edge as she leaned over Yakima, glaring down at him. "They always go after them, even if it's merely to retrieve a corpse. They never give up. If need be, they devote the rest of their life to the task of searching. My father abandoned Fort Hildebrandt—he abandoned me, my brother, and my mother, even though she was dead."

"He went back to fight in the War Between the States."

"What task is more important than finding your missing family?"

"He did look. I heard he looked hard. He sent out several patrols, went out himself a few times. But then there didn't seem to be any use anymore, and the war came." Yakima knew how sorry his explanation must have sounded to her. Suddenly, it even sounded sorry to him.

Would he himself have given up looking for his own family in a similar situation?

"After I've killed the son of a bitch, and every soldier at Hildebrandt, I'm going to dig up Firefly and bring him home to bury him in the Shadow Montañas, where he belongs. With his *real* family."

"The Shadow Montañas," Yakima whispered to himself.

He'd heard of the range in passing. He'd also heard that not much was known about it, lying as it did in a particularly remote part of Mexican Sonora, in the shadow of the Chiricahuas. It was said to be home of a reclusive band of especially fiercely territorial Apaches—the Winter Wolf People. Some said that the band and the small, unforgiving mountain range itself were mere legends. Only a few prospectors and early surveyors contended they were real.

Yakima studied the girl again with renewed appreciation and sense of foreboding. Had she become one of the Winter Wolf People?

"Who're them white men you're with?" he asked her.

"Why?"

"Never known Apaches to run with White Eyes. But then . . ."

She smiled. "You've never known them to be led by a white girl, either, have you?"

"You're the . . . leader . . . of the whole band?"

"Well, only a small band remains of the Winter Wolf People. There's only twenty or so warriors. The rest are old people, women, and children. They're hidden away." Her smile brightened, her long eyes lengthening, quirking up at their corners. "They follow me because I've proven myself to be tougher than any of them. I had to be to survive. To keep from being enslaved and impregnated again and again by a bunch of howling Apache devils. To keep from being treated like a filthy whore by those devils, I had to become a devil myself."

Her blue eyes flashed wickedly, cunningly. "It came to me easier than I ever would have thought. After I delivered my second child, I went mad. I killed both babies and my husband and I cracked the skull of a brave who tried to subdue me. I screamed and ranted and ran around like a chicken with its head cut off. The others jumped me, subdued me, locked me in a *jacale* while they figured out what to do with me.

"But an old medicine man ordered them to free me. I was a witch, he told them. I could see the past and the future, I could see into their minds, read their thoughts, and I would live forever in one form or another. If they killed me, I would come back to drive them mad and kill them and continue haunting them in the next worlds."

She'd picked up the knife and was testing its edge with the thumb of her left hand. Her tone was one of sheer delight, her eyes flashing what Yakima instinctively took to be pure, unfiltered, bona fide insanity. She was not only mad—probably driven mad by the captivity and the savagery she'd endured, including rape and other even more ghastly forms of torture—but she was intoxicated by that madness and the power she obviously wielded because of it.

"Since they couldn't kill me," she said, flicking the upturned point of the big knife across Yakima's left earlobe, "they followed me. And they've been following me ever since."

Yakima winced, felt blood well up from the notch she'd cut in his earlobe.

"And now white men even follow me," she said in a tone of self-adulation. "Confederate veterans of the War Between the States. They were on the run from the Union army, holing up in the Shadow Montañas . . . until I and my band crossed their path. We were about to kill them all, but then their leader and I decided to join forces. We are like-minded, Captain Chestnut and me."

"Like-minded how?" Yakima asked, staring apprehensively at the knife she was waving in front of his face.

"That's enough," the girl said, laying the big knife flat across his chest. "Enough talking."

She slid her face down close to his and studied him with a feline curiosity similar to that of the panther who'd visited him earlier. She turned her beautifully savage face this way and that. She placed her hands on his cheeks, and as he frowned curiously, tentatively up at her, she lowered her mouth to his and pressed her lips to his. She pulled her head back and then began running her left hand down his chest and across his belly.

"Do you have any strength left?" she asked in a bizarrely intimate whisper.

"Any what?" He grunted as she placed her hand over his privates.

"Oh, I think you do."

"Christ, what . . . what the hell you doin'?"

"I am seldom given the opportunity to fornicate." She was manipulating him. And even though his loins were responding despite the agony of the past many hours, he found it annoying, frightening.

Insane.

He looked down past the knife lying across his chest, his own blood staining the tip of the point, to her slowly moving, caressing hand.

"They must fear me, you see?" she said in a husky whisper. "If I were to lie with any of my warriors or with Captain Chestnut or any of his soldiers, they might lose respect for me, as men do with women they bed. They might lose their *fear*." She stretched her lips wide, showing all her fine teeth. "Oh, yes . . . you have quite a bit of strength left."

"You're . . . crazier'n . . . a . . . shit-house rat!" Yakima raked out.

"Told you."

He looked down at her hand again. Anger and humiliation burned through him. He gritted his teeth, wanting to close his hands around this beautiful savage's slender neck and squeeze the life out of her. But at the same time, as her hands warmed and manipulated him, firing up his nerves like miniature lightning bolts through his belly, his desire for her grew. Her *hoddentin* pouch dangled over his chest. He looked down at her bulging vest, the dark valley between the tops of her breasts.

"There, now," she said. "You're a strong warrior, aren't you? Strong enough to satisfy an Apache warrior queen?"

Yakima said nothing. His mind and body were at odds with each other. His mind wanted to kill her. His body, on the other hand, did not recoil when she stood, reached behind the small of her back, untied something, and let the skirt fall to her bare feet.

She kicked the skirt away and then reached up to untie the vest's whang strings. She waved both flaps of the vest, taunting Yakima, and then shrugged out of it, letting it drop to the ground behind her. The tips of her breasts were firm and pale, their cream color sharply contrasting the bronze of the rest of her long, voluptuous body. There was a narrow white strip running up between them, showing where the flaps of the vest did not meet. That strip was like the strips of white war paint on her cheeks.

For some reason, that pale strip, coupled with the others on her face, sent a rush of desire through young Yakima's belly and up into his chest to constrict his throat. His head swam as she lifted her left foot over him, straddling him, staring down at him, her long blond hair hanging down across her breasts, partly concealing her face in shadow.

Yakima looked up the length of her. Her swollen breasts

rose and fell heavily. He could practically smell the desire dripping off this wild blond animal.

Then she dropped down over him, and her hair tumbled across his face.

Ten minutes later, she slumped, sweating, across his chest. He could smell the wild musk of her and the deer tallow she'd combed through her hair. They lay breathing together heavily, Yakima's heart only just beginning to slow its fervid racing, when she suddenly straightened. She scooped up the knife from his chest and held it up near his throat, the upturned tip angling over his right shoulder.

"Mrs. Pendergrass would not approve of my manners," she said, snugging the sharp blade against Yakima's neck. "But you've suddenly become quite useless to me, Siwash. *Hasta luego*, lover!"

She gritted her teeth and had started to press the blade against Yakima's neck. When thunder pealed to the northwest, she lifted her head sharply, the knife sagging in her right hand. Yakima stared at the blade, more preoccupied with the instrument of his imminent annihilation than he was with a coming storm. But then he realized that what he'd heard hadn't been thunder.

It had sounded like an explosion.

Its echo had not stopped careening off the ridges before another one joined the cacophony. It sounded like a mountain howitzer or a dynamite blast. From the same general direction, men were shouting and horses were whickering loudly. Some loosed frightened whinnies. Hooves drummed, and there was the wooden knocking of corral rails as the horses ran.

Yakima's heart quickened. He stared hopefully toward the northwest. A detachment from the fort had come for him!

Pistols and rifles began thumping raucously.

"Bastards!" The colonel's daughter swung her enraged eyes back down to Yakima. "The bastards followed us here!" She raised the knife in both her hands high above her head, the point angled down toward Yakima's throat. "As though they could save you! Ha!"

She'd just started to plunge the blade downward when the darkness shifted behind her and an arm snaked around from behind her head. A gloved hand was clamped over her mouth, and she was drawn back sharply with a muffled scream, dropping the knife in the dirt just left of Yakima's head.

Chapter 24

The girl gave a loud grunt and sank her teeth into the arm of the man who'd grabbed her. The man yelped. The girl spun, stepped back, thrust her leg back, and threw her bare foot forward and up, sinking the toe of that foot into the man's crotch.

The man's breath exploded from his lungs as he jack-knifed. He managed to hold on to the rifle he was carrying while he clamped his right arm over his crotch. Recovering quickly, he raised the rifle and fired, but his bullet only plunked into one of the hanging dead men, causing the slack carcass to jerk and turn in the air.

"Bitch!" the man wheezed.

Yakima studied the man through the darkness until he turned his head with its flat-brimmed, low-crowned tobacco brown planter's hat toward Yakima. Holding his forearm over his crotch, the man shuffled toward him, the pinto vest that he wore over a cream shirt glistening in the flickering starlight. Seth Barksdale dropped to a knee beside him, raking Yakima's naked body with his pain-pinched gaze.

"Good Lord—what'd that she-cat do to you, kid?" he

said beneath the yells and gunfire rising in the northwest. His voice was pinched, face flushed with pain.

"Too awful to talk about," Yakima said. "You wanna cut me free or did you come all this way just to get kicked in the balls?"

Seth grabbed the girl's knife and, still wincing from the bruising she'd given him, wagged his head and said, "That's a polecat, that one. She's—?"

"The colonel's daughter?" Yakima said as he drew his left hand across his belly, Seth having cut it free of its stake. "Yessir."

"Christ!"

"Yep."

Seth had just cut both of Yakima's feet free of the stakes, and now the young half-breed sat up slowly. He was so stiff that he felt as though a metal rod had been run up his spine. Groaning and rubbing his cut and bleeding wrists, he turned toward the northwest, spying a couple of flashing guns.

"How many you got with you?" he asked Seth, who was kicking around at the perimeter of the camp—if you could call the little clearing in the circle of hanging dead men a camp. Seth quickly gathered Yakima's clothes from where the girl and her gang must have flung them when they'd stripped him. He was favoring his right thigh around which he had a neckerchief tied.

"Two," Seth said, kicking Yakima's summer-weight long-handles to him with his good foot. "Get dressed. Luz and Ramon are trying to divert them rawhiders' attention from where we are, but since the girl's on the run, we don't have long before they'll all be swarmin' over us like yellow jackets on a barrel of peach wine!"

"Only two?" Yakima had uncorked the canteen that the girl had left, and now he lowered the flask to stare up at his partner incredulously.

"The sergeant sent me out alone. I was just to get a handle on them bushwhackers' location and return to the fort, so we gotta pull our picket pins—damn it, Yakima, we don't have time for you to founder yourself on water!—or I'm likely to get thrown in front of a firin' squad!" He kicked the canteen, which Yakima had been greedily drinking from, from the half-breed's hands.

"Ow!" Yakima yelped, gritting his teeth at his partner.

Seth crouched over him. "You so addlepated you don't understand what *pull your picket pins* means?"

There was a crunching thud. Yakima and Seth turned to see a red-dyed Chiricahua arrow fletched with the feather of a red-tailed hawk protruding from one of the hanging dead men's calves—a limb the wildcat had not yet made a meal of—causing the dead man to dance slightly in midair, turning.

Something moved in the brush.

"All right, I get your drift!" Yakima said, suddenly not feeling half as stiff as he'd felt a second before.

While Barksdale squared his hips and triggered his Spencer repeater in the general direction from where the arrow had been flung, Yakima picked up his clothes strewn around him. Thick smoke from Barksdale's carbine peppered his nose and stung his eyes. The reports were like open hands slapping his ears.

Seth emptied the seven-shot repeater, counting the shots out aloud, and then yelled, "The powwow's about to commence, amigo!"

He swung around and, half dragging his right foot, ran into the darkness southeast of the clearing, nudging one of the hanging dead men with his shoulder and ducking and disappearing into the forest. "This way, Siwash!"

Clutching his clothes to his chest, Yakima ran after him. Since he hadn't had time to pull on his socks and boots, he was barefoot. Fortunately, his feet were still tough from all the time he'd spent barefoot as a younker, and the forest floor was not bristling with as much cactus as the lower desert.

Seth was a jouncing shadow before him, the white spots in his vest catching the starlight every now and then, as he moved down the forested slope. The cold, fresh air was tinged with pine resin. Yakima followed, leaping deadfalls and ducking under branches, wincing when his feet came down awkwardly on a rock or a pinecone.

He missed one deadfall, tripped, and rolled. His head swam. For a few seconds, he thought he would vomit from fatigue, thirst, and hunger. Fortunately, there was nothing in his stomach to expel. His head swam more violently, and his eyes blurred. He thought he was going to pass out.

He tried to heave himself back to his feet but staggered and dropped back down to one knee. Behind him, brush rustled and the soft thuds of men running toward him grew louder. An arrow buzzed through the air over his right shoulder and plunked into a tree bole.

"Goddamnit, will you quit foolin' around?" Seth said, suddenly crouching beside Yakima and snaking an arm around the young half-breed's waist.

Brusquely, he hauled the scout to his feet. When he saw that Yakima could stand without assistance, he drew one of his big Confederate pistols, clicked the hammer back, and said, "The horses are straight down the slope and behind that scarp you'll see humping up on the right. I'm right behind ya!"

Yakima ran heavy-footed down the slope, shivering, blinking his eyes to clear his vision. Christ, what a night. What a past two days capped by *one hell of a night!*

Had he really been ravaged by the colonel's daughter?

He jerked with a start when both of Seth's Confederate Griswold & Gunnisons began yammering and flashing. Beyond Seth there was a loud, agonized "God*damn!*"

Yakima turned around the large gray scarp jutting on his right. The horses whickered and sidestepped away from him, showing the whites of their eyes in the darkness.

"Easy, easy," he said, recognizing neither mount.

They were both outfitted with standard Texas-style stockmen's saddles with saddlebags, canteens, and bedrolls. Yakima dropped his duds on the ground and pulled his long-handles out of the messy bundle. If he tried to ride a high-backed Texas saddle buck naked, he'd pound his balls to jelly in six strides.

As he stepped into the long johns, he glanced around the side of the scarp. He could see Seth's silhouette against the flashes of the two Griswolds in his hands. When one pistol's hammer clanked onto an empty chamber and then the second one did as well, Seth whipped around and, breathing hard with anxiety, came limping through the pines, leaping deadfalls.

When he'd rounded the scarp, Yakima was shoving his clothes into the saddlebags of one of the horses.

"That oughta stave 'em off for about one minute!" Seth said, ripping the reins of the other horse off the branch he'd tied them to. "Can you ride, kid?"

Yakima had toed a stirrup, but in his weakened state he was having trouble holding the horse steady while trying to pull himself up into the leather. He was leaping up and down on his right foot when Seth came over, planted a hand on Yakima's butt, and heaved the young half-breed into the saddle.

"You want me to ride him for you, too?"

Yakima shook his long, sweaty hair back behind his face. "No, but you might have to steer him. I'm seein' a couple of everything. Even you. And that part of it's makin' me want to air my paunch!"

"Ah, Jesus!"

Seth grabbed Yakima's reins along with his own and stepped up into the saddle. As Seth jerked Yakima's mount along behind his own, brush snapped to Yakima's right. The long, oval face of a war-painted brave bounded out from the forest. The warrior lifted a savage screech and raised a Sharps carbine at Seth.

Before Yakima could yell a warning, a gun flashed straight out beyond Barksdale. The Indian's head jerked violently. He triggered his Sharps into the air between Seth and Yakima, and fell with a crunching thud. Something warm and wet had splattered onto Yakima's right thigh. He looked down to see a long, dark smear of blood liberally flecked with the white of the Chiricahua's blown-out brains dribbling down over his knee.

Seth pulled back on his horse's reins as their savior materialized out of the darkness. Yakima saw the one-eyed, straight-backed, proud-busted Luz Ortega ride up to Seth, holding a smoking Spencer. She wore a dark brown one-piece dress that was cut low between her pointed breasts and held fast to her waist by a wide black belt. A black bandanna was wrapped around her head, holding her hair back from her face. The skirt of her dress was pulled up above her knees, exposing her fine tan legs. On her feet were deer-skin moccasins.

"I see you found your foolish friend," Luz said, sparing Yakima a reproving glance.

"He's in a bad way," Seth said, glancing down at the dead Apache. "We're not gonna be able to ride all the way back to the fort tonight."

Luz gave Yakima another glance and a slow blink with her lone eye, the other one hidden behind a black patch. Then she turned her horse around sharply, her long black hair flying back behind her. "I hope you're not just trying to get into my bloomers," she said as she batted her heels into her horse's loins. "If you are, you're going to be badly disappointed, amigo!"

Yakima thought he heard Seth give a lovelorn snort, and they were off, galloping hell-for-leather through the dark night. Yakima barely managed to hold on to the saddle horn. Several times he found himself nodding off, his hands slipping, but he would catch himself just in time. The shooting receded behind them, though he was only half aware of it in his semiconscious state.

For some reason, he regained full consciousness while still in the saddle. It must have been all the jarring of his battered head as well as his nearly naked oysters being hammered by the unforgiving Texas saddle. He found himself clinging to the horse's mane as they twisted around the sides of mountains and through at least one wash.

It wasn't so dark, now that the half-moon had risen over a tall, black, eastern peak, but the horses had galloped sure-footedly during the entire ride. They must have been born, bred, and broken in these very mountains by Ramon and Luz Ortega. Any other horse would have thrown a shoe or broken a leg long before.

Yakima saw a shadow drop nearly straight down the side of a steep ridge. Horse and rider bottomed out on the trail ahead of Seth and Luz. The moonlight flashed off a straw sombrero and off the cartridge bandoliers the rider wore crisscrossed on his chest, over a dark serape with the arms cut off to reveal black-and-red calico shirtsleeves. The elder Ortega said something in Spanish that Yakima couldn't make out for the clattering of the horses' hooves and the squawking of the tack. Luz yelled something back at the man, who merely threw his arm angrily out before him and galloped on up the trail.

Yakima put his head down and gritted his teeth against his misery. He was only vaguely aware of his horse stopping and finally peace and silence closing around him save for voices pitched low. He was helped out of his saddle. His bare feet touched sandy ground, and, though he tried his hardest to remain upright, he dropped to his knees.

He had no idea how much time had passed before he smelled the distinctive smell of a female. Felt a female's warmth near him. His eyelids fluttered open.

He lay on the earthen floor of some ruin of a stone hovel that had no ceiling. A fire flickered in a stone hearth nearby. Two men milled in front of it, silhouetted against the orange flames. Yakima thought they were sharing a bottle encased in straw.

The woman was smearing some awful-smelling salve on Yakima's face.

". . . foolish enough to pull the kind of stunt he pulled," she was saying in a low voice with an edge to it, glancing at the two men over her left shoulder, "you should have left him there."

Chapter 25

"How are you feeling, Corporal Logan?" Samantha Tunney asked the wounded soldier as she sponged the fever sweat from his forehead with a cool, damp cloth.

"I'm burnin' up, but I still got a bone-deep chill inside, Miss Tunney." He shivered violently.

"It's a cool night, Corporal. I'm chilly, too. I'll add a little more wood to the stove."

Samantha set the cloth over the side of a stone washbasin and began to rise from her chair. Corporal Logan grabbed her right wrist and squeezed with surprising power for a young man so badly wounded. "Miss Tunney," he asked, swallowing heavily and casting his amber gaze at the girl from beneath a white gauze bandage wrapped around his forehead. "What does the surgeon say? Captain Phillips. Am I gonna die?"

Just then another solder cried out from down the long infirmary hall that was dimly lit by candle lamps hanging from the ceiling over the aisle running down between the two rows of starched-white, brass-framed hospital beds. Most of the twenty beds were filled with soldiers who'd been wounded in the attack two nights ago. This was the enlisted men's wing of the hospital. The officers' wing was on the other side of a white curtain farther down the hundred-foot-long, narrow hall. There were another five men over there. *A ridiculous separation,* Samantha thought. Wounded men were wounded men whatever their rank, and they needed the same quality of attention.

The three women who had been wounded badly enough that they needed hospital care were being treated over at the Sonora Sun Saloon, as the whores' cribs were outfitted with the most comfortable beds anywhere on the fort.

The soldier who'd cried out, Private Joey "Little Joe" Flennery, sat straight up in his bed on the other side of the aisle, about four beds down from Logan's, and said breathlessly, "Mama, I forgot to shut the chickens up! That coyote that's been prowlin' around. He'll get 'em, Mama!"

A white-jacketed orderly, Corporal Groundwater, pushed through the curtain from the officers' side of the infirmary. He waved to Samantha as if to say he'd see to Private Flennery. Corporal Logan hadn't seemed to hear Little Joe. He kept his worried gaze on Samantha, his hand firmly wrapped around her wrist. His bluish lips were shivering.

Samantha sank back down into her chair and leaned forward to give the wounded soldier a heartfelt, level stare. "Corporal Logan, you are not going to die. You are badly wounded, and you need your rest, but you are not going to die. I assure you."

"I'm afraid if I go to sleep I'll never wake up."

"Nonsense." She placed a gentle hand on the young man's forehead, away from where the Gatling gun had chewed a divot from his right temple. Logan had been one of the soldiers drilling on the parade ground when the marauders masquerading as a freighting detachment attacked the fort. "You need to sleep, Corporal. Sleeping will help you mend."

"Cap . . . Captain Phillips said I was shot . . . shot through both lungs." Logan winced, licked his lips. "I feel all chewed up inside."

"You'll heal, Corporal. Now, let me add some wood to the stove to get you good and warm."

Logan's eyes flashed worriedly, and he squeezed her wrist again. "You won't leave?"

"No, I will be right here for as long as you want."

"I feel so ashamed," Logan said, his eyes watering, "but I'm scared, Miss Tunney. I'm scared to death of dyin'!" He smiled at the humor in that. "Sounds kinda stupid, don't it? But I'm afraid if I die, the devil's gonna reach up and snatch me down to hell before the Good Lord can do anything about it. My pa, he always said if I didn't mend my ways I'd burn in hell for a thousand years."

"That's nonsense." Samantha glanced around to see if anyone was listening, and then she leaned closer to Corporal Logan and said in a lower, conspiratorial tone, "I'll share a little secret with you if you promise not to let the cat out of the bag."

The corporal's quivering lips curled a dubious half smile. "What's that?"

"There's no such thing as hell."

Logan looked scandalized. "There's no such thing as—?"

"Shhh!" Samantha pressed two fingers to her lips and looked around to see if he'd wakened any of the other wounded soldiers sleeping nearby. "It has to be our secret."

"How would you know such a thing?"

"I went to a really good school back East," Samantha said, giving Logan a devilish wink. "I had some of the best teachers anywhere, much better educated than the confidence men in clerical collars who go around frightening children with tall tales about burning oceans filled with screaming sinners."

"Really?" Logan lifted his head to regard her anxiously. "There ain't no hell?"

"None whatsoever." No, the only real hell was on earth.

The corporal rested his head back down on his pillow and stared with some relief at the pressed tin ceiling. "That makes me feel a little better about goin' to sleep."

"Sleep, then. Rest assured, I'll be right here if you need anything at all, Corporal Logan."

Samantha patted his shoulder and rose from her chair.

"Miss Tunney?"

"Yes, Corporal?"

"You sure"—he spread another smile, this time a shy, slightly devilish one—"you sure are pretty. It's hard to think you're the sergeant's daughter."

"Why, thank you, Corporal." She gave a lopsided smile. "I think."

"Uh . . . you won't tell the sergeant I said that, will you?"

Samantha winked as she flicked her thumb and index finger together up close to her mouth, as if to lock her lips. Logan grinned. Samantha moved away from his bed and over to the nearest of the four wood-burning stoves that stood about twenty feet apart along the infirmary's central aisle. Each stove was flanked by a large copper kettle filled with split wood.

She used a hook to open the stove's small, square door, which squawked on its hinges, and then shoved a couple of chunks of split piñon through the hole and into the smoldering coals. She used a poker to arrange the wood on the grate and then returned to Corporal Logan's bedside. "There, that'll warm you up in no time."

She sat back down on the chair, dipped the cloth in the cool water, wrung it out, and leaned over the bed to continue swabbing the corporal's face. She froze, frowning. He appeared to be staring into space, his eyes wide, unblinking. Samantha looked down at his chest. It wasn't moving.

"Corporal?"

Nothing.

She heard the quaver in her own voice when she said, "Corporal Logan?"

She waved a hand slowly in front of his face. His eyes did not follow it, nor did they blink.

Samantha felt a cold stone drop in her stomach. She set the cloth in the basin and gazed at the young man, staring off toward the other side of the room, his eyes glassy in death. She'd seen so much death in the past two days: four officers' wives, a dozen men. A dozen more badly injured—half of whom might still die.

Somehow she'd found a strength in herself not only to see her through it but to help the surgeons and the orderlies here in the infirmary, who were so badly overrun. Samantha wasn't the only civilian who was helping out. Several of the working girls from the Sonora Sun had also volunteered their services, as had most of the laundresses who worked at Soap Suds Row doing the fort's laundry. The women had spelled one another as they not only tended the wounded but cooked food and coffee, cleaned the surgeons' instruments, and helped prepare the dead for burial.

Samantha had found courage inside herself, one she'd never known to exist, to see her through. Of course, she'd been fortified by the presence of the other women, including the whores—they themselves called themselves whores, so Samantha had started to think of them that way herself with neither condemnation nor guilt—but they were off tending to other chores at the moment, including preparing a couple more bodies for burial the next morning, and boiling laundry.

It was only Samantha here in the enlisted men's infirmary tonight. Suddenly, she wished she had someone else here with her. Her heart swelled in her chest as she stared in horror at poor Corporal Logan, who'd been so afraid. Now his life had been taken away from him, and he probably wasn't even as old Samantha herself.

He'd never been married. Maybe he'd never even been with a girl. Being a shy boy, he might not ever have been kissed.

Now he never would be.

As Samantha's heart continued to break and she felt warm tears dribbling own her cheeks, she found herself wishing however absurdly that she'd kissed him before he died.

A hand closed over her right shoulder. She lurched with a start and turned to look up at her father standing over her, his bent-nosed, craggy, dark face shadowed by the leather bill of his blue kepi.

"The corporal's dead?" the sergeant asked.

Samantha sniffed, nodded.

"I'm sorry I startled you. I thought you heard me walk in."

"It's all right." She offered a wan smile as the tears continued to roll down her cheeks. Her heart swelled and convulsed for the poor, dead corporal who might never have been kissed. "I'm glad you're here." She turned to the dead soldier, bowed her head, and cried helplessly, squeezing the boy's left arm in both her hands.

The sergeant squeezed her shoulder with affection. "You did all you could for him. Captain Phillips told me he was badly wounded."

"I know," Samantha said through her sobs. "I'm just tired and overly emotional."

"You have every right. Come—let's walk you back to the colonel's quarters. My God, girl, have you slept in the past forty-eight hours?"

"Oh, yes, Miss Holliday relieved me for a couple of hours last night." Miss Holliday was one of the whores from the Sonora Sun. She and two others were assisting the fort's two surgeons in the operating room, helping to remove one man's spleen and to dig two bullets out of another soldier's chest, near his heart. The latter was not expected to survive the procedure. Samantha herself had helped with four surgeries since the attack, only two of which had been successful.

"Only a couple of hours?" her father said with an ironic chuff. "Sam, you need to get a full night's rest. The patients will be here in the morning."

"Some, maybe."

"Come," he said, squeezing her arm encouragingly, giving it a little tug, "let's you get you out of here."

"Yes, I suppose you're right." She glanced at the orderly who was listening to the heart of another patient through his stethoscope. She pulled the sheet up over Corporal Logan's face, caught the orderly's eye with a sad wave, gesturing at the dead corporal, and then turned to her father.

The sergeant escorted his daughter down the aisle toward the front door facing the parade ground. He crooked his arm for her and she hooked her own arm through it.

"Any sign of the scouts?" she asked as he opened the wooden door for her.

She stepped out onto the broad front gallery on which two oil pots burned and a water olla hanging from the brush ceiling squawked faintly on the wire it hung from. A refreshingly cool breeze was blowing in from the eastern desert, rife with the smell of creosote and sage. The breeze caused the flames in the oil pots to sputter and rasp, issuing black smoke that smelled like kerosene.

The "All-Clear" was being called by sentries from various points around the fort—haunting, lonely, forbidding sounds.

"No, I'm afraid not," the sergeant said with a sigh.

As they stopped at the top of the gallery steps, he glanced at her and then lifted his collar against the breeze. "Mr. Barksdale's orders were only to reconnoiter the gang, though. He was not to take action against them. He's merely supposed to report back when he gets a fix on the direction they're heading. When he returns with that information, I'll try to cobble together a patrol and see if we can't run that bunch to ground."

Samantha said nothing. The sergeant must have sensed the direction her thoughts had taken.

"You fancy that boy, don't you, Sam? The half-breed, Yakima Henry?"

"Fancy?" She shivered against the breeze and crossed her arms on her chest. "Oh, I don't know if you could say I fancy him." She paused, casting about in her mind for the right word. "But he does *interest* me, I guess you could say."

"He's a wild one, Sam," her father said with a sigh, removing his blue cape and placing it around her shoulders. "I hardly know anything about him. He seemed to have just wandered in from the desert looking for a job with the horses. A half-broke mustang, that one. When it turned out that he was not only good with horses but skilled at tracking and scouting, I quartered him with the other contract scouts. He's earned his keep. At least, he did."

"Is that all you can say for him?"

"Maybe it's all I want to say for him . . . to you."

"Why's that?"

"Because he's likely dead." The sergeant sighed. "And . . . maybe I'm a little worried you took a little too much after your mother."

"How's that, Serg . . . ?" She touched his arm, chuckling. "I mean, *Dad*." It still felt odd to call him that. In so many ways, he was still a stranger to her. She wondered if she'd ever be able to really get to know this man who'd helped give her life.

"Katherine was attracted to misfits and broomtails when she was your age. That's why she married me . . . and lived to regret it."

Samantha laughed. "And a broomtail is . . . ?"

"A horse that can't be tamed. A horse that's no good to anyone."

Samantha wanted to ask him a question she'd wondered about for a long time. She wanted to ask him how he'd gotten bucked down from a first lieutenant to a first sergeant. Hailing from a poor mountain family in Kentucky, he'd been promoted through the ranks to captain before the War Between the States had broken out and had been leading a California column out here in Arizona. No one in the family seemed to know why he'd been demoted, and no one seemed willing to discuss it. Least of all Joe himself. Deciding that this was not the right time to broach the subject, Samantha let it go.

Instead, she said with teacherlike admonishing, "To anyone but himself, you mean."

"He's sure not the kinda man a nice girl wants to marry and raise a family with." The sergeant plucked a slender cigar from his tunic pocket, scratched a match to life with his thumbnail, and cupped the flame to his mouth, puffing smoke into the cool night breeze. "I can see how a well-brought-up girl from the East could romanticize a man like that. So different from anything you've known. He's like some wild, exotic animal you've only read about in the magazines and dime novels. I've known plenty of Yakima Henrys. Plenty who weren't half Indian like he is. Men like his friend Barksdale. Wild, cantankerous men, who spend their lives drifting from town to town, fort to fort.

"They can never seem to get comfortable in any one place. Trouble is, they can never seem to get comfortable with themselves, but they think it's the place they're at or who they're with that's the problem. They need to keep looking, convinced that over the next mountain they'll find what they've been searching for. Men like that often make big mistakes—mistakes they regret and that make it all the harder for them to ever feel settled . . . inside or out."

Gila River Joe took a deep drag off the cigar and blew the smoke into the breeze as he stared off across the dark parade ground, beyond the darkened fort buildings mantled with the figures of armed sentries, toward the mountains rising in the south. "Men like that are damn hard on women. And damn hard on their children, if they stay with one woman long enough to have any."

Pensively, he studied the coal at the end of his cigar.

Samantha felt her heart swell again as she stared into the face of this forlorn man. Another tear formed in the corner of her right eye and then in her left one, as well.

She drew a breath. "She doesn't regret it, you know."

Joe arched an eyebrow. "What's that?"

"My mother doesn't regret one minute of the time she spent with you."

Joe returned the cigar to his mouth, rolled it around between his lips as he stared darkly off across the parade ground again. "How do you know?"

Samantha leaned over and whispered into his left ear, "Rest assured, Daddy. I know." She kissed his cheek.

Joe turned to her, his expression partly sad, partly skeptical. Samantha wrapped her arms around his neck, drew him close, and hugged him. She squeezed his lean, leathery body so close to her own that she could feel his heart beating against hers. As she did, tears flowed freely down her cheeks. She wasn't sure why. Her heart felt so tender tonight. Everyone seemed so alone and vulnerable, teetering so close to the edge of destruction.

More tears flowed down her cheeks when her father wrapped his arms around her and hugged her back tightly. "I'm proud of you, Sam. I couldn't be more proud." He paused, then said more softly into her ear, "I love you."

Samantha's heart hiccupped. She convulsed against her father, tears rolling down her cheeks and soaking both of them. When she'd finally gathered herself, she pulled away slightly, smiled into his craggy face with its sad brown eyes, and said, "Thanks for the advice about Mr. Henry."

Joe gave her one more squeeze and sighed. "Yes, but will you follow it? I mean . . . if given a chance . . . ?"

Samantha gave an expression of mock surprise. "Of course I will!"

Joe laughed as he led her off across the parade ground toward the colonel's quarters. "Like hell!"

Chapter 26

"I think he's going to live—the silly Siwash boy," said Luz Ortega as she walked up the side of the low bluff on which Seth Barksdale and her father sat on a flat boulder, staring off into the direction from which they'd ridden an hour earlier.

"He'll live," Seth said, drawing deep on the quirley he'd rolled from Ramon Ortega's peppery Mexican tobacco makings. "And he might be young and even stupid at times, but he's no boy. I doubt Yakima's been a boy since he was five years old."

Luz sat down beside Seth, leaning against him playfully to get him to slide over. "Only boys jump into fast-moving wagons filled with renegades and Gatling guns."

"There were only two renegades in the wagon," Seth said, studying the girl critically. He liked the way she was sitting so close to him. Almost as if she liked him or something, though she'd given little indication of that during the past two years he'd known her. Oh, she'd joked and flirted with him, but mostly just in the way cousins of opposite sex joke with one another. "And there was only one Gatling gun."

"One is enough," Luz said, leaning into Seth again and plucking his cigarette from between his fingers.

"Half-breed?" asked Ramon Ortega, who'd unofficially adopted Luz when he found her wandering alone in the desert when she was only six years old. Her Mexican *mestizo* parents—both had been part Yaqui—had been slaughtered by *rurales*.

"Yeah," Seth said, accepting his cigarette back from Luz. "Half white, half Cheyenne."

"The very worst sort of man," Ramon said in his heavy Spanish accent phlegmy from all the wine he'd drunk since they rode here to this little, ancient goatherd's camp. "A half-breed. *Mestizo*." He wagged his head sadly. "Not good, brother." He glanced past Seth at his daughter. "Uh . . . no offence, *mi haja*." My daughter.

Luz gave a caustic snort.

Ramon had known of this place and led them here to keep the marauders from attacking his and Luz's wild horse ranch at the foot of the Dragoons. He and Luz had flung dynamite sticks left over from their recent mining attempts to distract the marauders when Seth went in to rescue his half-breed partner.

"Ramon, for cryin' in the king's ale, you're a *mestizo* yourself," Seth pointed out.

"That's how I know!" Ramon—stocky, swarthy, bearded, going to middle-aged fat and smelling of alcohol—cackled. His hair was thick and curly, his straw sombrero hanging down his back. He held a Sharps carbine across his stout thighs. A straw demijohn of sangria jutted from between his legs, its cork hanging from a string down the side.

The former head scout at Fort Hildebrandt had been fired eighteen months ago for general drunkenness and insubordination despite his being the best tracker Seth had ever known. He could also speak the Apache tongue of Athabaskan fluently in half a dozen dialects, which made him an invaluable interpreter. Understandably, it had taken Colonel Alexander a good long time to fire the man. He'd only done so after he'd been caught literally with his pants down on Suds Row, screwing the wife of one of the line sergeants and nearly igniting a small war right there at the fort.

Seth glanced at Luz. They shared a smile. He offered his quirley to her, and she took it again. After the close call with the Apaches and the white marauders, and the colonel's crazy renegade daughter, it felt good to be here at this ruined little rancho with Luz and Ramon. Seth couldn't help himself. He was gone for the girl and maybe, just maybe, she returned his affection.

Anyway, he had other things to think about now.

He turned to her father.

"Ramon, tell me what you know about them marauders. How long they been up there? And just what is *where*, anyway?"

Ramon took a swig from his sangria and offered the demijohn to Seth, who waved it off. He offered it to his foster daughter, and Luz took a hearty pull from the bottle.

"They been up there a good month, at least," Ramon said, accepting the demijohn back. "I've seen them a few times, coming and going through the mountains. They always gave my place a wide berth—probably didn't want to draw too much attention to themselves until they did what they came here for, which apparently was to attack the fort." Ramon shook his head. "Ay-yeeee, brother, that girl's got balls, whoever she is! Leadin' them men—Apaches and white desperadoes—on a mission like that! Hell, not even ole Geronimo would have the *cajones* to do something like that. Attack a cavalry fort!"

The old scout took another sip of the sangria, smacked his lips, wiped his mouth with a grimy shirtsleeve. "I kinda figured they'd moved up there to the Johnson Ranch."

"That's where we were?"

"*Sí*, the Johnson Ranch. Herman Johnson and his three sons moved up there during the War. Came out here from Texas. Johnson didn't want his boys getting involved in that mess. Moved out here with a small herd of cattle. He figured with the Gadsden Purchase, this country would start opening up to white settlement and those settlers would need beef. He figured to get a leg up. His plan fell through when Geronimo stole all his cattle and herded them all down to Mexico. Ha! In one night they were all gone, brother! Johnson was madder than a dog with its tail caught in a door!"

"Is that who was hangin' from them trees around Yakima?"

"Most likely," Ramon said, nodding. "I don't know who else it would be. That was the Johnson ranch house them rawhiders had moved into, the Apaches forted up out in the yard. Looked like they'd built them a few wickiups, killed a mule or two."

"Who're the white men?" Seth asked.

"Their leader's name is Chestnut. Lamar Chestnut."

Seth, Luz, and Ramon leaped to their feet and swung around, facing Yakima, who'd crept up the butte behind them and stood eight feet away, fully dressed, a smoking cup in his hands.

"Mierda!" Luz intoned. *Shit!*

"Yakima, goddamnit!" Seth raked out, indignant as well as embarrassed.

"Oh, Christ," Ramon said, holding his sangria in one hand. He'd dropped his rifle when he bolted to his feet. He raked a fleshy hand down his face in chagrin. "I'm getting old. It's good I was kicked out of scouting before I embarrassed myself."

"I think you just did, old man," Luz said caustically.

Yakima raised his smoking tin cup to the girl. "Thanks for the coffee."

"Who the hell is Lamar Chestnut?" Seth wanted to know.

Yakima walked around the side of the boulder and stood with his back to the others, facing the inky black ridges jutting in the southeast, capped with a broad arc of sky trimmed with flickering stars. "Grayback."

"I figured that, but . . ." Seth let his voice trail off, thoughtful. He fingered the fringe of sandy hair hanging from his chin. "Ah, shit. I heard of a Chestnut. His family had a cotton plantation in south Georgia. Fought with that old warhorse, Jackson. Fierce fighter, Chestnut. Refused to turn in his saber to the Union after Appomattox. Took a platoon of Jackson's men and rode west, vowing to continue the war on the Western frontier."

He turned to Yakima, scowling. "How in the hell . . . ?"

"Miss Riona, or Nan'tan, as she prefers to be called these days, said they threw in together 'cause they were *like-minded*." Yakima turned to face the other two standing and studying him skeptically. "Yeah, *like-minded* was how she put it." He shrugged and sipped his coffee.

"How did you find this out?"

"Her and me," Yakima said, haltingly, "we had us a little . . . uh . . . *discussion*, you might say, before she tried to put the kibosh on me. Told me some things she probably wouldn't have told me if she'd known I wouldn't be snugglin' with snakes about now."

Ramon sighed and sank heavily back down onto his rock, taking another sip from the demijohn and placing it carefully at his feet before picking up his Sharps and brushing it off with his hands.

"What else did she tell you?" Seth asked, standing beside Luz, who still looked miffed. A prideful girl, Miss Luz.

"Their home country is the Shadow Montañas."

Seth furled his brow in exasperation. "The Shadow Montañas?"

"*Sí,*" Ramon said, nodding knowingly.

Seth turned to Ramon. "There's no such range."

Luz chuckled.

"Sure as shit," Ramon said.

Seth glanced at Luz, incredulous, and then stared at the old scout. "I heard they were only a legend. Or a lie. One and the same thing."

"Oh, they're there, all right," Luz said, dropping the Southern-bred scout's quirley in the dirt at her moccasin-clad feet and scrubbing it out with her heel. "I should know. I was born on the fringes of the Shadow Montañas."

"And I was prospecting in them when I found this wildcat." Ramon looked past Seth at Luz, and sighed with feigned misery. "*Dios mio*, my life has never been the same since."

"You're lucky it hasn't been, you old drunkard and whoremonger!"

Ramon sucked a sharp breath and wagged his head in mock distress. "She's going to kill me yet with her tongue."

"All right," Seth said. "Let's just say for the sake of argument that the Shadow Montañas really do exist and you three aren't just tryin' to pull the wool over this old grayback's eyes. Can you tell me how to get into them? If we need to?"

"There's no telling the way to the Shadow Montañas. Either you happen on them by chance, in which case you often don't even realize you're in them, or you are shown." Ramon yawned, brushing his hand across his mouth. "This old man needs to rest for a while. You young people can sit up and watch for those desperadoes . . . whoever they are and whatever they want. What I and Luz did tonight was only as a favor to you, Seth. As long as they don't take my horses, I don't care about them."

"What if they take your daughter, old man?" Luz said as, setting his rifle on his shoulder and cradling his demijohn like an infant in his arm, he began slouching down the slope toward the ruined hovel in which the fire flickered dully amongst the strewn stones.

"If they take my daughter," the old scout said wearily, "I will not worry because I know they will gladly return her to me soon and with great desperation." He sighed and kept walking down the slope, chuckling softly.

Seth looked at Yakima. "The Shadow Montañas?" He felt indignant because he considered himself a top scout who knew this country as well as anyone who'd been in it at least as long as he had, since the end of the war, and for all this time he'd believed the Shadow Mountains were the stuff of old prospectors' lies. He'd never known anyone who'd been in them or had even viewed them from a distance.

Yakima shrugged. "That's what she told me." He glanced from Seth to Luz standing beside the grayback. He groaned and rolled his head on his shoulders. "I think I'll head the way of Mr. Ortega. I could do with a bit more shut-eye. Besides, I'm sure you two together should be able to keep us from getting snuck up on."

He glanced at Seth again, then at Luz, then back to Seth and crooked his lips in a wry grin. Luz wrinkled her nose at him. Yakima tramped nearly soundlessly down the hill in his high-topped Apache moccasins.

Suddenly aware that they were alone together, Seth turned to Luz. She glanced at him, blinked her lone eye, then shook her long hair back from her face, adjusted her eye patch, and stared off into the darkness.

"You could show me where they are," Seth said with a half grin. "You and me—I think we'd work well together, Luz."

"You think so, do you?"

"Why not? Any other scouts been sniffin' around the Ortega *ranchería*?"

"Not lately."

"Anyone else? Soldiers from Fort Huachuca, for instance?"

Luz returned his smile. "I'm not sure I would tell you if they were."

"Why?"

Her smile faded a little. She held his gaze with a warm one of her own. "I'm afraid it might discourage you. If such a man as yourself—one so full of himself—can be discouraged."

Her response had been too complicated for the Southerner to take in all at once. He felt as though he'd been at once kissed and backhanded. "Wait—*what?*"

Luz laughed and looked away. "You'd better be careful, Seth, or I might start to think you're serious." She glanced at him, narrowing her one eye shrewdly. "And then what would happen?"

Seth blinked and looked away, his ear tips warming.

Yes, what would happen? Was this, like all of his former dalliances, merely a frivolous pursuit or did he feel that there could be some lasting bond between him and Luz—a beautiful *mestizo* raised in the Dragoon Mountains by an old Mexican reprobate?

He thought of the girl back home he'd been going to marry before the war broke out. Wichita Stonehall had been her name, and she'd been five years younger than Seth. Her father had owned a plantation in the next county south of the Roman Gate Plantation, the place where he himself had been raised amongst slaves after his mother died when he was only two years old.

Wichita Stonehall's round, pale face with her sweet golden eyes rose before the Tennessean's mind's eye. White as flour and delicate as a redbud blossom in the springtime. Sheathed in crinoline and lace, floppy hats large as side tables adorned with carnations. A rare, smoldering beauty Miss Wichita had been. With a heart as large as a wagon wheel. Schooled in the finest manners by her own private teachers in Atlanta.

Seth hadn't loved her, but that hadn't been the point. She'd had a good pedigree and would have born him strapping sons whom his own father would have been proud to call his grandchildren. Seth would have married Miss Wichita and raised his own family at Roman Gate.

But she had died during the war. A stray Yankee minié ball had torn through a window at Stone Hall, ricocheted off a brick hearth, shattered a Tiffany lamp, and punched a hole through Wichita's pretty head. Seth hadn't learned about it until after Appomattox, when he'd gone home to what had been left of Roman Gate. His aged father had survived the war, and his home at Stone Hall Manor had remained relatively intact. But most of his old man's sanity as well as his slaves, except for one devoted house slave named Aggy, had left him.

That's when Seth had come west with a cousin who'd later been shot when he and Seth and a gang they'd ridden with were robbing a Yankee bank in western Colorado Territory.

The odd thing was, when the shock of having lost so much had worn off and he'd found himself living a blood-and-thunder life in the West, he'd discovered that he really felt relieved not to have had to carry on with a life that hadn't really been his own. With a life that had merely been handed down to him by the dictates of deeply carved Southern tradition, as old as the mossy oaks that sagged like giant, weary birds along the banks of Mulberry Creek, coursed through the emerald hills of Roman Gate.

Luz was staring at him, her brow arched curiously.

"What was her name?" she asked softly in her sexy rasp.

Seth was a little taken aback by the question. Had his thoughts been written on his face?

Luz nudged him playfully with her shoulder. "Huh, amigo? Give me a name."

"Wichita. But—"

"Wichita," Luz said. "Pretty name. Was she a pretty girl?"

"Indeed, she was, but—" Seth cut himself off, drew Luz to him, and kissed her.

Luz responded, pressing her lips against his, opening them slightly, placing a hand on his knee. Seth was about to wrap his arms around her and kiss her with more passion, but she squirmed away from him, chuckling dryly.

"That's enough, now, huh?" She wiped her mouth with a sleeve of her brown wool dress. "We are going to get ambushed up here, if we're not careful. Remember how easily the boy snuck up on us?"

She turned slightly away, narrowing her eye as she stared off into the night. The wind touched her long, coarse, coal black hair. Several strands curled up against her cheek. Seth reached up to slide them back behind her ear.

She pulled back from him again, turning to him angrily.

Seth frowned, befuddled. "Luz, what the hell's wrong? I fancy you. I got no one else, and I don't think you do, either."

She reached up and removed the patch from over her eye, revealing the milky white, shrunken eyeball tucked back in the scarred socket. "Is this what you would like to make love to, handsome Southern boy? You don't think you'd get tired of looking at it? See? Look at it! Look at what the Apaches did to me for fun with a broken tequila bottle? You wouldn't be revolted?"

Seth felt himself inwardly recoil. He had to admit, it was a startling sight, especially on a face so otherwise beautiful. Sexy in a wild, natural way. His expression must have betrayed his startlement.

She laughed caustically, rose, and walked away. "I'm going to keep an eye on the other side of the yard."

Shouldering her Spencer carbine, Luz dropped down the slope and was gone.

Chapter 27

The next day around noon, Silas, the border collie who lived at the Black Mountain Stage Relay Station on Black Creek, in the foothills of the Dragoon Mountains, rose from his perch on the station house's shaded front ramada and strode furtively out into the sunlit yard. Silas had been sound asleep, but his keen ears had picked up a very faint slithering sound from out in the dusty station yard, and, opening his chocolate brown eyes, he spied the object of his desire.

Head down, moving slowly, with the fluid grace of a stalking panther, the shaggy, bur-infested collie made his way across the yard toward the main corral in which the pulling teams were housed. Silas's eyes were intent, jaws closed, the white tip of his otherwise black tail curled upward from between his hind legs. Silas slinked into the corral and made a mad dash for the zinc-lined stock trough filled with oil-colored water on which flecks of straw floated.

Silas's sudden, violent movement caused several of the stage horses to sidestep around and to whicker at the dog whom they always kept a leery eye on. When bored, as he almost always was when he wasn't sleeping, Silas had a penchant for secretly and silently nipping at their hocks just to see them scatter with their tails arched. Then he'd dash around behind the stable before either of the station's two hostlers, Dwight Feldon and Ernie Bunch, could see the true culprit of the horses' anxiety. Instead, they would blame it on a raven or a dust devil or the superstitious nature of the dim-witted beasts themselves.

This time it wasn't the horses Silas was after.

The collie abruptly halted his assault about a foot shy of the stock trough, dust rising thickly as his paws skidded. As the Mojave green rattler that had been dozing in the shade beneath the trough struck at the dog, Silas lofted himself into the air, turning his black-and-white body, and bounded over the trough. He landed on the other side of it, grabbed the snake's button tail in his jaws, and yanked the angry beast out from its hiding place.

Silas whipped the snake's head hard against a peeled corral pole. *Thunk!* Before the snake could gather its wits and strike, Silas shook the snake again in the way the stage drivers wielded their blacksnakes over the backs of their teams. This time the snake's head smashed against the stock trough with another dull *thunk!*

Silas dropped the snake and backed off, head down, tail up. He knew exactly how far a Mojave green rattler could leap. He waited, mewling with excitement, chocolate eyes blazing as he anticipated his forthcoming meal of his favorite dish—raw, freshly killed rattlesnake. Ready to leap and wheel, to parry another strike, he stared at the snake.

The snake didn't move. Silas growled again and sidestepped slowly around the inert viper.

It wasn't moving. Blood slithered out of its partly open mouth from which its pale, forked tongue also drooped.

Silas was a little disappointed. While he was eager to eat fresh rattlesnake under his favorite paloverde northeast of the station, he also enjoyed a good tussle. It didn't appear that he was going to get much of one today, however, as the snake appeared to be dead.

He'd become too damn good a hunter.

Oh, well.

Silas had taken one step toward the snake when he stopped abruptly and lifted his head, ears raised, the tips drooping forward. Silas's eyes were sharp, intent. He turned his head slowly from right to left, his right ear quivering as he strained to hear, his black nostrils expanding and contracting fervently as he sniffed the air.

Apache!

Just then Silas's keen ears picked up the distant rattling of a wagon. He looked toward the north along the stage road that curved amongst the chaparral in the blazing heat and sunlight of midday. He couldn't see it yet, but he knew it was a wagon, all right. Soon, he saw the white tarp draped over the box. It fluttered as the contraption came along the stage road, following the curves behind a hitch of four mules. Sometimes the creosote and cholla hid the wagon from view, but its clattering and the plodding of its teams kept growing louder.

And, still, Silas's nose as well as his mind was filled with *Apache*.

Silas hated Apaches as much as most white men. He'd seen what they could do. One had tried to pierce him with a bow and arrow once, when he lived over at the Brown Ranch, before it was a burned-out patch of fire-blackened ruins. Silas associated devilish howling and women's screaming and the smell of death and burning human flesh with the musky-sweet smell of *Apache*.

The wagon was almost to the station's yard now

Silas groaned, gave a quiet yip.

Apache.

Apaches didn't drive wagons. White folks drove wagons.

Still, his nostrils kept working the hot, dry air tainted with that sweet musk that Silas would remember until he took that last, long walk out into the desert to feed the coyotes. Giving another, low, anguished groan, Silas slinked out of the corral. Keeping his head and tail down, he headed back to the cabin, where the stage driver and the shotgun rider of the coach that pulled in half an hour ago were talking in speculative tones as they ate, likely discussing the wagon that was now rattling loudly into the yard.

Silas would have scampered up onto the porch and warned the two men about the Apaches, but they didn't like to be bothered when they were eating, and Silas didn't like to have things thrown at him. So he merely crouched back under the ramada floor that was suspended a foot above the ground by stone pylons. Here, in the cool darkness amidst the bones and rattlesnake skins of his previous hunts and late-night desert scavenging expeditions, Silas lay down and rested his chin on his front paws, staring out in the yard, softly, anxiously mewling.

Apache.

There was no sign of them yet, beyond the smell. The wagon swung into the yard in a flurry of clomping hooves, rattling wheels, and wafting dust and ground horse shit.

"What in tarnation?" said one of the men on the porch over Silas's head. The collie recognized it as the voice of the swing driver.

"Holy Christ!" bellowed the shotgun rider. "You want to slow that thing down? We're tryin' to eat lunch out here, friend!"

But the wagon didn't slow until it had stopped, the mules facing straight out away from the cabin. The back of the wagon and its rear pucker were facing the cabin, the men on the stoop, and Silas himself, whose heart was rat-tat-tatting in his chest. Silas continued sniffing and growling softly, his hackles rising, his lips starting to twitch up to show his teeth.

On the other end of the wagon, the mules snorted. One loosed a brief bray. There was the thud of boots hitting the ground, and a man's grunt, and then the driver of the wagon walked toward the back, half smiling under the brim of his dusty gray hat toward the cabin.

"Mister, that was just plain rude!" said the driver. "And

what're you doin' with that wagon? That's the old Conestoga that Ma Ford from the Lion Gulch Station drives to Wilcox for supplies!"

"Ma Ford don't need a wagon no more, old-timer," said the tall, thin-bearded, gray-clad gent from whose right hip hung a cavalry saber.

Boots thumped over Silas's head and another voice entered the fray. This voice belonged to the stationmaster, Meyer Cole. Silas could hear lower voices emanating from inside the shack—probably that of the cook, Meyer Cole's wife (whom Silas did not like one bit), the hostlers who tended the horses and switched stage teams, and the six passengers who'd rolled in on the stage earlier.

"Who's out there?" Cole said in his raspy old-man's voice.

"Got a delivery for ya, old son," said the man standing near the wagon's rear off wheel, smiling more broadly now, showing chipped brown teeth inside his thin light red beard. His nose looked funny with a scar across it.

"Delivery?" said Cole with an incredulous grunt. "I just got a delivery three days ago from Tucson."

"This one's special. It's death."

Silence.

"Wha . . . say again . . . ?" said Cole.

The tall man dressed in the gray hat and gray trousers reached over to pull a rope. The wagon's rear pucker opened, revealing the brass maw of a big gun that looked like a giant bug propped on two, short legs. A young woman was crouched behind the gun.

Apache!

Silas could tell by the smell emanating off her, though she was unlike any Apache the dog have ever seen.

This one had blond hair. But she was Apache, all right, complete with the weird markings on her face.

She glowered over the stout barrel of the gun.

"What the *hell* . . . ?" bellowed the shotgun messenger. Silas could tell from the sounds that the man had leaped to his feet, dropping his plate and eating utensils.

At the same time, the girl, who was crouched over the gun, began turning the crank. The six small barrels protruding from the end of the larger maw began spitting smoke and fire, raising what sounded like the largest thunderstorm Silas had ever heard.

And in his seven years of life, Silas had heard a few—and he hadn't liked a single one.

He liked this storm even less than the others. In fact, the others were mere spring showers compared to the din this particular storm was raising, accompanied by screams and shouts, the thudding of running feet, and the wails of a baby. Glass shattered and wood splintered and there was the cacophony of bullets pinging off iron from deep in the cabin's bowels.

Silas lay watching in shock for all of ten seconds, ears pinned to his head. But then all his nerves fired and a voice inside his head shouted, *Run, Silas! Run! Run! Run!*

Silas bolted out from the side of the porch and ran away from the source of the hellish racket. The snake popped into his mind. He knew it was crazy to do so, for the world sounded as though it were exploding behind him, but he'd left a good meal in the corral.

A dog never knew when a good meal would turn up again.

Silas turned on a dime and hightailed it into the corral. He swiped the dead snake off the ground, clamping his jaws around it, digging his teeth proprietarily through the scaly skin and into the still-pulsating flesh, the fine bones crunching softly.

Behind him, amidst the continuing thunder, he noticed that a baby suddenly stopped crying.

Silas ran across the corral, around a couple of buck-kicking, screeching horses, and out the far side, away from the din. He started into the desert, the snake drooping from his jaws. Something *snick*ed to his left, and he glanced that way to see an Apache arrow still vibrating from where it protruded at an angle from the ground.

Apaches! He knew it!

Silas yelped with a start and dropped the snake as he swerved away from the arrow. Not to be deprived, however, he swung around and dashed back to retrieve the viper, glancing at several Apaches riding into the yard from the direction in which the arrow had come. A couple of the braves laughed as they watched him, and Silas vaguely noticed that white men appeared to be riding with the Indians as he dashed under a paloverde and lit out into the desert as fast as his legs could carry him.

And they could carry him pretty damn fast!

Especially when Apaches were behind him.

At least he had a meal. Silas was scared, and being scared always made him hungry. . . .

Chapter 28

Crouching beside the wagon from which all hell had been blasting for nigh on a full two minutes, filling the swing station cabin so full of holes that the next breeze would likely turn it to jackstraws, Captain Lamar Chestnut pulled his fingers out of his ears.

He slowly straightened, coughing and waving the powder smoke out of his face. He stepped forward and looked to his left as the Gatling gun squawked on its swivel, and the still-smoking canister canted upward. The blond Apache girl stepped out from behind the gun and kicked the latch that opened the tailgate. She leaped down from the wagon and stood staring through the powder smoke at the cabin.

They'd confiscated the wagon from another swing station to the northeast, because the previous wagon's axle had cracked during the gang's wild-assed attack on Fort Hell. . . .

Captain Chestnut waved his hand to clear the smoke, choked again, and batted his eyelids against the sting. "You know, you could have done that job with half the bullets."

"Don't worry," Riona Alexander said. "We have plenty of bullets. Besides, I know a place down in Mexico where we can get more."

"Where's that?"

"A *rurale* munitions depot on the Yaqui River." She turned her war-painted face toward Chestnut. "Don't worry, Captain. I know what I'm doing."

She glanced at Chestnut's eleven men just now riding into the station yard from behind him while Riona's sixteen warriors, clad in brightly colored calico and smoke- and bloodstained deerskins, rode in from behind the corral to the north.

Her eyes burned into Chestnut. He caught himself nearly flinching against that hard, savage stare, which seemed so bizarrely out of place on a white girl. A beautiful white girl, at that, with hair as blond as autumn-cured hay. "You just keep your men on a short leash. The kind of bond we have is not one that can't be broken."

She was talking about the fighting between the two factions that occasionally broke out, though to Chestnut's way of thinking, that was as much the fault of the Chiricahuas as his ex-Confederates. Although the two unlikely groups had been halfheartedly waving a white flag over the past two months—since they saw the value in joining forces— trouble still occasionally broke out. Especially when bust-head or women were involved.

They were like dogs mixing with cats, or coyotes mixing with mountain lions. Chestnut knew the truce couldn't last forever, but for the time being, it was worth his trouble to try to keep them all together. Fighting as one, they were one hell of a fierce outlaw guerrilla group. And looking at Miss Riona, who was only about one-third dressed, wasn't half-bad, either. . . .

Tamping down the flames of anger burning behind his eyes, the lean, copper-eyed Chestnut pinched the battered, salt-crusted brim of his Confederate gray campaign hat and gave a courtly Southern bow. "Your wish is my command, my dear Riona."

"And don't horseshit me. You're getting more out of our little partnership than I am."

Chestnut scowled, the savage saber scar slanting across the middle of his nose turning white as flour while the rest of his face turned crimson behind his dust-caked, patchy light red beard. "Just how in the hell do you figure—?"

He cut himself off, knowing that his own anger was like raw meat to this blue-eyed wildcat standing before him. Instead, he drew a deep, calming breath and smiled over his shoulder at his men dismounting behind him, forming a semicircle on the south side of the covered wagon. "Gentlemen, light and relax a spell. Look over the cayuses in the barn yonder, see if there's anything we can't live without. Mr. Carlisle?"

"Yes, sir, boss!" yelled Harley Carlisle, who'd fought with Chestnut at Second Bull Run, Antietam, and Fredericksburg, as had most of the other men in his raggedy-heeled group of ex-Confederates turned frontier outlaws, who'd refused to turn over their sabers after the cowardly General Lee turned over his to that Yankee drunkard and scoundrel, U. S. Grant.

"Come on over here, will you, please, son?"

"Yes, sir!"

Carlisle, who walked with a slight limp after he broke his left ankle during the war, tossed his reins to one of his cohorts and hobbled dutifully over to where Chestnut stood at the rear of the wagon with Riona. When he saluted his former commanding officer, Chestnut returned the gesture and offered a warm smile.

"Sergeant Carlisle," Chestnut said, "would you do me the honor of going inside there and finishing off anyone who survived my partner's fierce fusillade and then see if there's a bottle or two of corn that somehow avoided being shattered? If so, bring it or them on out here with a couple of glasses, will you?"

He glanced at the small, square wooden table sitting on the station house's front gallery, abutted on one side by a hide-bottom chair and on the other by a badly faded and

torn old wingback brocade chair that had obviously seen
far better days before it had been relegated to the gallery.
The Gatling gun had emptied both chairs but had not entirely destroyed them with bullets.

"Of course, Captain!"

Carlisle with bearlike jaws carpeted in thick muttonchops saluted again, pulled his pearl-gripped Colt revolver—
one of many such arms the gang had plundered from
stagecoaches and bank safes—and strode up the gallery's
three steps.

He clicked back the Colt's hammer, gave his captain a
devilish grin over his left shoulder, and stepped over the
dead men sprawled on the gallery floor as he strode on into
the adobe pine-log cabin.

"I do believe I'll sit a spell," Chestnut said, loosening
the red bandanna knotted around his stout neck. "Hot out
here. Hottest damn country I ever did see." He mounted the
gallery, stepped over a dead man sprawled facedown in a
pool of his own blood, and after adjusting the Confederate
cavalry saber hanging down his right leg, sagged into the
hide-bottom chair, which groaned beneath his weight. "I'm
from southern Georgia, ya understand. Near Cairo. Been
out here since just after the war, and"—he shook his head
and studied the hazy, sunlit desert sprawled before and
around him—"I just don't cotton to it. No, sir—don't cotton to this dry land atall!"

Riona turned to the Apaches who were sitting their
mounts in the yard between the station house and the corral, where the frightened stage horses were still running in
circles, and made a horizontal sliding motion with her
hand. All at once, the Apaches swung down from their saddles and led their horses toward the corral and the filled
stock trough.

Turning to Chestnut, she said, "If you hate it so much,
Captain, why don't you go home?"

Chestnut opened his mouth to speak but was cut off by
a raised woman's voice inside the cabin. "No! No, stop—
please!"

The woman got only half of the *please* out before she was interrupted by the muffled bark of Sergeant Carlisle's pistol. The pistol's report was followed by a dull, wooden thump.

Chestnut's eye grew glassy as he stared into the hazy brown distance, listening. Then he smiled dreamily and said, "Ah, I love the sound of terror. Sheer terror. One of the unexpected joys of outlawry—don't you think, Miss Alexander?"

She was mounting the gallery steps, lifting her long, beautiful legs tanned to the color of varnished red oak, her short skirt billowing tightly about her upper thighs. She wore an obsidian-bladed stiletto in a slender leather sheath on her upper left arm, just beneath a tattoo of a wolf's head—the symbol of her people, the People of the Winter Wolf—and a bowie knife on her thigh. Her deerskin moccasins rose to just above her ankles.

"A bold confession, Captain Chestnut." She stepped over both dead men sprawled near the table, and slacked her long, high-busted frame into the chair, inspecting each arm as though the piece was familiar to her. "Brocade," she mused, quirking her mouth corners in a pensive half smile as though remembering long-ago days when such furniture hadn't seemed novel.

"Don't tell me it's not the same confession you could make, Miss Alexander."

Riona hiked an elbow onto the table and turned to him with a tolerant gaze. "The confession was bold for you. Me—I see no reason to mention anything so obvious." She blinked once, slowly, and then glanced at the dead man lying faceup at her feet. He'd been hit so many times that his upper torso looked as though he'd been smashed with a giant tomato.

Again, Lamar Chestnut felt himself recoil inwardly at the girl's flat, savage gaze. There was something even more off-putting about her than the fiercest of her male followers. Until he'd met her, Chestnut had never encountered anyone so lacking of any apparent soul.

Lamar could tell that all the Apache warriors in her ragtag albeit formidable troop feared and respected her. *Feared* more than respected—to the point that none of them seemed to want to be in close proximity to her for long or to make eye contact with her. The most vicious of the lot—a big, brooding, pockmarked warrior who was called Big Tree in English—kowtowed to her like a young child to an arbitrarily violent parent.

None, as far as Chestnut had ever witnessed, had ever come close to crossing her. Most didn't even speak to her but merely followed the girl's orders without hesitation. She commanded mainly with looks and gestures, though she seemed to be fluent in Apache. It was as though they were all being railroaded by a rabid mountain lion. Chestnut knew by the way she curled her upper lip and smiled devilishly as she gave the orders that she truly enjoyed wielding her invisible whip.

Once, while drunk on her favorite drink, *bacanora*, she'd mentioned that witches ran in her Celtic bloodline.

Chestnut didn't doubt it one bit.

Whistling sounded from inside the station house. Glasses clinked together. Boots thumped. And then Sergeant Carlisle walked out the door, stepping over the dead man sprawled in front of it, carrying three clear, unlabeled bottles in the crook of his left arm, another bottle under his right arm, and two stout shot glasses pinched between his first two fingers and thumb.

"Just happened to be a whole passel of bottles untouched by the Gatling's love kisses," said the sergeant, grinning inside his shaggy muttonchops. He had a nasty, knotted white scar over both cheeks marking the spot where a Yankee musket ball had passed through his mouth. The wound had laid him up for only a few hours. Although the sergeant looked like some weak, little, crippled gnome, Chestnut knew better, and always wanted Carlisle at his side when the chips were down and the bugles were blowing.

"There you are," the sergeant said, setting a glass in front of Riona and then in front of Chestnut. "Not corn, I'm afraid. I hope tequila will do." He splashed the clear liquid from the unlabeled bottle into each filmy glass. "I won't vouch for the quality, but I sniffed the lip, and it's tangle-leg, all right!"

"Probably brewed out in the barn," Chestnut said, smiling at Carlisle as though at a helpful waiter in a fancy restaurant. "Thank you, Sergeant."

"Do you mind, sir?" Carlisle gestured at the bottles in his right arm. "The men could use something wet to cut the trail dust, and we've been out of coffin varnish for nigh on three weeks now."

Chestnut glanced at Riona, who arched a menacing brow. "As long as you share with my warriors."

Chestnut chewed his lower lip. Riona's warriors and forty-rod mixed like kerosene and fire, but the girl had her boys on a short leash. Even pie-eyed, they wouldn't dare to disobey her commands. Besides, Carlisle was carrying only three bottles. That was just enough whiskey for each man, including Riona's bunch, to have one short drink.

"Enjoy, Sergeant, enjoy," Chestnut said, sipping from his own glass, and making a face as the potent firewater seared his tonsils and landed like a cup of hot tar in his belly. "Nothin' like the good corn I was raised with, but beggars can't be choosers, I reckon."

He glanced at the girl, who did not seem the least interested in her liquor. She sat with her heels propped on the belly of the dead man before her, elbows resting on the arms of her well-worn chair. She was leaning slightly forward, resting her chin atop her knuckles. Having allowed enough time to pass since she'd so casually chafed his balls earlier, Lamar thought he could safely return to the subject without overruffling either of their feathers.

"Miss Alexander, I'd like to return to the subject of our partnership, and"—he smiled—"who might be benefiting more than the other."

"You are," she said with the same brassy confidence with which she'd imparted her take on the subject before. "You want to start your own outlaw empire down here.

Well, you have a small herd of some of the fiercest fighters you'll ever encounter anywhere on your side. Of course, they're being led by me, but at the moment, as long as we agree on tactics and targets, you may consider them part of *your* army." She smiled frigidly. "Which we, of course, share joint leadership of."

His smile still in place, though it had stiffened some, Chestnut sipped the rotgut again and blinked slowly as he looked over the table at the blond Apache queen. "Miss Riona, I do believe you're underestimating not only the prowess but the efficiency, bravery, and brutal savagery of the Confederate fighter."

"If you're so brutal and cunning, Captain, why is it that you seem to have lost the war?" She returned his wooden smile complete with the single, slow blink of her hard blue eyes.

Chestnut drew a deep, calming breath and eased his tired muscles into his chair. There was no point in arguing over such a trivial matter.

Their small armies had thrown in together against a common enemy—which was everyone who stood between them and their desires. His desire was to build and run his own outlaw army. He might have been on the losing side of the War of Northern Aggression, but he'd never let the Union forget him, by God. Not until long after he was dead with plenty of gold and silver cached away in Mexico, and Union notches on his belt.

As for Miss Riona herself—she seemed merely content with killing as many blue bellies as she could and cutting a wide swath of terror across Arizona Territory.

Like minds think alike, Chestnut thought.

He swallowed down his pride. He had more pressing and time-sensitive matters on his mind than whose army was more adept at their business. They'd already proven that together they were a damn near unstoppable force. The girl and her Gatling gun had really taken his breath away at Fort Hell.

"What do you suggest we do now that every soldier in

Arizona will soon be trailing us . . . after the dust we kicked up at Hildebrandt?" Chestnut frowned as he refilled his empty shot glass. "And who, by God, came in and snatched that half-breed out from under us?"

The Apache queen's cheeks flushed slightly at that, as though she was embarrassed by what had happened. Chestnut would like very much to know just what *had* happened. He hadn't seen Riona for some time before, during, or after the explosions that had turned out merely to divert their attention from the direction of where Riona's warriors had staked out the half-breed as bait for the wildcat who'd been slowly devouring the ranchers.

Bad bit of business, there. The ranch had been a nice hideout. Neither Riona nor Chestnut had figured on someone from Hildebrandt following them so soon after the devastating attack. It had revealed a chink, however slight, in their armor.

That chink would need patching. The flush in the girl's cheeks told Chestnut she thought so, as well.

Riona closed her eyes, regained her composure, and said tightly, "We'll lead those soldiers into the Shadow Montañas."

"We're going back there?" Chestnut had been yearning for the Mexican senoritas and mescal. They'd spent enough time holed up in those savage, isolated mountains with Riona's band of Apaches who worshipped her as though she were some kind of goddess.

Which, Chestnut supposed, she sort of was. And she sure as hell looked the part, he'd give her that.

She stared off across the desert, toward where a hawk was winging low over a distant arroyo, hunting. "They won't know the country. We will. It will be as easy as target practice. We rest there in our home country, and lay in some ammunition. In the spring, we will head to Mexico and raise hob with the *rurales*—just to make sure we haven't lost our touch over the winter, you understand. By then, the dust should have settled in Arizona, so we'll head back to Hell and finish off what is left of the fort . . . and my father.

I left him alive to ruminate on what he did to me and my brother and mother . . . and what his daughter has become because of it."

Her eyes narrowed as she stared off over the rim of her still-full shot glass.

"And then we return my brother to his home in the Shadow Montañas."

She threw back her tequila, downing the shot in one fell swoop. She chucked the glass over Chestnut's head, wiped her mouth with the back of her hand, and rose from the chair, her breasts jiggling around behind her taut vest. "Let's get moving, Captain. We don't have time to waste sitting here like we're waiting for the opera to start!"

She laughed.

As she stomped past him, Lamar regarded her uncertainly.

Crazy. The girl is truly crazier'n a peach-orchard sow. . . .

Chapter 29

The next night, Ramon Ortega reined his big roan mustang gelding to a halt on the winding horse trail that he, Luz, Yakima, and Seth were taking down out of the Chiricahua Mountains, and said quietly, "Hold on, folks. Geronimo's got that light in his eyes."

Seth glanced at the roan, Geronimo. "What light is that?"

"The light he gets when he smells somethin' he don't like."

"What don't he like?" Yakima asked.

"Despite his name, Geronimo don't like the smell of Apaches—Chiricahua or any other kind. He also don't like the smell of death."

Ramon held the big roan on a short rein. The horse was prancing around, lifting his long, fine snout to sniff the air. It was almost dark, but the remaining green-and-salmon light spearing around from behind the dark western ridges shone in the fidgety horse's eyes. The other horses also began twitching their ears, and Yakima reached forward to keep his sorrel from giving a whinny.

"How do you know which one it is?" Seth asked.

Ramon glanced at the Southern scout. "One and the same, ain't they? Pretty much?" He canted his head down into a shallow canyon off the right side of the trail. "Down there, at the mouth of that canyon is the Black Creek Stage Relay Station. Geronimo's tellin' me somethin's wrong. Follow me."

Ramon turned his horse around and galloped back up the way they'd come. Seth, Yakima, and Luz turned their horses and followed the stocky, bearded scout, who rode his horse like two hundred pounds of loose suet shoved into deerskins, down off the opposite side of the trail from the stage relay station.

Ortega halted the roan on a slight shelf bulging out from the shoulder of the gravelly bluff, and swung down from his saddle, quickly shucking his Henry repeating rifle, for which he'd traded the quartermaster sergeant at Fort Huachuca five good, mountain-bred, and thoroughly gentled cavalry horses.

Seth leaped down from his own mount, shucked his Spencer repeater, and tied his horse to a cedar near Ortega's roan. Ramon quietly racked a round into his rifle's breech and trudged back up the hill over which their tan dust was still sifting. Ramon was pushing fifty, he might even have been older, but he was damn hard to keep up with.

Seth glanced at Yakima, who gave an amused shrug.

"Give me your pistol," the half-breed said, holding out his hand.

Seth scowled. "Huh?"

"Them rawhiders got my pistols. Hand over one of those old Southern guns. You got your rifle."

Seth sighed and gritted out under his breath, "Have I mentioned what a fool stunt you pulled?"

"When?"

Seth glowered at him. Yakima, who was looking a hell of a lot better than he had looked when Seth found him staked spread-eagle and stark naked in the circle of hanging dead stockmen, grinned. Seth cursed under his breath, gave Yakima one of his Griswolds, and then followed Luz up the slope to where her father knelt near the ridge top. Luz hadn't said anything to Seth since she showed him her grisly eye socket late the night before. Since Seth hadn't known what to say to her in the ensuing sixteen hours, he'd said nothing, though he'd thought about it plenty.

Now, however, he was more interested in her father's horse. More specifically, what the horse had smelled. There was a good chance the marauders had figured out which direction they were headed and had somehow gotten around them with the intention of cutting them off before they could make it back to Hildebrandt.

Or this might be an entirely different set of Apaches altogether. God knew there were plenty of Apaches in the Arizona Territory.

Seth knelt beside Luz, who did not turn to look at him. Yakima dropped to a knee to Seth's left.

Though Ortega was no longer a contract scout, this was his country. His and Luz's ranch was within three miles of here. Seth deferred to Ramon's greater experience and knowledge of the terrain.

"How you want to play it?"

Ramon said softly, "There's no point in all four of us waltzing down there. One should go and report back what he finds." His beard lifted and his dark eyes flashed an ironic smile as he shifted his gaze between Seth and Yakima. "Me—I got bad knees. Can't walk for shit. And I hope neither of you two gentlemen would send a girl."

Yakima said, "I'll go."

"No, you won't," Seth said. "You only have a pistol."

"A pistol's all you need if you're good enough."

Seth saw no reason to send Yakima, who still had to be feeling the effects of his two long days and nights staked out on the ground in the marauders' encampment.

Seth turned to Ramon. "What's the best way down to the station?"

"Drop down the other side of this rise. A few yards lower, you'll see a game trail. Follow the game trail along the side of the wash. It will lead you to the edge of the station yard. You'll see a corral and the back of a barn in front of you. I didn't see any light down there, but the station sits on open ground. You'll see the cabin just beyond the barn."

"How long should it take me?"

"An hour to get down and back." Ramon winked. "If you learned half of what I taught you."

"About trackin' or whores?"

Luz gave a wry chuff.

"About respectin' your elders," Ramon rasped out in mock anger. "Haul your skinny Rebel ass. If you're not back in an hour—"

"I know, I know," Seth said.

They'd assume the Apaches had gotten him and would soon be scouring the hills for his friends, and they'd ride the hell out of there. It was the code of the contract scout. Seth might have risked his life to rescue Yakima, but he'd also been doing his reconnaissance job, as well, by finding out where the marauders had gone.

Dangerous work, scouting . . .

Seth scrambled quietly up and over the rise and down the other side, moving slowly, planting each moccasin lightly as he moved down the rocky slope, heading toward gauzy darkness at the bottom. He could tell even in the darkness that the canyon formed a *V*-like shape. He was heading down toward the closed end of the *V* into a dark tangle of brush and rocks. The tan slopes rising to each side were set against the lilac sky of early evening.

A coyote was yapping somewhere off in the hills to Seth's right. There was a faraway, short-lived squeal— likely a rabbit that had just become some stalking night predator's supper.

Seth found the trail that ran along the edge of the arroyo and followed its meandering course along the side of the wash, which was lined with mesquites, catclaw, and Mormon tea. Through the brush he occasionally caught glimpses of the white rocks paving its bottom.

He moved slowly and deliberately, crouching low over

the rifle he held in both hands and sliding his gaze from up the slope on his left, across the trail before him, and into the wash. If Apaches had taken over the stage station, they could have posted pickets anywhere.

As he continued cat-footing southeast, the hills leaned farther and farther back to each side of the wash until they disappeared altogether. The wash became an even shallower ravine twisting off to Seth's right, and a structure of some kind loomed ahead on his right. Soon, he could make out the rails of a corral and the silhouettes of the horses milling inside.

He dropped to a knee beside a paloverde and stared straight out ahead of him. A soft mewling rose to his left. Seth jerked with a start and turned to see a beast of some kind hunkered low about ten feet away.

A fox? A coyote?

The beast mewled softly once more. Seth could see the flash of dark eyes and the ears that were not standing up straight, like either a fox's or a coyote's.

Bobcat?

The beast moved toward him, continuing to growl and mewl warily, and then, when it was six feet away, Seth saw the tentatively wagging tail. The dog stretched its head toward Seth, sniffing busily, as though trying to get a read on what it was sniffing—friend or foe?

"Go away," Seth whispered. All he needed was to have his position given away by a damn mutt. "Git!"

He waved the dog away with his left hand. The dog lurched back with a start, raising its tail and its hackles, and started barking.

"Goddamnit!" Seth said, gritting his teeth and lowering his head, looking around frantically. "Go away, you god-blasted—!"

Something hard, round, and cold was pressed up tight to the back of his neck and slightly to the left. A low, burly voice said in his right ear, "You gotta be one hell of a tin-horn to let your position be given away by a damn dog, Barksdale. I oughta fire you right here and now."

Seth's heart quickened hopefully. "Sergeant Tunney?" He glanced behind him as the short, lean gent pulled the big Walker Colt away from his neck and lowered the pistol to his side, depressing the hammer. "What're you doin' out here?"

"Just about to ask you the same thing."

"Gonna have to ask you again, since you avoided answerin' the question the first time I asked it."

The sergeant, sitting back in a rocking chair by the snapping hearth in the station house, puffed his pipe. His cartridge belt, Colt, and bowie knife were hanging on the back of the chair near his right elbow. "What're you doin' out here, Barksdale? You're supposed to be headed back to Hildebrandt by now. In fact, I expected you back there *before* I pulled out this mornin'."

"Ah, leave the poor boy alone, Sergeant," said Ramon Ortega, ambling around the bullet-riddled, bloodstained shack like a kid looking for a cookie car.

The sergeant took another draw off his pipe, which he'd carved himself from mountain oak and a staghorn, then pointed the stem at the squat Mexican, who was rummaging around the cluttered shelves in the kitchen of the cabin. "If I want any shit out of you, Ortega, I'll knock you down and stomp on your head."

Ramon sighed as though deeply saddened by the remark. "You can't let bygones be, can you, Sergeant?" He shook his head. He'd been referring to his carnal knowledge of the laundress who'd gotten him fired from Hildebrandt, which the sergeant admittedly still held against him because Ramon was better at tracking Apaches than most Apaches were. The bottle had gotten to him, however, as it does to so many men of one particular genius or another.

"What the hell you lookin' for over there?" the sergeant barked at his old friend.

"The stationmaster, ole Meyer Cole, always kept a bottle or two of tequila hid where his old lady couldn't find 'em."

"You don't need anything to drink, old man!" Luz admonished him in Spanish. She was sitting at one of the two long wooden tables near the front wall, far to the right of the eight soldiers from Hildebrandt who were drinking coffee, smoking, and playing Red Dog by the light of the cabin's single lamp.

So much smoke hung over and around the blue-clad soldiers that that lamp looked like a train light in heavy fog. Occasionally, when the breeze sifted through the bullet holes in the walls and sent a draft through the cabin, the lamp bounced on its wire, squawking and scattering shadows like large black rats around the hovel.

Though the soldiers had removed the bodies and scrubbed away as much of the blood as they could, the stench of blood and powder smoke was still heavy even with the perfume of burning piñon.

The sergeant said, "Listen to your daughter, you son of a bitch!"

"Ah, here we go." Ramon smiled, heavy-lidded, for he'd just pried up a loose floorboard by the dry sink near the large black range and makeshift bar, and was pulling up a half-filled bottle of *aguardiente*, which Cole had likely bought cheap from whiskey traders peddling their wares between Nogales and Tucson. The sergeant remembered that Meyer Cole had been nearly as much of a drunk as Ramon, and a crafty one, whose perpetual stagger his wife attributed to the ague.

The sergeant would miss Cole and Cole's old wife, Hilda. They'd weathered the Apache storms out here for a lot of years, manning this station since before the war. They'd come to a bloody end, and an ironic one, given that it had most likely been Colonel Alexander's daughter who'd slaughtered them.

Worse than any Apache, that girl.

The sergeant turned his attention to Barksdale, who sat on a sofa built of mesquite branches and stuffed hide cushions across from Joe, the scout's back to the soldiers and to Luz, who was smoking a cigarette and drinking coffee.

"Answer my question, boy."

"I followed them bushwhackers into the Chiricahuas, Sergeant. I reckon I got carried away and followed 'em a little farther than I first intended."

"I reckon you did get carried away!"

The sergeant glanced at Yakima Henry, who was sitting on the far side of the sofa to Barksdale's left. The half-breed was hunkered low, his head nearly below the couch back, his legs stretched far out in front of him, and his moccasin-clad feet crossed at the ankles.

The Sharps carbine he'd found in the cabin rested across his thighs. Young Henry held his hat in both hands, turning it slowly, studying the brim.

He was bored, didn't like sitting around overmuch, though there was plenty of sitting around at Hildebrandt. Wild as a coyote. Strung taut as piano wire. Given seasoning, and as long as he continued to abstain from spirits, he could be every bit as good as Ramon.

But the sergeant had to admit to himself that when he'd seen the young half-breed alive, he registered a vague disappointment. Though Henry had the makings of a top-shelf scout, Joe's daughter was enamored of him. That was the trouble with having a daughter, he realized now. You started thinking more like a father than a chief of scouts.

Damn unprofessional.

Still, Joe sort of wished the Apaches had finished the half-breed off. It wasn't as if they wouldn't sooner or later, anyway. Henry wasn't the type of man who lived too deep into his twenties. Why couldn't his wick get blown before he could take advantage of Samantha's big, romantic heart and jade her against the good ones back home?

"Oh, him?" Seth said, glancing at Yakima. "I just found him walkin' out of the woods."

At the table, Luz chuckled softly as she blew out a long plume of smoke.

"What's next, Sergeant?" Seth asked, changing the subject. He'd taken one of his Confederate pistols apart and was oiling the parts. "We goin' after them?"

The sergeant sighed and looked at the eight card-playing soldiers sitting at the table near the front wall, oblivious of the conversation in their portion of the cabin. Three more were keeping watch outside. With the garrison so depleted at Hildebrandt, Gila River Joe had dared take only eleven of the best riders and shooters. He'd sent couriers to Tucson, Grant, and Huachuca for reinforcements, but those wouldn't arrive for at least a week.

So he'd put Geist in charge of Hildebrandt, though he'd had to argue with the colonel some to do it, and led the eleven-man detachment out himself. He'd figured that Henry and Barksdale were singing with angels. He was *half*-relieved they weren't, because it would make his mission at least slightly more doable.

"What's next?" the sergeant said, glancing down at the black-and-white-spotted collie asleep on the rug near his mule-eared cavalry boots. The dog was snoring softly into his paws. "What's next is we follow the marauders and wipe 'em out. Even if we have to follow 'em down into *Manana* Land, we scour 'em from the desert."

"Even the colonel's daughter?" Ramon asked, sitting across the table from his daughter, nursing the bottle he'd found and avoiding Luz's stink-eye. "Nah, you're gonna bring her back, right?"

The sergeant knocked the dottle from his pipe and tossed it into the crackling fire. "Nope."

Chapter 30

Relighting his pipe, the sergeant returned his gray-eyed gaze to Ramon, who continued to scowl at him over his shoulder.

"What are you going to do if you are not going to bring her back, amigo?"

Ignoring the question, the sergeant said, "I'm told they're headed for the Shadow Montañas. Tell me, Ramon, I've been hearing about those mountains since I first came out here in fifty-seven. Some say they're real, some say they're legend. Which one is it?"

"Oh, they're real, all right." Ramon swung half around and hooked an arm over the spool back of his chair. "I've been in them. At least, I *think* I was in them. With the Shadow Montañas, it's kind of hard to know *where* you are . . . for sure." He spread his pudgy, dark fingers in front of his face. "It's all up and down, that country. And the light plays tricks. So, too, do the shadows from the surrounding ranges. But you don't want to see so for yourself. They are in *Mejico*, Sergeant-Who-Was-Once-My-Friend."

He showed his scraggly teeth in a grin.

"I know they're in Mexico. But if that's where them damn killers are headed, that's where we're headed."

"We?" Ortega smiled without humor and wagged a finger. "Don't forget I am no longer employed by the U.S. Army."

"No, but you're employed by me. You're the only man here who says he's been to the Shadow Montañas."

"What—are you calling me a liar, my former friend?"

"No, I'm calling you a contract scout. You'll get paid once you've helped me run down those killers. And after I've gotten back to Fort Hildebrandt, the usual pay per day for however long it takes."

The sergeant waited, staring at Ortega, who snootily gave the sergeant his back as he turned to face his daughter.

The sergeant said, "Oh, come on, you old *javelina*. Don't tell me you can't use the money. With all the bust-head you throw back!"

The sergeant couldn't tell, but Ramon must have been staring at Luz, who stared back at him expressionless, casually puffing her quirley and blowing the smoke over her father's head. Luz slid her eyes away from the old former scout, and then Ramon ran a thick paw through his tangled mess of dark brown, silver-streaked hair as he looked down at the table.

"It's too dangerous. I have become a fearful man."

"I've never known you to turn down a challenge, amigo," the sergeant said, rocking slowly in his chair.

"It's too much of a challenge. That country is different than how it used to be. So many Apaches from so many different bands—all on the run from either the U.S. soldiers or the *rurales*. They are like cornered mountain lions. Many different bandito factions, and they are damn near as mean and nasty as the Apaches. They will kill a man from a distance just for target practice."

Ramon turned around in his chair again. "And the *rurales* themselves are as bad as the banditos and the Apaches put together!" He pointed at Gila River Joe. "You remember the trouble we've had with them, my former amigo!"

The old scout held the sergeant's emotionless gaze for a time before he turned back around to face the table. Luz stubbed her quirley out on the tabletop.

The sergeant sat back in his chair and puffed his pipe, rocking slowly, glancing down at the collie. Meyer had once told the sergeant that the dog could smell an Apache from miles away. Now the sleeping dog was groaning and softly yipping, twitching its limbs and flapping its tail as it dreamed.

About Apaches, no doubt.

Ramon turned back around in his chair. He stared at the sergeant shrewdly, grinned.

"I will show you the way to a painful and violent death in Mexico, Sergeant—if that is what you want—if you can do one thing." He half raised his arm and slowly opened and closed his hand. "Beat me at arm wrestling."

"You want me to arm-wrestle you?"

Ramon spread a grin. *"Sí."*

The sergeant was suddenly aware that all eyes in the room were on him. Even the dog lifted his head from his nap, and gave him an expectant stare.

"Don't tell me you are afraid of old Ramon, Sergeant Tunney," Ramon said, jeering.

The sergeant removed his pipe from between his teeth and said with a slow, tolerant blink, "Amigo, have I ever been afraid of you? When in hell was the last time you beat me, anyway? Back in sixty-four?"

"I believe it was sixty-three. If I beat you tonight, however, I do not lead you into the Shadow Montañas. If you beat me"—he gave a courtly dip—"I am your servant, my former friend."

Luz looked around her father at the sergeant. "He is drunk. He is a bored *pendejo*! He will be worthless on the trail, I warn you, Sergeant. Forget him. The fool's place is at home with his horses."

Tunney ignored the girl. He felt himself warming to his old friend's challenge. It had been a couple of years since they'd indulged in an arm wrestling match, which was somewhat of a tradition amongst soldiers with so much free time on their hands. Every fort had its arm-wrestling championships and the champion whom every other soldier wanted to beat.

The sergeant emptied his pipe into his hand, tossed the dottle into the fire, and poked the pipe into his shirt pocket. He rose from his chair. The dog mewled, watching him, apparently feeling as though it had found a new master— though the sergeant had no idea what the dog saw in him. Maybe it was because he was the first white man the dog had seen since the massacre.

Tunney smoothed his thin, close-cropped, salt-and-pepper hair down behind his temples and, strolling over to the table, rolled up his shirtsleeves.

"Old fools acting like foolish boys," Luz said, abandoning her chair and rolling her eyes as she strode to the door. She went outside.

Tunney slacked his sinewy one hundred and forty pounds into the young woman's chair, across from Ortega, who was also rolling up his own shirtsleeves. Instantly, all eight of the soldiers rose from their chairs to gather around the two challengers, loudly placing bets. The sergeant was quickly pronounced the odds-on favorite, either because most of the soldiers were afraid to bet against him or because they genuinely deemed him to be the more capable opponent.

One of the only three in the room who bet against him was the half-breed, Yakima Henry, who'd risen from the couch but remained in the parlor area, folding his arms on his chest and leaning back against a ceiling support post, a faintly wry expression on his jade-eyed face.

The sergeant sensed that Yakima knew of his feelings of ill will. Joe didn't like that. It was an unprofessional way to behave. Besides, Henry was a damn good scout.

It was just Samantha. . . .

When all the bets had been placed, Joe and Ramon raised their right arms in the middle of the table and clutched palms. Corporal McAdams yelled, "Go!" and both challengers gritted their teeth, gazing devilishly into each other's eyes.

Immediately, the sergeant felt a substantial loss of strength in his old friend's arm. He thought he could probably win the match in the first fifteen seconds, because he had Ramon's hand halfway to the table. But not wanting to embarrass the old Mexican scout, he eased up some. He made a face, as though Ortega were countering him handily, and watched the back of his own right hand begin angling down toward the table.

Ramon grunted. "Thought it was going to be easy, did you, Sergeant?"

Tunney only groaned and feigned a slightly worried look as he stared at his hand, which Ramon now had halfway to the scarred tabletop.

"Come on, Sergeant!" yelled Private Tannehill. "I bet a whole dollar on ya! Come on, Sergeant—you can do it!"

The sergeant put some steel into his arm and watched the entwined hands rise back until they were nearly vertical again. The cheers grew.

Joe stared into Ramon's dark eyes that glinted copper in the guttering lamplight. The sergeant felt a strange sadness, looking into those eyes. There'd been a time, not all that long ago, when their matches were a genuine contest of strength and will—the men so evenly matched that it was anyone's guess which one would win on any given night. They were roughly the same age, so the years weren't responsible for Ramon's decline.

It was the drink, but perhaps also a loss of fighting spirit. But that was probably the drink, too. The Mexican scout had made the challenge only because, in his half-inebriated state, he'd wanted to want it. Like old times. Just as he wanted to feel the compulsion to lead the sergeant's patrol after the marauders.

The truth was, however, Ortega didn't know if he really had that much gravel in him anymore.

That was why he wanted the sergeant to force him to go. Not only for the sergeant's benefit—he knew Ramon could still track; that wasn't something a man ever lost—but for Ramon's benefit, as well.

The sergeant pushed the old scout's pudgy brown hand with its dirt-encrusted nails and the grime-caked knuckle down toward the table.

"Ah, shit!" Ramon cried, staring in horror at the sergeant's knobby, long-fingered hand, which was almost as tan as Ramon's, down toward the table.

The cheering rose.

The sergeant felt guilty for toying with his old friend, so he finished him. More cheering. Money changed hands. The sergeant rolled down his shirtsleeves, strapped on his gun and knife, ordered a change of sentries, and followed them outside, the collie dogging his heels.

"I almost had you, Sergeant!" Ramon said behind him, jeering, splashing *aguardiente* into a glass. "Next time, eh? *Saludos!*"

"I never thought I would live to see it," Luz told the sergeant later, as Joe leaned back against the corral rails, smoking his pipe, the bowl of which he concealed in the palm of his right hand.

"What's that?"

She'd come from the cabin and was wrapping a blanket around her shoulders against the desert night's chill. "You becoming sentimental."

"How's that?"

"I was watching through the window. You made it look like more of a fight than it was."

The sergeant hiked a shoulder and, puffing his pipe, looked off. "Not even an old mossy horn like me could rub his nose in it."

She leaned her back against the fence beside him. The dog was scratching and sniffing around the yard, growling quietly. He still scented the Apaches.

"I hear your daughter is at the fort. Was she hurt in the attack?"

"Nah, just frightened. But she's holdin' up well. In fact, she's tendin' the wounded over at the infirmary."

"I didn't know you had a daughter." She glanced at him. "Would never have guessed you'd ever married."

"Yeah, I got shanghaied back when I was too young to know better than to loiter around the docks after dark." Joe chuckled deep in his chest at that.

"I hear she's beautiful."

Joe turned to her, narrowing a suspicious eye. "Who told you that?"

"Seth."

"Mm-hmm." Joe turned away.

"And I hear she has an eye for the half-breed."

Joe looked at her again with the same suspicious expression as before. "Barksdale's just a whole sewin' party full of camp gossip, ain't he?"

"I'm sorry," Luz said, sheepish. "I didn't mean to rub your nose in it. He's not so bad. He's young, and he has some Indian blood, but the best of us do." She smiled, trying to lighten his mood.

"She's an Eastern gal. A girl of privilege. Her stepfather is the lieutenant governor of New York State. She grew up reading books and going to balls with other young ladies of privilege. She's been groomed to marry a boy with money and . . . and manners. Not some half-breed contract scout who's likely never stepped foot east of the Mississippi."

The sergeant puffed his pipe and shook his head, his ears warming with anger as well as embarrassment. He was not normally an emotional man.

"Easy, Sergeant," Luz said, shaking her hair back from her face and adjusting her eye patch. "It's likely a passing attraction. He is rather handsome. I'm sure she'll marry just the kind of boy you'd like her to."

"Damn romantic notions is what she's plagued with. Takes after her mother that way. Read too many dime novels about the Wild West, growin' up."

"She takes after her mother, huh?"

"That's right?"

"*Only* her mother?"

The sergeant glanced at her, incredulous.

"You came to the frontier from the East, as well, did you not?" Luz said.

"Hell, I was raised in the hills of ole Kentuck. We were so poor that I ran barefoot until I joined the army."

"You wandered a long ways from Kentucky. It takes an adventurous man to stray as far from his home as you have . . . and stayed to become somewhat of a legend. Eh, Gila River Joe?"

"Girl, you're startin' to rattle me."

Luz chuckled, turned, and planted a moccasin heel on the corral's bottom rail. "I apologize. I just came out to make conversation, because I wasn't sleepy." She shook her long hair back behind her shoulders and canted her lone eye toward the starry sky.

The sergeant relaxed and leaned back against the corral again. "Ah, hell. That's all right. To tell you the truth, Luz, I reckon you're right. Samantha does take after me as much as her mother. But that worries me even more, because she's likely to make the same mistakes we did."

"Well, then, she'll make the same mistakes and learn from them."

"I reckon so. Sometimes I wish . . ." He let his voice trail off, silently admonishing himself for the thought.

"For what? That you didn't get to know her?"

"Well, it pesters me. And I'm not used to bein' pestered by . . . by *private matters*."

"Welcome to the human race, Sergeant."

Joe chuffed a dubious retort to that and looked down at the toes of his boots as he rocked back on his heels, pensive. He supposed he couldn't insulate himself forever. After all, Samantha was the fruit of his loins. He was the girl's father. About time he faced up to what all that entailed, including the worry.

He turned to Luz. "What about you?"

"What about me?"

"You're two years older than Samantha. How come you

ain't hitched yet? I got a feelin' you could be . . . if you'd just give the boy the time of day once in a while."

He canted his head at the cabin. "It's Barksdale I'm talkin' about. He's a might distracted whenever you're within hailin' distance, I've noticed."

Luz rested her arms over the corral's top rail, leaned forward, and studied the ground. The slight breeze nudged her hair back behind her ears. "Then he is a fool. Ramon needs me. And I have more in common with horses than that pretty Southern boy."

She turned and started striding back toward the cabin, wrapping the blanket around her shoulders. "Good night, Sergeant."

"Night, Luz."

She stopped and turned back to him. "Sergeant?"

"Luz, you've known me long enough to start callin' me Joe."

"I want you to know, Joe, that I know what you are trying to do." She canted her head toward the cabin. "With the old *pendejo* in there. And while he would probably prefer dying with you in the Shadow Montañas, I'd prefer he hung around for a while longer. And died back at the rancho . . . with me."

The sergeant studied her for a time and nodded.

"I want him along because he knows the way to the Shadow Montañas. That's my first and foremost reason, anyway."

"I understand that. Still . . ." She turned and started walking toward the cabin again, before the sergeant's voice halted her once more.

"You comin'?"

Luz turned to face him, smiled. "Someone's gotta keep an eye on you two old seed bulls."

She headed on into the cabin and quietly latched the door behind her.

Chapter 31

Three days later, the column of nine uniformed soldiers, including Sergeant Tunney, who rode at the head of the bunch, plodded up a gradual slope and into the ruins of an ancient Mexican village.

There was little left of the place except for maybe six adobe shacks hunched amidst the rocks and cactus and prickly pear south of the San Pedro River.

The village, Sierra Paquime, had long ago fallen victim to one of many revolutions that exploded in northern Sonora. And the residents who'd survived a particularly ferocious battle fought here between peon revolutionaries and an army of killers hired by local *hacendados*, wealthy Mexican landowners, had been finished off by disease or by the Apaches and Yaquis, who also preyed on northern Sonora and Chihuahua.

All that had remained for some time were a few poor farmers raising a smattering of goats and chickens, and a locally famous watering hole housed in what the sergeant had always assumed had once been the grand casa of an estancia hugging the outskirts of the village. At least, the house had been grand by outback standards—three stories high, built of whitewashed adobe, and with wide balconies running along the outside of both the second and third stories.

These days, the roof was missing at least half of its red tiles. Both balconies were sagging ruins, wrought-iron rails drooping toward the ground. Most of the planks from the balcony floors had tumbled away and were rotting in the high weeds growing up around the base of the chipped, cracked walls. Now a plank sign over the gray, timbered door, which was currently propped open with a rain barrel, announced in crudely painted letters simply: CANTINA.

The estancia's barn sat just beyond the cantina. It, too, was a ruin of gray wood and adobe bricks with half of its roof caved in. But the windmill that stood between the old casa and the barn was still functional, the wooden blades, kept in generally good repair, spinning in the afternoon breeze, which was cool at this relatively high altitude. The sun shone as though through a lens. The stock tank of sunbleached adobe forming a broad circle at the windmill's base rippled with dark water flashing the brassy Mexican sunshine.

Tunney rode his bay up to one of the two hitch racks fronting the casa. Several horses were tied to both racks, shaded by a sagging brush ramada. There were several more horses in a corral near the barn, all wearing saddles. Most pilgrims passing through Sierra Paquime stopped for the local *aguardiente* brewed and served inside the cantina by an impossibly fat, toothless Mex named Antonio Chacin—or for a roll in the hay with one of Chacin's whores, also as locally famous as the man's tarantula juice.

But most, once fortified by either one of the place's highly touted delights, rode on soon afterward. Banditos and Indians in this neck of Sonora, who rode by night, discouraged the wise from lingering around Sierra Paquime for more than a few hours at a time.

An old legend said that bad luck hung over Sierra Paquime like a particularly black and long-stalled storm cloud. That bout of ill fortune had come when, many generations ago, the Franciscans who had originally established the village spread a disease to a band of Yaqui who had called the area home, annihilating the entire band—men, women, and children. It was said that even the Yaquis' animals had died.

It was also said that, as she lay dying, a Yaqui sorceress had cast an evil spell over the village. That's why the once prosperous place had endured so much bad luck over the ensuing years, and why it had been reduced now to a haven for drunkards and fornicators.

It was also a good place to water cavalry remounts and to glean bits and pieces of what might or might not be useful information.

"Corporal McAdams, order the men to dismount and water their animals, including my own, over at the stock tank. We'll take a fifteen-minute blow, so smoke and relieve yourselves and fill your canteens and do whatever you else you gotta do and be ready to ride in fifteen minutes, understand?"

The corporal saluted with two fingers touched to the brim of his broad campaign hat to which trail dust and sweat clung thickly. "Aye-aye, Sergeant!"

Tunney returned the salute, dismounted, and tossed the reins of his own horse to the corporal.

"Oh, and, Corporal?"

"Yes, Sergeant?" McAdams said as he stepped down from his own McClelland.

Tunney glanced at several of the other seven men chuckling amongst themselves and glancing toward the brush shacks flanking the roadhouse. "Don't let any of our soldiers wander back to the hog pens. I don't want anybody bringing the Cupid's itch back to Hildebrand. You understand that, too?"

The corporal glanced over his shoulder at the other men

and spread his scraggly mustache with a knowing smile. "You got it, Sergeant. Under no circumstances, Cupid's itch!"

"They venture back there, I'll guarantee you that in two days they'll likely be burnin' so bad against their saddles that they'll be tryin' to shoot themselves."

"Aye-aye, Sergeant!"

While the corporal led Tunney's horse off toward the stock tank, barking orders to the others, the sergeant stepped between the two hitch racks, doffed his hat, and ducked through the low door into the cantina. Once inside the smoky place, whose flagstone floor had been pummeled into gravel over the years, he set his dusty, sweaty campaign hat back on his head. This was not a place of polite convention.

The room was long, running nearly the whole width of the building. Tunney thought it might be the only part of the building still in use, though stone stairs trimmed with an iron railing ran up to the second story. The only light was that which angled through the glassless, unshuttered windows.

There were twenty or so crude wooden tables outfitted with chairs of every fashion. A bar of oak planks ran along the wall on the far side of the room from the door.

Only about five of the tables were occupied. Faces turned toward him. Skeptical eyes flickered, took his measure, and lips moved, muttering. The other customers were wondering what an American soldier was doing down in Mexico. The sergeant knew he shouldn't be here, but the colonel had sent him on a mission, and the mission had led him to Mexico. So be it. He intended to fulfill that mission without waiting for special permission from the War Department. He was here and he wasn't going anywhere until he'd fulfilled his mission—though he'd never before considered himself an assassin.

The fat man who ran the place sat at a table near the bar, abutted by a cracked, pocked, and pitted adobe wall on

Tunney's right. From the wall hung a faded oil painting of
a naked Mexican woman sprawled in a hay cart. The woman's body was fine, but her face looked mannish. The sergeant was no art expert, but even he could tell the perspective
was completely off. Her breasts were larger than the cart's
wheels.

Chacin was facing Tunney in his ancient, high-backed
leather chair with arms fashioned from bullhorns. The
chair must have come with the house. Another man sat facing Chacin, though he'd now turned to look at the sergeant skeptically. Both he and Chacin had wooden cups on
the table before them, and wheat-paper cigarillos drooping
from their thick, cracked lips.

Sitting there with Chacin, who weighed a good three
hundred pounds at least, the other man looked like a child,
though his snow white soup-strainer mustache suggested he
was as old as the sergeant. His sagging, leathery skin was as
dark as an Indian's and he wore peasant's rags and a sombrero hanging down his back.

Chacin clapped his hands together, causing the loose
flesh of his face and his belly to wobble. "Sergeant! *Dios
mio,* senor—how long has it been? So good to see you
again, amigo. Come, come. Have a drink on your old friend
Chacin!" He beckoned, though he did not take the Hercu-
lean effort necessary to rise from his chair.

The sergeant had been down here before, against the
laws of his own country as well as Mexico's, hunting
Apaches as well as desperadoes with federal warrants on
their heads. That was all right. The *rurales* and *federa-
les* often hunted north of the border, as well. But the sergeant had gotten to know Chacin better than he'd wanted.
The man was a smarmy confidence man, blowhard, and
pimp.

Despite the cantina owner's good-natured smile, the
sergeant sensed that his heart was as black as his eyes, and
that he'd shoot his own mother for overcooking the frijoles.
But since the roadhouse was the last outpost, abutting the
vast desert to the south and east, Chacin was privy to the

comings and goings of men of every stripe. And thus, he was a valuable acquaintance.

If you paid him enough, he'd divest himself of his secrets, which he considered just as much his assets as his *putas* and his home-brewed mescal and *bacanora*.

"No drink today, amigo," said the sergeant, walking over and pulling out a chair from a table near where Chacin sat, spilling over the sides of his chair. Chacin's hair was long and liberally stitched with coarse gray strands. Mare's tail mustaches of the same color drooped down over his mouth to brush his lumpy chest. He was barefoot and had thick nails yellow and striated as clamshells.

The sergeant straddled the chair backward and pitched his voice low so he wouldn't be heard above the murmur of surrounding conversations. "I'm lookin' for a gang led by a blue-eyed blond Apache—*female*—and a tall, rangy *americano* outfitted in Confederate gray. Wears an old sword. Has a scar across his nose. I'm sorry I don't have time for polite preamble, but there you have it. I know they been through here, so let's not beat around *that* bush. They're doin' a good job of covering their sign, but not *that* good."

Joe winked and dipped his fingers into his shirt pocket.

Chacin looked slightly offended, as though the sergeant had tracked mule dung on his rug. If he had a rug, that is, which he didn't.

He lowered his head and pitched his voice softly as he said, "Yes, you have always been a direct man, Sergeant Tunney. So, yes, let's not beat around the bush, as you say. If their trail is so clear to you, and you know that they have been through my cantina, why do you need to talk to me about this . . . this blond, blue-eyed Apache and this Confederate soldier and his sword?"

"Because it'll save me time trackin' 'em if I know which direction they headed when they left here. The south trail or the north trail?" The sergeant pulled his fingers out of his shirt pocket and held up a single gold coin between the thumb and the index finger of his right hand. "That oughta be enough jingle for a single, two-word answer. South trail or north trail?"

Suddenly, the sergeant realized that Chacin was no longer looking at him. The cantina owner was looking over the sergeant's right shoulder. Tunney also realized that the rest of the room had fallen silent as a Mexican graveyard at midnight.

Tunney slipped the coin down into the palm of his hand. Slowly, he turned his head to stare over his shoulder at the four men standing between him and the open front door.

Three were to the left of the door. The fourth one was to the door's right. They were silhouetted by the bright light pushing through the door and the windows. But the sergeant could still see that they were all dressed in gray.

For a second, he'd thought it was Confederate gray. But then he saw the red stripes running down the outside legs of their light blue trousers, and he realized he was staring at four *rurales*. Four shaggy-headed enforcers of the so-called peace out here in rural Mexico, though it was well-known on both sides of the border that the Mexican rural police force was every bit as corrupt and sometimes even as savage as the desperadoes and Apaches they'd been organized to combat.

These four stood ten feet away from Gila River Joe, staring at him through heavy-lidded eyes, wobbling a little from side to side. Joe glanced to his left, saw the table they'd apparently been sitting at when he'd walked in. The table was mostly in shadow, so he hadn't gotten a good look at them.

They wore the traditional high-crowned straw Sonora hats with the silver eagle insignia pinned to the crowns. Three were tall—at least, taller than Tunney, who was only five-eight. The second man from the left was about Joe's size, though a soft paunch pushed out his dove gray, gold-buttoned tunic, the collar of which was liberally festooned with gold stitching.

The second man from the right of the group spread his

lips around the fat cigar he was smoking and showed four gold upper front teeth.

"Sergeant Tunney," he said slowly, gold teeth glinting above the fat cigar he'd rolled into the far right corner of his mouth. He blew out a wobbling wheel of gray smoke. "What a vision you are!"

"Right back at ya, Arellano."

The *rurale* leader turned his chin to one side and dropped it slightly toward the two gold bars on his shoulder. "*Captain* Arellano."

"Shit, the upper ranks must be thin down here in *Mejico*."

Most likely, Joe thought, Fernando Arellano had shot the captain whose place he'd taken, which was often how one moved up the ranks of the rural Mexican police.

"I told you the last time I saw you, Sergeant, that if I ever saw you again on my side of the border I would keel you."

"Yeah, and that was when *you* were on *my* side of the border."

Captain Arellano hikèd his left shoulder slightly. "We'd been chasing bronco Apaches and had merely gotten lost. You, however, are too far south—and you have been to this country too often—to be able to use that as a believable excuse."

"I don't give a copper goddamn what you believe. I'm down here trackin' a band of Apaches and Anglo despera-does led by a young white woman. The Apaches call them-selves the People of the Winter Wolf. Bad apples. They attacked Fort Hildebrandt, killed a lot of men as well as several women. Opened up on us with a Gatling gun. I'm down here to feed 'em to the coyotes. I do apologize if we didn't take the time to confer with your government on the matter, but there wasn't time."

Captain Arellano didn't appear one bit impressed by the story. He might or might not have believed it. He continued to flash his gold teeth and puff his stogie out the side of his mouth. "I told you I would keel you, Sergeant Tunney, and I would send your head back to Fort Hilde-brandt in a croaker sack."

"All right," the sergeant said, nodding grimly. He paused, shrugged, blandly studied the four men lined up before him.

Then, suddenly, he hardened his jaws and thrust his head forward on his shoulders. "You gonna pull those pistols or you just gonna stand there grinnin' like mules chewin' cholla?"

Chapter 32

Very, very slowly, the captain's lips closed over his mouth. His eyes hardened.

The other *rurales* slid their suddenly anxious gazes toward Arellano, as though they hadn't expected the bold challenge from a lone, diminutive cavalry sergeant old enough to be their father. The sergeant had barked out his challenge angrily, for his temper had grown short as his years had grown long.

Gila River Joe had always had a furious temper. He suckled his hatreds as a doting mother suckles her young. It was one of many things that had always set him apart, even back home in Kentucky. It was this innate pugnaciousness that caused him to go his own way, to live his life on his own terms as well as those of the U.S. Cavalry, without which he was sure he'd be either lost and friendless or in prison.

Gila River Joe had hated Fernando Arellano since the moment he first set eyes on the man's sneering, savage face.

As though he were reading the sergeant's irascible mind, the captain's own eyes gained an uncertain cast. He'd underestimated his enemy. He'd expected the sergeant to back down. After all, they were in the captain's territory. Only, the sergeant was not a man to give quarter *anywhere*. Arellano could see that now. And now the captain's underlings were waiting for him to give some indication of what they were to do with this pinched-up little man's ballsy challenge.

There was really only one thing Arellena *could* do. Joe read that in the man's eyes beneath the wide brim of his straw sombrero. So Joe was ready when the captain let the stogie slip out from between his lips. Before the cigar even hit the floor, Arellano was reaching for both of the ivory-gripped, silver-chased Colts he wore up high on his lean hips.

Half a second later, one of the other *rurales* screamed.

The scream was drowned by the thunder of the sergeant's big Walker Colt, which leaped in the sergeant's hand, stabbing smoke and flames straight out from Joe's right shoulder. His first slug plumed dust from the captain's tunic before Arellano had even half raised his own revolver.

Joe's second bullet snuffed the wick of the man to the captain's right. While the other two men each snapped off a shot, they were too frightened and moving too quickly for careful aim. One of the bullets shattered a bottle on the bar behind the sergeant, while the other plunked into the table at which Chacin and the man with the soup-strainer mustache sat, evoking a shrill curse from the cantina owner himself.

Joe dispatched the last two *rurales* without blinking and watched as one danced on out the open cantina door and into the yard and dropping in a cloud of wafting dust. The other one fell across a near table, upending the table and the two bottles and four glasses sitting there. The glass shattered on the cracked stone flags.

Chacin was cursing wildly behind the sergeant, who, spying movement to his right, wheeled in that direction, clicking his big horse pistol's hammer back once more. One of the other customers had just leaped to his feet, yelling his own Spanish curse and drawing an old Colt Patterson from a holster thonged low on his left thigh.

As he began to raise the gun, the sergeant aimed hastily and fired.

As the pistoleer bounced off the wall, his sombrero tumbling off a shoulder, Joe slid his smoking revolver toward the wounded man who had been sharing his table with the other. This man had half gained his feet, but seeing the fate of his *compañero*, and the smoking horse pistol aimed at his heart, he froze with his hand on the walnut grips of his own holstered revolver.

Quickly, as the sergeant squinted down the Walker's barrel, the other man removed his hand from the grips of his gun and straightened, sliding his hands up high above his head. He lowered his right hand to briefly make the sign of the cross over his striped serape before flinging the hand high once more, the dark eyes in his gaunt, unshaven face were beseeching.

As Joe slid his pistol from left to right and back again, making sure none of the other drinkers were about to blow out his lamp, he heard running footsteps. He glanced out the window to see Corporal McAdams and the other soldiers sprinting for the cantina, pistols drawn.

Joe depressed his Colt's hammer and turned to Chacin, who had fallen from his throne to the floor and lay flopping around like a turtle on its back. He was breathing hard and sweating.

Joe crouched over him. He dug the gold coin out of his pocket and, holding it between his thumb and index finger, showed it to the man. "Which trail?"

"Ah, *mierda*," Chacin wheezed, grabbing a near chair to help hoist him to a sitting position. In Spanish, he said, "*Dios mio*, you fool. Look what you've done. You'll be hunted by every *rurale* in the territory after this. If they don't catch you, the bounty hunters will!"

"Which trail?"

Chacin glanced around anxiously, to see if anyone was listening. But all the other customers had gathered in a murmuring crowd around the dead *rurales*. "The south trail, for chrissakes!" Chacin said softly in English.

Corporal McAdams burst into the cantina, waving his pistol around. The Mexicans who had gathered near the dead *rurales* stepped back, several raising their hands. McAdams's gaze found the sergeant, and the young corporal beetled his brows with mute exasperation. He was panting from the run, shuttling his gaze around the smoky, bloody room.

The sergeant holstered his pistol and stepped around him. He moved on out the door and pushed through the other soldiers who'd gathered there, staring into the cantina. One of the privates was staring down incredulously at the *rurale* whom the sergeant had blown into the yard.

The scouts as well as Ramon and Luz Ortega galloped into the yard from the northern trail, reining their mounts down near the sergeant, who was striding toward the stock tank, where the cavalry remounts stood ground-tied.

Dust billowed and the tired horses blew. The scouts looked around wildly, holding pistols or rifles at the ready.

Barksdale cast his wary gaze at Gila River Joe.

"What in the hell was that all about, Sergeant?"

"Diplomacy." The sergeant continued striding toward the horses, sliding a fresh, loaded cylinder into his Walker's action. "We're hitting the south trail. And from now on, we're traveling only at night."

"Why's that?" asked Yakima Henry, off-cocking his carbine's hammer.

"My attempt at diplomacy came up lacking." Joe glanced behind him and beckoned to the other soldiers. "Come on, you shavers. Get mounted. You act like you never seen a dead *rurale* before!"

Five nights later, just after midnight, Yakima Henry strode along the side of an escarpment somewhere in southwestern Chihuahua. He walked slowly, staring into the dark, jagged-shadowed desert dropping away to his right. His moccasins made little noise as he set each foot down, holding his Sharps carbine straight down by his side so that the milky light of the moon did not reflect off the barrel.

Aside from the soft rasps of his own breathing, silence enveloped him. The sky was a vast Christmas tree adorned with a plethora of burning candles. There was the smell of rock and sage and piñons, the occasional musk of some dead, rotting thing concealed amidst the wiry brush and rocks around him.

Yakima stopped, crouching low. He stared into the moonlit valley twisting below to his right. Down there, maybe a hundred yards ahead, a shadow moved. There was a muffled clop. Yakima dashed four feet down the slope and pressed his shoulder against an irregular finger of rock jutting up out of the side of the ridge he was on.

He glanced at the moon quartering over him. Satisfied that he was in shadow behind the rock, he doffed his hat and slid his gaze out around the rock's left side into the canyon that was all pearl light and murky indigo shadows. The golden tan of the desert visible through the soft light.

Yakima spied an old Indian trail that threaded the bottom of the canyon, following its twists and turns. Along that trail, a shadow moved slowly. No, two shadows. As Yakima stared, he was gradually able to make out the silhouettes of two riders moving slowly toward him.

His heartbeat quickened. His hands began sweating inside his gloved hands wrapped around the carbine.

For two and a half days, the patrol hadn't seen anyone along the trail they'd followed southeast of the cantina in which the sergeant had snuffed the *rurales*' candles. Before that, they'd spied only one lone Mexican prospector with a beard that hung to his belly. More important, they'd seen little sign of the marauders they were supposedly following, and everyone in the detachment was beginning to wonder if the cantina owner hadn't sent them on a wild-goose chase.

All except for Ramon Ortega, that is. The old scout and interpreter was stubborn in his conviction that they were heading in the right direction, insisting that he could see sign that the others—namely Yakima and Seth—couldn't see because they were "green as cottonwood saplings."

Now Yakima's heart beat hopefully. While the older scout's condescension rankled him, he hoped like hell they weren't on the wrong trail. This was vast country. It felt larger and more rugged and dangerous than Arizona did, and if they were not on the killers' trail now, they'd likely never be able to pick it up. They'd have to ride back to Fort Hell with their tails between their legs, the idea of which graveled the hot-blooded half-breed even more than Ortega's insults.

But those two riders moving slowly toward him might validate the old scout's blather.

Yakima lifted his gaze to the ridge rising across the canyon on his right, to the northwest. Seth was over there somewhere, helping him scout the canyon. Yakima hoped his partner saw the riders and took care not to let himself be seen. Ortega himself was off scouting a lesser canyon feeding into this main one, in case the killers had left the main trail. They were traveling lightly, having forsaken their wagon back in Arizona and hauling the Gatling gun via mule.

Yakima glanced at the two riders as they slipped into the shadow of the far ridge. Quickly, the scout moved out from behind his covering rock, dashed carefully down the slope he was on, weaving amongst boulders and jutting escarpments and cactus clumps, before bottoming out on the canyon floor. Moving within the shadows, he crawled snake-like for thirty yards along the canyon floor and held up in the shadow of a stone formation in the shape of two mushrooms.

He crabbed around the base of the monolith until, doffing his hat again, he was staring out around its left side.

The trail passed maybe ten feet beyond.

Shit, that's too close, he silently scolded himself. An Apache could likely scent him from that distance!

He glanced around, looking for optional cover. Soft thuds grew. He turned back to the trail. The two riders were moving out from the shadow of the high ridge and into the moonlight, heading directly toward Yakima along the curving trail. One of the horses was nearly all white.

It was too late for the half-breed to move now. He had to hold his position and hope like hell he wasn't winded by the animal-like Apaches, whose sniffers worked as well as those of black-tailed deer.

The riders kept coming. Moonlight shone silver on the long blond hair and war paint of the rider on the right, as well as on the white-splashed black coat of her unmistakable tobiano mustang—a fine, rare mount—and on the gray tunic of the man on her left. Yakima's heart thudded sharply, painfully. Not only had he come upon the detachment's quarry; he'd come upon the quarry's two leaders!

Suddenly glad he'd gotten as close to the trail as he had, Yakima slowly brought his rifle up, snaking the barrel around the left side of the boulder. You cut off a snake's head, the body will die shortly.

That girl and the ex-Confederate were the head of a very deadly snake.

"Come on," Yakima silently urged as he pressed his cheek up to the Sharps's breech, gently rocking the heavy hammer back to full cock. "Keep coming."

They were within fifty yards now and approaching slowly, steadily along the trail, turning slightly with the trail itself. The broad white patch on the tobiano glowed in the moonlight. Occasional large rocks, cacti, and creosote obscured them. In about ten seconds, they'd be well within Yakima's fail-safe range even with a rifle he was not accustomed to and in the murky, moonlit darkness.

Yakima held his breath, trying to quell the hammering of his heart.

But then the girl threw up her right hand, drew back sharply on her tobiano's reins, and both riders stopped suddenly, partly concealed by a massive-cracked boulder.

Shit!

Chapter 33

Yakima waited.

He caressed the cocked hammer of his carbine with his thumb, keeping his head as low as possible while still aiming down the carbine's barrel. From his angle, he could see nearly all of the gray-clad rider, but only the top of the girl's blond head and her left shoulder, and her horse's black, white-splashed hip.

The moonlight seemed to magnify them. He could hear their voices pitched low in the quiet night. They were conferring. The man muttered something. The girl responded.

Suddenly, she laughed loudly. Then she turned her tobiano around sharply and yelled, *"He-yahhh!"* her voice echoing loudly around the canyon, as did the soft thuds of the hooves, which had been wrapped in leather or rawhide so they'd be less likely to leave prints.

"Come and get me, lover!" she cried. And that, too, echoed like the yammer of some demonic coyote, causing Yakima's ears to warm and his jaws to tighten.

Her laughter dwindled, as did the soft thuds of the padded hooves.

"Lover?"

Yakima jerked so violently, startled, that he slammed his head against the rock jutting on his right. He turned to see Ramon Ortega lying about six feet away and slightly behind him, staring off toward where the riders had disappeared, the girl's voice just now fading to silence.

The round-faced Mexican scout was staring at Yakima, his mustache dangling down over the corners of his mouth, dark eyes twin pools of reflected milky moonlight. "Lover? Is that what she called you?"

"Where in the hell did you come from?" Yakima was embarrassed not only by the girl but that the old scout had managed to sneak up on him. If he'd been an Apache, Yakima would likely be sporting three or four Chiricahua arrows and a cut throat by now. He himself enjoyed sneaking up on folks but didn't care to have the tables turned.

"From behind you, fool!" Ramon stared off toward where the galloping riders had disappeared. "I told you, didn't I? I told everyone. We're close."

"Yeah, but now they know we're here."

"They always knew. They were leaving just enough sign so that the best tracker in all of Apacheria—maybe in the entire Southwest—could track them. But not too much. You and that velvet-voiced grayback—you couldn't have tracked them. Only me."

Ignoring the insult—one of many he'd endured over the last several days—Yakima said, "They wanted us to follow 'em—that what you're saying?"

"Sure. They wanted us to follow them right into an ambush! They would have tried ambushing us long before now, but, fortunately, I made certain we did not make an easy target."

"Well, how are we gonna not follow them into that ambush now—now that we're close?" Yakima wanted to know, genuinely impressed with the old Mex's savvy. He was not so brash that he did not realize that he could learn from those with more knowledge than he.

"We're gonna find out where they're holed up and do

something about that Gatling gun before *they* can do something about *us* with the Gatling gun. *Comprende*, Siwash?"

"You think they're forted up somewhere close?"

"Hell, yes. *Cristo!*" Ramon chuffed a wry laugh, doffed his sombrero, and ran a hand through his thick, curly hair. "I think I know *exactly* where they are. There is a little village. An outlaw village, mostly. I think that is what they're forting up in out here . . . temporarily, between raids into the Arizona Territory."

"Can't be." Yakima shook his head, donning his own hat and letting the chin thong sag to his chest. "She told me they were holed up in the Shadow Montañas. She had no reason to lie, since she'd figured on . . ."

He let his voice trail off. Ramon was regarding him again with that look of a father grown weary of his children's dim-wittedness. "Look around you, Siwash."

Yakima glanced around at the high, dark, serrated ridges jutting around him, blocking out the stars. Slowly, his lower jaw sagged. "Don't tell me . . ."

Ortega grinned. "*Sí*, we are in the Shadow Montañas. We have been in the Shadow Mountains for the better part of two days."

Yakima must have made a face, because the old scout, staring at him, chuckled dryly. They'd been traveling after sundown, so it had been hard to get a fix on their surroundings. But somehow, even under cover of darkness, the old scout had led them to their forbidden destination—a place that some didn't believe even existed.

Yakima looked around and suddenly the landscape grew in significance. He felt a chill of excitement, like that of a child suddenly realizing that he'd left the known world behind and entered into a land of danger and mystery. A land of folktales, like those Cheyenne tales that Yakima's mother had told him around winter campfires in their tipi when he was a boy.

Only, these tales told of dark and malevolent things. They told of Apaches, of slow torture and a violent death in a place far from home, if Yakima could call Fort Hell home, which he did in lieu of any other.

Soft foot thuds sounded from the other side of the mushroom rock formation. "Don't shoot—it's Seth!" Barksdale's voice raked out, breathlessly.

The Southerner jogged, crouching low, around the formation and dropped to a knee ahead of Yakima and Ortega, who'd removed a flat, hide-covered flask from the well of one high-topped moccasin, and plucked the cork from the lip.

"What the hell was that all about? We stumble into a canyon full of witches?"

"Only one witch," Ramon said, holding up a single finger either to indicate the number of witches or to indicate his pause for a libation. When he'd taken a long drink, he sighed and said, "A witch in love with green-eyed Siwash here, apparently."

"Ah, stow it, Ramon."

The Mexican scout knocked Yakima's hat from his head. "You call me Senor *Orr-tega* out of respect, Siwash. *Sabe?* Or I will twist your ears full around to make you look funnier than you already look with those green eyes, and send you howling back home to your mother!"

He tugged on Yakima's right ear.

"Ow . . . goddamnit!"

The elder scout canted his head toward a high stone shelf revealed by the moonlight ahead and east. "Come on, *putas.* We climb up there to that ridge and see where they are heading. The canyon curves around to the east. I just want to make sure we are where I think we are before the sergeant and I plan our attack."

For all his excess weight, the old scout lithely climbed to his feet and set off jogging, whang strings dancing along his buckskin vest and trousers. His high-topped moccasins moved soundlessly around the rocks and brush. Yakima and Seth followed in single file—Yakima behind the lead scout, Seth bringing up the rear.

They climbed the slope, which was gradual at first but

quickly grew steeper. As they climbed up and over and around boulders, Ortega started wheezing, breathing hard. Yakima could smell the man's sweat-soaked calico shirt and his deerskin trousers—and the *aguardiente* oozing from his pores. Ortega stopped at the bottom of a particularly high shelf of rock jutting over them, and leaned forward, hands on his thighs.

His broad-brimmed, short-crowned straw sombrero tumbled down before him and was caught by his chin thong. He tossed his head with its sweat-matted tangle of curly hair toward the formation.

"You go," he told Yakima. "I'll be right behind you."

Seth pulled up beside the scout, whispered, "You all right, Ramon?"

"Of course I'm all right. If you'd been eating and drinking and fornicating as much as I have over the past year, you'd be out of breath, too. Go! I'm coming. But watch yourselves. We may be close to their village. If so, that blond Apache demon has likely got her own scouts out! If so, I want *us* to see *them* before *they* see *us! Sabe?*"

Yakima was already halfway up the escarpment, which jutted up near the crest of the canyon's northeastern ridge. He'd slung his carbine behind him; it jostled heavily across his back by its leather lanyard. The formation was steep, and he climbed it by grabbing knobs and cracks and little shelves and pulling himself up with his hands while pushing off similar cracks and protrusions with his feet.

The top of the formation, which was near the top of the ridge of the canyon, was only three feet away. That three-foot stretch wasn't an easy climb, however. Sheer, flat rock stretched across the gap.

Gritting his teeth, Yakima stretched his right hand toward the lip of the formation. But as he did, the darkness shifted before and above him. A large brown hand dropped down over the top of the scarp. A scrap of rawhide trimmed with wolf teeth encircled the wrist just below the hand.

Yakima grunted with a start. Before he could pull his own hand away, the Apache's hand had closed around

Yakima's, as though the hands belonged to two old friends greeting each other after a long separation. There was a soft grunt above Yakima, and Yakima was suddenly pulled free of the side of the scarp and hoisted upward.

The Apache set Yakima down atop the scarp. When the young half-breed had his feet firmly planted, he saw the beefy Chiricahua staring at him blankly. The warrior had a broad, dark face and bulging cheekbones. His dark eyes reflected the pearl moonlight. He had a slew of tattoos on his neck.

Porcupine quills dangled from the Chiricahua's ears. A medicine pouch hung down his broad chest clad in brown-and-white calico. Around him hovered the dead mule stench of Apache.

The broad nostrils flared. The lips bunched. The warrior lurched toward the half-breed scout. Yakima stumbled backward and grabbed the wrist of the hand wielding a homemade bowie knife, which had been sweeping up from below toward Yakima's bowels.

He stopped the glinting blade eight inches from his lower belly, took another grunting step backward, and dropped to his butt.

At the same time, he kicked up with both legs, throwing the Apache up and over him.

The Apache gave a shrill scream of surprise. He went sailing off into the starry sky above and beyond Yakima, and then he arced out over the canyon. He was gone as quickly as he'd appeared.

Yakima lay on his back atop the narrow formation, breathing hard, clutching the man's knife still warm from the Indian's own grip in both his hands. He sat up and stared off into the canyon from which, a second ago, he'd heard a crunching thud and then a brief rattle of falling gravel.

The Apache had landed on the canyon floor.

"What in the name of God and the devil and Madre Maria was that all about?" Ortega raked out from below the scarp.

Yakima gained his feet quickly, dropping the knife and

sliding his rifle around in front of him. He raised the Sharps toward the ridge. He half expected to see more Indians leaping across the ridge and onto the scarp, the flat top of which was only a little larger than a bar door.

When he saw no more Chiricahuas, he glanced down over the ridge at his partner and Ortega. Both men were glowering up at him over the barrels of their rifles.

"Scout," Yakima said quietly.

"Do you think you made enough noise, Siwash?"

"I couldn't help it," Yakima said. "He was about to gut me!"

"Did I not just tell you, Siwash, that I wanted *us* to see *them* before *they* saw *us?*"

"You did, but—"

Yakima cut himself off. Ortega just glared up at him, shaking his head disdainfully.

Yakima climbed carefully down the scarp and stood between Seth and Ortega, looking sheepish. "What now?"

"What now?" The elder scout grinned suddenly, shrewdly, showing his crooked, tobacco-stained teeth to Seth and Yakima. "Now we report back to the sergeant that I am where I so brilliantly thought I was!"

Riona reined her tobiano mustang to a halt and curveted the horse to face in the direction from which she and Lamar Chestnut had ridden. Chestnut halted his own horse and looked at the war-painted blonde. "You sure someone was back there?"

"Of course I'm sure."

"How do you know? I didn't hear nothin'."

"No, you wouldn't hear nothin'." She glanced at the bearded man gazing through slitted lids at their back trail. "Just make sure your men are on high alert. The soldiers will be attacking us soon."

She reined her regal, long-legged tobiano around and batted her heels against the horse's flanks, trotting and then galloping on down the canyon. The moonlight silvered the trail along the base of the high western ridge. Riona could hear

Chestnut galloping behind her. She could hear his tack squawking, hear his breath rasping in and out of his lungs.

Hearing his raking, male breaths and smelling the male odor of him mingling with the stench of his sweat touched her low down in her belly. She had to resist the natural female urge to sleep with him.

The urge was a fire burning inside her—which was all the hotter for having lain with the Cheyenne half-breed. That had stirred her desires. She knew, however, that Captain Chestnut would not be anything like the young, green-eyed half-breed, in whom she'd sensed the heart of a fierce Cheyenne warrior—fiercer, even, than the hearts of any of the Apaches she knew. He himself was not aware of the primitive Indio lurking inside him. His white half had suppressed it.

Still, that heart beat inside him, confusing him with a wash of mixed-up emotions, most of which he knew subconsciously that he had to keep on a leash for fear it would ruin him. He lived in the white man's world, after all. But if, like Riona, in whose own heart thudded the heart of a savage Celtic sorceress, he had lived amongst his own, primitive kind . . .

Riona curled the sides of her mouth at that as she rode, enjoying the thumping of her stallion's back against her rump. If the green-eyed Yakima Henry were to live and fight with his own kind, all hell would break loose, and the whites would have a *real* battle on their hands with the Siwash tribes.

Warm, male hands of desire rubbed the insides of Riona's thighs. She could hear Chestnut galloping behind her. She could hear the man's occasional grunts, which were nudged out of him by his horse's lunging gate on the uncertain terrain. She could hear the rattle of his sheathed saber against his leg.

As the trail began to climb and the black ridges lowered to either side of her, Riona shook her head. No. She could not give in to those ancient urges. Not now. Not yet.

Not with the lowly likes of Lamar Chestnut. Christ—what

was she thinking? After giving herself to him for even an hour, he would think he owned her. He'd think that her warriors were his. Worst of all, his desire for her would have been quelled, and he would no longer be wet mud in her hands. She would have to work all the harder at bending the ex-Confederate to her will.

Ahead of her, the trail continued to climb. The steep ridge walls continued to lower and to fall away to both sides. Riona and the beautiful tobiano rode up onto a high plateau amidst low, moon-lined, and shadowed boulders. The trail curved slowly through the rugged country until she could see the moonlight glowing on the ancient village sprawled ahead of her, nestled in a broad crease between two buttes that resembled dinosaurs slumped in sleep.

Riona threw her head back and made a garbled bird sound, like the hushed cry of a *zopilote*, signaling her approach to her warriors. She paused beside a boulder snag, and when a brave rose from a niche in the rocks, holding a Spencer carbine across his chest, she told him about the imminent attack and ordered him to spread the word to the other People of the Winter Wolf nestled in the rocks around the village.

Then she rode on, passing the outlying shacks and corrals and stock pens. She rode past a bulky brown adobe church and looked up over the stout oak doors to see the maw of the Gatling gun mounted in the belfry. She smelled cigarette smoke, and paused before a man in Confederate gray trousers and gray campaign hat leaning in the doorway to the right of the church's heavy doors.

The man straightened, stepped out into the moonlight, gazing sneeringly up at the half-naked blonde on the regal tobiano. "Evenin', Miss Riona. How're you this evenin'?" His name was Garvey. He wore tattered sergeant's chevrons on the sleeves of his patched gray coat that had been faded to nearly white. He pinched his hat brim to the girl.

"Try to stay awake," she told him, snootily, drawing back on her frisky stallion's hackamore reins.

"I'll be givin' my orders to my men," Chestnut snarled

behind her, reining up. "Pretty Miss here thinks them soldiers are behind us. Pass the word and stay awake." He glanced up at the maw of the Gatling gun peeking out of the belfry. "Who's manning the cannon?"

"Burroughs."

"Make sure he stays awake. And make sure he doesn't have any whiskey or women up there."

"He don't, Captain," Garvey said. "I was just up there."

About the only permanent residents here were a large family of Mexican chicken farmers. The family's children consisted of five pretty, young women of various ages who enjoyed cavorting with the graybacks—Riona's Apache warriors frightened them.

"See to it he don't," Chestnut said.

"Ah, hell—there ain't that many of 'em, are there, Cap?" said Garvey.

"No, but I want you fellas to be ready for what few there are. Mostly, I don't want any o' them blue bellies to get away and ride back to Arizona. Not after they've found out where we're holed up down here. Understand?"

"I understand, Captain."

Chestnut returned Garvey's salute.

Riona heeled her mount on down the broad street lined on each side with sun-faded adobes that had at one time housed shops and living quarters behind long, dilapidated brush ramadas. The lone remaining business establishment in the village was of course a cantina, which survived on the patronage of various itinerant outlaw factions, the current one headed by up the blond Apache queen and the bearded grayback.

Riona had thrown down her straw sleeping pallet in a back room.

She knew that the goatish Chestnut often quartered up with one of the Mexican girls in an abandoned chicken coop. Thinking of him grunting around with those girls often made her belly hot.

Riona pulled the tobiano over to the hitch rack fronting the cantina. There were three other horses tied there, all with the elaborate, silver-trimmed saddles of vaqueros. Riona swung down from the tobiano's back and turned to see Chestnut pulling his own grulla up to the cantina.

"Don't you have better things to do this evening, Captain?" she asked him dryly.

"Than have a drink with my purty partner while we await an attack by them blue bellies?" Chestnut chuckled as he stepped down from his saddle. "Nah." He shook his head, grinning at the girl. "No, not really."

"They won't attack in the dark," Riona said. "I'm going to catch a few hours' shut-eye."

Though she scowled in disdain at the man, Riona felt the familiar pull in her loins. She swung her head abruptly toward the cantina and then, giving a caustic chuff, mounted the galleria and pushed through the batwing doors.

She moved on into the room, vaguely noting the four vaqueros sitting to her left. *"Fuera de aqui!"* she shouted.

To a man, the brightly dressed vaqueros scrambled to their feet and out the door, knocking over a tequila bottle in the process. The bottle leaked its contents onto the floor.

"A bottle," Riona told the short Mexican standing at his plank bar on the room's left side, looking as frightened as he usually did when Riona was around. "In my room," she added, and kept walking.

When she reached her curtained doorway, she stopped and half turned to see Chestnut still standing near the batwings, canting his head to one side as he gave her a sidelong, dubious look. She hated herself for it, but she was glad he was there.

"If you're coming, come now, Captain," Riona told the grayback. "Or stay out."

The blond Apache queen pushed through the curtain into her room and immediately began shucking out of what few clothes she wore.

Chapter 34

Captain Chestnut walked down along the plank bar and beyond. He stopped just outside the curtained doorway, frowning.

"What you doin' in there?" he asked.

No reply. He could hear her moving around. There was the soft sibilant sound of a bedcover being thrown back.

"Hey?" he said, cocking his ear to the curtain.

He glanced behind. He could hear the hooves of the vaqueros' horses thudding into the distance. The short barman, his black bangs hanging straight down over his forehead, gazed fearfully back at Chestnut and quickly crossed himself.

Chestnut smiled. He winked at the barman lasciviously.

Cautiously planting his right hand over the pistol positioned for the cross draw on his left hip, Chestnut cursed and pushed through the curtain. He stopped just inside the doorway and looked to his left. The straw pallet lay along the wall on that side of the room. There was a candle burning in a small shrine set into the back wall. It offered the room's only, watery light.

Riona lay on the pallet, covered with a striped blanket. Her clothes were piled on the earthen floor in front of her. She lay propped on one elbow, her head resting on the heel of her hand. She was staring at Chestnut, catlike. By the thin, guttering light of the candle he watched her slowly blink.

He looked again at her skimpy deerskins piled on the floor. His heart thudded. A warm coal shifted in the fledgling fire of his nether regions.

"Shit," he said, chuckling dryly.

He unbuckled his cartridge belt and let it and his pistols and saber fall to the floor at his boots.

Yakima slipped between boulders atop the ridge southwest of the little Mexican village. Below him lay the church in which, an hour earlier, he and Seth had spied the maw of the Gatling gun winking in the murky light of the false dawn.

Seth was on the ridge on the opposite side of the village, presumably doing what Yakima was doing—working his way carefully through the Apache and ex-Confederate sentries posted around the village. The sergeant had ordered his young scouts to take the belfry in which the Gatling gun was being housed and to cause a diversion just as the sun raised its lemon head in the east.

That was when Gila River Joe and the blue bellies were going to swarm into the village from opposite ends and attack their quarry—despite the fact that the detachment was only eleven-men strong. And that was not counting the old Mexican scout, Ramon Ortega and his daughter, Luz, whom the sergeant had ordered to remain back in the canyon beyond the village, excluded from combat.

Those eleven soldiers were not raw recruits fresh from Jefferson Barracks. Most had been on the frontier for a long time, and had chosen to remain in the army because they'd warmed to the challenge of riding and shooting, and they were just plain good at fighting Indians.

Probably not much else. They probably wouldn't have made good citizens. But they were relatively reckless and damn good at fighting Apaches. . . .

Yakima paused beside an arrow-shaped boulder pointing eastward, and looked around.

There was a wash of violet in the eastern sky. The stars overhead were like dim candles against it. The sun would likely be up in half an hour. Yakima had been moving painfully slowly since he'd left Seth and moved around the village from the opposite side. He'd seen two Chiricahua sentries but had managed to slip past them without being detected. Now, only a hundred yards from the back of the church housing the cannon, he felt an urgency to increase his pace.

The sergeant was depending on him and Seth to somehow take out the Gatling gun. The two scouts had decided, after they'd scouted the reconnoitered village and found the Gatling gun's location, that only one should try to take it out. Or, even better, confiscate it. They'd decided that only one person should attempt an assault on the church, because one man was half as likely to be detected moving over the rocky buttes into the town.

They'd flipped to see who would take the gun. Yakima had lost.

He straightened and, holding his carbine back behind him, started moving out from behind the arrow-shaped boulder. A shadow moved to his left. He stopped, dropped to a knee, heart thudding. Someone was moving toward him, meandering through the rocks. Yakima could see the Chiricahua's long hair waving across his shoulders as he moved, the lilac sky behind him.

Suddenly, the brave gave a grunt and, holding a carbine, leaped up onto the arrow-shaped boulder. Yakima turned his head sharply to see over the boulder. The brave stood there, holding his rifle at port in one hand, fingering the pistol on his left hip as he stared down toward the village.

Slowly, the brave turned his head. In a second, he'd see Yakima. Not so much thinking as reacting, the young scout reached up behind his neck and plucked the bone-handled Arkansas toothpick from its sheath and, staring transfixed at his target, gave the savage little sticker a flick behind his right ear. The blade flashed dully in the eastern light.

The Indian grunted and dropped his carbine onto the boulder with a wooden thump and clatter. The Chiricahua raised both hands to his throat, gurgled, and then dropped to his knees. He rolled forward off his left shoulder and off the boulder to hit with a thud at Yakima's feet.

As the brave continued to grunt and gurgle, one hand wrapped around the horn handle of the knife in his throat, Yakima gritted his teeth and looked quickly around. Had anyone heard the rifle or the Indian's death throes?

Quickly, Yakima planted his left foot on the brave's chest and held him down as he pulled the toothpick out of his throat. He rammed the blade through the Chiricahua's chest, the blade crunching as it plunged between ribs and through sinew before puncturing the fluttering heart.

The brave sighed and relaxed against the ground. Yakima could see his eyelids fluttering, and then they closed halfway down over his glassy eyes and stayed there.

Knowing there was a chance the sounds had been heard, Yakima quickly wiped the blade on the Chiricahua's calico shirt, sheathed the knife, and stole down the side of the bluff. As he meandered soundlessly around the boulders, the bulky brown church grew gradually before him. He paused several times despite his heart's anxious thudding. Hunting animals for food since he'd been old enough to heft a weapon, he'd learned the art of patience. Getting in a hurry would not only end up wasting your time but could also get you killed.

He glanced back in the direction from which he'd come. The boulders and rocks and tufts of brush and cacti were slowly becoming more defined as the sun gained the eastern horizon. The ground between them was turning olive, and the stars were dimming.

He didn't have much time.

Still, he drew a deep breath, calming his war-drum heart, and willed himself to remain calm and methodical.

He continued on down the slope. After pausing behind a dilapidated, wheelless hay cart, and looking around him carefully once more, he pushed off his heels and ran at a low crouch, eventually gaining the back of the adobe church and pressing his back to the cracked and pitted wall.

There was a door to his left. He moved to it, wrapped his hand around the iron handle that was only partly attached to the rotting wood, and pulled. It raked slightly on the jamb, so Yakima opened it very slowly and stepped inside, where it smelled like bat guano and dank earth and mice. Somewhere inside the building, he could hear a man and a woman grunting together. The ceiling at the other end of the church creaked. He could hear the faint sound of dust sifting from the rafters.

Yakima closed the door, waited for his eyes to adjust to the darkness, and then moved along the wall that lay on his left. Obviously, the church hadn't been used in a long time. It was as empty as an abandoned barn. There were windows in the thick walls, but they all were shuttered except for one up near the front and on the opposite side of the church from the half-breed.

Both of this window's shutters drooped on their hinges toward the floor. Out the window, Yakima could see a periwinkle blue creeping into the sky.

Birds zigzagged past the window, chirping in the rookery for breakfast.

Yakima gained the front of the church. The man's and the woman's grunts grew louder. Wooden stairs rose near the front of the church, to the right of the heavy oak doors, both of which stood partway open. Squeezing his Sharps in both gloved hands, Yakima set his right foot down on the bottom step. He eased his weight on that step by slow increments. Still, it squawked.

At the top of the stairs, the grunting stopped.

"Willard!" a man called softly down the stairs.

Yakima removed his foot from the step and crouched behind a stout ceiling beam as another man voice, his voice also pitched low, said from between the front doors, "What is it?"

"You keepin' watch?"

"Yeah, I'm keepin' watch."

"Anybody out there 'cept you?"

The second man paused, shuffled his feet as though looking around. "Not so far. Better hurry up, though. There's bound to be folks soon. It's gettin' light."

Upstairs, the man sighed, chuckled, whispered something to the girl. The girl whispered back to him in a heavy Spanish accent. She giggled. As the man started sighing, the girl began groaning, and then they were going at it again full force.

Yakima glanced out the gap between the doors. He could see the profile of the man standing out there, the collar of his coat raised against the chill. He held his rifle under his right arm. A cigarette drooped from between his lips. Smoke wafted around his hatted head.

Beyond him, the sky over the white adobe buildings on the other side of the street was turning pink.

As the man and the girl continued grunting in the belfry, Yakima turned once more to the steps. Avoiding the bottom step, he set his right foot down on the second one. This one creaked only slightly, probably not loud enough to be heard above the fornicators' love cries. Yakima continued slowly up the steps, one at a time, keeping his weight to either the far right or the far left, where the stringers offered the most support.

As he rose up the steep stairs, Yakima saw the girl's narrow brown back vertically bisected by the fragile-looking spine. The bones of her spine and the muscles around her shoulders moved beneath her skin as she rose up and down on her knees. After another step, Yakima saw the boots and the gray-clad legs of the man she was straddling.

The girl's dress was bunched around her waist, her torso and legs bare. Her thick black hair was pulled up and loosely tied atop her head.

The man's trousers were bunched around his ankles, the buckle and tongue of his black belt drooping down over the first riser. Four steps from the top, Yakima paused, leaned his rifle against the adobe wall on his left, and drew the walnut-gripped Remington .44 he'd taken off one of the sergeant's dead *rurales*.

His heart thumped with anxiety as well as excitement. This was what the young half-breed lived for. A dangerous challenge. Could he silence both the man and the girl before they could yell out and foil the sergeant's plan?

In two seconds, Yakima had a plan. In the next second, he was acting on it, wrapping his left hand around the girl's head and closing his palm over her nose and mouth, drawing her back against his left thigh. She gave a mumbled exclamation. He could feel the wetness of her mouth and lips against his palm, but he held her head fast against him, muffling her cries.

He clicked his Remington's hammer back and aimed it down at the man she'd been screwing, who'd just spotted the half-breed crouching over the girl. The pink-lipped mouth inside the scraggly black beard opened wide, and just as the man began to haul a scream up from his throat, Yakima stuck the barrel of his Remington into the man's mouth.

The man made a loud gagging sound and flailed with his hands.

At the same time, the girl managed to pull her head free of Yakima's grip and screamed, *"Ayudame!" Help!*

The man beneath Yakima reached for his own pistol in a holster beside him, and as his head jerked, Yakima inadvertently squeezed his Remington's trigger and felt the warm wetness of the man's blood wash over his hand and arm and fleck his face as the heavy thump shook the bell tower.

Chapter 35

The girl screamed shrilly and for such a length of time that Yakima ground his molars against the painful rattling of his eardrums. She wheeled away from Yakima and fell partway down the stairs. Turning away from the dead ex-Confederate, Yakima saw the man from outside running toward the bottom of the stairs.

"Goddamnit!" the grayback yelled, raising his revolver.

Yakima raised his own blood-slathered Remy but held his fire when the girl bounced up in front of him, in the direct line of fire between him and the grayback. The grayback's own revolver thundered. The screaming girl's head exploded, the grayback's bullet punching through it, changing course, and plunking into the adobe wall to the girl's right.

As the girl's corpse fell forward down the stairs, the grayback bunched his lips and recocked his revolver. Before he could squeeze the trigger, however, Yakima triggered his own gun, watching in grim satisfaction as a quarter-sized hole appeared in the man's forehead an inch above his right eye. Blood and viscera spewed out the back of the man's head as his body stumbled backward, dropping his pistol and both arms—a puppet suddenly being released from its strings.

From somewhere below the belfry, a man's agonized scream rose. Believing the cry had something to do with him, Yakima quickly holstered his Remington and manned the Gatling gun, whose stout barrel poked out over the belfry's low adobe wall, beneath the peaked wooden roof.

The gun's swivel chirped as Yakima aimed the barrel into the blue-gray street fronting the church, his right hand on the wooden-handled crank. Three figures appeared atop roofs on the street's opposite side—two Apaches and a grayback, all bringing up carbines. Yakima turned the Gatling gun's wooden crank, and the maw spat smoke and flames and slugs that plunked into the three men on the opposite rooftops, lifting them up off their feet and blowing them backward as they screamed and dropped their rifles to clutch their oozing wounds.

Two more figures appeared lurching out of alley mouths below Yakima and left. A rifle flashed and barked, the slug ricocheting off the front of the belfry. Yakima swung the maw in that direction and cranked out several more rounds, blowing up dust at the two men's feet and then punching dust from their clothes as the slugs cut through them and hurled them back against building fronts.

The man's scream rose again, louder this time. Yakima turned to his right to see a man stumble out of a door on the opposite side of the street and onto a brush-roofed galleria.

As the man stumbled down the galleria's steps and into the street, triggering one of his two pistols into the ground, blowing up dust, Yakima blinked at him.

The man was tall and pale and naked as the day was born. Stringy light red hair hung to his neck, and a sparse beard covered his pinched face with close-set eyes and a jutting chin. He had a bulging fish-belly-white paunch, and his legs were as skinny as cottonwood saplings. He dragged his toes out into the middle of the street, threw his head back, and loosed another agonized bellow at the lightening sky.

"Bitch!"

As he turned toward Yakima, the half-breed could see blood dribbling from two wounds in his chest and upper belly.

He loosed a shrill curse, adding, "That bitch done killed me, partners!" He bunched his face, gritted his teeth, and rolled his head around on his shoulders. "I want her and her dog-eatin' heathens *dead*!"

Several men came running up the street beyond the naked, bleeding ex-Confederate. They ran with rifles held at port, staying in the thick shadows along the edges of the street.

Yakima crouched lower over the Gatling gun's maw, tightened his grip on the handle but held fire, frowning, when another figure stepped out of the cantina. The blond Apache walked spryly down the gallery steps and into the street. She held a pistol in her right hand.

The bleeding, naked man had dropped to his knees, half facing her, cursing and groaning, while trying to raise his own pistols. His arms only flopped like broken wings. The girl stopped before him and casually aimed her pistol at his head, dipping her head slightly to aim down the barrel.

Bang!

The red-bearded man's head jerked violently as a long plume of blood and goo painted the dirt street behind him.

"Hey!" one of the men running toward the girl shouted.

More men were running toward the cantina now—graybacks as well as Apaches. They were coming from all directions, shouting incredulously, even the Chiricahuas. The sun just then lifted its bright buttery head above the eastern ridges, and it was as if the lights had just risen on some bizarre passion play.

The girl swung her pistol toward the two men running toward her from Yakima's right. She fired her pistol once, and received a groan for her efforts. She fired a second time and that bullet plunked off a ramada support post.

The man she'd been aiming at, on the far side of the church from where Yakima stared befuddled down from the belfry, stood near a rusty tin tub hanging from a post and shouted, "You double-crossing whore!" and triggered his rifle toward the girl.

He'd just snapped the shot off, pluming dust just beyond the girl, when an arrow flung by an Apache on the street across from him whistled wickedly and punched through his head. The arrow sticking out of both sides of the gray-back's head looked like one of those fake arrows that Yakima had once seen in a Wild West show in Oklahoma, when he was a kid on his first trail drive.

He just stood there, lifting his chin high and dropping his arms and sort of dancing around as though he'd been struck by lightning or had heard the call of his Maker.

Before he fell, what sounded like the yapping of a dozen coyotes celebrating a kill rose in the morning-silent, gold-lit street. Deerskin-clad Apaches, black hair held back by red or blue flannel headbands, converged on the cantina from nooks and crannies along the street as well as from rooftops. The same went for gray-clad, bearded men wielding pistols or cavalry carbines.

They were all yelling and shooting or flinging arrows at one another in the street beneath Yakima. A few triggered shots toward the belfry, causing Yakima to flinch and keep his head low to avoid flying lead. Both groups seemed to think that the man in the belfry was part of the coup, but they were so distracted by one another that the bulk of their attention was directed toward the street around the cantina.

As the shooting and whooping and screaming continued, dust and powder smoke billowing, Yakima released the crank handle, poked his hat brim up off his forehead, and just stared down into the street. A boot stomped behind him. He grabbed the gun's crank again and swung the maw toward the blood-splattered stairs but held fire when Seth yelled, "Don't shoot!" and called out his name.

The scout climbed the stairs, glancing around skeptically at the two dead bodies and the blood on the walls to both sides of him. When he gained the balcony, Barksdale stared down at the dead white man who lay with his pants and underwear around his ankles, staring up at the sky, his blood-filled mouth drawn wide.

Slowly, Seth turned his pale blue, befuddled gaze to Yakima, and beetled his sandy brows beneath the brim of his tobacco brown planter's hat. "You . . . uh . . . You wasn't supposed to start this dance till the sun rose. You jumped it a might, didn't you?"

Yakima released the Gatling gun's maw and keeping his head low so he wouldn't get it shot off, he stretched his gaze over the belfry's low wall and into the street. "Does it matter?"

Now there appeared to be more dead men than living ones down there. Bodies lay strewn around the front of the cantina—both Apaches and graybacks. The shooting wasn't as wild as it had been just a minute before, because there were no longer as many men shooting. In fact, the shooting was now fairly sporadic, and it seemed to be coming from a small group to Yakima's left.

It appeared that three Apaches were chasing two white men, both white men running and yelling and flinging shots behind them. Just now one of the white men's pistols clanked, empty, and he shouted a shrill curse and bolted into a break between adobe buildings, and disappeared. The Apaches ran after him, triggering carbines and whooping and hollering like the devil's demon hounds.

The shots dwindled, as did the whooping and the screaming.

An eerie silence rose from the street, as did the thick webs of powder smoke. One man was groaning, but then the groans stopped suddenly, and there was only the chirping of distant birds.

Yakima and Seth shared a glance. They shrugged. Yakima straightened, looked around carefully, and then said, "Well, hell . . ." He stepped over the naked grayback and moved over to the blood-washed top of the stairs. He grabbed his Sharps and aimed it straight out from his right hip as he started down the creaky steps.

A minute later, he and Seth moved through the church's front door and walked out onto the street.

Dead, bleeding men lay strewn like jackstraws. The air

was peppery with the smell of burned powder. Flies were already swarming.

Someone moved in the shadows on the street's east side, near the cantina. Seth must have seen it, too, because they both raised their rifles at the same time. Sergeant Tunney waved an arm as he moved toward the front of the cantina, keeping his back against the front of the building just beyond it. The sergeant was holding his Walker Colt half out in front of him. Yakima then saw other blue bellies, too. They were moving slowly up the street and stepping out of breaks between buildings, looking owly and cautious and holding their carbines at port.

The sergeant stepped up onto the ramada of the cantina. He moved slowly toward the door, then quickly stepped inside and to the right, his back to the front wall.

Presently, the sergeant's voice rose from inside the place. And then a woman's voice rose, as well.

Yakima and Seth shared another skeptical glance. They shrugged and walked over to the cantina. They mounted the galleria and stood side by side, staring through the open front door and into the dingy shadows.

The blond Apache, Riona Alexander, sat at a table with her back to the cantina's left wall. A dead grayback and a dead Apache lay nearby, both holding pistols in their outstretched hands. Flies buzzed over them. Riona had a bottle and a shot glass on the table before her, and she was leaning back against the wall. She was bloody, as though she'd been bullet-burned a couple of times.

Her blue eyes, however, were sharp beneath the red flannel wrapped around the top of her head, holding her long blond hair back behind her shoulders.

"You'll have to take me back, Sergeant," she said, sort of smirking up at Tunney standing over her, about two feet away from her table. "I'm surrendering." She raised her hands. "As you can see, I'm unarmed."

"Why would you want to go back, Riona?"

She laughed, throwing her head back slightly and scrunching up her wicked eyes. "Why, to be reunited with my beloved father, of course!" Suddenly, her expression hardened. "And to ask him why he didn't keep looking for us."

"I can't take you back," the sergeant said, holding his cocked Colt straight down by his right leg.

Riona stared at him. She chuckled a little uncertainly, arching one eyebrow. "You're . . . going to let me go . . . ?"

"You won't be going back to him, Riona. All you want to do is torture him. The kidnappings were bad enough. And then the war . . . all that time, wondering. And then the attack. His own daughter . . ."

The girl slapped the table and leaned forward, flaring her nostrils like an enraged, headstrong filly. "He should have kept looking for us!"

"Yes, well, he didn't," the sergeant said fatefully.

"You must take me back to him. I want him to see what he created!"

The sergeant only stared at her.

She stared back at him and something very close to fear edged into her eyes. "Sergeant . . . remember how we once played baseball . . . and croquet . . . back at Hildebrandt? On the parade ground? Do you remember that picnic we had in the Chiricahuas, by the waterfall?" She smiled and squinted, canting her head to one side. With her war-painted, bronzed face, it was a bizarre impersonation of an innocent child. "We called you Uncle Joe—Angus and I . . . ?"

There was a long pause. The two just stared at each other. Flies buzzed around the dead men.

Yakima looked at Seth. Seth returned the glance. They gave their gazes back to the cantina as the sergeant said, "I am sorry, Riona."

He raised his pistol.

The girl screamed and jerked back in her chair.

The sergeant's Colt roared. The whole room jumped from the concussion of the thundering report.

Riona's head bounced off the wall behind her. She stared up at the sergeant for a few seconds as the light slowly leeched out of her eyes and blood trickled down from the hole in her forehead. Slowly, she leaned to her left and slid down along the blood-splattered wall behind her until she dropped out of her chair and hit the floor with a thud.

The chair fell over on top of her.

The sergeant holstered his pistol. He turned and walked toward the two young scouts staring at him.

His haggard face was taut, his eyes weary and haunted. He didn't seem to see either of the scouts as he moved through the door. Yakima and Seth made way for him, and Yakima turned to watch the old frontiersman, who seemed to have aged a good decade in the past minute, step down into the street and walk down the center of it to the southwest.

Keeping his head forward, he walked. The other soldiers, who'd gathered around the dead Apaches and graybacks, stared wonderingly after him.

The sergeant kept walking away from them until he got to a stock tank. He sat down on the tank, reached into his breast pocket for his pipe and his tobacco pouch, and slowly, deliberately began filling the pipe. The dog he'd befriended at the Black Mountain Relay Station yipped anxiously as it poked its head out from between adobe hovels on the opposite side of the street from Yakima.

The dog looked around cautiously sniffing. It spied the sergeant, wagged its tail, and slunk on over to Gila River Joe.

It lay at the old warrior's feet, curled its tail around a back leg, and rested its chin on its front paws.

Joe thought of Samantha back at the fort. For long stretches of time over the past twenty years, he'd forgotten he'd even had a daughter. Now he could think of little else *except* his daughter. He felt a driving need to return to Samantha, and to hold her very tightly in his arms.

When he'd lit the pipe, he blew smoke out his nostrils and said softly into the funereal silence, without turning his head, "Let's clean up here and start on back to the fort. We've got a long, damn ride ahead."

ABOUT THE AUTHOR

Peter Brandvold has penned over seventy fast-action Westerns under his own name and his pen name, **Frank Leslie.** He is the author of the ever-popular .45-Caliber books featuring Cuno Massey as well as the Lou Prophet and Yakima Henry novels. Recently, Berkley published his horror/Western novel, *Dust of the Damned*, featuring ghoul-hunter Uriah Zane. Head honcho at "Mean Pete Publishing," publisher of lightning-fast Western e-books, he lives in Colorado with his dogs.

CONNECT ONLINE

peterbrandvold.com

peterbrandvold.blogspot.com

Also available from
Frank Leslie

BAD JUSTICE

Framed for the murder of two U.S. Deputy Marshals, Colter
Farrow heads to Utah Territory where a desperate town marshal
offers him a job as—of all things—a lawman. But regardless of
which side of the law he stands on, Colter makes enemies fast...

DEAD MAN'S TRAIL

When Yakima Henry is attacked by desperados, a mysterious
gunman sends the thieves running. But when Yakima goes to
thank his savior, he's found dead—with a large poke of gold
amongst his gear.

THE BELLS OF EL DIABLO

A pair of Confederate soldiers go AWOL and head for Denver,
where a tale of treasure in Mexico takes them on an adventure.

THE LAST RIDE OF JED STRANGE

Colter Farrow is forced to kill a soldier in self-defense, sending
him to Mexico where he helps the wild Bethel Strange find her
missing father. But there's an outlaw on their trail, and the next
ones to go missing just might be them...

DEAD RIVER KILLER

Bad luck has driven Yakima Henry into the town of Dead River
during the severe winter—where Yakima must weather a killer
who's hell-bent on making the town as dead as its name.

**Available wherever books are sold or at
penguin.com**

National bestselling author
RALPH COMPTON

"A writer in the tradition of Louis L'Amour and Zane Grey!" —*Huntsville Times*

Available wherever books are sold or at
penguin.com